"THANK YOU FOR RESCUING ME."

He shook his head. "I told you to stop thanking me."

She couldn't help it. Bret had planned to kill her, or worse, and her time had definitely run out. "Okay."

Amusement darkened Raze's eyes. "Any idea what he wanted from you so badly?"

She hunched into herself, her gaze dropping to her knees. "No."

Silence ticked around the dismal apartment. She shivered.

"For an ex-FBI shrink, you're a terrible liar." Lazy contemplation leavened his tone.

She fought another shiver, this one from something other than fear. A tension, one she barely recognized as sexual, heated the air around her. Her gaze slammed up to his face.

He continued to scrutinize her, seeming perfectly comfortable in doing so.

Heat rushed through her, rising up and filling her face. "Stop staring at me."

"Can't help it. You're something to look at."

Look who was talking. Raze Shadow was six and a half feet of hard-muscled badassery with hard-cut features and the most unique light blue eyes she'd ever seen. Add in the thick dark hair, the weird ability to move without making a sound, and an intensity only the most dangerous of people could ever hold? Yeah. She'd stare at him all day . . .

SHADOW FALLING

Scorpius Syndrome

REBECCA ZANETTI

ZEBRA BOOKS
KENSINGTON PUBLISHING CORP.
http://www.kensingtonbooks.com

ZEBRA BOOKS are published by

Kensington Publishing Corp.
119 West 40th Street
New York, NY 10018

All Kensington titles, imprints, and distributed lines are available at special quantity discounts for bulk purchases for sales promotion, premiums, fund-raising, educational, or institutional use.

Special book excerpts or customized printings can also be created to fit specific needs. For details, write or phone the office of the Kensington Sales Manager: Attn.: Sales Department. Kensington Publishing Corp., 119 West 40th Street, New York, NY 10018. Phone: 1-800-221-2647.

Zebra and the Z logo Reg. U.S. Pat. & TM Off.

First Printing: September 2016
ISBN-13: 978-1-4201-3796-5
ISBN-10: 1-4201-3796-4

eISBN-13: 978-1-4201-3797-2
eISBN-10: 1-4201-3797-2

10 9 8 7 6 5 4 3 2 1

Printed in the United States of America

*This one is dedicated to Caitlin Blasdell,
who's been my agent from the very beginning
of this exciting journey.
There aren't enough words to describe
how grateful I am to work with you,
or how much I appreciate everything that
you do for me.*

ACKNOWLEDGMENTS

I have many people to thank for help in getting this book to readers. I sincerely apologize to anyone I've forgotten.

Thank you to Big Tone for taking the kids to basketball and football while I wrote this book, for cooking interesting concoctions of noodles and, well, more noodles for dinner, and for being a better hero than I could ever create. Thanks to Gabe for the entertainment and love, and thank you to Karlina for the adventure and love;

Thank you to my talented agents, Caitlin Blasdell and Liza Dawson, who have been with me from the first book and who have supported, guided, and protected me in this wild industry;

Thank you to the Kensington gang: Alicia Condon, Alexandra Nicolajsen, Vida Engstrand, Michelle Forde, Jane Nutter, Justine Willis, Lauren Jernigan, Ross Plotkin, Stacia Seaman, Steven Zacharius, and Adam Zacharius;

A huge thanks to Jillian Stein and Minga Portillo for all the amazing work;

And thanks also to my constant support system: Gail and Jim English, Debbie and Travis Smith, Stephanie and Don West, Brandie and Mike Chapman, Jessica and Jonah Namson, and Kathy and Herb Zanetti.

Chapter One

*In his own mind, a sociopath is
the sanest person in the room.*

—Dr. Vinnie Wellington, *Sociopaths*

The nightmare clawed through Vinnie, ripping and gnashing until she awoke, her mouth opened in a silent scream.

Thank God. Finally, she'd been quiet. They'd had to move her quarters three times already because her night terrors scared the hell out of normal people. Now she lived in the bottom far corner of a sparsely populated residence in Vanguard territory, which was seven square blocks of relative safety in a dark world.

She leaped from the bed, her bare feet slapping ripped linoleum. Her lungs compressed and tremors shook her legs. She couldn't breathe. God, she couldn't *breathe*.

Bending over, she planted a hand on her chest.

Air.

She needed air.

Launching into motion, she ran through the dilapidated tenement to the creaky sliding glass door and yanked it open. Rain, cold and drizzly, cascaded inside on a burst of wind. Undaunted by the storm or the darkness outside, she pushed through weeds choking torn concrete and stumbled onto the abandoned road.

Sharp rocks and pieces of debris cut into her feet, but she paid no heed. Crossing the worn asphalt, she reached the chain-link fence protecting all seven blocks of Vanguard territory.

Her hands wrapped around the chain link near her face, and even in her panic, she remembered not to reach up to the barbed wire.

Thunder bellowed above as what was once the City of Angels gave itself over to the short but devastating rainy season. She held tight and lifted her head, allowing the rain to barrage her.

"You're early tonight." A voice, low and masculine, cut through the storm from the other side of the fence.

She blinked and stared into the darkness. The streets, abandoned to weeds, stretched in every direction across the empty, dark land. "Where are you?" she whispered.

He came into view, silent like any predator, stepping right up to the fence. "You're getting wet, Doc."

She wiped water from her eyes. "I didn't scream this time."

"I know." Raze Shadow, one of the elite Vanguard lieutenants, had rescued her from hell a week ago while on a mission.

If he hadn't heard her scream this time, was he just patrolling nearby? She shivered. "How is patrol going?"

His eyes, such a light blue as to be odd, lasered through the dark, touching on her toes and wandering up her bare legs and soaking white T-shirt to her damp face. Somehow, even in the cold and through the fence, the gaze heated her skin. "Go back inside, Vivienne."

"No." She couldn't. She just couldn't return to the nightmare and that dismal apartment. "I'm fine." Except her left foot hurt. A lot. She lifted her leg and stretched her ankle, squinting to see through the darkness.

Raze tucked an AK-47 over a shoulder, his gaze dropping to her aching foot. His shoulders straightened. "Damn it. Stay there." Long strides took him down the length of the fence until she couldn't see him any longer.

The wind whistled a lonely tune over the barren land, and somewhere in the distance, a lion roared. Probably Marvin. She hadn't seen the beast, but some of the other Vanguard residents had warned her about him. He'd escaped some zoo when the world had died from the Scorpius bacterium, and now he hunted survivors and other predators alike.

Cold blasted through her thin shirt and she trembled.

"Vivienne?" Raze gave her warning that he was near.

She turned, and he came into view on her side of the fence. "That was fast."

"Humph." He reached her in two strides. "It isn't safe out here."

"It isn't safe anywhere," she whispered.

His chest settled. "Inside."

The cold pricked over her skin and she nodded, turning. The second her damaged heel touched asphalt, the injury stung. She sucked in air.

He planted a large hand on her shoulder. "You okay?"

She stiffened. He'd taken great pains not to touch her during her one week in Vanguard territory, always remaining distant but polite. "Yes." She gritted her teeth and took another step, trying to balance on her toes.

He exhaled loudly. Shaking his head, he lifted her and pivoted toward the building. So easily.

Warmth and male surrounded her in the closest thing she'd had to protection in months. Her heart stuttered and her body softened into his strength. For the moment, safety surrounded her in the form of hard muscles. Yet Raze

Shadow was nowhere near safe. "What's your real first name?" she babbled, suddenly aware of her thin T-shirt and panties. She should've worn yoga pants to bed.

"Raze." He kept his gaze straight ahead.

No. Raze was short for Razor, which was his nickname from the military because apparently he was a master with a blade. The man didn't owe her his real name, so she refrained from asking again.

His strides were long, and even holding her, he made no sound. She held herself stiff, trying not to brush against his hard body. The second she softened, she'd try to burrow right inside him, and when he rejected her, as he surely would, she'd want to cry. There was no crying after the apocalypse. "Why are you babysitting me?" she asked.

"You need babysitting." His voice was deep and dark with an inflection of power. The voice of a man in control of his environment. She'd heard the same tones from seasoned soldiers, retiring neurosurgeons, and hard-edged survivors. He carried her through the glass door and into the dingy apartment, which was such a far cry from her former condo in Boston that it wasn't even funny. "Lantern?" he asked.

"Um, on the counter?"

He moved the short distance to the L-shaped area that had once served as a kitchen, somehow able to see in the dark. The fridge was gone, the sink didn't work, and the oven now held extra socks. Once electricity had stopped flowing, kitchens for the most part had become useless.

Setting her on the chipped counter, he twisted on a halogen lantern and immediately crouched down, one broad hand wrapping around her ankle. "What the hell, woman?"

She winced. "I panicked."

"No shit." He opened the oven and drew out a pair of socks, having been the person who'd put them there in the first place when he'd helped her to move. Gently, much more gently than a man his size should be able to touch, he wiped grime and blood off her aching arch.

She tried to remain still, but tingles wandered right up her foot to her leg and then to her girly parts. Only Raze Shadow could remind her of her femininity while surrounded by such destruction.

"Seems okay—just scraped." He looked up, all intent. "We're out of antibiotics and you can't injure yourself like this."

A panic attack didn't wait for reason. "All right."

He slowly shook his head. "You need a roommate."

Not a chance. Often she awoke screaming like a banshee and she couldn't do that to another person. Even if she could find somebody willing to stay with her, which was doubtful. "Okay."

"Stop agreeing with me." His voice remained level, always in perfect control.

"Okay."

He sat back, still on his haunches, a shield over his expression. As usual. "You've been here a week and nobody has pushed you, but this isn't working."

She swallowed and tried to sit back. Such complete focus from him launched butterflies—the crazy wild ones—through her abdomen. "I'll be okay."

"Stop saying okay."

"O-all right."

His eyebrows drew down. "If you talk about what haunts you, you'll get rid of the nightmares." He placed both hands over her cold knees, instantly warming her legs.

His touch sent electrical zaps through her skin and she tried to focus. "I don't want to talk about it." Hell, she didn't even remember most of her time in captivity. The president of the United States, one of the most dangerous Rippers of all, had held her captive and drugged the hell out of her. "I don't remember."

"You remember." Raze's attention didn't waver.

Yeah, but if she shared the agony of that time, she might reveal too much. "Listen. I was held captive and beaten a little bit, but that's all. In fact, although it sucked, it wasn't so bad until he used the drugs from the CIA to try to get me to cooperate." As odd as it sounded, she'd been given food during her imprisonment, which was more than most people had these days.

Raze cocked his head, just so slightly, to the side. "I saw the vials. Those kinds of drugs rarely get the desired results, so for him to shoot you up like that was crazy."

"He's a Ripper, which by definition means he's insane." The Rippers were survivors of the Scorpius bacterium whose brains had somehow been altered by the disease so they now lacked empathy. They were still humans, still capable of feelings and thoughts. However, some became serial killers ranging from crazy wild to brilliantly deadly. "How do you know so much about those kinds of drugs?" she asked.

"Training in the military." His sharply cut face didn't give anything away. As usual.

Right. She didn't want him probing into her life, so she should offer him the same courtesy, even though curiosity had always been her cross to bear. The rain droned outside, lending intimacy to the room. She cleared her throat. "Thank you for rescuing me last week, by the way."

He shook his head. "I told you to stop thanking me."

She couldn't help it. The president had planned to kill her, or worse, and her time had definitely run out. She'd never forget the sight of Raze Shadow bursting through the door of her makeshift prison to rescue her, so big and strong . . . and gentle when he'd released the restraints. "I may never stop thanking you," she mused.

Amusement darkened Raze's eyes. "Any idea what President Bret Atherton wanted from you so badly?"

She hunched into herself, her gaze dropping to her knees. "No." Silence ticked around the dismal apartment. She shivered.

"For an ex-FBI shrink, you're a terrible liar." Lazy contemplation leavened his tone.

She fought another shiver, this one from something other than fear. A tension, one she barely recognized as sexual, heated the air around her. Her gaze slammed up to his face.

He continued to scrutinize her, seeming perfectly comfortable in doing so. The atmosphere shifted with the sense of male intent.

Heat rushed through her, rising up and filling her face. "Stop staring at me."

"Can't help it. You're something to look at."

Look who was talking. Raze Shadow was six and a half feet of hard-muscled badassery with cut features and the most unique light blue eyes she'd ever seen. Add in the thick dark hair, the weird ability to move without making a sound, and an intensity only the most dangerous of people could ever hold? Yeah. She'd stare at him all day if he remained unaware of it. But Raze noticed everything. "Stop watching me."

He straightened and leaned back against the wall. "There's nowhere else to look."

Cold instantly assailed her without his nearby warmth. She shoved herself off the counter, and the second her feet touched the ground, pain sparked along the arch of her foot. "I appreciate your help tonight."

He grinned, transforming his face from predatory to stunning. "That's a brush-off."

Yes, it was. "I should get some more sleep." Not a chance in hell.

"You're done sleeping." He glanced toward the rainstorm outside. "I have another round of patrol to do—any chance you want to get out of here and get some air?"

Her lungs seized. "No." The idea of leaving the safety of the gate stopped her breath. There were Rippers, scavengers, gangbangers, and even Mercenaries out there. The Mercs were a group from northern California who were even more feared than the insane Rippers.

He scowled. "Okay. It'll be dawn in about two hours. Pack your things and I'll help you move to the main headquarters."

She bit her lip. While she'd like nothing more than to leave the apartment, she didn't want her nightmares to keep the elite soldiers at the headquarter building awake. "I don't think—"

"You're about to start working for Vanguard, and being at headquarters makes the most sense." Raze rotated and moved, all grace and muscle, toward the slider. "Be ready in a couple of hours." Without making a sound, he slid into the night and closed the door.

Thunder rumbled outside. She hesitated, looking at her meager possessions. It was lonely so far away from most people, and she did start work the next day.

As she reached to gather her socks, her mind flared awake. There weren't any empty apartments at headquarters.

Just where did Raze think she was going to sleep?

Raze nodded to a soldier guarding the rear exit of Vanguard territory and strode into the darkness, appearing to be patrolling. The rain drowned out most of the night sounds, but in the distance a wolf howled.

Wolves in east central Los Angeles. How crazy had life become?

With ninety-nine percent of US citizens killed by Scorpius, nature had quickly retaken the earth, and animals now reclaimed territory.

He wiped rain off his cheek and caught Vinnie's scent.

Though he'd barely touched her, even now he could smell calla lilies. A soft, sweet, delicate reminder of the woman he'd just left behind.

Her softness, her very fragility, called to him in a time when such traits invited death. She needed protection, and a part of him wanted to provide exactly that. Unfortunately.

Making quick tracks, he scouted the area to the north of Vanguard, moving between abandoned buildings smelling of rot and decay. Most of the Rippers and homeless would be seeking shelter from the storm, but again, because they were nuts, a few roaming Rippers might attack anyway.

His senses remained on alert as he passed a looted jewelry store, an empty quick-loan store, and an abandoned convenience store. Beady green eyes stared out at him from the corner.

Cat's eyes. A huge black cat sat in the still intact window just watching him.

He jerked his gaze away. He might have fought hand-to-hand with knives an ocean away, he might have been tortured and nearly killed on one tour, but cats freaked him the hell out.

He crossed over rubble and dodged around a several-car pileup in the middle of what was once a busy street. Rust covered the vehicles, and part of a decomposed body was visible in a Chevy.

The tiniest of scraping sounds came from Luke's Bar on the corner. No light, no movement, but a couple of breaths. He stopped moving and focused all of his senses.

He could make out the breathing of one person only. His senses had been honed in the military, but he could still be walking into a trap. Yet he didn't have a choice this time, so he crept quietly and remained on high alert.

He reached the heavy metal door and pulled it open, waiting for his eyes to adjust before walking inside.

A lantern ignited.

"You're late," Ash said from behind what was left of the bar. Pieces had been removed, probably for firewood, leaving only a thin strip running end to end, attached with bolts to the floor.

"You're inconvenient," Raze drawled, keeping his expression bored. The door shut behind him and he surveyed the room.

Ash rolled his eyes. The twenty-something former meth dealer still had the blank eyes and fidgety fingers of a man who'd sampled too much of the goods.

A cracked mirror decorated the dingy wall behind him, which was lined with empty shelves that had once held liquor. Dirt, blood, and moss covered the floors, while a couple of tables without chairs were broken on the far side of the room. A jukebox—a real one—still sat in the corner.

It was probably too heavy for any of the early looters to take.

Ash shoved back his jacket to reveal a Glock stuck into his waistband. His greasy hair cascaded out of a knit cap, which didn't cover enough of his long, crusty face. Apparently it was difficult to find medicine for impetigo nowadays. "Well?"

Raze kept his arms loose at his sides. "Well what?"

"Where's the woman?"

"Not here," Raze said.

Ash shook his head, his entire rail-thin body moving with the effort. "We made a deal."

"No. We don't have a deal," Raze said silkily, allowing every violent urge he was feeling to show in his eyes.

Ash swallowed, his Adam's apple bobbing. "I represent Greyson and you know it."

Raze didn't move a muscle. He'd learned early on that his ability to hold perfectly still constituted a threat in some circles. Especially the despair-riddled streets of an inner city—before and after the end of civilization. "I know Grey wouldn't mourn your death."

Ash snarled. "I'm important to Grey and the Mercs. He'd rip your skin from your body if you harmed me."

"I doubt that," Raze said evenly.

Ash paled even more. "Are you bringing the woman or not?"

Raze took in the rapidly lightening sky outside. It was time to get back to Vanguard. "I have until the end of the week. So get the fuck off my back and stop coming into my territory."

Ash cackled, revealing stained and crooked teeth as he no doubt realized Raze didn't plan to kill him this time. "Your territory? You're claiming Vanguard territory as your own now, are you?" He snorted. "You don't have territory, dumbass."

Raze straightened.

Ash breathed out and backed into the counter behind him. "I'm just sayin'. You belong to the Mercenaries and don't you forget it."

"I don't belong to anybody." Fury threatened to grip him, so Raze focused on the world around him. The room was rank with the smell of sewage and raw fish. He glanced at the window to see morning arriving in full force. "I have to go." He turned for the door, keeping Ash in his sights.

"One week, Shadow. We'll give you the plan next time we meet."

"Give me the plan now." Heat circulated through Raze's chest, leaving a piercing pain. Even so, he shot Ash a hard look and waited until the guy turned pale.

"Nope. Grey wants to keep you on your toes," Ash said.

"Tell Grey I'm looking forward to settling up with him."

Ash smiled and flashed his disgusting teeth. "Oh, I will. You will turn over Vivienne Wellington, or you know what happens. Grey wants confirmation you're on track."

Raze breathed in and said the words that would finish off any soul he still had. "I'll deliver her to him, per our agreement. I'll see you in five nights for your fucking plan. Midnight." Without another word, he turned and strode into the storm.

Chapter Two

A sociopath is both born and made.

—Dr. Vinnie Wellington, *Sociopaths*

Vinnie held her meager possessions in a canvas bag near the sliding glass door, her eyes closed, her breath even. In for seven counts, out for eleven. She'd learned the trick while earning her doctorate, and she'd relied on it more than once during her time working for the FBI.

Her eyelids slowly opened. The storm had ebbed, leaving tracks of churning gray clouds separated by startling blue sky. The LA summer would soon arrive, and rain would be a distant and fond memory.

Water was scarce.

But now, with the sun trying valiantly to shine down, the scraggly weeds and crumbling asphalt road only appeared all the more despondent. As if even nature didn't want to try to exist within the enclosed barbed-wire fence.

A lone flower, purple and attached to what must be a weed, bloomed in the middle of the overgrown path to the road.

Vinnie studied the brave petals. The flower reminded her of a poster she'd seen in an FBI office a lifetime ago—the caption had been something about perseverance, with a flower growing from a rock cliff.

Her very life existed on a damn cliff these days, and she was no flower. Not even close.

Whispers tickled through her mind in different voices and she shoved them away. Her heart rate picked up. The drugs the president had forced on her had affected her brain, and this was just another aftereffect. The voices would be gone soon.

They had to be.

Or maybe the drugs had changed her brain chemistry enough that she'd go insane from the misfiring of neurons. Totally possible.

She'd studied the insane partly out of curiosity and partly because her aunt had killed herself after a horrible bout of depression. Vinnie had been five years old and hadn't understood the facts until much later in childhood—and then she'd been fascinated with psychology in general.

That fascination was turned into determination by the brutal death of her mother at the hands of a serial killer.

Raze came into view from around a corner, moving in that smooth lope that fascinated her. She had no doubt he'd purposely let her see him just to keep from startling her. If Raze Shadow wanted to sneak up on a person, he'd do so without any warning.

She shivered and yanked open the door with one hand. The glass fought her, scraping along small rocks and dirt until finally giving in with a shudder.

He reached her, still wearing the dark jeans and black shirt from the night before. The clothing accentuated hard muscle and long lines, and the gun at his hip gave him the look of a vigilante soldier.

Which was who he'd become in this new world.

"You ready?" he asked, stopping a few feet away.

She swallowed. "Yes, but I need more details."

One dark eyebrow rose. "I'm escorting you to head-quarters, where you won't be so alone and can deal with your issues. You start work there today anyway."

She shook her head. "No. I meant, where am I sleeping?" Warmth climbed into her face. Yes, she could've worded that better, but her skin heated whenever the man was near, and she couldn't help her thoughts. Hell, she couldn't stop any of the thoughts zinging through her drug-addled gray matter. "Is there an apartment at Vanguard headquarters available?"

His gaze darkened. "They're trying to find you a place, but if they can't figure it out, you can have mine. I'll bunk with another soldier."

She blinked. Well, geez. Talk about not even trying to get into her pants. Not that she wanted any pressure right now, but it'd be nice if the guy at least noticed she had working girl parts. "That's perfect. Thank you."

He gestured her ahead of him after quickly scouting the area. "Let's move."

She deserted the tenement building without a backward glance, stepping through the damp weeds to follow him onto the road heading north along the fence line. Stacks of tires, turned over semis, and old vans lined the street outside the fence, forming a makeshift barrier from attackers.

The minute they reached the end of the building, Raze turned her onto another old road toward the middle of the territory. Away from the boundary and danger. They moved past more apartments and barrels set out to catch rainwater before reaching an old gymnasium that now served as a mess hall. The main medical facility was located next to it in a weathered brick building that had once been an elementary school.

At this early dawn hour, only patrolling soldiers were

up and about. Raze gave a guy nod to a couple and they returned the gesture.

Men of few words, definitely.

She stepped over a large puddle as they turned again, maneuvering down a street between row houses and a rambling building now serving as training facilities. It used to be a bunch of old businesses. The silence began to wear on her. "Are you training scavengers today?"

"No."

She nodded and tried to let the silence stand. Nope. "What are you doing today?"

"Probably scouting outer territory for threats." He blinked several times, as if finally sensing her discomfort. "Um. So, you're a profiler? I mean, you *were* a profiler?"

"Yes, except we're not really called profilers." That life already seemed so long ago. "I worked for the FBI Behavioral Analysis unit." She missed her friends there, in fact. They'd all succumbed to Scorpius.

"Ah." He gently pulled her to the right and away from a gaping pothole filled with rainwater. "You seem young to already be with the BAU."

She nodded. "I was a special agent for three years, but I mainly worked on cold cases, not in the field. I had some luck with the cases and was fast-tracked to the BAU." Her insight into the criminal mind had bordered on psychic even before Scorpius.

"Why the BAU?" he asked quietly.

"I wanted to make a difference to society, and with an analytical mind, I figured that was a good way to do it." She gave her routine answer without a hitch in her breath.

He glanced sideways at her just as they reached another road and turned left to go by a warehouse that housed vehicles and fuel. The headquarters, where the elite soldiers lived, was next to it in a building of heavy red brick. "That's not all, is it?"

She paused. Raze Shadow could see beneath the surface, now couldn't he? "No. That's not all."

He took a step away from her, giving her space. "It's none of my business."

No, but something in her, something so alone, wanted to confide in him. Wanted to share. "Remember Scott Rysen out of Boston?"

Raze frowned. "The Back Alley Butcher?"

She sighed, her stomach turning over. "That's what the press called him. My mother was his third victim when I was eight years old."

"Ah, shit, Vinnie." Raze ran a hand down her arm, slowing his stride.

Raze's touch settled something inside her, and she breathed in his masculine scent.

"I'm sorry. Your dad?" he asked.

"Cop who threw himself into his work." She forced a smile. Man, she'd loved her dad, even though he'd definitely had problems. "Died of cirrhosis of the liver a week after I graduated college."

Sympathy glowed in Raze's eyes. "I'm sorry."

"It's in the past." She hustled her pace and stumbled over a pothole. Raze reached out to steady her. His hand, so large and heated, enclosed her upper arm. Tingles shot through her entire body. As soon as she'd righted herself, he released her and took his warmth with him. She frowned. Realization dawned. "You haven't been infected, have you?"

He kept walking, scouting the area around them, even though they were inner territory. "No. Why?"

Because he rarely touched her. She shrugged her shoulders. Talk about ego. Maybe he just didn't like her. Or perhaps he felt no attraction to her. "Just asking."

"Why?" They reached the back entrance to the two-story building and he paused, turning to face her.

She swallowed and fought the urge to step back. He was

just so . . . big. "The way you try to stay away from me, I, ah, was confused. I mean, it seems like we're kind of friends, as much as you can have friends in this crazy lonely world these days, but you always back away, and I—"

He held up a hand. "Whoa."

She winced, pricks of heat dancing through her. Man, why wouldn't her mouth just stop? Before the drugs, she could've played poker with the best of them. She had been calm, cool, and totally in control. Now? She couldn't even keep a thought to herself. "Sorry."

He crossed muscled arms. "For what?"

Her mouth gaped open and she quickly shut it. Words tumbled out anyway. "For going on and on. For making you uncomfortable. For—"

"Whoa," he whispered. Again.

The soft rasp licked down her body. She jerked her head, trying to find some control. "Sorry." Turning to go, she tripped, and he reached out to steady her again. Somehow, his hold was both protective and restrictive.

He shook his head. "Vivienne, I'm not afraid of getting infected."

Oh. An odd hurt spiraled through her chest. "I see." So he just didn't want to be around her.

"I know it's going to happen at some point, but still, I'd like to hold off as long as possible."

She nodded. Once a person survived the contagion, he was always a carrier and could infect other people, just like carriers of staph or MRSA could. Some people who survived the infection became sociopaths, some went as far as to become serial killers, while others did not change in a bad way. Many still changed, however. "Are you up to date on your vitamin B injections?" she asked.

"Yes."

Well, good. For some reason, vitamin B helped the body protect itself from the worst of the Scorpius brain damage.

Everyone took shots. Those who hadn't been infected took them to build up B in case they got sick, and those who had already survived took the B to keep sane. After infection, extra B during the first twenty-four hours was crucial. Unfortunately, nobody knew how long the treatments had to go on.

Science and technology had ground to a halt as most of the world died.

She turned toward the center door, a slider. "Well, then. Let's go see if I have a place to live." Steeling her shoulders, she took a step forward.

And forgot he still held her arm.

His grip didn't lessen, so she had to step back to keep her balance. Slowly, with obvious gentleness, he turned her to face him.

She shivered in the cool air, which was such a contrast to the warmth of his touch. "It's okay. No worries, Raze."

His upper lip curved. "There are plenty of worries, Vivienne, but you infecting me ain't one of them." He rocked back on his heels, so damn solid in a world of uncertainties.

"Then why are you so distant?"

A veil dropped over his startling eyes. "I'm not distant, but I need freedom of movement in case an attack comes, which it often does."

"Oh." A warning whispered through her. Another voice, this one stronger than most. He wasn't telling the truth. Well, not the whole truth. "Okay." She didn't have any reason to challenge him, and she couldn't let anyone know what was going on with her brain or how she knew things she really shouldn't. Hell, even she didn't understand.

She'd survived Scorpius, which was known to alter brain chemistry. Then she'd been shot up with the most creative drugs ever used by the CIA, which definitely could have changed the way her neurons fired. Combine the two? Yeah.

There was no telling how damaged, or changed, her brain was now.

On the bright side, she had no interest in killing victims or turning into a cannibal, so she wasn't a Ripper.

Raze's hold remained firm while he moved toward the door, and she fell into step, walking in front of him when he opened it. A former soup kitchen, the central ground floor room of headquarters now held a hodgepodge of tables and chairs. A long counter ran along the west wall, even now laden with unplugged Crock-Pots of some type of soup.

From the smell it was burned tomato, and only two people sat around a rickety old picnic table, empty bowls in front of them. Lynne Harmony and Jax Mercury.

Jax glanced up, his all-encompassing gaze hitting them both, flicking behind them, before returning to their faces. His coloring spoke of his Latin American heritage, while the glint in his eyes showed a predator, one trained and deadly. He'd put together the Vanguard territory to protect survivors when Los Angeles had fallen to Rippers, looters, and criminals. Rumor had it he had been a gangbanger growing up and then had joined the military when given the choice between Army or prison. "Mornin'."

Raze nodded, while Vinnie forced a smile, her stomach twinging. What if Jax didn't want her at headquarters? "Hello."

"I heard you're moving in," Lynne said, the circles under her intelligent green eyes testifying that she'd probably been up all night working on her research to synthesize vitamin B in the body despite the meager equipment available.

"Um, yes. If that's all right?" Vinnie halted near the table.

Lynne nodded, her fingers tapping on a bound-leather journal. "Makes sense, if you're going to start helping with research. I could really use more information on the socio-pathic mind."

"Sure." It'd be nice to be of value again. Vinnie tried to

keep her eyes on Lynne's face and not the telltale blue glow emanating from beneath her white T-shirt.

The former head of the CDC's infectious disease unit, Lynne had contracted Scorpius and then been infected with an experimental strain of the bacterium that had turned her heart and surrounding arteries and veins blue. Many people mistakenly blamed her for the outbreak, and many others believed she somehow contained the cure.

All Vinnie knew was that Lynne and Jax had helped rescue her from the most powerful Ripper on the planet, and that secured her loyalty without question. "I'm, ah, not sure where I will be staying."

Jax stood, grabbing both empty soup bowls. "You're bunking with Raze. Only room available." He turned and stalked across the room to dump the bowls in a rubber bin. "Raze? You done scouting?"

"No. I took a second shift that starts in thirty minutes." Raze glanced at what appeared to be a military watch on his wrist.

Jax nodded. "I'll be back to join you. This decision is on you and don't forget it."

"Copy that," Raze said, his expression giving away nothing.

Vinnie looked from one to the other. Decision? Were they talking about her? She opened her mouth to ask, and a sharp shake of Raze's head stopped her words in her throat.

Jax looked back at Lynne. "Blue? Get some damn sleep before you fall down." He pivoted and headed toward his office and war room, which were connected by a newly cut door in the building.

Lynne stood, her lips twitching into a smile. "You smooth talker, you. Take me now."

He stopped at the doorway, all hard-muscled male.

Vinnie swallowed, heat sliding down her back. Tension filled the air.

Jax turned around and studied Lynne for a moment. Then smoothly launching into motion, he retraced his steps, no expression on his hard-contoured face. The legends whispered about him far and wide, the dangerous leader of the Vanguard, the man who killed easily, could be seen in every step.

He reached Lynne, towering a good foot over the pale brunette.

Vinnie's knees wobbled with the need to do something, but her feet remained frozen in place. She cut a glance at Raze, who was watching the two with heavy lids, appearing almost bored.

Vinnie turned back to Jax.

With a shockingly gentle movement, he slid a knuckle under Lynne's chin and lifted her face. "I'm sorry. What I meant to say was that you're working too hard, you need sleep, and I'm worried about you. If I lose you, there's no fuckin' reason to keep going." Leaning down, he planted a soft kiss on her mouth, released her, and turned to head back to the doorway.

"That's better," Lynne called out, a pretty pink covering her cheeks just as he disappeared into the other part of the building.

Vinnie exhaled. Wow. All righty, then. Reality slammed her, and she turned to Raze. "I am not living with you."

He glanced down, no expression on his face. "I know. I'll move my things to Tace's apartment later tonight." He shared a look with Lynne. "It's probably a good idea anyway."

Lynne sobered. "Yes. It can't hurt anything."

Vinnie glanced from one to the other, easily catching undercurrents in the conversation. "Who's Tace, and what's wrong with him?"

"I'm the combat medic here, and I'm probably turning into a Ripper," said a low voice with a Texan twang from her right.

She turned toward the western doorway, which also

appeared newly cut into the wall, to see a six-foot, dark blond-haired, blue-eyed guy wearing a stethoscope and a black cowboy hat. "Oh. Hi."

He lifted an eyebrow. "You don't remember me."

She blinked, her heart dropping. "No. Sorry."

"It's okay. Those drugs they pumped into you would scramble anyone's brain. I was on the mission to find Lynne when we rescued you." He leaned against the doorway, and the blue of his shirt enhanced the color of his eyes. "I'm glad you're better."

Was she better? Maybe not. "Thank you for the rescue."

He half-bowed. "We're here to help."

She glanced from Raze to Lynne and then back to Tace. Well, if no explanation was coming, she'd just have to ask. "Why are you turning into a Ripper?"

"I was infected and we were out of vitamin B." He lifted a large shoulder.

Her breath caught, but she tried to keep her expression merely interested. Vitamin B injections were crucial in the first twenty-four hours of infection, and only very rarely did a victim retain sanity without the B. "You seem to be doing all right and beating the odds."

His upper lip quirked. "Thank you, ma'am, but I can assure you, I am not the same man I was. Not even close."

Raze stepped alongside Vinnie. "As long as you're not trying to take my skin and wear it as a suit, I don't care if you're a little off. Where did you get the hat?"

Tace ran a finger along the brim. "A couple of the kids found it scavenging near Malibu the other day."

"They need to be careful over there. The rains are loosening the cliffs, and without a workforce to shore them up, those houses will soon be tumbling into the ocean." Raze rubbed his chin. "We should hit the entire coast as soon as possible before we lose all those houses and anything useful remaining there."

Tace nodded. "I agree. We'll come up with a new plan

tonight that incorporates that territory. Who knew the rain would be so terrible this year?"

"It just figures." Raze gestured toward the door where Jax had disappeared. "I'll show you your new digs, Vinnie." His tone didn't invite discussion or argument. Distance once again separated them, no matter how close they stood to each other.

Her knees weakened, but she began to maneuver through the mix of tables.

"Why don't we meet in about an hour?" Lynne called after her. "Unless you wanted to go back to sleep?"

Not a chance. "I thought you were going to get some rest?" Vinnie asked. Jax Mercury had been fairly clear with his order, no matter how sweetly he'd ended up delivering it.

"Nope." Lynne turned and walked toward Tace. "Come down when you're ready and we'll dig into your brain."

Vinnie started and quickly recovered, not missing the narrowing of Raze's eyes. "Ah, great. I'll be down shortly." Nobody, and that meant absolutely nobody, was going to dig into her brain. God only knew what they'd find.

Chapter Three

Insanity is merely a matter of perception.
—Dr. Vinnie Wellington, *Perceptions*

Raze led Vinnie, *Vivienne*, through the doorway toward the war room and entered what used to be the building's vestibule. He had to keep his distance and stop thinking of her as Vinnie. The name was too cute, too likable. Not for a second could he like her.

Stairs, brick and worn, led to the upper two floors, which held ten apartments each. He climbed quietly and reached the top floor, turning right and walking halfway down the hallway to shove open a doorway.

Vinnie tromped behind him. "You don't lock your door?"

"Nothing to steal." He moved aside to let her walk into the tiny efficiency. An L-shaped kitchenette took up the area to his left, his bed the right, and a couch sat under the far window. A bathroom, now defunct, opened beyond the kitchen, where he stored extra boots if he came across any.

"It's, ah, lovely," she said.

Humor attacked him and he grinned. Damn it. So fucking likable. "Thank you." The sofa was an atrocious purple pleather, the bedspread threadbare, and the floor cracked concrete. Even the kitchen counter was a faded lime green that somehow conflicted with the useless avocado colored oven. A gaping hole remained where a fridge had probably once been, and another hole near the baseboard had been plugged with old T-shirts. "I'm glad you like it."

She clutched her hands together and moved inside, taking a second, as if summoning courage. "What did Jax mean that this was 'on you'?"

Raze eyed her, the sense of obligation creating a heaviness in his chest. He was being pulled in too many directions, and he needed to shut down and complete the mission. That's all this was. "Bringing you into headquarters is on me. If you end up trying to kill anybody or go nuts, then I take the fall."

"What does that mean?" she whispered, her pretty eyes widening.

Raze gave her the truth in gentle terms. "In Jax's world? He'd probably shoot me."

She blanched. "Then I should go."

Shit. He'd upset her. "No, honestly, it's all good. Don't worry about Jax. It takes a while for him to trust anybody." Even Raze didn't have Jax's full trust, and after he did what he had to do, Jax *would* try to kill him. That wasn't on Vinnie, though.

She looked around again. The room seemed brighter with her in it. "I feel bad taking your home." Her voice was a low, sweet murmur.

The apartment was so far from home it wasn't funny. His body awakened at the concern in her voice. When was the last time anybody around him had truly given a shit? Somehow, even though he was rock cold, she managed to warm him. "Don't feel bad. This place sucks." Not that Tace's was any better.

Raze studied her, once again taking a hammer to the chest. God, she was beautiful. Long blond hair, dark blue eyes, so damn tiny she'd be a master at hide and seek. He'd always had a thing for petite blondes, and throw in obvious intelligence and a wary cautiousness? Yeah. She filled his damn dreams.

Which was why he hadn't slept more than an hour at a time since rescuing her. Of course he'd been hunting her for months now, hadn't he? Not for a second had he considered he'd end up genuinely liking her, much less wanting to shield her from the world.

Two seconds inside the apartment and the room seemed warmer. The smell of calla lilies, her scent, already was seeping into the air. The woman wrung her hands together, so nervous she was making him uncomfortable. "Vinnie? You're safe here."

What a fucking lie. She wasn't safe . . . because of him.

She nodded. "I just hope I can help out a little." Her blue eyes darkened as she looked at the bare countertops. "You don't have any pictures anywhere."

"No." He shrugged. "I was on a mission halfway around the world when Scorpius hit and haven't been home since."

"Home?" she asked.

He breathed out. "Wyoming. I grew up in the mountains before entering the service."

She smiled. "You're a cowboy?"

The smile shot through him like fine whiskey and put his muscles on alert. His groin hardened. "I'm no cowboy." He chuckled. "We did own a small ranch, though. Also, our mom owned a small restaurant in an even smaller town. We served a lot of ranchers." From ten years old, he'd known how to sling hash. Sometimes he missed those days.

"Do you still have family there?" she asked, her body finally relaxing.

He didn't have time to share with her. The less she knew about him, the better. Yet the hope in her eyes did him in. "No. Our father died in the service when we were young, and my sister and I were raised by our mom. Great lady." To this day, his heart hurt at losing her. "Cervical cancer took her when I was twenty and Moe was sixteen."

Poor Maureen. She'd gotten so lost.

"Moe is your sister?" Vinnie asked.

"She was," Raze said, his pulse quickening. He had to get out of there and stop sharing with the shrink. While she might be vulnerable, pure intelligence shone in her stunning eyes. "I have to go meet Jax and will be back later for my stuff." Almost running, he shot out the door and closed it behind him, taking several deep breaths. A mission. That's all she was. Just another mission.

The second he turned her over to Grey, he'd forget all about her. Just like any mission.

Liar. Even now, as he stormed back down the hallway, he knew he was a damn liar. He'd never forget Vinnie Wellington. Taking the steps down two at a time, he launched into the vestibule just as Jax emerged from his offices, gun in hand.

Jax lifted a dark eyebrow. A scar cut under the left side of his rugged jaw, showing he'd beaten death more than once and would more than likely do it again. He'd changed into worn jeans and a black shirt, stretched tight over solid muscle. "You okay?"

"Fine." Raze reached for the gun at the back of his waist and checked to make sure the safety was off. "Ready to roll."

Jax studied him with deep brown eyes, as if trying to see inside his head.

Raze stared back, accustomed to the Vanguard leader's scrutiny. Of course they didn't trust each other. This deadly new world made for odd allies, and for the moment they could cover each other's backs. If, or rather when, Jax discovered Raze's true mission, they'd be instant enemies.

The thought charged into Raze's gut like an ax handle he'd taken to the ribs one time years ago. It'd been so long since he belonged anywhere, and Vanguard was a good place. As good as possible these days anyway.

Jax turned to look up the stairway, his movements quick and graceful. "She still having nightmares?"

"Yes."

"She tell you why Atherton wanted her so badly?" Jax slid that hard gaze back onto Raze.

"Nope. We're not girlfriends, Jax." Raze pivoted to open the outside door.

Jax may have muttered *asshole* behind his back, but Raze didn't give a shit. He was a helluvalot worse than an asshole.

"She was with President Atherton a long time, Raze," Jax said.

"Yeah, but she's not working with him. She wakes up screaming his name in terror," Raze snapped. "You can trust her, Mercury."

"I don't trust anybody," Jax retorted easily. "Especially a former shrink who can read us all with a glance. If she does anything to harm Vanguard, I'm taking it out on both of you, and I hate the idea of harming a woman, so I'll probably kill you instead."

"You could try," Raze said evenly.

Jax kept moving forward. "It'd be a helluva fight, Shadow. But you gotta know, in this time and this place, I apparently have more to lose than you do."

"Right." Yet that wasn't exactly true. "You have trust issues. Maybe Vinnie can help you work on those."

"Asshole." Jax didn't bother to mutter this time.

The Vanguard headquarters opened up to a former parking lot, now empty, that reached the long chain-link fence and a large gate. Downed vehicles protected them on the other side, while across the deserted road, a three-story brick building still stood.

"You figure out how to get rid of that damn building

yet?" Raze asked as Jax followed him into the early dawn
light.

"Yeah. C-4 or a bunch of dynamite. If you find any, hand
it over," Jax all but growled as they made it across the parking lot.

Right. If he found C-4, he'd save it to defend himself
from Jax's attack when it came. Vinnie was under Jax's protection, and once Raze took her, Jax would fight hard and
without mercy to get her back—whether he trusted her or
not. "I would assume all the C-4 and dynamite has been
looted or secured." But who knew? They'd found weirder
stuff in innocent-looking suburban homes.

"Nah. There's more out there somewhere. We just need
to find it tomorrow when we go scouting." Jax whistled and
the gate rolled open. "We have a briefing with Vinnie after
lunch today to discuss President Atherton and what she
knows about his organization, motives, and next moves. She
had better be of value or she's out of headquarters. For now,
I need you to walk the perimeter with me to look for holes
in the fence and weak points. I have an itch between my
shoulder blades—I think an attack is coming."

Raze nodded. "Copy that." Oh, an attack was coming,
but it was from the inside. From him.

Chapter Four

Some of the most insane persons on earth appear perfectly normal. It is the glint in the eye that gives them away.

—Dr. Vinnie Wellington, *Sociopaths*

Vinnie tried to remember what lecturing felt like. Before Scorpius, she'd given lectures all over the country to law enforcement organizations when she wasn't hunting serial killers. She could talk to these people. A scratched whiteboard waited at her back, while some of the most dangerous people still alive sat in front of her on folded chairs.

Jax Mercury looked just as deadly in the soft afternoon light as he had in the morning. Shaggy black hair, hard brown eyes, and sharp Latino features. Lynne Harmony sat next to him, cultured and educated, her gaze intense and curious. Blue from her famous heart showed through her T-shirt in an electric glow. The second she'd entered the room, Jax had put her safely between him and the door.

What would it be like to have somebody so intent on protecting her? So damn determined? Vinnie felt a small spurt of jealousy that she quickly quashed.

Tace, the medic, sat next to her, while Sami, a pretty

brunette with sparkling eyes, kicked back on his right. Raze leaned against the side wall as if preparing for an attack.

Did he ever sit?

Of course, he was right between Vinnie and any threat, whether he'd intended to place himself there or not.

"You ready?" Jax asked quietly. His gaze was shuttered, his body on alert.

One of her gifts, one she'd honed with training, was reading body language as well as digging into subtext. Jax didn't know her, didn't like her, and wasn't going to trust her.

If he had any clue how crazy she was, he'd throw her right out.

"I'm ready." She nodded and tried to ignore the sight of her stepmother sitting behind Jax. Lucinda had married Vinnie's father when Vinnie was thirteen, and they'd had a fairly decent relationship until Lucinda had succumbed completely to schizophrenia a few years after Vinnie's dad had died. Regardless, Lucinda had died years ago and wasn't present in Vanguard territory. Nope. Not at all. And ghosts didn't exist. So Vinnie needed to get a grip on her hallucinating brain somehow.

They were on the first floor of Vanguard headquarters, in Jax's offices, where a large conference room was surrounded by lockers holding weapons.

"Okay." Jax scrubbed a hand down his face. "Lynne has educated us about Scorpius and the bacterium's effect on the brain and body, so we can skip any more information there. I understand that sociopaths and serial killers might have different brains than normal people. For now, I need you to give us a brief lesson on the way sociopaths and serial killers think before we move on to discussing President Atherton."

Vinnie swallowed. The Vanguard leader wanted her to distill seven years of higher education and five years in the field into an hour briefing? "No problem." She reached for a blue marker to twirl in her hands. "Simply put, sociopaths don't feel anything, especially empathy. They can fake emotions, and well, but they don't really *feel* them."

Her stepmother nodded vigorously. Today her blond hair was streaked with purple and dangling elephant tusk earrings hung from her ears.

Vinnie kept her gaze on the real people and not her new hallucination. "Serial killers range from the disorganized kind who just want to harm or kill to the brilliant, calculating kind who live for the game of hunting people."

Raze crossed his arms and settled his back against the wall. "It's impossible to tell one until they act, right?"

"Correct. Before Scorpius we looked at nature and nurture. What was their nature, genetic makeup, and so on, in addition to how they were raised. Were they abused?" She settled into knowledge she still held. "Even though Scorpius changes the brain and has created killers out of people who might never have killed, we still need to look at background and behavior in order to figure out predators."

Lynne nodded. "We have to wait until people snap."

"No." Vinnie shook her head. "People actually very rarely just snap. There are always warning signs. Behaviors to watch. Anger, acting out, careful planning, and so on. The problem is, often those things are muted or hidden until something bad happens, and then we see the signs."

"But some Rippers are obviously nuts," Jax said.

"Yes. The bacterium changed not only the physical aspects of the human brain, but the way neurons fire and so on. Heck, we don't really know how the infection changed parts of the brain we've never understood. Not all sociopaths are serial killers, though."

"But Rippers are serial killers, right?" Jax asked.

Man, she hated that nickname for the killers. Jack the Ripper shouldn't live on in infamy. Yet it was too late to change. "Yes. The common name for serial killers these days is 'Ripper.'"

"Go on," Jax ordered.

She breathed in and then out to calm her heart. "Serial killers can be organized, disorganized, or a mixture. The disorganized ones are the people running naked in the street and biting their victims or shooting guns wildly." She sighed. "Keep in mind that Scorpius strips the brain and helps to create sociopaths. Again, not all sociopaths turn into killers."

"For now I'm just worried about the ones who do," Jax said slowly.

"Okay," Lynne said. "Why do they kill? I mean, are they all hearing voices in their heads?"

Vinnie coughed. "No. There are many reasons. Some killers have visions or hear voices from God, some are hedonistic, some are on a mission to rid the earth of certain people, often prostitutes, and some killers just need the power of controlling others. These reasons often overlap."

"Can they be cured?" Raze asked.

Vinnie shrugged. "The prevailing thought is that they cannot be cured. But we've never dealt with the situation of a bacteria stripping brains and helping to create these killers. Who knows?"

Lucinda nodded wildly.

She wasn't there. The woman did not exist. Vinnie kept herself from looking at her very dead stepmother.

Jax ground his fist into his eye. "The headaches from Scorpius probably don't help."

"No," Vinnie said.

He dropped his hand to the table. "Let's move on to the president. Bret Atherton is a brilliant and organized killer."

"Absolutely." Vinnie nodded.

Lynne Harmony blanched. "He's convinced he's doing the right thing by hunting me. And you," she said, eyeing Vinnie. "Thus he's on a mission?"

Vinnie nodded. "A mission combined with the need for

power and control. You and I both escaped him, and he can't let that happen. Even though he has no empathy, he has a hell of an ego. He'll come for us both." Lynne had dated Bret Atherton before he'd turned into a Ripper; Vinnie, on the other hand, hadn't known him until she'd been taken by him after he'd already succumbed.

"Can he be manipulated or controlled?" Jax asked quietly.

Lynne cut him a shocked look.

Jax kept his gaze on Vinnie. "He's evil and he's the enemy now, but somebody has to lead the country, and he's good at it. He's working to bring the branches of the military under one umbrella, and we need that. The devil you know . . ."

Vinnie swallowed, her mind spinning. "His ego would allow for manipulation, and he's always going to think he's the smartest person in the room." A flashback of his kicking her leg while she'd been shackled to the wall rippled through her mind, and she shoved it away. "He might work with you for a while, thinking he's in control, but at some point he's going to want you dead. All of you."

Jax nodded. "I know. But I was thinking we'd let him organize the military before taking him out."

Vinnie shook her head. "You won't have time, I don't think. He's coming for us as soon as it's feasible."

"He'll need to regroup first," Tace mused, his Texan accent tingeing his words. "He lost forces in the fight we waged in Vegas to rescue you, and it looked like the military wasn't under his control quite yet."

"Agreed," Jax said, his gaze sharpening. "Why did Bret want you, Vinnie?"

She shrugged. "He read many of my FBI files and thought I was psychic. He wanted me to find Lynne for him."

"Are you?" Sami asked.

"No." Crazy maybe, but not psychic. Probably. "Definitely not." She heard voices and thoughts that didn't exist. "I was just good at my job hunting serial killers, and I have, I mean *had*, great instincts."

Raze lifted his head. "You don't now?"

"No," she whispered. "My brain is a mess from the drugs Bret injected me with. My instincts are all over the board." Now she was apparently hallucinating.

Lynne tapped her fingers on her faded jeans. "It'll take time for your brain to heal, but it will. Your instincts will return."

"You don't know that," Vinnie said. It was nice of the scientist to try to reassure her, but reality was reality. Her brain had been infected with Scorpius, and nobody had a clue what a bunch of truth serum drugs would do to an altered brain like hers.

"You said there wasn't a cure for serial killers. Is there a cure for a sociopath who hasn't turned into a serial killer?" Tace asked, his eyes burning.

"No," Vinnie said. "There's never been a way to turn a sociopath into a normally functioning person. But keep in mind, we've never dealt with Scorpius before, or Scorpius-created sociopaths, so maybe there's a chance we can reverse the effects. Lynne? You understand the physiology."

Lynne tilted her head. "The changes to the brain seem permanent, though most of our information is based on behavioral observation rather than physical examination. The infection spread so quickly there wasn't enough time to study the progression of the disease before the world went dark."

Jax looked around at his lieutenants. "All right. So we face a threat from President Atherton and one from the remaining members of the Twenty gang."

Vinnie paused. "Who?"

"My former gang. Before I went into the military, I was with a gang called Twenty right here in LA. President

Atherton reached out to them and they helped kidnap Lynne. During the rescue, I killed their leader."

"And several of their members," Tace added.

Jax nodded. "The remaining members will want retribution, so everyone stay alert on patrol."

How was it possible they had so many enemies when there were so few people left on earth? Vinnie shook her head and replaced the marker. She'd forgotten to use it.

Jax cleared his throat. "Tace and Sami, go inner territory and scout for problems. Report back in a few hours. Blue? You still have research files to go through from the last raids, so take the afternoon, and I'll meet you for dinner around dusk. Raze, you haven't slept in too long. Catch some shut-eye."

Raze pushed off from the wall. "I'm fine."

Jax studied him for a moment. "Fine. Finish surveying the northern fence for needed repairs." He turned his sharp focus on Vinnie. "Everyone out so I can speak with Dr. Wellington."

Lynne stood and leaned over to peck a kiss on his forehead before following Tace and Sami out of the offices and into the vestibule of the building.

Raze didn't move.

"Please sit," Jax said, waiting until Vinnie had taken Lynne's vacated chair. "Out, Raze. I won't scare your lady."

"I'm not a lady," Vinnie said quickly, her knees weakening. Thank goodness she'd sat. She shook her head. "I mean, I'm not his. Definitely not his. That would be impossible so soon, don't you think? Plus, I've had the infection and he—"

"Vinnie," Raze said.

She gulped. "Sorry. Mouth goes off and I can't stop it."

Jax kept his focus directly on her. "No worries. Shadow? Get to work."

Raze waited for Vinnie to nod at him. "If you scare her,

you'll answer to me." He turned and loped gracefully out of the room.

Jax smiled, transforming his face from deadly to charming. "He's sweet on you."

She pressed her lips tightly together and noticed belatedly that her hallucination had gone, too. Maybe even crazy Lucinda was afraid of Jax. Hopefully she wouldn't appear again. "Uh-huh." She rubbed sweaty palms on her borrowed yoga pants.

"Are you willing to work for me?" Jax asked, his gaze searching.

She nodded. "I want to work and feel needed." More than anything, she wanted a home.

"Okay. I'd like you to keep me updated on sociopaths and serial killers." He sat back and steepled his fingers beneath his chin. "In addition, people here need a shrink. I understand that isn't what you did with your degree, but you can do it, right?"

"Yes," she murmured. Maybe she could find a place for herself and be useful, despite the hallucinations.

"Good. Folks here are scared and hurt, and many have lost way too much. We lost one of our leaders a couple of weeks ago, and morale is shitty." Jax dropped his hands to his faded jeans. "Tace set up an office for you at the back of the combat infirmary, and he put a sign-up sheet outside for folks to make appointments."

Warmth slid through her. "All right."

"I'm ordering my closest lieutenants to meet with you as well. Tace has been infected with Scorpius, and we didn't have any vitamin B to make sure his brain remained intact. Watch him."

Vinnie nodded, her mind spinning. Jax didn't trust her, but he wanted her to spy on his people?

"Sami has secrets, and if they're dangerous to Vanguard, you're to tell me." Jax's face hardened even more.

"I can't break confidentiality," Vinnie countered.

"If there's a danger to others, you will." Jax leaned toward her. "Raze is hiding his agenda, and if you find out what it is and it's a threat, you also have to tell me."

"I have a duty to report if there's a threat to others or to a patient," Vinnie said. Of course that was in the old days, before Scorpius. "Anybody else?"

"Yes. Watch out for a young girl named Lena. She brings gifts that are a little spooky, and she doesn't speak. Maybe you can help her find her voice again." Jax rubbed his whiskered chin. "There's also a pregnant girl, about two months along, who's sixteen. She doesn't know that no live birth has occurred since Scorpius."

Vinnie blinked. Panic exploded in her chest. How could that be? "Not one live birth?"

"No. It's only been six months, so who knows? But Scorpius took care of all pregnant women, or at least their babies." He sighed. "Lynne is working around the clock to see if vitamin B can somehow save a fetus."

Vinnie coughed. "If not—"

"Yeah. If we can't reproduce, then Scorpius won after all."

A pit opened up in her stomach. "I'll go check out my new office." She stood and then paused. "Why did Raze think you'd scare me?" Besides the obvious fact that Jax was scarier than hell.

Jax stood and towered over her. "Because he knows if you screw me over, or if you harm one of my people, I'll end you." He didn't smile. "I think Raze was afraid I'd tell you that."

Chapter Five

❦

Only the insane truly fall in love.
—Dr. Vinnie Wellington, *Perceptions*

Raze shook out his wet hair as he jogged up the headquarters steps to the living quarters. He'd taken a shower in the drizzly rain after yet another full afternoon of scouting Vanguard territory for threats, and he'd forgotten to eat dinner again. After nearly fifty hours without sleep, grit scratched his eyes and his temples thrummed with a low-grade headache.

Threadbare and stained carpet lined his way. He turned down the second-floor hallway, where ten or so metal doors, new ones installed by Jax, were set every few yards. Behind them lived the elite soldiers of Vanguard.

God, he hoped Tace wouldn't mind him crashing on his couch for the night. Raze hadn't seen Vinnie since her briefing, and he wanted to keep it that way.

The woman just messed with his equilibrium.

The smell of lemon competed with the scent of mold as he reached Tace's door. Somebody must've tried to clean the carpet with lemon. Nice. It was a nice touch.

He lifted his hand to knock just as a cry came from within. Pausing, he stiffened and braced to kick open the door.

Another cry. This one high-pitched, female, and filled with pleasure. Then a male grunt. Tace.

Jesus. Ever since Tace had survived the Scorpius bacterial infection, he'd started fucking his way through all the single, willing women. Soon there wouldn't be anybody left in Vanguard he hadn't screwed.

Raze rubbed his aching eyes. He needed sleep, damn it. He eyed the other doors. While close proximity had forced him to befriend Tace and Jax, he'd purposely kept his distance from everyone else. He kind of knew Sami, but he didn't feel right knocking on her door.

His shoulders hunching, he turned back to the hallway. Maybe he could grab a cot in the soldier infirmary downstairs.

As he reached his former doorway, a soft cry emerged.

He stopped cold.

Vinnie was shacking up with some guy in Raze's apartment? Heat flushed through him so quickly his ears burned. Oh, hell no. He pivoted to kick the damn door right down when another cry came. This one pained. Scared.

He paused. Oh. Shit. He mentally debated with himself for all of two seconds before twisting the knob to the right. Unlocked. The woman hadn't even locked the door.

Taking a deep breath, he stepped inside and closed the door, waiting until his eyes adjusted before walking around the dented coffee table to the bed. The scent of calla lilies filled the room. Weak moonlight filtered through dusty blinds, assisting him.

Bedclothes tangled around Vinnie's moving legs as she fought the nightmare, her hands striking out in the air. Her blonde hair was splayed over the pillows, twisting along with her head. She mumbled something, and even several feet away Raze could see tears glistening on her smooth skin.

He reached her and sat on the bed, taking a firm grasp of her arms. "Vinnie."

She lurched up with a sharp scream.

He grabbed her close, tucking her into his warmth and putting his mouth to her ear. "You're safe."

The two words, spoken with soft certainty, stopped her movements.

"I've got you and nobody is gonna hurt you," he continued, keeping his voice level, trying not to notice how soft her skin was beneath his palms. "Take a deep breath."

She obeyed instantly, drawing in a shaky breath and letting it out. Her entire body shuddered, but she didn't move closer. God, she was small. Her head remained down, nearly touching his chest, and she didn't look up. The sob that escaped her next ripped through his heart.

He knew what she needed.

Without question, he could help her. He fought himself, and she didn't move. He didn't know her, not really—he had no right to try to comfort her. With what he had planned for her, whether he had a choice or not, he had no right to help her now.

She sobbed again.

Ah, hell.

He picked her right up, covers and all, and set her in his lap. Cupping the back of her head, he pressed her face into his T-shirt. "You're safe," he whispered, tightening his hold.

She broke.

Sobbing, barely coherent words bursting from her, she cried against his neck. "Drugs, and faces, and people. Dead. Hear thoughts. Going crazy."

Some of the words he could make out, but many were just burbles. Most people, when they lost it to pain or fear, just cried. Not Vinnie Wellington. No, she let loose with tons of words, crying and talking intermittently.

The woman couldn't even cry like a normal person.

Why the hell that warmed his chest and tickled his mouth into a small smile, he'd never understand.

Yet he gathered her closer and rubbed her back with his free hand, murmuring platitudes and agreement.

She probably was going crazy.

That was okay. There were worse things to be. Like a lying, conniving, backstabbing bastard like him. Yeah. Crazy was a lot better than evil.

Finally, she wound down.

He patted her back, careful to keep the movement light. Her bones were so small and fragile. "Do you want to talk about it?"

She shook her head against him.

He grinned. "Sometimes it helps."

"None of it makes sense," she mumbled, her mouth against the skin above his shirt.

He bit back a groan of pleasure. Her lips were usually pink and full, and he'd had more than one unwelcome fantasy of her using them on him. "Nightmares rarely do."

She drew in air, and her breath heated his neck. "I keep having dark flashes of my time in captivity, and then ghosts talk to me. They're everywhere, but they're not real."

He rubbed circles between her shoulder blades. "You see the ghosts?"

"No. I think I see people who aren't there, but they're not ghosts. In hallucinations, I hear their thoughts and feel their pain," she whispered.

"That's just a nightmare, sweetheart." After her time of being held captive and then injected with truth serums, she could probably be diagnosed with PTSD. Heck, anybody who'd survived the last six months on earth could be. "What would you tell a patient?" he asked.

She shook her head.

"Come on. If you were a patient, what would you say?" He increased the pressure of his massage and she leaned into him with a soft groan.

The sound shot straight to his cock.

"To take it easy and let the mind do its job." She rubbed her nose against his collarbone.

Pleasure relaxed his usually tense muscles. "Good." His voice cracked. He cleared it. "Let your brain work out the problem whatever way it needs to so you get better. You'll be okay."

She lifted up, finally, to face him. "You're kind of bossy."

He bit back a smile. "I'm sorry."

A cute, very cute wrinkle marred her forehead. "I kind of like it." The wrinkle turned into a frown.

Shit. That was a hell of an opening, but he couldn't take it. Not a chance. Even so, his gaze dropped to her pink lips.

"You can't kiss me," she blurted out.

He stiffened and then drew back. Of course he couldn't. What kind of asshole would take advantage of a woman at her most vulnerable? "I know."

She shook her head. "I've had the infection. You haven't. The bacterium lives in saliva as well as other fluids in the body."

He'd forgotten. For a moment, with her in his arms, he'd actually forgotten Scorpius. "Yes, I know, Vinnie." He tried to cover for himself, even as his mind spun out of control. He was trained and he was dangerous. Yet two seconds with this woman and he'd forgotten everything but the way she smelled and felt.

"Good." She relaxed. "I don't want anything to happen to you. Ever."

Her words were always so honest, which made her vulnerable. Way too vulnerable. "You're so fucking soft." The words burst from him without thought. "How the hell did you chase serial killers?"

She blinked. "I'm not the same person I was before Scorpius and being kidnapped." She spoke slowly, as if realizing the truth at the same time. "Before, after having pretty much raised myself, I was strong and made an effort to keep people at a distance. To use my brain, you know?"

He couldn't imagine her being anything but an open book. "We've all changed." Even those who hadn't been infected had been changed by this dying world.

"I know. But now I can't even keep my thoughts in my own head. Everything just blurts out." She sighed. "You're becoming a confidant, and I know you don't want that."

No, he didn't. Not at all. It wasn't fair to her, and he had to get out of there. "Go back to sleep, Doc." He gently laid her beneath the covers and smoothed tangled hair back from her head.

She blinked, those blue eyes glimmering through the night. "Would you stay? It's not dangerous for you unless we kiss."

He stilled. Bed. She was offering him a bed. He was way too damn tired to fight both her and exhaustion. "If I do, I won't be able to leave when you fall asleep. I'm working on no rest for way too long, and if I lie down, I'll be out in a minute."

She scooted over and pulled up the covers. "You need sleep."

And she needed to know somebody had her back, now didn't she? He hesitated only a moment before standing and shedding his damp jeans and shirt. Then he slid inside and gathered her close.

She snuggled into him with a soft sigh, her butt moving way too close to his dick.

Warm woman and the scent of calla lilies filled his senses even as his eyes closed. Holding on to her as if she was a lifeline to the decent guy he'd once been, he allowed himself to drop into a dreamless sleep.

Vinnie closed her eyes and tried to even out her breath and fall asleep, but the hard body enfolding her held too much intrigue. And he was *hard*. Smooth muscle, powerful lines, sinewed and strong. While many bodies had grown streamlined and become more powerful after surviving Scorpius, Raze was all man, perfectly *un*infected.

She'd seen pictures in sports magazines of bodies like his, but she'd never had one wrapped around her before.

For once, she'd managed to keep her mouth closed and hadn't asked him all the questions roaring through her damaged brain. He breathed softly against her hair, relaxed in sleep and yet still somehow on alert.

She could feel his concentration, lumbering beneath the surface of slumber.

He hadn't wanted to comfort her, and she had felt his hesitation. But something good lived in Raze Shadow, and he'd been unable to turn away from a woman in pain.

Oh, a conflicting force drove Raze, and he hid it well. But at some point, his true agenda would become clear.

"See if you can read his mind," cackled a familiar voice.

Vinnie's eyelids opened and she saw Lucinda perching cross-legged at the edge of the bed. Shoot. She'd hoped somehow Raze's presence would keep the hallucinations at bay for the night. *No*, she mouthed.

Lucinda shook long blond hair and her dark blue eyes seemed to deepen. "You can read minds now," she said, voicing one of Vinnie's unspoken fears.

No, I can't, Vinnie mouthed back, careful not to make a sound. If Raze awoke and saw her talking to imaginary people, he'd tell Jax, and then she wouldn't get to work at headquarters and be around people. *Go away.*

Lucinda pursed her lips. "I read minds my whole life."

You were schizophrenic, Vinnie mouthed back. *It wasn't real.*

"Now who's seeing people who aren't real?" Lucinda returned, smoothing down her long velvet skirt. "Your father's people hail from mystic gypsies and you know it."

Vinnie rolled her eyes. *We're from Sweden.*

Her stepmother shook her head again. "No. Your

Great-Grandma Vinilula was a gypsy. My ancestors were gypsies, too. That's why your dad and I were drawn together."

You imagined that gypsy connection. Now go away. Vinnie closed her eyes. Lucinda had died ten years ago in a mental hospital, when Vinnie was in her early twenties. *You can bother me after I get some sleep.* She yawned and her jaw cracked.

"I'm not leaving until you try to read his mind. He's sexy. I bet he's dreaming about—"

Fine. Vinnie clenched her jaw. *I'll try.* She deepened her breath and tried to focus on Raze's mind.

Nothing. No sights, no sounds, no images.

Relief washed through her and she opened her eyes. *His mind is a steel trap.* There was no way she could read minds. All the images and thoughts lately that weren't her own were a byproduct of the truth serum drugs and not a new ability. Thank goodness.

Lucinda crossed her arms over a fluffy peasant blouse. "Try again."

No. Vinnie closed her eyes and wished the hallucination away. She knew she should be worried about her tenuous mental state, but for the moment she just felt too warm and too good with the dangerous soldier holding her close. Life sucked right now, so why not take a pleasurable moment and enjoy it?

"If you're going to sleep with that man, you should really wax your legs," Lucinda whispered.

"I'm not going to sleep with him," Vinnie mumbled.

"You're sleeping with him now. I was talking about sleeping, and you were thinking about sex. Interesting," Lucinda stage whispered.

Vinnie cringed and then remembered Raze couldn't hear Lucinda. *She* couldn't even hear her stepmom because the woman didn't exist. God, life had gotten confusing. Besides, sex was off the table. "He hasn't been infected," Vinnie whispered.

"He will be."

Vinnie's eyelids opened again, but the end of the bed was now empty. Well, it had been empty the entire time, but at least she'd stopped seeing dead people. For now.

I see dead people. The line from a famous movie whispered through her mind, and she chuckled just like an insane person would.

Raze murmured and pulled her even closer into his warmth, his long length bracketing her. She wiggled a bit and then stopped as her rear end brushed across a definite erection.

Whoa.

"Don't worry about it," Raze mumbled sleepily. "I'm too tired to do anything, so stop talking to yourself and go to sleep." His breathing instantly leveled out.

She hadn't exactly been talking to herself. Well, she had, but not really. Right? "I'm crazy," she whispered into the night.

For once, the night didn't answer.

Chapter Six

Whether it's a virus, bacteria, or evil thought . . .
something minute will take us down.

—Dr. Frank X. Harmony, *Philosophies*

Raze slowly returned to wakefulness, feeling more refreshed than he had in months. A slight weight pinned him down and he frowned, instantly flashing into full-awake mode.

He lay on his back with Vinnie sprawled over him, her long hair covering his left shoulder and arm. Her nose was pressed against his jugular and her thighs bracketed his—

Shit. His full-on erection. Nestled right between her legs against very thin panties.

He ached to press inside all that wet warmth.

Her shirt had ridden up past her waist, and he tried to gently tug it down, his knuckles brushing smooth skin. His body shuddered, flaming awake. God. When was the last time he'd gotten laid? He actually couldn't remember.

She lifted her head and blinked several times. During daylight, she was stunning with a fragility that called to everything in him. Yet half-asleep, soft and vulnerable, she held a beauty that was all female.

He watched as she awoke, her blue eyes focusing until

the very second she felt him against her sex. Her mouth formed a silent *o*.

Any sane woman would've scrambled off him and ducked under the covers toward the wall.

She proved, once again, that she was nuttier than a fruit-cake as she rested her chin on her arms, her gaze evenly meeting his, her body fully on top of him.

He lifted an eyebrow.

"We'd have to use a condom if we had sex, so that you wouldn't get Scorpius," she murmured.

He tried not to move, but his cock jumped against her as if in perfect agreement.

A red, bright red flush shot up from her chest to cover her pretty face. "Oh my God. I'm so sorry. Ever since the drugs, every little thought in my head pops out. Sometimes it's not a thought even in my head. It comes from nowhere." Tears filled her eyes. "A couple of times I've wondered if it's other people's thoughts. But it can't be. So I—"

"Vinnie." One word stopped her tirade.

"What?" She frowned.

I'd love to have sex with you. I'd die for a condom. Don't fucking move or it's over. The thoughts ran through his head like rapid fire. "It's okay. Don't worry about the thoughts. Let's get breakfast." If she rubbed against him again, he wasn't entirely sure he wouldn't toss her on her back and take his chances with Scorpius.

She blew out air, and her gaze lowered to his chin. "You don't like me."

"I like you fine." Yet he had to betray her, and sleeping with her would only make things worse.

"What are you hiding?" she whispered.

His gut clenched. "What do you mean?"

She looked up. "I'm pretty good at reading people and always have been. You're hiding something, and I wish you'd just say what it is so I can stop imagining worst-case scenarios."

The truth was the worst-case scenario. "Sometimes the ends justify the means," he said, wanting nothing more than to give her honesty.

She tilted her head to the side. "Are you here to betray Jax Mercury?"

"No, but he'll probably see the situation that way," Raze said, focusing his gaze on her. For the first time he wondered if he could really turn her over to Greyson, but it was the only way to get Maureen back. He'd taken care of his sister his entire life and he couldn't stop now. But an overwhelming sense of responsibility for the small blonde in his arms caught him by the throat and squeezed.

Vinnie licked her lips.

He groaned.

She smiled and her eyes lit up. "You do kind of like me."

God, she was too cute for words. Brilliant, insightful, and cute—an unthinkable combination, and one he couldn't turn away from. Slowly, deliberately, he slid his hand down her back and flattened his palm over her firm ass, pressing her onto his aching cock. "I like you a lot," he rumbled.

Heat sparked in her eyes and her breath caught. "I guess so." Her thighs widened and she dropped her knees on either side of his legs.

The heat from her core washed over him with a temptation that edged on pain.

He was two seconds away from coming in his shorts. A guy had to have some pride. If there was a private shower somewhere, he'd find it and jack off until he could think again. As it was, he was out of luck, so he needed to get himself under control. "Enough, Vinnie."

She rubbed against him, arching like a cat. "Are you sure?"

Hell no, he wasn't sure. "Yes." He released her and dug

both hands into her hair, lifting and easily controlling her head. "Don't trust me, and for God's sake, don't give yourself to me. Trust me."

She laughed out loud. "What a contradiction you are."

"Look who's talking," he said, frustration lowering his voice to a near growl.

"What makes you think I won't tell Jax you're going to betray him?" she asked without an ounce of coyness.

"He already knows I have an agenda and doesn't trust me," Raze said evenly. "I'm needed right now because his forces are down, or he'd probably just shoot me in the head and neutralize any threat."

Vinnie sobered. "That's just sad. Why don't you tell me your agenda and I'll help you? So long as nobody gets hurt."

"You'll know soon enough, baby." He rolled to the side and dumped her on the bed, his entire body aching for relief. "We need food. Get dressed and we'll head down." He had to stop saying *we*. There was no *we*.

She grumbled but did as he said, rolling to the floor and heading for the defunct bathroom. The sound of her brushing out tangles in her thick hair filled the apartment with a domestic feel. A happy shout came from her. "You have the good toothpaste."

"Yep. There's water in a jug under the sink." He drew on fresh jeans and a faded Metallica T-shirt before taking his turn in the useless bathroom to brush his teeth.

When he emerged, his shaggy hair smoothed back, she smiled. "You didn't shave."

"No." He'd shaved the other day, so the shadow lining his jaw could stay for a couple more days. The room already smelled like her. Calla lilies with a hint of spice. "Thanks for letting me crash here last night. I was exhausted."

She nodded and tugged the door open. "It's your place."

True, but now if felt like *their* place. He grabbed his gun off the top of the cupboard and tucked it into the back of his waist before following her into the hallway. They made it to the end just as Jax Mercury and Lynne Harmony stepped from the landing, plates of scrambled eggs in their hands as they headed to their apartment.

Lynne stopped and eyed Vinnie and then him. "Good morning," she said, her green eyes twinkling.

Jax's rough face, as usual, held no expression. "Sleep well?" he asked silkily.

Raze held his gaze and fought the urge to explain that nothing had happened. "Yes. Good morning." He grasped Vinnie's hand and tugged her past the couple.

"Morning," Vinnie said as she passed. "Don't worry. We didn't have sex, although he had a raging erection." She gasped and jerked free of his hold, running for the landing.

Raze continued after her, ignoring Jax's low chuckle behind him. The woman really had to learn to censor her thoughts before they entered the world.

"We go on mission in an hour," Jax said from behind him.

"Copy that." Raze followed the scent of calla lilies.

Jax Mercury watched his new psychiatrist and his most dangerous soldier escape around the landing before shoving open his door with his hip.

Lynne followed behind him. "That was interesting."

He shut the door and strode to the ratty sofa and rickety coffee table to set down his plate. A pretty green blanket stretched across the back of the sofa, while a fairly new and almost matching bedspread covered the neatly made bed. He surveyed a couple of new prints on the walls. "Have you been decorating?"

She put her plate on the table next to her father's treasured journal and sat in a comfortable leather chair facing the sofa. "A little."

The place had felt like home, as crappy as it was, from the first step Lynne Harmony had taken into his life. "It looks nice." He'd grown up on the streets in a gang and then had entered the military before Scorpius infected the world, and while he'd dated plenty, he'd never had to search for flowery words. "I, ah, like it."

Lynne smiled then, her eyes sparkling. "I'm glad." Her blue heart glowed through her white blouse. She'd given up trying to hide the blue after he'd rescued her from her crazy ex-boyfriend.

Jax tossed plastic utensils to her before taking his seat. He glanced at a picture of his brother, Marcus, pinned near the door. "I had Byron sketch some pictures of Marcus to send out with scouts. Just in case they come across survivor encampments. To see if anybody has seen Marcus." It was a long shot, but Jax had recently discovered that his little brother might still be alive, so he'd tried to figure out a way to find the man. Thus far, nothing had panned out.

"We'll find him," Lynne said softly. "I just know we will."

"Faith is not wanting to know what's true," Jax murmured.

Lynne tilted her head. "Nietzsche?"

"Yep."

"He was wrong about that one. Faith is good, and we will find your brother." She smiled.

Her belief helped him. He concentrated on her. "How are you feeling?"

"I'm fine." She dug into the watery eggs.

"Your wounds have healed physically, but I want to know about your mental state," he said evenly, taking a bite of eggs. Yep. Watery without any salt. He sighed.

She lifted an eyebrow. "I'm well. Bret only had me for a few hours before you blew up his world."

It had been a week since she'd been kidnapped by the

president. Jax had saved her, but he had failed to kill the bastard. "I needed more explosives."

She tilted her head to the side, easily reading his emotions. "It's not your fault I was taken. You saved me, remember?"

"Everything that happens to you is on me," he said, forcing himself to eat another bite of the eggs. Oh, an educated and cultured woman like Lynne wouldn't completely understand his claim, but she'd support him. He was raised on the streets and understood this new life much better than she did. "You shouldn't have been in danger."

"Danger is everywhere," she breathed.

"Not for you." Jax finished the crappy breakfast. "We don't have a clue where Atherton or his forces are, but we'll find him." While Jax wanted to be strategic and use Atherton, if they came face to face again, the president would bleed. No way could Jax let a threat to Lynne continue breathing.

"I know, but keep in mind that the military, what there is of it, answers to him." She choked down more eggs. "I'm worried that he knows where we are now, you know? I think Tace is right and Bret will attack at some point."

Oh, the bastard would definitely attack at some point. "Maybe, but we've shored up the perimeter for now, and Atherton needs to consolidate his forces before launching an attack. Hopefully we'll be long gone from here when that happens, because I'd rather attack him on my terms." Jax needed to move everyone out of inner city Los Angeles and go north to more fertile land soon. Food was becoming scarce. "We need to pick up a farmer or two."

"We have a couple," Lynne mused, eating more eggs. "We just need to find good land."

"We will." Jax studied the woman who'd stolen a heart he hadn't realized he had. "How is the research going?" Lynne was the former head of infectious diseases at the

CDC, and lately they'd raided several local labs and obtained reams of research files.

"It's going well." Her frown belied her words. "The last lab had some interesting theories on how to create permanent vitamin B in the body without monthly injections."

"Good, so why are you frowning?"

"I need a lab. A good working lab." She sat back in the chair. "The newest batch of research materials has references to the Bunker. I'm starting to think the place might actually exist."

Jax rubbed his chin. "It kind of makes sense. I mean, the government had to have some sort of plan in case of a plague, right?" The Bunker was an almost mystical place whispered about in survival camps. A place beneath the ground with generators, labs, food, and medicine. But nobody knew its location or if it really existed.

"We have to find it. I need a lab." She eyed the remaining scrambled eggs on her plate.

"Eat it all, Blue." He couldn't afford for her to get ill.

She sighed and picked up the plate to finish off the eggs. "You're tense. I mean, more than usual. What's going on?"

He shook his head. "Nothing."

"Don't lie to me." She pushed her empty plate away. "We're past that."

"There are some things you don't need to know." She was good and kind and he didn't want her carrying a burden that belonged to him.

She blew out air. "You're planning something that has you tied up. So don't do it."

"How did you know?" Jax asked, more than ever intrigued by her ability to read people, especially him.

"We sleep together every night and see each other every day. There's love here." She picked at a loose string on her jeans. "If I had to guess, and apparently I do, this has something to do with Raze Shadow. You seem tense around him, but I know you like him."

His woman was both brilliant and insightful. Usually he liked that about her, but sometimes it was a pain in the ass. He gave in and told her the truth. "I like parts of Raze, but he's definitely a threat. His reason for being here is a bad one for us or he'd share it. I'm finished waiting for him to come clean or make a move. So he has to be neutralized."

"That's a lovely word for stopping his heart," Lynne snapped.

Jax nodded.

"When?" she mumbled, her body stiffening.

"Today, scouting." Jax kept his voice even and his face determined.

She looked him right in the eye. "Whatever his agenda, even if it's bad, he won't carry it out. He won't let harm come to Vanguard. I just know it."

"I can't take that chance." Heat slammed through Jax to roll into a hard pit in his gut. He loved her and he trusted her, but leadership of Vanguard belonged to him. "I have a job to do, Lynne." That was the end of it.

Lynne ran her hand over her dad's leather journal. She seemed to take some sort of comfort from the ramblings inside. "You'll do the right thing today. I know you will."

"Agreed."

Chapter Seven

<hr>

We never truly know the people closest to us.

—Dr. Vinnie Wellington, *Perceptions*

Raze met Jax outside the brick headquarters in the parking area that fronted the building.

"You ready?" Jax asked.

"Yes."

They maneuvered between a tipped-over soccer mom van and a rusting semi truck to reach a small waiting Datsun, dented and yellow. A young soldier jumped out of the back, nodded at them, and hustled back inside the gate.

Raze paused. "I thought we were patrolling the eastern fence on foot?"

"Nope." Jax slipped into the driver's seat and ignited the meager engine.

Raze paused, the hair rising on the back of his neck. "I don't like surprises."

Jax turned to face him out of the rolled-down window. "Then the postapocalyptic world must really suck for you."

Whatever. Raze crossed around the front of the truck and stretched into the passenger seat. "You have no clue." Was Jax on to him? The weight of the weapon at his back pressed in, and he moved his right foot out so he could reach his knife if necessary. "Where exactly are we going?"

"To find explosives." Jax jerked the gear shift into place and turned the wheel to head east along a road they'd cleared months ago. Dawn cracked over the horizon and dew still clung to the earth. "I've had the younger kids going through old phone books, and they found several construction companies outside of Compton. We need explosives, Raze."

Yeah, or this was just a good way for Jax to shoot Raze in the back of the head without any witnesses. Soldiers failed to return from missions every day. "I'll keep an eye out, then. Why just the two of us?"

Jax lifted an eyebrow. "You think we need backup?"

"No." Hell no. If they were working together, they'd be the most dangerous force in Vanguard. Were they on the same team? At least for the day? "But it's the first time we haven't taken additional backup."

"No room in the truck."

Yeah. That was Jax Mercury . . . a man of few words. Of course Raze could relate. "Fair enough." He tugged his gun free and rested it on his jean-clad leg, watching out the window for threats. The roads had been cleared around Vanguard territory, and most buildings had been torn or burned down, leaving clear views in case of attack.

They left Vanguard territory and turned into what used to be Watts. Vines and weeds were already climbing up dilapidated small homes, while vehicle carcasses rusted across empty lots and in the middle of streets. The smell of nature, dust, and death filled the air.

For a while, as Scorpius infected the land, there had been community burn piles for bodies. Then there weren't enough people healthy enough to gather the dead.

Now many of the dead decomposed wherever they had fallen.

Raze swallowed and calmed his system. The dead weren't his problem right now. He had to deal with the living.

The houses turned to small businesses, all crumbling and dark. A man, dressed in what might've once been a flowered dress and ski gloves, barreled out of a shack with "Pete's Ink" burned into the shingles. A straggly beard covered his jaw and wild red striations marred the whites of his eyes. His hands gripped what appeared to be Barbie dolls.

He yelled something unintelligible and ran toward the truck.

Jax punched the gas. "Insane bastard." Sorrow darkened his tone rather than anger.

"Should we shoot him?" Raze asked, turning to watch the Ripper run across concrete, rocks, and glass behind them, screaming incoherently.

"No." Jax sighed. "Not today anyway."

Raze nodded. Sometimes he didn't feel like shooting anybody either. "Do you think there's a cure? I mean, do you think it's possible we'll ever find a cure for Scorpius?"

"No." Jax jerked the wheel to avoid a crumpled Honda motorcycle. "I don't think we can make the insane sane again, you know? Maybe we'll come up with inoculations to protect people from being infected, but I figure once it's done, it's done."

"You've been infected."

"Yeah, and I had B the second it happened, so hopefully I won't go nuts. But who the hell knows?" Jax glanced up at the sun. "Vinnie has had the fever."

Raze nodded, noting the Ripper had stopped following them. "I'm not planning on hitting that, so it doesn't matter." He kept the language crude on purpose so Jax would drop it.

"You could use a condom."

Jesus. "I don't need a pimp, Mercury."

"I'm just saying. Life is short, and she seems to like you for some damn reason. You moved her into your place." Jax slowed down to drive around a couple of facedown bodies partially decomposed in the center of the street.

"I'm bunking with Tace. Not interested in Vivienne." Not for the right reasons, anyway. Raze jerked his head toward a bunch of smashed mirrors up ahead. "Avoid the glass."

"Copy that." Jax had to drive up on a sidewalk and over lumber. The truck jumped and hitched, but they made it back to the street all right. "Did Vinnie say how yesterday afternoon went with the patients?"

Ah-ha. So Mercury wanted the dish on everybody. Suspicious bastard. "No, and don't push her." Even as he said the words, Raze bit back a wince.

"No need to be overprotective," Jax drawled.

"I'm not, but you haven't heard her screaming late at night."

Jax slowed down and squinted out the window. "Pine Street." He turned and drove down a street canopied by palm trees. "It's interesting you've heard her scream so often. You time your patrol to be within hearing distance?"

"Just doing my job, boss." Raze stretched his neck as homes, nicer than the earlier ones, started to line the street. Brick homes, small but probably well kept at some point. "We're going the wrong way."

"No." Jax tugged a page from the phone book out of his pocket and unfolded it on his leg. Glancing down, he pursed his lips. "Twenty-seven-O-Two Jacoby Street." He drove farther down Pine Street and then turned at Jacoby, which held more homes. "Humph."

Raze eyed the silent brick sentinels. "We could raid here. Looks fairly untouched." They could really use prescription drugs as well as canned goods. And condoms, although not for him.

"Agreed." Jax downshifted to move around a green barrel. "I don't like having somebody I barely know cover my back—it makes me twitchy."

Raze preferred not to know anybody right now. Even so, he understood the sentiment. "Fine. What do you want to know?"

"Not your biggest dreams or fears, asshole. How about telling me why you went into the service."

That made sense. As former soldiers, they had that in common. So Jax was looking for common ground? Raze kept his focus on the threats outside the truck. "My dad died in the service, and my mom worked hard but didn't have much money. The service seemed like a good idea, and I enjoyed it. Made friends, and I miss my good ones every day." So damn many people had died from Scorpius. "You entered the military because a judge made you, right?"

"Yep. Either prison or military. Either way, I had to leave gang life or I'd be dead."

It seemed like that background had actually served Jax well after the world became infected. Raze cleared his throat. "Speaking of gang life, any news on your brother?"

"No. I've sent out sketches with his face, but nobody has seen Marcus." Jax slowed down to cross over a bunch of crumbled bricks in the center of the road.

It'd be a miracle if Jax ever saw Marcus again. The gang leader Jax had killed when rescuing Lynne had hinted that Marcus, another gang member, was still alive. It was likely that the gang leader had just been messing with Jax's head. "I hope you find him," Raze said.

"Me too. What about you? Siblings?"

Raze purposefully kept his body from stiffening. "A younger sister named Maureen."

"Ah. Where is she now?"

"Not with us," Raze said. He couldn't exactly tell Jax that Maureen was being held by the Mercenaries up north.

"I'm sorry."

"Me too. She was everything good in this world, you know? I pretty much raised her since our mom had to work so much, and she ended up so damn smart. Got a scholarship to Harvard."

"Wow."

Raze nodded. "Studied food production. Wanted to end world hunger."

"Sounds like she was a sweetheart. I would've liked to have met her." Jax slowed down. "There it is." He pulled into an empty driveway with 2702 on a plaque near the dusty red door. Another sign had been mounted on the house near the driveway: "Jack's Construction—Go around back."

A home business. Raze's heartbeat sped up a little. "Unless scavengers bothered to look in the phone book, if they could even find one, this type of business wouldn't be easy to find."

"Nope. Let's hope Jack didn't take his goodies with him if he left." Jax stopped the truck and jumped out.

"Let's hope Jack left," Raze muttered, exiting the truck, leaving his door open for a quick getaway. He settled his stance and took a moment as Jax did the same thing, not moving.

Birds trilled above, their chirping cheerful in the chilling quiet. No sound came from the ground or from the homes around them. No children laughing, no lawn mowers humming, no cars honking. No life.

Raze caught Jax's eye and gave a short nod.

Jax nodded back, any congeniality gone from his stone-cold face. Leading with his gun, he kept to the brick and started making his way down the rest of the driveway past the house.

Raze stayed on his six, emerging onto a square of concrete with a metal shop on the far side. The twenty-foot garage door was closed, as was the bright yellow man-size door to the side.

The wind picked up, scattering palm leaves against the house, while the birds continued to chatter. So long as they kept up the noise, he wasn't too worried.

Jax kept his gun low and sidestepped across the empty lot to twist the doorknob of the shop. It turned easily and swung open. He leaned against the far side.

Raze hustled his way, his peripheral vision working hard, and stopped on the other side of the door. "I'll go low." He waited until Jax had nodded, took another glance around at the trees lining the wooden fence on either side of the property, and then bunched his legs. Turning, he ducked into the room and went low.

Jax moved in sync, his gun high.

Sunlight filtered through a series of windows from the back, revealing a stunning 1969 Boss 429 Mustang.

Jax whistled.

Raze nodded, his gaze on the shiny chrome as he straightened. "What a beauty," he whispered.

"Man, I wish we could take her." Regret crossed Jax's face, so real and heartfelt, it almost made Raze laugh out loud.

"Me too," he whispered back. New red and chrome lockers and tool storage units lined both walls, while the floor was sealed concrete, clean and nearly sparkling. "I'm thinking if there was a work truck, it's long gone."

Jax nodded and began filtering through the lockers, every once in a while glancing with longing at the Mustang.

After twenty minutes of searching, all they found were a couple of hammers, a can of nails, and a box of girlie magazines. Jax loaded them up and headed outside.

Raze cut him a look.

"What? We have teenagers, you know. Every teenager

should have a skin magazine." Jax's stride didn't waver as he continued out to the truck.

Raze shook his head. What a bust. "This was a waste of time," he muttered, carefully closing the door behind them. Maybe someday he could return for the car.

Jax nodded and dumped the loot in the back of the crappy truck. "Yep. We have five more businesses like this to hit. The shop was so clean, let's skip the house. They took everything of value."

Raze nodded and slid back into the passenger seat. Unfortunately, the best loot was found at homes with dead bodies. He was so damn tired of dead bodies.

They worked methodically through the list of home-based construction companies, finding many more tools, some pot, more magazines, cigarettes, and even a generator before reaching Plympton's Hard Tools on the far side of Compton.

While they didn't speak much, they moved in sync, both having been trained well. Jax had been Delta Force, while Raze had been SEAL Team Six. Something else they didn't discuss.

Plympton's was comprised of two metal shops behind a double-wide trailer not nearly as nice as the other buildings. A work truck had been abandoned near the trailer and gave up tools, electrical wire, and cocaine.

Raze lifted his eyebrows. "Do we want the coke?"

"Yep. Take all drugs." Jax squinted toward the first shop. "We can't be picky when it comes to pain management and bullet wounds."

True. "If I get shot, don't even think of using coke," Raze said, gathering the bundle to slide it beneath an old tire in the back of the truck.

"Copy that."

They walked side by side toward the first shop, more

than used to entering new buildings together. Before Raze could open the door, Jax moved, smoothly slicing a hand-cuff over his wrist.

What the hell? Raze kicked out, nailing the Vanguard leader in the leg.

Jax grunted, jumped forward, and secured the other cuff to the side of the metal door. Then he backed up, weapon out.

Raze went still. He'd gotten caught up in the day and had forgotten to watch his back. How the hell had he gotten so damn complacent? "What the fuck?"

"You don't sound surprised," Jax said, his aim steady.

"I'm not." If he went for the knife in his boot, Jax would shoot to kill. Raze's gun was at his waist, and he was fast, but Jax was probably fast, too. "You going to leave me here?" His heartbeat sped up, and he tried to control his breathing.

Jax slowly shook his head.

Ah, hell. Jax would go for the sure result. "You're just going to shoot me and go," Raze said evenly.

"That's the plan."

Raze kept his gaze level. If he could talk Jax into just leaving him cuffed, he could eventually get free. If Jax shot him in the head, then nobody would be able to help Maureen. He had to live. "I helped you save Lynne from Atherton. Why are you doing this?"

"Let's not play games." A muscle ticked at Jax's jaw. "Give me some credit. You had to expect this."

"No." Sure, he'd expected it, but he'd gotten careless in the hunt for explosives. Jax and his crew had drawn Raze right in, and sweet Vinnie was the cream on top. "I didn't think you had it in you. To kill a guy you'd fought next to."

Jax snarled. "Reminding me of lost comrades is a shitty thing to do."

"Shooting me in the head is worse," Raze countered dryly.

"Tell me the full truth, and I won't shoot you. Why did you walk into Vanguard territory and offer to help? More importantly, how did you come by the intel about President Atherton that helped us rescue Lynne and Vinnie last week? You knew way too much about him and his troops." Jax's aim didn't waiver a millimeter.

"I've been traveling and gaining intel," Raze said, giving part of the truth. "I'm not going to harm you or yours, Jax." Except Vinnie. He was going to betray her, and that would hurt.

A ruckus started up behind the other shop.

Raze reached for his weapon, able only to turn a little, while Jax slid to his right.

Instantly, four men ran around the far side. The lead two held guns, the next two knives and leashes. Jax settled his stance, switching his aim to the men.

The long leashes were attached to women running on all fours, who careened around the building, snarling.

"What the fuck?" Jax muttered.

The lead guy, a man in a pale green suit, smiled. "You're trespassing." Without blinking, he fired.

Chapter Eight

We find our friends by chance in the oddest of places, and only we can decide to keep them in our hearts.

—Dr. Frank X. Harmony, *Philosophies*

Vinnie tried to roll up the sleeves of her borrowed sweater, leaving clumps at her wrists. Maybe the scavengers could look for some petite clothing on their next run. At least the yoga pants only went to her ankles and not beyond. Of course they were supposed to end right below the knee.

She hurried across the soup kitchen in the direction in which Lynne had disappeared and crossed into what looked like a former medical office. Long reception desk, waiting room with old magazines, and dark carpet. "Lynne?"

"Back here," came the call.

Vinnie nodded and inched around the desk, heading down a hallway. A door to her left held a couple of hospital beds and, farther down, an opening led to a kitchenette. Well, what used to be a kitchenette. Now a couple of old microscopes sat on a table surrounded by reams of paper and articles.

Lynne glanced up from a microscope, her eyes focusing. "How are the new digs?"

"Fine." Vinnie moved inside to take a plastic orange seat.

"Good. You know, when I first got here, Jax and I shared an apartment." Lynne rubbed her pointy chin. "Not that I wanted to."

Vinnie sat back. "He, ah, forced you?" She'd been told that women didn't barter for sex and were never forced in Vanguard, unlike much of the remaining world.

"Kind off." Lynne shoved curly brown hair off her forehead. "I mean, he gave me the couch if I wanted it, but we had to share the room for safety reasons." She blushed a deep pink. "Then I decided to stay and share for other reasons."

Right. Vinnie scrutinized her. Love shone in her eyes. Of course in drastic times, being tied to a guy like Jax Mercury also meant safety. "You make a nice couple."

Lynne rolled her eyes. "We make an explosive couple, but I like us."

A former head of a CDC unit and a special ops solider? Yeah. That probably did lead to an explosion or two. "Does your blue heart hurt?" Vinnie gasped and covered her mouth. "I'm so sorry. Since the drugs, sometimes my mouth gets ahead of my brain and I just can't control it, I really didn't mean—"

Lynne held up a hand and grinned. "Take a breath." She glanced down at the glowing blue through a pink T-shirt. "The blue doesn't hurt, although sometimes it feels, well, weird."

Vinnie leaned forward, her gaze fastened on the glow. "Weird how?"

Lynne lifted a shoulder. "I don't know. Just like my chest feels heavy or constricted."

"That could be anxiety." Or heartburn. Or any number of things.

"I know, but I can't help wondering."

"Why is it blue?" Vinnie asked. "I've never understood that fact."

Lynne shook her head. "When we first started experimenting with vitamin B to cure Scorpius, I was injected with an experimental concoction, turning my heart blue. We were never able to duplicate the exact formula again, although since it didn't cure me, I'm not sure it matters."

"Why blue though?"

She sighed. "I have both photosphores and chromatophores in my heart, which without the initial bacterial infection would be impossible. Squids and octopi have the same materials, essentially, and they can turn different colors—usually blue."

Vinnie nodded. "I see. Both squid and octopuses are high in vitamin B."

"Yes. I'm hoping that the government, while it still existed, stored squid somewhere . . . maybe in this Bunker we're all looking for." Lynne rolled her neck. "So, enough about me. I'm weird, right?"

"So am I. My brain is different," Vinnie whispered. Damn it. There went her mouth again. "Since having Scorpius and all the mind-control drugs. I can sense odd things, and I hear voices sometimes."

Lynne's gaze sharpened. "That's interesting."

Vinnie chuckled. "That's the scientist in you talking."

"Sure. I mean, you can relate. You were kind of a scientist, right?"

Vinnie bit back a full-on laugh. "Said just like a medical and research doctor to a psychologist."

Lynne winced. "I'm sorry. I do think psychology is a science. I mean, kind of." She buried her face in her hands. "I'm an ass."

"No, you're not." Hell, many scientists didn't consider psychology to be a science, and that was fine with Vinnie.

"Without understanding humans and behavior, what's the point of the rest of science?"

Lynne slowly lifted her head. "Sure. Let's go with that."

Vinnie eyed the row of worn-looking microscopes. "We can tell who's been infected and who hasn't, right?"

Lynne nodded. "Yeah. With a simple blood test, even just a couple of drops, I can see the infection." She breathed out. "We've thought about requiring Vanguard citizens to take the test so we know who the survivors are, but that seems like such a breach of privacy, you know?"

"Yeah."

Tace loped into the room, his black hat still in place.

"How often are you going to wear that?" Lynne asked.

The Texan shrugged, his big body filling the doorway. "Makes me think of home."

Vinnie nodded, noting he didn't say *feel* like home. But *think*. "I was hoping maybe we could find time to chat."

A slow smile lifted his full lips. "Aw, shucks, ma'am. You hitting on me?"

She blinked, her breath catching. "No. Not at all. I want to dig into your brain." She clapped a hand over her mouth. What the hell?

"I figured," Tace murmured. "Didn't mean to tease you, darlin'."

She straightened up and focused. "The amusement and the flirting. Is it real? I mean, do you feel it?"

His smile slid away. "No. Not really. I remember feeling it, and I know what to say and when to say it, but I don't actually feel it. Not anymore."

Lynne stood and ran a hand down his arm. "You will. Keep in mind, you only contracted the fever a couple of weeks ago and you haven't had time to heal. The B is in your system now and we'll shore it up. Trust me."

He nodded and patted her hand. "I do trust you." The wink he aimed at Vinnie was slow and surprisingly sexy.

"For now, why don't you dig into my brain, Doc?" He glanced at Lynne. "I'm surrounded by doctors. Well, kind of."

Vinnie bit back a chuckle as Lynne frowned. Apparently medics didn't really consider scientists to be doctors. "Aren't we chock full of preconceived notions?" she murmured, fairly certain that all science really stemmed from psychology. All discovery originated in the human brain or, at the very least, the observations of the human mind. "Are you a medical doctor, Tace?" she asked.

"No, ma'am." He pushed his hat farther back on his head. "I was a medic in the army, so I'm trained in combat. We have three real doctors inner territory, but none of them had much combat training. Now they have plenty."

Vinnie nodded and pushed out another orange chair. "Too bad we don't have a couch." She smiled.

He wiggled his eyebrows. "I could find a couch if you'd rather snuggle with me."

Lynne sighed and smacked his arm. "Knock it off." She retook her seat. "Why did Bret Atherton think you were psychic, Vivienne?"

Vinnie's shoulders went back and her breath caught in her throat. She turned her gaze on Lynne, reminded again of just how smart Dr. Lynne Harmony was. "Bret had access to my FBI files, and I had successfully solved a string of serial killer cases."

"And?" Tace said, dropping into a seat.

She took a deep breath. "I was good at my job." She'd always been able to read people and get into their minds, but there was nothing otherworldly about it. "After Scorpius spread, the government, such as it was, needed a couple of Rippers chased down, and they came to my unit for help." Whispers tickled across her brain, sounds and feelings, more voices. Was she partially schizophrenic?

"You found the Rippers?" Lynne asked.

"Yes." Vinnie took a haphazard stack of papers and patted them into a neat pile. "I used my knowledge of human and sociopathic behavior to calculate where they'd go. One of them was a guy named Spiral."

Lynne sat back. "He brought down the Internet."

Vinnie sighed. "Well, he created a computer virus that did so, but he didn't work alone. Eventually, the Brigade caught him, and he died in a firefight."

Lynne gasped and grabbed Vinnie's wrist. "You saw the Brigade? Did you meet Deacan McDougall?"

Vinnie tried not to wince from the firm hold. "Yes. Four months ago I worked with McDougall to bring down Spiral." McDougall was the leader of the Brigade, the USA's front line of defense against Scorpius, and was one seriously badass guy with a Scottish accent. "Knowing McDougall, he's still in charge of the Brigade, but I'm not sure they answer to the president or his elite force."

"I'd heard they'd gone rogue," Tace murmured.

Lynne's eyes widened and she removed her hand. "Sorry." She winced at the red marks on Vinnie's skin. "Was Nora Medina—I mean McDougall—with Deke?" She visibly held her breath.

"Yes. Dr. McDougall was with Deacon, and as they gathered information on the infection, from data to possible cures from around the globe, she worked on putting it all together." Vinnie clasped her hands in her lap, out of reach.

Tears filled Lynne's eyes. "So Nora and Deke were alive—at least four months ago. I knew it."

Vinnie nodded, her heart softening. "I take it you're friends?" She kept the tense in the present because if anybody could survive out there, it'd be McDougall.

"Yes. Nora is my best friend, has been for years." Lynne smiled, her lips trembling. "I actually used emotional blackmail to get her to remarry Deke when I was first infected with Scorpius and turned all blue."

Vinnie's eyebrows lifted. "Well, if it helps, they seemed very happy." As happy as two people could be when most of the world was dying or chasing them.

"Good." Lynne sniffed. "I, ah, am going to use the restroom. I'll be back." She stood to leave and tripped over Tace's boot.

He caught her with one hand before she could hit the floor and then waited until she'd straightened before releasing her. She sighed and continued walking, bumping into the doorframe as she exited.

Vinnie watched her leave, bemused.

"She's a total klutz," Tace confirmed. "All right. My brain? I don't feel anything, even much pain, and I'm not nearly enough bothered by that fact. Am I a sociopath?"

Vinnie reached for another stack of papers to settle into some semblance of order. "I doubt it. Sounds like a normal reaction to the Scorpius bacterium, especially if you haven't had time to heal yet. Do you get urges to kill anybody?"

"No. But I'm fine if I have to do it." He shrugged. "Before being infected, it would've bothered me a lot. Now?" His hand rested on the table, and his fingers began to tap. "I shot a guy the other day without thinking twice about it, and I also seem to be obsessing about things." His shoulders hunched, and his hand inched toward the papers.

Interesting. Just how bad was it? Vinnie reached for more papers to stack, watching him carefully. She made the newest stack smaller and then tilted it just a bit toward the other two stacks.

A flush worked its way up Tace's hard face.

She sat back to give him room. Images and thoughts, all male and irritated, wandered through her consciousness. No way was she reading minds, but she sure could read people all of a sudden. She shook her head, trying to banish the idea of psychic powers, and yet she knew what Tace would do even before he suddenly moved.

He shuddered.

She kept perfectly silent.

"Hell." He grabbed the off-kilter stack, aligned it with the other two, and then dispersed papers until they were even. "Scorpius gave me OCD."

"You weren't, ah . . ."

"Freaky organized before being infected? No, ma'am." Tace shoved the hat back on his head, lines cutting into the sides of his mouth. "Aren't most sociopaths obsessive compulsive?"

She eyed the perfect stacks of paper. "No. Not at all." Sure, some were, but many normal people suffered from different degrees of OCD. "If you were a patient, I'd say that if the OCD isn't altering your life to a large degree, then some biofeedback is all you'd need. No medication, even." Of course the disease could progress.

His eyebrows lifted. "I am a patient, right?"

She opened her mouth and then shut it again. "I, ah, guess so." While she'd thought she'd just be consulting with Jax and his team about serial killers and likely scenarios when there were specific threats, it did make sense that she act as a psychologist. God knew survivors probably needed counseling.

"So shrink my brain."

She rolled her eyes. "Jax said there's an office somewhere here in headquarters."

Tace pushed away from the table. "I have a room toward the back that used to be a doctor's office. I've made it into your place now. Let's go and I'll show you."

She stood, her body settling. For months she'd wanted to belong somewhere. She could do that here, and she could actually help people. Once she got her own brain under control. For the first time in way too long, hope began to unfurl inside her, and she followed Tace from the kitchenette.

A shout echoed from the other room and she turned so quickly, her ankle protested.

Tace pivoted and ran for the reception room.

She followed and quickly jumped out of the way as two men hurried in carrying another man, this one bleeding profusely from the leg.

"Was patrolling east and looking for ammunition. Ran into an ambush," said a heavyset guy sweating under the strain of carrying the injured man.

"Put him in the first examination room," Tace said over his shoulder, running down the hallway.

The men complied, and Vinnie followed to see them dump the guy on a cot before backing away. The smell of dirt and blood filled the air.

The injured man appeared to be about eighteen, with short blond hair and a goatee. His ripped T-shirt had a faded picture of the Grateful Dead on it.

Lynne rushed in behind them and grabbed a pair of scissors off the counter to cut open the leg of his jeans. "Wait outside, guys," she said calmly, bending closer to tear the denim away from the wound. "Was he shot or bitten?"

"Shot," the heavy guy said before exiting.

Tace finished dumping something from a bleach can over his hands in a sink set in the corner. He grabbed a surgical knife.

The kid mumbled something from the cot. Pain slid across Vinnie's mind. Thoughts scattered like buckshot. *Mom. Help me, Mom.*

The thoughts weren't hers, but she felt them, and deep. The kid's mom wasn't anywhere near, but Vinnie was. She rushed forward and took his free hand. "You'll be okay. I promise," she murmured.

Tace sliced into his skin and a shriek of pain cut like a blade into Vinnie's brain. She blinked and stopped breathing.

The kid convulsed and screamed.

The echo roared through her head and landed hard in her stomach.

"Oh, God," the kid moaned a second before he went limp into unconsciousness.

Relief filled Vinnie for about two seconds. Then darkness attacked her just as the boy's hand relaxed beneath hers.

She barely felt her body hit the floor before she was out.

Chapter Nine

———••◉••———

If you find trust, you're not a sociopath. Well, probably.

        —Dr. Vinnie Wellington, *Sociopaths*

Raze ducked against the metal building, and a bullet clipped his shoulder. Pain cascaded over his skin from a superficial wound. He and Jax fired simultaneously, each hitting his target center mass and dropping the two men with the guns.

Jax tossed him a set of keys, and he quickly uncuffed his wrist.

Blood slithered and settled across the concrete. The two remaining men stiffened, their knives glinting in the dim light, while the leashed women started to screech. What the holy fuck?

"Rippers," Jax muttered, angling toward the garage.

"Yeah." Raze angled the other way, splitting the focus of the enemy. "I'll get behind them." If they could get the guys to go back to back, they'd have a better chance.

"I'll take the Rippers," Jax hissed.

Although Raze appreciated the thought, considering Jax had already been infected with Scorpius and Raze hadn't, he shook his head, moving smoothly in a circle. "Take down the standing men and deal with Rippers last." The women both gurgled white foam, definitely beyond helping.

Jax kept moving until his back was to the closed garage door.

Raze tried to focus on any sound beyond the garage in case there were more of them, but the snarling and hissing of the Rippers blocked any other noises.

Above them, the birds had gone silent.

"We have guns and you have knives," Raze said quietly to the guy following his every move. He was about six foot and two hundred and forty pounds, most of it gone to fat. But he was solid, and he'd provide a good fight. He wore faded white shorts and a wrinkled blue golf shirt, while his shaggy hair reached his shoulders. "I really don't want to shoot you today," Raze added.

The woman on the leash jerked against it.

"Stop." The guy pulled up on the leash.

Raze's gut boiled. "Why don't you put her down?" The poor woman.

"Because she bites when I tell her to bite."

The Ripper sat down on her ass and wrapped her arms around her knees, rocking back and forth.

Raze sidestepped a couple of yards, his gun held evenly, until he was opposite Jax with four enemies between them. "Get out of here and I won't shoot you," he said.

"I can't do that," the guy in the polo shirt answered, raising his knife higher.

Raze widened his stance, adrenaline flowing through his veins. His vision focused and his body settled. "Gun versus knife? Gun wins."

"Maybe." The guy lowered his chin. "Now, Henrietta."

She leaped sideways and then charged Raze, directly in front of the other female Ripper. Raze squeezed the trigger and the body kept coming, plowing into him, knocking him down. He let gravity take over, landed on his back, and tossed the woman over his head. Rocks cut into Raze's shoulder, digging in with pain.

Two gunshots echoed over his head from Jax.

Like a blur, the remaining woman on the ground propelled herself forward and latched onto Raze's ankle before he could move.

Agony lit his leg and he jerked away, bringing his gun hand up.

The Ripper tore way, taking a chunk of Raze's skin with her.

Raze fired, hitting the chick between her half-crazed eyes. The body fell back onto the ground and blood oozed beneath the head, filling the cracks.

Jax hustled toward him, bending down to check the ankle just as Raze sat up. A chunk of flesh was missing, clearly outlined by sharp bite marks.

Raze coughed, his head swimming. He'd been infected. Emotion swamped through him from panic to fear and finally to anger.

"Hell, man," Jax breathed, glancing up with darkened eyes. "We have to get you back to headquarters."

"I thought you wanted me dead." Raze allowed him to set a shoulder beneath his arm.

"That was before. If you survive the bite, you'll need vitamin B. You'll tell me everything I want to know," Jax said almost cheerfully.

"Fuck." Raze allowed Jax to help him up before jerking his head toward the closed garage. He had to survive to save his sister. "We have an hour, Jax. Let's see what they were so intent on protecting."

Jax glanced at the silent building and then down at Raze's profusely bleeding ankle. "One look and we go." He tugged off his T-shirt and leaned down to tie it tightly around the wound.

Pain shot through Raze and he caught his breath. "Thanks."

Jax helped him around the downed bodies to throw open the door. The shop was about forty-five by fifty feet, with a concrete floor and haphazard shelves lining each wall. Blankets were strewn across the floor, along with empty cans of beans and corn.

The smell of body odor and piss was suffocating.

Jax turned toward the far wall and let out a small whistle. "Look at that."

Three boxes of dynamite sat next to an oversized generator, several lanterns, more cans of food, toilet paper, and a bunch of other boxes.

Jax pushed Raze to the nearest wall. "I'll get the truck." He glanced at his wristwatch. "You have about an hour before the fever strikes, and we need you contained at that point."

Contained? Just the thought made him want to puke. Raze reached up to push the garage door opener. Nothing happened. Heat climbed into his face. Of course nothing happened; there was no electricity. His brain was already getting muddled.

Jax lifted an eyebrow but didn't comment. Instead, he leaned down and forced the door up, grunting with the effort. The door slowly rose, fighting him, but finally he lifted it to the point the truck could get under it. "Stay here."

Raze nodded and half-limped, half-hopped toward the boxes. No damn bite injury would keep him on the sidelines. If this was his last day on earth, he was gonna be useful.

Nausea filled his stomach, and his head began to ache. Tingles of heat pricked just under his skin. He'd known someday he'd be infected, but he thought he'd have a little more time. Now he had to survive the damn fever, or everything he'd worked for would be lost. He couldn't lose. Not now.

So he ignored the pain and heat, reaching for a box of dynamite.

Jax backed the truck into the garage, guiding it around the dead bodies without running them over.

Raze swayed. His vision fuzzed, and his ankles felt like jello.

When the truck stopped, he shoved the dynamite toward the cab. "Good call on the small construction companies," he said as Jax joined him after fetching the weapons from the dead men.

"Thanks. Let's get all of this loaded, and fast. If we don't get vitamin B into your bloodstream within the hour, you'll be one dangerous Ripper." Jax grabbed two of the closed boxes. "If you don't die, that is."

Raze nodded, an odd and heated pressure pushing against the back of his eyeballs. "If anything happens to me, there's a letter hidden. Please read it." At the very least, Jax needed to know what he was up against.

"At your place?"

Dots swam across Raze's vision. What did he say? "Urg."

"Roger that." Jax bent at the knees to lift the generator. "Give me a hand with this before you lose your strength."

"I won't." Raze moved to help, sweat breaking out down his arms.

"Uh-huh." The muscles down Jax's arm rippled when he stood, and a cut from a fight the other day split open on his bicep.

They loaded the generator and then all the boxes, with Jax keeping an eye on his watch. Finally, he headed toward the driver's side. "Get in. We need to speed."

Raze's vision wavered, and he took careful steps to slide into the passenger side of the truck. A roaring started up between his ears. His blood? How infected was he? How soon would he lose consciousness?

Some folks, more than he liked to admit, had been ready to give in to Scorpius. It was so hard to live these days. Not him, though. Damn, he wanted to live.

Sweat slicked down his arms and dotted his forehead. His legs went numb and chills attacked him. Slowly, trying to be cautious, he secured his seat belt in case he went into convulsions.

Jax shoved the truck into gear and tore out of the square, jerking the wheel to avoid dead bodies. "We don't have time to bury or burn them."

Raze clutched the door handle, his breath panting out. "I know." Hell. Was it possible he'd succumb faster than most? "Hurry up, Mercury." Fire licked up his throat, burning his tongue.

Jax pressed on the gas, and the truck lurched onto the street, barreling by empty land before reaching the first of several residential areas. The sun rose high in the sky, and though they ought to be sticking to the back roads, he drove hell-bent in a straight line for headquarters.

"Take a better route," Raze ground out. "If we're attacked, I'm about to be useless to you."

"No time," Jax hissed back. "You're sweating like a bastard."

Yeah, he was. Sweat trickled down Raze's face and he wiped it off. "If anything happens to me, there's a letter—"

"You already told me," Jax said, leaning forward in his seat to drive around a downed tree.

He had? "Oh." The windshield bubbled in front of him. Hell. Now he was hallucinating. "I just want you to understand. Want Vinnie to understand."

Jax cut him a sharp look, his face morphing into odd lines like a clown in a carnival mirror. "Understand what?"

"Not what." Raze shut his eyes to stop seeing things that weren't there. "Why. Understand why." Cramps attacked his stomach, and he partially doubled over.

The truck pitched over several branches left lying in the deserted street, and Raze jerked back in his seat, his entire body suddenly awakening to something beyond mere pain.

He grimaced and dug his nails into the handle. "Was tortured in Somalia once," he gritted out.

"Yeah?" Jax slowed down to drive around the burned-out shell of a Mercedes.

"Yeah." Raze leaned back his head and allowed the pain to flow through him. Fighting it would only make him lose. If he accepted the pain, he could control it. "Electricity. And bats. Metal bats."

"Fuck, that hurts." Jax punched the gas again. "I've dealt with the electricity, but nobody ever hit me with a bat. With boards full of nails, though."

"Nails suck." Raze blew out through his nose because his mouth felt like he'd sucked on glass. Would his tongue swell until he couldn't breathe? Totally possible. He had to talk about something, anything but death. God. What would Jax want to talk about? "So, you and Blue Heart?"

"Lynne. I'm the only one who calls her Blue."

Right. He knew that. "You and Lynne. Is it the real thing?" Whatever the real thing was, if it even existed. Could it exist in the world as it was now?

"Yeah. I mean, I think so." The side of the truck scraped against a rock wall as Jax avoided an overturned ice cream truck. "Before I was fighting just because Rippers and LA gangbangers needed to be fought. Now I fight because I have Lynne. When I almost died in Nevada, her face was the last thing I saw in my mind. That's real, right?"

"Hell if I know," Raze breathed. It sounded real. In fact, it sounded kind of nice. An image of Vinnie's face swam across his vision. Pretty. So pretty. "Sounds real, though."

"Yeah, and it's what I've got."

An ache bloomed out from Raze's spine to ricochet off every nerve he had. "I figured Lynne was using you for protection and safety." It'd be a smart move.

"Yeah?"

"Yep. But then I got to know her, and she lights up when you walk into a room." Only one person, his baby sister, had ever been glad to see Raze Shadow, and he was going to save her if it was the last thing he did, which it probably would be. When he betrayed Jax by saving her, he'd be a hunted man.

"How you feelin'?" Jax asked.

"Like I got bit by a Ripper," Raze returned, keeping his eyelids shut. "It's more painful than I figured."

"It gets worse."

That's what he was afraid of. "We close?"

"Yep." The truck slowed, and the sound of Jax rolling down the window filled the cab. He gave a whistle—the emergency one that said to open the gates, and now.

Raze nodded. Now would be good.

The world fuzzed, even with his sight gone.

Raze jerked against the seat belt as the truck lurched forward, and he fumbled with the clasp. Before he knew it, the truck stopped and his door was wrenched open.

"Got bit," Jax yelled, running around the truck.

Raze opened his eyes just as Tace pulled him free, muscles bunching across his arms. Sunlight smashed down, making the world waver as if he'd taken several acid hits. He laughed.

"Hell. How long?" Tace asked, taking one arm while Jax grabbed the other.

"About an hour," Jax said.

They moved him inside the soup kitchen toward the medical triage, all but dragging him the last few yards and then dumping him on a bed.

"Secure him," Tace said.

"No." Raze tried to lift himself up. "No restraints. I won't fight the fever."

"Okay." Smooth as silk, Jax fastened his left arm while Tace got the right.

"Fuck." Raze fought against them, kicking his legs, but the men worked together and soon had him secured on the bed. "Assholes."

Tace disappeared and returned to slide two needles into his arm. "Morphine and vitamin B. We'll keep you injected throughout the rest of today and tonight, but it's still going to hurt. Scorpius burns from the inside."

"I know." Raze forced his body to relax as the morphine tried to take hold. He could fight it, but why? So he allowed the medicine to somewhat numb him and ease a bit of the panic.

"Oh my goodness. What happened?" asked a female voice, one that slid right through him to land hard somewhere he didn't know existed. Somewhere inside him that had been closed off forever.

He blinked sweat out of his eyes.

She peered down, beautiful blue eyes concerned, her stunning blond hair pulled back at the nape. "Oh, Raze. What in the world happened?"

He tried to reach up and touch her—to feel that softness one more time. "Vinnie. I'm so damn sorry." Then darkness yanked him away.

Chapter Ten

Sometimes a demon just wants to snuggle.
—Dr. Vinnie Wellington, *Sociopaths*

Vinnie smoothed Raze's hair back from his heated forehead as he kept eerily still. His muscles twitched once in a while, but even unconscious, he seemed to be in perfect control. Most patients thrashed around and cried out.

Not Raze.

The fever swelled from him, and perspiration dotted his now pale face.

She sat next to him, gently patting and soothing him. An hour or so ago, she'd tried to leave, and he'd mumbled her name until she'd returned to his side. Her hands trembled, but she kept her touch light. "You're all right," she whispered, trying to guess at his fever. It was high. Way too high.

Tace reached her and handed over a semicool washcloth. "We've been keeping some of the rainwater in the basement."

She placed the faded blue cloth over Raze's forehead, trying to will him to live. He was the strongest man she'd ever met, and that had to count for something, right? "Is it still raining?" she whispered.

"No. We're probably finished with the rain," Tace

whispered back. "Should conserve water, but he needs to be cooled down." The medic leaned back against the wall and crossed his arms. "The fever is really high. That's a warning."

"I know." Her stomach cramped. "The higher the fever, the more likelihood . . ." Of death. The more likelihood of death.

A soldier like Raze, one who'd faced death more than once, just couldn't succumb to a tiny bacterium. It wasn't right. The idea of facing Vanguard and its people without him providing his natural shield made her want to cry. Or run.

Tace grabbed scissors from a small counter and reached Raze, quickly ripping open his sweaty T-shirt. "Put the washcloth on his chest."

Vinnie's eyes widened. She hadn't taken a good look at Raze's chest the other night. Ripped and predatory, his muscles showed strength, while a myriad of scars proclaimed a life of battle. Burns ran up his arm and over his shoulder, whitened with age. She flattened a hand on his heated flesh, counting two bullet holes, a knife wound, and a couple of other punctures she couldn't identify.

Tace reached for the cloth and dropped it on her hands. She rolled the faded material over and flattened it on the scars. "He's not moving. That's weird, right?" she asked.

"Yes, ma'am," Tace murmured. "That's the tightest control I've ever seen. Elite soldiers, the really dangerous kind who face torture, are trained to control themselves even in drugged or nearly unconscious states. That man is well trained."

She swallowed. It was more than that. "He's strong. Incredibly strong, body and brain." She smoothed the washcloth over his hard body, her lungs compressing. Oh, he was amazing to look at, but that strength? She wanted that. Not only to have it but to hold it. Life was so terribly dangerous, and he could keep her safe.

Man, she was a wimp. "I can keep myself safe," she muttered.

A snort sounded to her left, and she turned her head.

"You're a total wimp," Lucinda said cheerfully, floating around the bed. "You should get a brawny guy like this to cover you. That Lynne Harmony knew what she was doing when she landed Jax."

"He's not a fish," Vinnie hissed to her annoying hallucination.

"Huh?" Tace asked, his gaze sharpening.

"Nothing." Vinnie turned back to Raze's too-silent form.

Her stepmother sighed, and Vinnie could swear she felt the breath stir her hair. "He's not going to survive," Lucinda said mournfully. "How about the Texan? He's blond and cute. Good body. A little dark and moody, but so is the entire world."

Vinnie ignored her. "He's going to be okay." She said the words out loud, just in case Raze could hear her. "He's strong enough to survive this fever. He *has* to live." Statistically, it was unlikely he'd survive the night, but surely Raze had beaten statistics before. The scars on his body proved that fact.

"What is it with you and men who keep secrets?" Lucinda muttered. "Remember that boy who kept stealing your underwear?"

Vinnie rolled her eyes. "He was twelve."

"He was wearing them," Lucinda countered.

"Who was twelve?" Tace asked, glancing around the room.

Vinnie coughed, turning to face him. "Sorry. My mind wandered."

"Uh-huh." Tace's sharp gaze narrowed on her. "When you fainted a while back. What happened?"

What happened was she'd forged some sort of link with the kid in excruciating pain, and she'd actually felt the agony. Her body had shut down in protection. "Ever since I was kidnapped, I've felt weak. I just got dizzy for a moment," she lied.

Tace's eyebrows drew down. "Humph."

There was a sound by the door, and Jax strode inside. "Is Raze still secured?"

"Yep." Tace didn't move from the wall, shifting his focus to the Vanguard leader. "He's out cold, Jax. We won't be able to question him for several hours, probably not until morning."

Vinnie's breath caught. "Question him? What do you mean?"

"Keep me apprised," Jax said to Tace, his gaze squarely over Vinnie's head.

"You got it," Tace said.

"I've already searched his quarters. If he wanted to hide a letter, where would it be?" Jax asked.

Tace rubbed his chin. "Raze scouts the entire territory, but if he died and wanted you to read it, it'd be somewhere you'd eventually find it. My guess? Not in his room but somewhere close by in headquarters."

Jax slowly nodded.

"What letter?" Vinnie asked, wanting to stand and face Jax but needing to keep touching Raze. She'd figure out why later. "Jax?"

Jax glanced at her hand resting on Raze's chest. "Where do you think he'd hide a letter, Dr. Wellington?"

For some reason every time he used her former title, she felt self-conscious. "I have no clue, Master Sergeant Mercury."

He smiled, a flash of white against his bronze face. "Fair enough. One of you call me if he regains consciousness." Gracefully pivoting, the Vanguard leader strode out of sight.

Raze shifted his weight and Vinnie gasped, turning back to him. "Raze?"

"Maureen," he groaned. "Get Maureen."

Vinnie reared back.

"Interesting," Tace drawled. "Who the hell is Maureen?"

Now that was the question of the evening. "Raze hasn't ever mentioned her?" An odd burst of heat exploded in Vinnie's chest.

"Nope, but we've all lost people to Scorpius. He's certainly alone now, so I wouldn't worry about it," Tace said.

"I'm not worried about it." Vinnie drew in air, and she was sorry Raze was alone. Her first memory after being rescued from Bret Atherton was Raze carrying her to safety, and she'd pretty much attached herself to him at that point. "I'm a duck." She'd imprinted on him just like a baby duck.

Tace chuckled from behind her. "You are not a duck. We form attachments out of necessity and loneliness. Raze seeks you out more than you do him."

Vinnie frowned but her heart leapt. "That's true."

Lucinda popped up at the other side of the bed.

Vinnie jerked her head and then tried to cover the weird movement. Tace was already suspicious.

"I think he just wants in your pants," Lucinda said slowly, her gaze on Raze's bare chest. "Use a condom. I taught you to always use a condom."

Vinnie bit back a groan. Of all the people to haunt her, why did it have to be her crazy stepmother?

"Of course, like I said, he probably won't make it through the night," Lucinda muttered.

He had to live. Raze just couldn't die. Vinnie would figure out later why that mattered so much to her.

"You always did like the lost causes." Lucinda sighed. "But this one? Even if he survives, he'll definitely break your heart. It's written all over him."

"I know," Vinnie murmured softly, her gaze on the warrior fighting so valiantly. She didn't need any psychic ability to see that one coming. "We are who we are, and we've done what we've done. Heartbreak makes no difference."

Lynne Harmony poked her head inside. "Tace? How's the patient?"

Tace kept his gaze on Raze. "Still alive."

"Good." The brilliant scientist's eyes darkened. "Keep giving him vitamin B through the night, and when he awakens tomorrow, if he does, please let me know before you talk to Jax." On that ominous note, Lynne moved out of sight.

Vinnie focused on Tace. "Why? Why would she want to know first?"

Tace stared down at his fallen comrade. "I assume she wants to prevent Jax from torturing Raze for information." The Texan lifted a shoulder. "But I could be wrong."

Lynne Harmony nodded at the few folks eating sandwiches in the old soup kitchen as she passed through and entered the stairwell. She'd been almost positive Jax wouldn't shoot Raze on the mission, but a part of her had wondered. Jax Mercury protected the Vanguard citizens with an absolute focus and no mercy.

Love mellowed most men.

Not Jax. If anything, he gripped life harder than before committing to her, his determination almost frightening.

She reached their door and nudged it open. Her entire life she'd solved puzzles but had rarely understood people. A man like Jax was so far out of her wheelhouse, she didn't have a clue how to solve him. How to help him.

But God, did she love him.

He sat on the sofa, long legs extended, boots on the cracked coffee table. His dark hair brushed his neck, while his golden-brown eyes saw everything. A black T-shirt stretched across his broad chest, and he'd pulled the material out of his ripped jeans. "Where have you been?"

Her mouth watered. Whatever fate had brought her to the sexy soldier deserved a kiss. So did he. She shut the door and crossed to him, leaning down to press her lips against his.

He manacled her waist and pulled her onto his lap, taking over the kiss.

When he finally allowed her to back away, she could barely breathe. She smiled. "That was nice."

He lifted one dark eyebrow. "You didn't answer my question."

Sometimes she forgot the sharp intelligence behind that handsome face. "I was back in the makeshift lab working on the research materials we found at the Los Angeles labs." She'd found several notations about making vitamin B permanent in the body, but even more exciting, she'd found hints of a cure for Scorpius. "There were several mentions of the Bunker in a log left by a Dr. Jonas, but no concrete evidence that it exists."

Jax smoothed the hair back from her face, his fingertips calloused but his touch gentle. "Do you think it does?"

"I do." She leaned in and nuzzled the whiskers on his chin. "The more I read, the more it makes sense."

"If there was a Bunker, and it contained emergency labs and resources, then the scientists there would've immediately begun working to cure the Scorpius bacteria once it began infecting so many people," Jax said thoughtfully.

"Exactly." Lynne smoothed her hands over his wide chest. "Some of the inventory logs I've studied showed materials arriving from a place called TB, and that has to be the Bunker, right? I mean, why else just put the initials? All of the other labs are clearly identified."

"The mysterious TB," Jax said. "If there's a secret lab, and if they had a cure, they would've shared it with the military at least."

"I know." Lynne's shoulders slumped.

Jax brushed his thumb across her lips and sent tingles

through her entire body. "My best guess is that there is a Bunker created by the military, but that Scorpius got the researchers, too."

"Or maybe there isn't a cure, and the researchers are safely underground with tons of medicine and food," Lynne said.

Jax nodded. "That's possible as well."

"We need to find the Bunker. If nothing else, they have to have some research about pregnancies. I'm worried that the rumors are true and there have been no live births since Scorpius." Lynne rubbed her eyes. "It's only been six months, but all pregnancies terminated. We haven't had enough time yet to see if we'll be able to procreate after being infected."

He sighed. "We have one pregnancy here, and that's it."

"Yes. Jill Sanderson." A sweet sixteen-year-old girl who was about two months pregnant. "So far, she's doing all right."

Jax frowned. "As far as we know. It's not like we have ultrasound equipment."

Lynne leaned into him. "You didn't kill Raze."

"He got bitten." Jax flattened his hand between her shoulder blades.

"You could've left him," Lynne said gently.

"No. He's vulnerable now, and I need to find out his agenda." Jax leaned in and let his mouth wander along her jaw.

Pleasure rippled through her, and she tipped her head back to allow for more access. "You like Raze," she murmured. "It's okay to like him and still not completely trust him. He hasn't trusted you yet."

Jax stopped and leaned back, capturing her gaze. "You need to understand that I'll end him if necessary. Whether I like him or not is irrelevant. If he's a threat to you, a threat to Vanguard, then he dies."

Lynne swallowed. She did understand that fact. "I'm sure he'll come through."

"We'll see." Jax tightened his hold. "If I decide he's more liability than asset, it's a done deal. Get on board now, Blue."

Chapter Eleven

*When the end for humanity arrives, it'll be in
the form of a whisper and not a shout.*

—Dr. Frank X. Harmony, *Philosophies*

Needles poked through his skin from the inside. Raze
opened his eyelids as he shuddered, heat and freezing cold
sweeping through him.

"You lived." Jax Mercury kicked back to his right, boots
on the bed and a sandwich in his hand. "I bet against you.
Sorry about that."

"Who bet for me?" Raze croaked out, his vision wavering.

"Tace bet you'd make it." Jax dropped his feet to the
floor.

Raze drew in a deep breath. "The fever broke?"

"Yep."

His entire body thrummed with residual pain, and his
muscles felt like he hadn't moved in a year. He tried to sit
up and failed to move. A quick glance down confirmed his
suspicions. "Why am I still restrained?"

Jax finished his sandwich and dusted off his hands. "You
know why."

Ah, hell. Race had been tortured before, more than once,

but never when he'd been already so worn down. He glanced around the room, noting the door had been closed.

"You've been out for about eighteen hours. Tace is guarding the outside, and we've forced Vinnie elsewhere for the day." Jax cocked his head to the side.

Raze blinked. "Did she put up a fight?"

Jax rubbed his cheek. "The woman has a decent right cross, truth be told."

Raze's lip quirked. Sweat rolled down his cheek. "She stayed with me the entire night." As he'd drifted in and out of consciousness, the one constant was Vinnie. Her voice, her scent, her soft touch. "All night," he murmured, a possessiveness rolling through him he'd have to figure out later. When his brain worked fully.

"Yep."

Raze sighed. "Jax, I've been tortured by the best, and I've never broken. Not once. You'll kill me before I break." Unfortunately, it was the damn truth.

"I know." Jax leaned forward. "That's why I'm not going to torture you."

Raze lifted an eyebrow. "All right."

"It's too bad about Vinnie, though. She would've been a welcome addition around here." Jax's gaze gave nothing away.

Raze grinned. "You are so full of shit. No way would you torture a woman."

Jax slowly nodded. "Yep. You read me right. I mean, I would torture a woman if I absolutely had to, but in this case, I don't even know what you're hiding."

Raze lost his smile. "So?"

"So one word from me, and Tace will work her over until you give me what I want." Jax's voice remained almost pleasant, but a thread of heat wove through the tone. "He's not right, and he'll do it."

Raze studied the man. "You wouldn't."

"I would." Absolute conviction showed on Jax's face. The white scar along his jaw seemed to stand out in warning. "Two months ago, and Tace would've been in here arguing with me to let you find your way. After Scorpius? He'll torture her in ways I can't even imagine, I'm afraid."

A ball landed in his gut and exploded. "Don't do this," Raze hissed, struggling against the bindings, which held tight. If he had to kill both Jax and Tace to save Vinnie, he'd do it.

"Then tell me what I want to know. Where's the letter?"

Raze stilled. "Letter? What letter?"

Jax sighed heavily and strode for the door to open it. "Tace?"

Tace poked his head in, surveyed Raze, and then nodded. "Yeah?"

"It's time for that talk with Dr. Wellington," Jax said, his gaze remaining on Raze.

"Tace, don't even think about it," Raze growled. "I'll take your head off myself if you even give her a slight scare."

Tace's gaze remained steady, and his eyes had turned a darker blue lately. "You can't frighten me with threats. Nothing scares me since Scorpius. That part of me, the part that feels, well, doesn't. Sorry."

Raze jerked against the straps, but they held tight. He wasn't the first soldier to require restraints during the Scorpius fever. "Even after Scorpius, you're not a guy who'd torture a woman."

Tace gave a crooked smile. "I'm not sure, but I think we're about to find out."

"Wait a minute." Raze stopped fighting.

Jax snorted. "Too late."

"For what?" Raze gently tested the restraints this time. No give.

"For you to convince us that you don't care about the

good doctor. That she's not your concern, yada, yada, yada," Jax said. "You already showed your true reaction."

Which was exactly why Jax had hit Raze up when he'd first awoken from fighting for his life. There just wasn't time to think things through. "You're a real prick," Raze said slowly.

"Yes," Jax said.

Raze eyed both men. "I have no plans to harm Vanguard or its people. My mission is my own, and believe me when I tell you two things. The first is that although I do genuinely like Vinnie, my loyalty and focus are elsewhere. I'll sacrifice her for my mission." At one point that had been the absolute truth. Now he wasn't sure, but he kept doubt off his face.

"And second?" Tace asked.

"If you touch Vinnie, if you harm her in any way, I'll make sure you do feel again. And Tace? You'll wish to God you didn't." Raze meant every damn word.

"Where's the letter you mentioned?" Jax asked again.

When the hell had he told Jax about the letter? Raze shook his head. "I have no clue what you're talking about. If I said something while delirious, there's no truth to it. You have to know that."

"Go, Tace," Jax said softly. "Come back in an hour."

"Wait." Raze tried to rear up. "Give me a couple of hours to figure things out. Just to let my brain start working again."

Jax shook his head. "Sorry, buddy. It's now or never."

Raze paused. "Why?"

Jax shrugged.

Shit. "Where's Dr. Harmony?" Raze asked, his chest swelling.

"She's inner territory at the main hospital," Jax said.

Raze stopped breathing. Jax had sent Lynne inner territory

because she would've stopped any harm from coming to Vinnie. "She won't forgive you for torturing a woman."

Jax grimaced. "She'll forgive me, but it ain't gonna be easy for a while."

"You're that confident of your woman." Raze shook his head, going with the only ace he had. "She's a healer, Jax. No way will she be all right with you harming Vinnie."

"Then she'll have to get herself all right," Jax said simply. "The world has changed, and the rules are gone. She's my life, and she agreed to that, so there's no going back. Like I said, it ain't gonna be easy, but at the end of the day, she'll still be in my bed." He opened the door wider. "You could have that with Vinnie, if you do the right thing here. Don't you want that?"

"If Tace touches her, I'm coming after you." Raze would've threatened Lynne, but Jax would just shoot him right then and there, which would screw up his mission for sure.

"Of that I have no doubt." Jax followed Tace out and shut the door.

Raze yanked against the restraints. The idea of the sweet blonde being physically tortured because of him filled him with a rage he'd never experienced. Nobody could harm her soft skin. She'd been through enough, damn it. He had to get free before Tace reached Vinnie. He just had to.

Vinnie waited in the large gathering room off Jax's office—the same room in which she'd given her lecture the other day. She sat in the same chair, her focus on the door.

Tace Justice strode inside and tossed two books on the table. The medic looked long and lean in ripped jeans with a button-down green shirt covering his wide chest. "Look what I found."

She gasped and reached for the books. *Sociopaths* and *Perceptions* by Dr. Vinnie Wellington. "Where in the world did you find these?" She held the treasured volumes to her chest. The second she'd finished the first book, she'd dedicated it to her father. He would've been so proud had he lived long enough to see her books on a shelf. God, she missed him.

Tace pulled out a chair and dropped into it. "Raiding party hit a library on the west side early this morning. They brought back the entire reference section for our doctors, and your books were included."

She rubbed the weathered binding of *Perceptions*. "We have to get the rest of the books. Literature, romances, thrillers. They matter, too."

"Agreed. A group is heading back tomorrow." Tace rested his elbows on the table.

"How's Raze?"

Tace tapped the tabletop. "Raze is awake and doing better."

Vinnie pushed away from the table.

"You can't see him yet."

She faltered. "Why not?"

"He and Jax are having a chat," Tace said, his gaze never leaving her face. The medic seemed to overwhelm his chair in a way he hadn't just a few days ago. Was he getting bigger? More muscular?

"A chat between Raze and Jax right now doesn't sound good." Vinnie stood.

Tace leaned forward and suddenly took over the atmosphere. "Please retake your seat, darlin'."

The Texas twang held a hint of threat. A new one. Vinnie didn't move. "Excuse me?"

"I need you to sit. Now."

She studied him. Rugged face, deep blue eyes, black cowboy hat. Superior fighting shape. While she could make it to the door, he'd catch her before she reached the infirmary. If he chased her. His expression showed quite clearly that he would.

He nodded. "You know how animals, the predatory kind, always chase prey? I mean, even if they're not hungry at the moment, but prey is there and runs? Instinct makes them give chase."

Her stomach rolled over. She sat.

"Thank you."

"Do you think you're a predator?" she asked gently.

He stilled and then broke into a smile. "Ah, sweetheart. You're shrinking my head right now."

Well, maybe. "Seriously. Do you have the urge to, ah, chase people?"

"Not usually, but if you'd run when I told you to sit, I would've taken you down three steps before you reached the doorway." He leaned back, almost appearing relaxed. "It's instinct, and it's new, but it's there."

They'd have to explore that issue later. Her head ached. "Is Jax hurting Raze?" If so, she'd have to get past Tace somehow. She needed to start carrying a weapon.

"No." Tace drew imaginary circles on the table but kept his focus on her face. "I promise."

She studied his body language as well as his voice inflection. He seemed to be telling the truth. "Then why do you want to keep me here?" she asked.

"Jax needs to find out why Raze is here helping Vanguard," Tace said. "In fact, supposedly there's a letter Raze composed in case of his death. Any idea where he would have hidden it?"

She slowly shook her head, her mind reeling. "Maybe

Raze just wants to help. Maybe he's looking for a place to call home."

"That's you, not him," Tace murmured. "You're the one wanting to set down roots."

Her mouth opened and then closed. "Aren't you?"

"Hell, sweetheart. I'm just trying to keep myself from becoming a Ripper. I don't give two squawks where I am when I do that." He glanced toward the light coming through the doorway. "It's midafternoon. Guess I won't scout today."

"How long are you supposed to keep me here, and why do you think Raze will talk to Jax?" Something wasn't adding up.

"You need to stay here for the afternoon, and I know Raze will talk to Jax because he doesn't have a choice if he wants to be released." Tace held up a hand when she began to argue. "Plus, and here's the rub, Raze *wants* to talk to Jax. He's definitely on a mission, but he wants to belong, and he needs to trust somebody. Jax is a good guy and Raze knows it."

Now that did make sense. "That's all there is to the situation?" she asked.

"Yes, ma'am," Tace said, all charm.

"I don't believe you," Vinnie said, the hair on her arms rising.

Jax Mercury strode into the room, finishing what looked like a ham sandwich. "Dr. Wellington? Please profile Raze Shadow for me." He drew out a chair to sit.

Vinnie swallowed. "Where is he?"

"Resting peacefully," Jax said. "I questioned him, he refused to answer, and then I came here."

"You, yo-you didn't hurt him?" Vinnie whispered.

Jax sighed. "That's a man who won't break physically. Period. I don't torture people, but even if I did, it would be a waste of time with Raze. Which is why I need you to profile him for me. Thank you." He waited.

She eyed the door. "I find it odd that you'd give thanks after issuing an order. You didn't ask. You told. Which is fine, I guess, because we all kind of work for you. But I—"

"Vinnie?" Jax murmured.

She snapped her mouth shut and took a moment. "Sorry. I babble."

"That's all right. So? Profile?" Jax asked, impatience lining his face.

Well, if Jax and Tace were sitting in front of her, then they weren't harming Raze in any way. "He's a soldier because he wants to be one. He's loyal and ambitious." She pursed her lips together. "Something is driving him, and he doesn't like it, but he's determined to succeed at whatever his mission might be."

"What else?" Jax asked.

"He likes you. He likes being here and working with the group, and I think he appreciates the order you've created. He defends the weak, and the fact that you do the same makes him respect you," she said.

"Then why doesn't he trust me?" Jax asked, lines cutting into the sides of his mouth.

Vinnie pushed hair away from her eyes. "He does trust you, but whatever this mission is can't be compromised. Something more important than you, than trust, is driving him. He won't take the chance unless you get through to him somehow."

Jax's lips thinned into a firm line. "Then I'll have to get through to him." He looked at Tace. "It has been about an hour since I left him."

Tace stood and withdrew a big black gun from the back of his waist.

Vinnie swallowed. "Um, what—"

Tace brought the gun down on his right knuckles. Blood sprayed.

Vinnie jumped up, her lungs seizing. "What are you doing?"

Tace smashed his hand twice more while Jax watched impassively.

"That should do it," Jax said.

Tace nodded and turned toward the door.

Jax pointed to Vinnie's seat. "Please sit back down, Doc. I'd like for you to profile Tace now."

"No," she said wildly. "What the hell was that about? Why would Tace hurt himself? What does it have to do with—" She sat back as realization dawned. "You're a fucking asshole."

Jax lifted an eyebrow. "Okay."

"Y-you want Raze to think Tace tortured me," she whispered, her legs itching to run for the door.

"It's better than actually torturing you, right?" Jax said, his chin down.

She glared. "You wouldn't torture a woman, Jax Mercury." She'd bet every advanced degree she'd earned on that fact.

"Even to save Lynne? To protect her?" he asked softly.

Vinnie's mouth opened and then shut. Good point. As a last resort, there probably wasn't anything Jax wouldn't do to keep Lynne alive. "You'd think of another way first, I'm sure."

"Which is exactly what I just did," Jax said. "Now you're going to stay here until Tace convinces Raze to talk."

Vinnie's nostrils flared, and she wanted nothing more than to kick Jax in the balls.

"I wouldn't," he said, easily reading her.

She swallowed.

"If Raze wanted to hide a letter, where would it be?" Jax asked.

Vinnie pursed her lips. Well, he had visited her in her old apartment, and he'd also helped her to move from there. "I have no clue," she said. Jax wouldn't get her cooperation against Raze, especially since the Vanguard leader was currently emotionally tormenting the man.

A Vanguard soldier, blond, male, and about forty years old, slid open the back door. "Jax? This reverend guy has been waiting to talk to you for a couple of hours."

"Reverend? *We* have a reverend?" Jax asked. At the soldier's nod, he motioned. "Send him in."

Vinnie pushed her chair away from the table.

"Stay here," Jax said, his gaze on the door.

She settled back down.

"Give me a read on this guy. Let's see what you can do, Doc," Jax said.

The man walked inside. He was tall and thin with dark blond hair swept back from a sharply cut face. Deep green eyes showed intelligence and strength. "I'm Reverend Lighton," he said, his voice deep and melodious.

"Uh-huh." Jax pointed to a seat. "You wanted to see me?"

Vinnie watched Lighton approach. Easy gait, calm manner, gaze unblinking. She sat up, her instincts humming. His gaze was too unblinking.

"I'm sorry to bother you, but my main congregation is having concerns, and I promised to speak with you." Lighton sat and clasped his hands on the table.

Jax lifted one eyebrow. "You're a reverend?"

"I am now. Scorpius has created new lives for us all." Lighton crossed his legs.

Jax studied him. "Fair enough. You mentioned concerns?"

"Yes." Lighton barely shrugged. "Most of my congregation hasn't been infected by Scorpius, and they're concerned about staying safe. I'm not sure what to tell them."

Jax leaned back. "I suggest you tell them to wash their hands."

Lighton's eyes widened. "Is there anything else we can do?"

Jax shook his head. "I'm not ready to run two separate camps. We don't have the manpower or resources, unfortunately. If folks want to strike out on their own and create their own Scorpius-free zone, then that's up to them."

Lighton sighed heavily. "I understand and will pass on that information. Thank you for your time. If you require clergy here at headquarters at any time, please call on me. I have the education, experience, and now the calling." He smiled at Vinnie, stood, and quickly exited.

Jax glanced at Vinnie. "Where were we?"

She pressed her lips together. It wasn't her place, but . . . "You can't trust that guy."

Jax glanced at the closed door. "He's harmless."

"No." She reached out and grabbed Jax's hand. "He's not harmless. He's on a mission, and he was here to check you out. His body language was slightly off, and you need to keep an eye on him."

Jax studied her, his gaze thoughtful. "I'll keep that in mind."

Vinnie hadn't read Lighton's mind or anything, not like she'd done the other day when that kid had passed out. But she definitely had some weird stuff going on. Was she becoming psychic? Had Scorpius really changed her mind?

"Doc? You still with me?" Jax asked.

She started. "Yes. Sometimes I daydream."

"Great. For now, tell me more about serial killers and whether or not I should let the president live. If he's doing a good job, I may need him to keep doing it, if I can protect you and Lynne from him."

She shook her head and concentrated on the current conversation. "He won't ever give up on reclaiming us." Then she spent almost an hour going through history, facts, and statistics with the Vanguard leader. After a while, she forgot he scared her.

Finally, the same soldier as before poked his head in. "We have a problem, and it's about to erupt into a full-out brawl."

"Shit." Jax stood and motioned toward Vinnie. "Stay here and guard her. She doesn't leave this room."

The soldier nodded. "Understood."

Chapter Twelve

Faith secured by force is fractured.

—Dr. Vinnie Wellington, *Perceptions*

Jax met two other soldiers outside the back door, one of them Sami. "What's going on?" he asked.

She gestured toward inner territory. "Apparently we have a new group called the Pure that wants to be left alone. They're trying to put up a fence around a couple of the apartment buildings in the southeast quadrant."

Ah, damn it. Jax moved into a jog. "Tell me they aren't led by a new reverend."

She nodded, her black ponytail bobbing. "Yep. Reverend Lighton. The guy was a condom salesman out of Portland before heading south when Scorpius hit."

A fucking condom salesman? "Jesus." This was the last thing Jax had time to deal with. The guy had seemed decent, but it sure hadn't taken him long to cause problems. Dr. Wellington had been correct about him.

Apparently Vinnie knew her shit. He could use her mind for sure.

Jax turned the corner and took in the situation. The Pure group had taken over the three apartment buildings in the far right corner of Vanguard territory. Somehow, during the night, somebody had placed fences around three-quarters of the apartment buildings, including barbed wire over the top so nobody could climb over. "Were they up all damn night?" Jax snapped.

"Must've been," Sami said.

Six Pure members stood near the fence, all armed, two of them behind a massive gate.

Several of Jax's soldiers stood on guard and fanned out, facing the fence.

Tension and stress rode the air.

"Did they get that gate out of our western storage warehouse?" Jax asked when he was a few yards from the men.

"That's the only explanation," Sami said, halting next to him.

Reverend Lighton strode out the front door of the crumbling brick apartment building. "Master Sergeant Mercury. I'm so glad you're here. Please tell your men to stand down."

Jax held a hand up. "Everybody point your weapons at the ground. Right damn fucking now."

Instantly, his men complied.

The men at the fence looked toward Lighton. He nodded, and they lowered their guns.

That wasn't good. Not at all. "Take note of who you see on Lighton's crew," he whispered to Sami.

She nodded, her brown eyes beyond alert. "Got it."

"What the hell is going on, Lighton?" Jax asked, crossing his arms.

Lighton moved closer to the fence. "We're just trying to protect our people. That's all."

"Yet you failed to mention the entire fence situation when we met earlier," Jax said, his temper simmering.

"You didn't seem receptive to any plan to protect these pure people, so I went ahead with doing it myself." Lighton gestured widely. "Scorpius will kill them, so I have to take precautions. It's my duty, and I'm bound by God."

The men flanking him nodded, fear in their eyes, determination on their faces.

Ah, hell. "How exactly do you intend to get food and medicinal supplies?" Sami called out.

"We're part of Vanguard, and we require extra precautions. Many of us will still conduct our jobs out there, including me. But we need a safe place for the women and children who don't work outside to remain untouched by the bacteria. If you had loved ones who were uninfected, you'd want them to be here," Lighton said.

Jax shoved anger away as most of the people facing off kept perfectly still. His soldiers were well trained, but he recognized the ones backing Lighton. Also well trained. "This is unacceptable."

Lighton held his arms wide. "'The Lord watches over the sojourners; he upholds the widow and the fatherless, but the way of the wicked he brings to ruin.'"

"Psalms 146:9," Jax said. "'Beloved, do not believe every spirit, but test the spirits to see whether they are from God, for many false prophets have gone out into the world.'"

"You're quoting John. Interesting." Lighton shook his head. "I'm merely a simple man doing God's work. Not once have I said I'm a prophet."

Yet he was acting like one, now wasn't he? Jax turned slightly toward Sami. "What's the danger if we go in, guns blazing? How many people are quartered there?" Not that he had a prison cell anywhere. His only recourse would be to kick Lighton and his followers out.

"I don't know," she whispered. "That apartment building is where we've housed the orphaned children."

Shit. "Kids, widows, and armed soldiers." Jax shook his head. "Advice?"

Sami studied the tense soldiers all around. "Schedule a

meeting with Lighton. Let everyone walk away right now so both sides can save face and nobody gets shot. Especially any kids in that building behind him."

Jax gritted his teeth. "I don't like backing down." It wouldn't set well with his soldiers.

"Then don't." Sami shuffled her boots. "Tell Lighton he has one day to tear down the fence and come to you with a plan for his people."

"You think he'll tear it down?"

"No. Do you?" Sami asked.

Jax eyed a fluttering curtain on the third floor. "No, but I also don't want the folks inside to think I'm the bad guy or to be afraid of me. Lighton is capitalizing on fear already." Fear of Scorpius.

Sami nodded. "I met with him last week and thought he was a nice guy. I missed this."

"So did I." Jax counted the guns he could see. Too many. "Vinnie Wellington caught it, though." The shrink had been correct about Lighton. Jax should've listened to her.

"I want to work with you and not against you," Lighton said gently.

Jax lifted his chin. "You and I are not equal leaders here, buddy. This isn't détente. You have twenty-four hours to take down the fence and come to me with a plan for your people. In addition, I want a list of who you're including as your people." He turned away, as if finished with the matter.

Sami loped into a walk next to him as thunder rolled in from the Pacific. "Our soldiers will watch for trouble."

"I know." Jax kept striding south and glanced up at the darkening sky. It was going to rain again. "You go back to headquarters and find a list of who you think lives in those apartment buildings. I'll check out all the warehouses on the perimeter to see what they've taken." Something told him it wasn't going to be pretty.

* * *

Voices and the sound of dishes clanking echoed through the infirmary from the adjoining soup kitchen. The soldiers must be having dinner, but the last thing Raze wanted was to eat. He might never eat again.

For an hour, he'd fought against the restraints shackling him to the bed. He nearly had his left hand free when Tace loped inside, blood dripping from his knuckles. Against all reason, going on his gut, Raze burst out laughing.

Tace paused.

Raze coughed a few times and then settled down. His intestines hurt, his muscles ached, and his head pounded. Even so, his fuckin' brain worked. "You smashed your knuckles for no reason, dickhead."

Tace frowned and glanced down at his bleeding hand. "Humph." He flipped a chair around to straddle it. Mild curiosity and no real emotion showed on his face. "How did you know?"

Raze took a shaky breath and then two more until his lungs worked properly. "Two reasons. One, if you hit her hard enough to smash your knuckles like that, she'd most likely be dead. I know you wouldn't kill her. She's too valuable to Vanguard."

Tace wiped his thumb across his purpling knuckles. "Reason two?"

Raze studied the man he didn't really know but had already trusted to have his back. "Neither you nor Jax would ever harm a woman. Especially a sweet, innocent, brilliant one like the good Dr. Vinnie Wellington." He'd settled into that fact the second Jax had left the room an hour ago, so his mind had been much more peaceful than Jax had intended. "Now get me out of these restraints so I can figure out what to do." Maybe he could get Jax's cooperation to retrieve Maureen. He just needed to clear his mind from the fever and think, damn it.

Tace reached over and released the restraints. "Hey. You were almost out of this one."

"Almost." Raze shoved himself into a seated position. "When will my head stop pounding?"

Tace shrugged. "About a week, but then the headaches come on regularly. At least for me. Maybe they won't for you because we shot you up with vitamin B immediately. Do you feel crazy?"

"No. Just tired." Raze glanced down at his bare chest. He'd survived Scorpius. While he had no idea what would happen to his brain next, he'd lived. Thank God. "Where's my shirt?"

"Ruined."

"Great." Raze scrubbed both hands down his face. "I liked that shirt."

Tace headed for the door. "Bummer. Stay here and get your bearings. I'll fetch you some soup for a late dinner. You were out all day."

"Not hungry."

"Need to eat," Tace returned, striding out of sight.

Raze pushed off the bed and stood. His legs straightened. Good. While he certainly shouldn't have been granted the grace to live, he was alive, so he was going to do what he needed to. Then he hitched toward the door, sweat pouring from him by the time he entered what used to be the reception area for the free clinic.

An explosion boomed from the other room.

What the hell? His body took a second to catch up to reality. He lurched into motion, fighting gravity.

He ripped open the cabinets behind the counter for the hidden guns known only to the elite soldiers. Screams came from the other room.

His hands shook, but he had to do something.

He grabbed a Glock and inched toward the wide opening between the infirmary and the mess hall. Smoke and rushing bodies instantly filled his view. He crept into the main rec room just as Tace barreled in from the opposite side, a gun in his hand.

A fire burned in the middle of the room, and smoke billowed in black clouds. "Status?" Raze barked.

"Don't know." Tace moved with him in perfect sync as they began stomping the burning mass.

"Where's Jax?" Raze growled.

Tace coughed. "Don't know that either."

Raze looked down. Glass, rags, and unidentifiable material. "A Molotov cocktail?"

"Three of them, actually," Tace said.

People jumped up from tables, eyes wide, several armed. Smoke and debris made it hard to see, even with the daylight pouring in, and a couple of civilians ran into each other.

Sami jumped from the stairwell leading to the soldier apartments, her dark hair swinging wildly in a ponytail. "What's going on?"

The front door opened and two women ran in, armed and dressed for guard duty. Barb, a tight blonde with a scar on her jaw, shook her head. "They cut the fence in the west and killed two guards. Throats sliced—no shots fired. We've been infiltrated." Smoke slammed into her, and she turned her head. "Open the doors wide," she ordered the other woman.

Raze met Tace's gaze. "Did anybody see anything?" He slowly glanced around at the rapidly assembling group, looking for somebody he didn't know, a feat impossible with the still-dark smoke.

Sami slammed a clip into her gun. "I'll go cover the west side."

Raze stopped her with a hand on her shoulder. "Go careful. Somebody got inside, and they could be waiting." He jerked his head at a kid who'd emerged from the back of the war room, hair mussed and glasses askew. As the resident genius with machinery, Byron was often on call to the head-quarters, and Raze had started training him in combat. Jill Sanderson, his pregnant girlfriend, hovered at his side, wires in her hands. "You armed?" Raze asked.

"Yeah." The kid drew a gun from the back of his jeans and coughed out smoke.

"Good. Cover Sami and scout the west side."

Jill Sanderson paled, but she didn't move.

The kid turned and brushed a kiss across her cheek. Whatever he whispered made Jill nod and step back. The smile she gave him was fake but brave.

Byron nodded and instantly ran to Sami's side. "Let's go."

Raze pivoted to see Vinnie herding several of the scav-enger teens toward the far counter and away from the steaming smoke. The woman needed to get away from the line of fire.

"Raze?" Tace asked.

"I know. We've got a threat here. I can feel it." Raze inched away from Tace, taking point across the room.

Tace moved the opposite direction, his gaze sweeping.

Fuck it. Raze couldn't see well enough. "Everybody kneel down, hands behind your head. All weapons on the ground." Enough bark filled his voice that several people dropped to their knees. Too many still stood, confusion buzzing through the smoke. "Fucking down. Now!" Several more obeyed.

He caught movement across the room. "Tace!" he hissed.

"For Twenty," a man yelled, swinging an automatic and firing.

People screamed and flattened on the ground. Time slowed for Raze. From the corner of his eye, he saw Vinnie tackle a bunch of kids to the ground, protecting them with her body.

Tace moved faster than wind and slid feet first into the

shooter. The bullets rocketed up and hit the ceiling, and the guy fell on top of Tace, who flipped them both over. Without pausing, Tace drew a blade from his pocket.

Raze turned around, senses on alert, eyes burned by the smoke. There had to be another one. His gaze caught a kid's, one he didn't recognize. The kid wore dark clothing with a turtleneck covering his neck. Hiding a tattoo? Raze bunched to attack, and the kid grabbed a woman by the hair, pressing a gun into her throat.

What was the woman's name? Raze couldn't remember it, but she was about thirty and worked as one of the cooks at the headquarters building. Her terror-filled eyes pleaded for help, and she cried out when the kid yanked back her head.

Then she screamed. Loud and with enough terror to skitter chills down Raze's back.

Panic filled the kid's eyes.

"Shut up," Raze snarled.

The woman hitched and then fell silent, tears sliding down her pale cheeks.

The gun lay heavy in Raze's hand, the feeling too familiar. Although the weakness in his limbs from the fever was something new. "Let her go and I won't kill you."

Terror and determination crossed the kid's face. "Let Chade up."

"Chade is dead," Raze said, not needing to turn and look. He'd already seen the smoothness of Tace's movement with the blade, and he'd heard the knife go in. "You can still live. Maybe find a different way to survive in this world than shooting kids and scaring somebody's mom." He had no fucking clue if the cook was a mom or had ever been a mom. But to this kid, she was mom age, and that was good enough.

The kid faltered. "Twenty sent me. Sent us. This is retribution for the members you all killed."

"I know the drill. This is for your colors." Raze angled to the side to get a better view. He'd never been in a gang, but he'd studied membership and group dynamics in the military. Movement sounded behind him, and he caught sight of Vinnie shepherding the civilians out of the room. Good. The fewer folks in the path of bullets, the better.

His heart beat rapidly, and he took a couple of deep breaths, trying to stay calm. "The Vanguard leader, Jax Mercury, used to be Twenty, you know." Where the fuck was Jax?

The kid's chin lifted, his dark gaze hardening. "There's no used to. You're Twenty or you're not." The more the kid spoke, the younger he seemed. Raze had thought sixteen at first, but maybe fourteen? Even younger, possibly.

"There's a better life and a different way," Raze said.

"There's no other life." The kid shoved the gun harder against the cook's jugular, and she rose up on her toes, crying out.

Raze took another step to the left, ignoring the fear overtaking the atmosphere. His knees wobbled, but he kept moving steadily, his focus on that gun. If he kept asking questions, maybe he could distract the kid. "How long have you been in Twenty?"

"Long enough." The kid twitched his head to the side, and Raze could sense Tace stepping closer.

Raze took another step toward the kid. "You have a big choice to make now. This is no way to get your colors. The time for that has passed. Now we need to work together to survive Scorpius." The kid was too young—this had to be his mission for colors. Shit. He might have just earned them. The scent of blood mingled with the smoke, and several bodies lay on the ground. "Let the lady go."

The kid looked at him and slowly backed toward the door, dragging the cook. He was about an inch taller and definitely stronger. His eyes transmitted his intent the second he decided to kill. "Twenty forever," he yelled.

Raze lifted and shot with one smooth motion. The bullet struck between the kid's eyes, killing him instantly. He flew back into the side wall. Blood spurted. The cook screamed and lurched toward the eastern residence hallway and kept running.

The blood in Raze's veins cooled. His chest hurt. He strode toward the kid, who lay lifeless, his eyes still open. Dropping to his haunches, Raze gently closed his eyelids. The hole in his head was small and perfectly shaped. Raze cleared his throat and pulled the kid toward him, reaching for the back pocket.

Tace stood above him. "Raze, man. Don't do it. It's over."

Raze ignored him and found a wallet, yanking out the cloth material. He ripped open the Velcro and slid out a picture of the kid with a family. Mom, Dad, two sisters, all smiling in front of a Christmas tree. Fuck. Raze reached in for the only other item in the wallet, a student ID card from Breton Middle School. *Middle school.* Clearing his throat, he read the card. "Phillip Lopez. Sixth grade, last year." Tucking the wallet between the kid's hands, he stood. "He was fucking twelve years old."

Tace set a hand on his shoulder. "He was going to shoot Mary."

Raze jerked his head in a nod. "Yeah." Twelve years old. He'd just plugged a hole into the head of a twelve-year-old boy, and Raze didn't even belong in Vanguard. He didn't belong anywhere. Weight descended so heavily on his shoulders, he nearly staggered. "He gets buried in the graveyard tomorrow morning when the storm stops."

Tace dropped his hand. "I'll get a sheet and make sure he's ready."

Fire burned deep and hot in Raze's chest, torturing him from inside. He had to get out of there. Away from people and away from death. But he turned around to view the wounded. "How bad?"

Lynne Harmony ran inside, her hair a wild mess and sleep in her eyes. She instantly started checking the five or so people on the ground. Blood seeped into the cheap vinyl floor. "Three dead and two unconscious. I need Tace."

Tace ran toward the injured. "I've got it."

Raze's hands began to tremble, and he slid his gun into the back of his waistband. Twelve. Years. Old. Pain pounded in his temples, and bile rose in his throat. He needed to puke.

Jax barreled in from the rear door and took in the scene. "Jesus."

Raze nodded.

"You okay, Raze?" Jax asked, his gaze dark.

"Yes." Darkness claimed him, and Raze never felt the ground he hit.

Chapter Thirteen

————◆◆◆————

*There's no doubt that life has the power to deliver
such agonizing blows as to create insanity.*

—Dr. Vinnie Wellington, *Sociopaths*

The smells of smoke, blood, and death hung like too-heavy
curtains throughout headquarters, even hours after the explosion and fight. Vinnie's eyes teared as she moved inside.

She blinked through the smoke still hanging in the air.
Everyone had deserted the rec room and headed either outside for duty or inner territory for their apartments. It had
taken hours to patch people up and clean the area, and she
hadn't seen Raze the entire time. "I'll be back."

Jax looked up from scrubbing blood off the floor. He'd
heard the shots from across Vanguard territory and had
come running back in time to see Raze hit the floor. "You
should get some rest, Doc."

"I know." Her mind was way too busy to go to sleep. "I
just want to check on Raze first."

Tace cleared his throat, his blond hair askew and a dark
shadow covering his jaw. He had tended to the wounded
with brisk efficiency if not empathy. "We're not going to try
to stop you, but Raze needed a little space, and you should
give it to him."

She rubbed her chin. Raze had killed a kid, and leaving him with the demons in his own head seemed like a bad idea. "He's been alone for hours," she murmured. "And he's still recovering from the infection."

"Your funeral," Tace said, assisting a limping man toward the residence hall.

Perhaps, but from their first encounter, she hadn't been able to ignore Raze Shadow's pain. Why, she had no clue, but they'd come way too far for her to turn her back on him now and allow him to deal with the tragedy on his own. He'd saved her a week ago from a madman, and she could do the same for him. She tried to rationalize her motivations as she turned away from the open door and headed for the stairwell, but deep down, emotion and heart propelled her forward.

They were in this together, whether that made sense or not.

Right or wrong, she went with her gut.

She climbed the stairs, her neck muscles competing with her shoulder blades to pound out pain. She rolled her head and tried to find some sort of relief.

After the attack, Raze had quickly regained consciousness, and Tace had taken him to the showers to clear his head. Then Raze had disappeared upstairs hours ago to sleep, if he could.

He'd saved her life and possibly her sanity, and if nothing else, she could help him through the crisis of killing a kid. She'd figure out what to do next.

Lucinda popped up out of nowhere. "Run back to the mess hall, sweetheart."

"No," Vinnie snapped. "I'm not leaving him in pain. No way."

"That man is on a mission, and you'll be collateral damage," Lucinda spat. "Run away from him now."

"He's a good man who saved my life," Vinnie countered,

stopping in front of the door. "He's shown me kindness over and over again."

Lucinda shoved her way in front of the door, shimmering like liquid in a snow globe. "Once again, you're being stupid with a man. That soldier will strip your heart from your chest and roast each piece over an open fire."

Vinnie frowned. "You're even crazier in death than you were in life."

"You're the one seeing me. For once, use your head. Go the other direction, away from the bad boy with the great abs." Lucinda smacked her hands together.

Vinnie paused. "I can't leave him alone. He's hurting." She'd never been able to turn away from a person in pain.

"He'll break you," Lucinda muttered.

"He already saved me from being broken. No matter what, he took me out of that hell hole and away from the drugs. I owe him." More than that, she wanted to help him. Something inside her, something deep, soft, and female . . . needed to ease his pain. She trusted him, and that meant something to her.

Lucinda puffed out of the way, her irritated hiss echoing as she departed.

Vinnie pushed open the door.

He sat on a folding chair, facing the window, his back to her. Darkness streamed inside, filtered only by a slight moon, lending a sense of intimacy to the ragged room.

"It's late," she murmured, crossing inside and shutting the door.

He turned, his face stoic but his eyes ravaged. "I killed a kid."

"I know," she whispered, taking several steps toward him. "I'm so very sorry."

"I'm not who you think I am," he murmured, overpowering the chair with his bulk and the room with the sense of male. Tension swelled around, making the air feel heavy.

"You don't know what I think." She kept her voice low, soothing, even while her mind rebelled and tried to take over. Kicking off her borrowed shoes, she scrunched her toes in surprisingly soft socks. "I read people pretty well."

He crossed his arms over his still bare chest. "Read me."

Her mouth watered and her body flushed. "You are way too hot to be shirtless." Damn it. Her mouth needed to wait for her mind. "The way your jeans are unbuttoned invites heated thoughts."

He didn't smile, and the agony in his eyes didn't abate. "Profile me," he commanded softly.

She breathed in and walked toward him, stopping less than a foot away. Why was he asking her to do that? His expression was a challenge—or an angry dare.

The energy around him vibrated with an intensity that warned anybody sane to get the hell out of there. She stepped closer, close enough to touch, and all but bathed in it.

"Vinnie." One word, deep voice, raw feelings.

"I'm here." She took that final step, knowing there was no turning back. "One time my family visited a refuge in southern Idaho. It wasn't a zoo, but tigers lived there. Real ones. Maybe illegally?" She wasn't quite sure.

"And?" Every vibration from him suggested a predator about to attack.

"There was one tiger. Fully grown and truly pissed off after a porcupine attack. He had all these quills stuck in his face, and you could sense his pain. But he wouldn't let anybody get close enough to touch him. To heal him," she whispered. "You remind me of that animal."

Raze lifted his chin, his gaze meeting hers evenly. Although she stood and he sat, they were almost eye to eye. "You can't heal me."

"I can," she said. "I don't know how, and you're a threat to my heart, but I can heal you. I can make you feel better."

Her words weren't making much sense, but she felt them as much as thought them. However, she couldn't read his mind, no matter how hard she tried. "You're a good guy, and you've had to do some bad things. But this is your moment."

"My moment." His upper lip curled back. "How so?"

"Tell me the truth. Give me honesty."

"I can't."

This now became *her* moment. She could get angry and storm out, she could cajole, or she could go with her heart, which made absolutely no sense.

As usual, since Scorpius, her heart won. She moved between his legs and threaded her fingers through his thick hair, tilting his head. Tomorrow they might be enemies, but she needed this night. Craved this night. Maybe just the one, but she was taking it.

"Vinnie," he breathed in a clear warning. His glittering blue gaze dropped to her lips. "Run."

"Too late." She lowered her head and brushed her mouth across his.

He didn't even twitch, and the world seemed to hold its breath.

She murmured and swept her mouth along his firm lips again. The man had survived Scorpius; he had nothing to fear from her. "I can't hurt you now, Raze."

He took a sharp intake of breath. "Not true. You're the most dangerous woman I've ever met."

Although said with a dark growl, the words filled her with power. "You feel it too, right?" As impossible as the world had become, this feeling between them, whatever it was, felt *good*. There was actually something good. She began to lean back, but he stopped her with both hands on her hips. Her entire lower half heated, and a pulse pounded between her legs. She could barely breathe with his hands on her.

"I feel it. Us." His hold tightened with definite strength. "I'm not the good guy who'll tell you to go once we get started, Vinnie. You give me one taste of you, and I won't let you leave until I'm done. Until I have all of you. I'm not that strong."

"You're strong." Warmth speared through her, and her breasts began to ache.

"Not strong enough to let you go, so if you wanna run away, I'm telling you this is your one chance." In contrast to his words, he drew her closer in to heat and power.

"I'm staying," she breathed. "But we can just cuddle. You have to be weak from the fever." Thank God he'd survived.

"I could never be that weak, baby."

His shoulders relaxed as if giving in. "You never profiled me."

"Sure I did," she said. In fact, she probably knew him better than he knew himself. It was time for Shadow to stop running and start feeling again. "I just didn't share my thoughts."

He stood and lifted her on his way up.

She yelped, then settled into his arms. Her breath caught in her throat. "Are you all right? I mean, you just had the fever, and you passed out, but I'm glad you had a shower. A shower is good. Scorpius is tough to handle, but now we can have sex. I'm happy we—"

His mouth over hers stopped her rambling.

Shock stilled her for the briefest of seconds. Heat. Raze Shadow was all heat as he worked her mouth, shooting tingles down her jaw to zing through her body. She edged closer to him, trying to get inside so much warmth.

The room spun, and she ended up on her feet again, the mattress pushing against the back of her knees.

His fingers were gentle as he reached for the hem of her shirt and tugged it up and over her head. The cotton bra covering her breasts had a back clasp that he released with a quick flick of his fingers.

She gasped, trying to remain sane. "Not your first bra."

He ran the bra straps down her arms, his eyes flaring. "God, you're beautiful," he breathed.

Her knees weakened, and she fought the urge to cover her chest. Instead, she indulged herself and flattened her palms over the hard ridges of his abdomen. Ripped and predatory, Raze Shadow was all man.

She wanted this night. Hell, she *needed* this night. A happy hum rolled up her throat. Muscle, power, and heat filled her palms. She traced his muscles up his chest, paying attention to each wound and scar. Talk about beauty.

He glanced down at her hands. "I'm damaged."

"You're perfect," she murmured, leaning in and kissing above his heart. His scars showed a warrior's life, one he'd survived. Sometimes survival held a primal glory all its own.

He slid his hand into her hair, threading his fingers through the strands. A quick twist of his wrist jerked her head up, and he took her mouth again. He kissed her so hard and so thoroughly, she forgot where they were. Who they were.

She fumbled with his zipper and drew it down. His penis sprang free, full and erect.

He kicked out of his jeans, his free hand shoving her pants to the floor. Laying her gently on the bed, his body over hers, he broke the kiss. "Don't let me hurt you."

She curled her fingers over his shoulders, meeting his gaze. "I won't."

A wrinkle set between his eyes. "I, ah—"

"Condom?" she whispered.

He stilled. "Got one." Leaning to the side, he fetched a foil package from the back of his jeans. His erection rubbed against her. Catching her raised eyebrow, he blinked. "Tace shoved it in my jeans after my shower."

She'd have to thank Tace in the morning. "I've never had a one-night stand."

Raze paused. "I don't know exactly what this is, but it ain't a one-night stand. That much I do know."

She cleared her throat. "It has been a while. I mean, I don't do one-night stands. Oh. I told you that. Well, I didn't have a lot of time to date, but I did date, you know, sometimes. Anyway, I haven't—"

His lips settled against hers. "Relax."

"Right." She allowed her body to go lax in direct contrast to her pounding heart. "Okeydoke. I'm ready."

He smiled then, a full flash of teeth that revealed a dimple in his left cheek. In their limited time together, she'd never seen the dimple. She stared, beyond fascinated. "Raze?"

"Okeydoke?"

She nodded.

His light blue eyes sparked and then deepened. "Baby, you're nowhere near ready."

She sniffed, still staring at the mysterious dimple. "I most certainly am." Her gaze narrowed, and she lifted it to meet his eyes. Her entire body thrummed with an ache only he could satisfy, and her thighs were already damp with arousal. If her nipples got any harder, they might cut his chest. "Why don't you think so?"

He chuckled. "The second you can't think or speak, I'll know you're ready."

"Oh yeah?" she said softly, more than a little intrigued. "Show me."

Chapter Fourteen

*Becoming part of another person holds
equal amounts of risk and reward.*

—Dr. Vinnie Wellington, *Perceptions*

Raze stared at the fragile beauty beneath him, partially understanding her need to get things going and complete the act. It would certainly change things between them, and then they could relax and do it again. But he couldn't allow her to miss out on what he suspected would be something intense.

Even though he certainly lacked his usual strength, no way was he missing out on her, since she was offering.

She looked up at him, pretty eyes thoughtful and more than a little challenging.

Oh, she was definitely still in her own head. He'd have to do something about that.

She smiled, a dare in the curve of her sweet lips. "I like to talk, Raze. You know that."

"True," he murmured. "Tell you what. How about you profile me, and we'll see how long you can keep up the chatter?"

She rolled her eyes. "Fine."

"Oh baby. Don't throw down a challenge like that." His

cock surged against her sex, forcing him to keep still and not shove inside what had to be heaven.

"You're a fighter," she started, caressing down the ridges of his arms and over his biceps. "How did you get the burn scars?"

"Ran into a burning barn to save my sister. Long time ago." Just having Vinnie's sweet hands on him was enough to give him strength.

"So, you're a hero. You became a soldier."

"I'm a soldier." He moved in, licking across her neck and down.

She shifted against him. "Um, you chose that life to serve, and it ended up being more painful and a lot darker than you'd planned."

He kissed the hollow of her neck, wandering down. "Mmm."

"Yet you're good at it. Sometimes you're proud of your skills, and sometimes you're afraid that you're too good at fighting and killing," she breathed, arching into him.

The woman was damn good at profiling. "What else?" he asked just before capturing a nipple with his mouth.

She gasped and dug her hands into his hair. "You missed having a father, which is part of the reason you followed his legacy into the service."

Raze flicked the hard nub with his tongue and then leaned back to study the red tip. Beautiful. "Yes." He moved to her other breast, only partially listening to her. This was wrong, but he was committed, so he wasn't going to miss out on a second with her sweet body. She was so open and giving, something shifted inside him.

"You became the man of the family and took that seriously." This time it took her a few seconds to start talking again. "You lost your mother more recently, and when that happened, you became even more of a parent to your sister than you were while she was growing up."

"Yes." He licked across her abdomen and then down, shoving her thighs wide with his shoulders. "Pretty." Gently, he placed a soft kiss on her clit.

She arched off the bed and pulled his hair.

He grabbed her hands and pressed them to the bed on either side of her hips. After a brief resistance, she relaxed. "Go on."

"Um."

There he had her. "Tell me more." He made sure his breath warmed her.

"Ah, you, um, you're driven. Something has a hold of you, and you're fighting it, but it's winning." She gasped the last few words.

Too close to the truth. He flicked her clit with his tongue and slipped a finger inside her.

She nearly came off the bed. "Raze."

Enough talk. He went at her with no mercy, nearly getting drunk on her taste. She moved against him restlessly, murmuring incoherently, finally out of her head. Power surged through him, and he gave her as much pleasure as he could, taking what he needed. Her cries filled him, and her movements spurred him on.

For the moment, in this time and place, she was his.

Her thighs quivered against his shoulders. Ah. She was close. He slowed down and took his time, lost in the moment. Her body trembled.

She smacked the top of his head.

Whoa. He glanced up, one finger inside her, a frown making his forehead ache. "Did you just hit me?" The woman was in an incredibly vulnerable spot, and if she wanted to play, he'd flick her somewhere she'd never forget. He gently slid his hand free. "Vinnie?"

"I want to be with you. Or I want you to be with me. Not alone." She gasped the words.

He lifted his head. His heart thumped hard. God, she

was stunning. Her light hair was splayed out on the pillow. Pink tinged her cheeks, and desire darkened her eyes. Her lips were rosy from his kiss, and her nipples were pointed and red.

She was everything beautiful in the world, and she was offering herself to him.

Moving up her, he kissed both breasts, her collarbone, her chin, and then finally her mouth. He must've dropped the condom wrapper. Glancing around, he found the foil next to her elbow. Ripping it open, he used his teeth to remove the rubber, edged to his side, and rolled it on.

Then he moved over her, keeping his weight on his elbows. He'd told her he wouldn't let her go, but he needed her with him. If this was a mistake, they both needed to make it. "Are you sure, baby? It's okay if you aren't. We can just play." In fact, he'd be fine returning to where he'd just been.

Her face softened.

Ah, hell. She had him now, and she knew it. Damn it.

"I'm sure," she whispered, her small hands resting on his shoulders. She bent her knees, creating more room for him.

He closed his eyes. This was such a huge mistake, but it was too late. He slowly pushed inside her, pausing several times to let her body adjust. Wet, slick, dangerous heat surrounded him, tighter than any glove. God. She was heaven. Finally, perspiring from holding himself back, he pushed all the way inside.

Her moan mixed with his groan.

He opened his eyes and dropped his forehead to hers. "Are you all right?"

"Yes." She traced his torso, down his rib cage, to his hips. "You're huge."

He barked out a laugh. Cute. Smart, sweet, and cute. "I'm not a good guy, sweetheart." Where the warning came from, he'd never know.

She lifted her head and licked across his lips.

Fire rushed down his torso to land in his balls.

"You're better than you believe, Raze Shadow. Trust me." She wiggled her ass just enough to shoot sparks up his spine.

He moved then, pulling out to the tip and then shoving back inside.

Her head dropped to the pillow. "I figured we'd be like this. More than just, well, *this*."

Yeah. He got that. But he didn't want to understand her, and not just because she was a little crazy. The more he knew her, the better he understood her, the more he wanted her beneath him longer than just this one night. She was wounded and she was vulnerable. Everything in him craved to make her right. To protect her from the world out there, and shit, that didn't make a lick of sense.

Her nails dug into his flesh. "Now who's thinking too hard?"

He nodded. "Good point." He pulled out and thrust back where he wanted to be forever.

"More."

That he could give her. Reaching beneath her, he grabbed her ass and lifted her into him. She moaned and tightened around him. He pulled out and sank into her, pounding hard, keeping control until he felt her tense beneath him. Her body trembled and her thighs slapped against his hips.

Her eyes shut as she went over, her soft cry of ecstasy burning into his heart. The waves pummeled around his dick, sending him over the edge. He gave one last, hard, complete thrust, burying himself as deep as he could. The orgasm rushed down his spine and exploded inside him, shattering every thought he'd ever had.

Finally, he regained some sense of control and opened his eyes. Emotion washed through him, and he batted back any feelings he didn't want. Even so, he couldn't help but grin. "So that's how to get you to stop talking."

She snorted a laugh, delight crossing her face. "I guess so. Think you can do it again?"

Perfect. Damn, if the petite woman wasn't too perfect. He studied her contented face. What the hell was he going to do now?

She snuggled against him, apparently not giving a shit that he was still inside her. "Raze," she murmured sleepily, her eyelids closing. "I'm glad I found you."

The sweet words held truth and no coyness. With them, she pretty much reached in his chest and manacled his heart.

When he'd first seen her, she'd worn a ripped and dirty pencil skirt with a white blouse, and she'd been shackled to a wall. Bruises had matted her face, and her hair had been a wild mess. She'd been smacked around and injected with drugs that had altered her very reality. Yet pure defiance and raw intelligence had glowed in her stunning eyes. Spirit and heart . . . that was Vinnie. That day she'd impressed him.

Now, all sweet and trusting beneath him, she claimed him.

He slapped his hand against the wall to shove them both down the bed a little.

The woman didn't even stir, trusting him completely.

Now what the hell was he going to do?

Jax tried to keep his gaze stoic as Tace threw down a card on the cracked table in Jax's apartment. He drew in a breath. The smell of cheap booze competed with the scent of lavender in the spartan room. Where the hell Lynne had found dried lavender to put in a bowl, he'd never know. His place now had girlie items like bowls of purple stuff, and he'd never admit how much he liked having her touches all around him. At least not to Tace. Lynne already read him like a worn journal.

A woman's cry came through the walls.

"Jesus." Tace reached for a glass of rotgut whiskey and shifted in his seat. "We should've played gin downstairs in the offices."

"I didn't know Raze and Vinnie were going to go at it like fuckin' rabbits." Jax picked up a ten and discarded a three of clubs, trying to tune them out. "I wouldn't have figured her for a screamer."

"Me either." Tace took the three and studied his hand. "I'm surprised Shadow is strong enough to make it happen after just awakening from the fever. Scorpius is a bitch."

"He'll drop again." Jax poured more of the booze. They were almost out of their secret stash; it was time to go raiding again. "Don't you remember?"

"Not really," Tace said, discarding a two.

Jax reached for the pile. "I do. It was a shitty series of feeling better, dropping from exhaustion, and then feeling better before dropping again. Totally sucked." He discarded a seven. "How are you feeling, anyway?"

"Cold. Not crazy and not mean, but cold." Tace took the seven. "Gin." He kicked back in his chair.

"Shit." Jax tossed his cards down. "You just got better. Give it time, and your brain will return to normal." Maybe. Who knew? "Just let me know if you feel homicidal."

Tace shrugged. "I don't really *feel* any way, so maybe that's good."

The door opened, and Lynne slid inside. Dark circles marred the hollows beneath her eyes, and her pale skin seemed nearly luminous in the soft lantern light.

Jax frowned. He'd told her to get some rest early this afternoon, and of course, she'd ignored him. Several of the most dangerous men still alive followed his orders without question, yet the pretty scientist had no problem defying him. He kinda liked that about her, but he couldn't allow her to become ill. If he had to shackle her to the bed to get her to sleep, he would. The idea hardened his groin.

"What are you grinning at?" Lynne asked.

He kept her gaze and didn't answer.

She shuffled her feet. "Something about that look worries me."

Smart girl.

"You look exhausted," Tace said, shoving to his feet.

Lynne nodded. "A raiding party found a Scorpius research lab on the north side that had been making dental molds and retainers before being turned into a lab."

Tace shook his head. "The government used every lab available when things got bad. We have to give them that much."

"They didn't do enough." Jax motioned to Lynne. "Come have a drink."

Her eyes lit up, and she walked past Tace to accept a tumbler.

A man's groan echoed through the flimsy walls.

Her face turned pink. "Raze and Vinnie?"

Another sigh, and something loud banged against the wall. Jax nodded, amused at her pretty blush. After the things he'd done to her in bed, ones she'd enjoyed, it was a sweet surprise to see her embarrassment. "I think Raze and Vinnie are getting acquainted."

Lynne tipped back the drink. "Good. That's good. Connections are what keep us together as a society."

Her cultured and educated tone shot straight south through Jax's body to land hard in his balls. They drew up tight, and his zipper cut into his dick. "Why don't you come closer and connect with me?" he rumbled.

Tace turned and headed for the door. "That's my cue. Night, folks."

Jax grabbed Lynne and tumbled her down onto his lap. "Tace? Check on Sami, would you? She's been out of sight too often lately." His young lieutenant had attended every mandatory meeting, but when she wasn't on patrol, she'd been somewhere else. He hadn't had a chance to question her after dealing with Lighton earlier.

"She's hiding out. In fact, she's hiding a whole lot." Tace partially turned. "At first I didn't care, but now I'm thinking she's a mystery I need to solve."

"Good. Solve her." Jax waited until Tace nodded and had disappeared into the hallway.

Lynne pushed both hands through his hair. "Now aren't you glad you didn't kill Raze?"

"No, but I'm glad I have time to figure out his angle," Jax said, his gaze dropping to her inviting mouth. "I thought I told you to get some rest."

"Did you?" She stretched against him with a soft purr. "I must not have heard you."

He scoffed. "Funny."

Another grunt, this one deep, announced the couple in the other room was close to the finish line.

Lynne chuckled and buried her face in Jax's neck. "This is good."

Jax rubbed her back. "Maybe."

"You can trust Raze."

"Love all but trust a few," Jax murmured.

She snuggled closer. "Shakespeare?"

"Yeah." It had been a while since he'd quoted Shakespeare to her. In fact, it had been a while since he'd pulled out a quotation for a moment, something he used to do a lot.

Lynne tugged down his shirt and kissed his Vanguard tattoo. "I want one of these."

"You got it." The idea of marking her in such a way tightened his entire body. But first, they had to be on the same page about Vanguard in general. "If I have to take care of Raze, then Vinnie's not gonna like it, and I need her cooperation."

Lynne sighed against his jugular. "Come up with a better plan. Figure Raze out, help him, and then we all live happily ever after."

Jax lifted her and turned for the bed. "At this point, I'm just glad we're all still living."

A crash banged against the wall. Jesus. Those two might kill each other, and then he wouldn't have to worry about it, anyway.

Chapter Fifteen

Everything on earth can be explained in terms of atoms and matter . . . except love.

—Dr. Franklin X. Harmony, *Philosophies*

Vinnie awoke slowly, wrapped safely in warmth. Her eyelids slid open. Cracked ceiling, moldy smell, cold air. Oh. For the slightest of moments, she'd forgotten about Scorpius and the world pretty much ending. She stretched and caught herself. Whoa. Little aches and pains flared to life in unexpected places.

She smiled.

Then she stilled at finding Raze Shadow sitting across the room on the sofa, watching her. He'd pulled on a fresh-looking pair of dark jeans and a white T-shirt that clearly emphasized the muscles in his chest and arms. "Morning." He didn't smile.

She sat up and tucked the sheet around her. "Hi." Her gaze barely met his, so she focused on his chin. What she wouldn't give to see that dimple of his again. "How are you feeling?"

"Fine."

Ah. "Headache?"

"No." The pinched skin around his eyes proclaimed that a clear lie.

"Muscle weakness?" she asked, her heart kicking strongly into gear. Her hands fluttered around the blankets.

"Nope."

She breathed in and lifted her gaze. "Say what you need to say, Shadow."

His chin lowered. "Excuse me?"

She faltered. This wasn't how a morning after went, now was it? She'd never had a casual affair. Either he needed to crawl back in bed and vow his eternal love, or he needed to run out the door and avoid her like the rogue he was. But sitting there and watching her so calmly? Um, no. "You're freaking me out."

His lips came together, and a frown drew down his eyebrows. "Why?"

"Because you're just sitting there." Realization slapped her in the face. Oh. Maybe she was the one who was supposed to leave. It was his place. Heat spread from her chest into her face. "Um, give me a few minutes and I'll get out of your hair." He wouldn't try to watch her dress, would he? She wasn't even sure where she'd put her underwear. God, this was excruciating.

Lucinda hovered outside the defunct refrigerator, her white hair glowing. "I told you this would be a mistake."

Vinnie looked up at the ceiling. Her stepmother was not there. She was *not*.

"Stop ignoring me. You made a mistake. Now tell him it's over," Lucinda snapped.

"He already knows that," Vinnie whispered.

Raze cleared his throat. "What?"

"Nothing." Now she was talking to her hallucinations in front of Raze. "That was fun—last night, I mean—but today it's daytime, and let's forget it." She lowered her gaze to meet his and ignored the sight of Lucinda doing the cha-cha by the counter. "I'm seeing things, and I'm hearing things, and you know this was a mistake. Nobody else knows, so let's just pretend it didn't happen. I'll try to find a different place to stay, and if there isn't one in headquarters, I'll go back to my apartment. I actually didn't mind—"

He launched himself off the sofa and reached her in two long strides, lifting her, sheet and all.

"Eek," she murmured as he turned and sat with her in his lap. "Um—"

"I'm not sorry it happened," he rumbled, his breath brushing her hair.

She blinked up at him, her traitorous body snuggling right in. "Yes, you are."

He frowned again, giving him the look of a pissed-off warrior. "Last night doesn't change anything, but I'm not sorry it happened."

What in the world did that mean? Her ears rang. "Well, it changes things a little. We've seen each other naked. Although we could pretend we haven't, we have, and I think that's the very definition of change. I'm not—"

"Vinnie."

She gulped in air. "There was a time I was almost laconic. I mean, I'd watch everything and everyone before making a sound. Methodical, you know? I liked to—"

"Vinnie." His dimple winked again.

Fascinating. Totally fascinating. That dimple grounded her and gave her something to hold on to. Not many people had seen it, probably. "You're patient." Man, he held an abundance of patience and understanding.

"Yes. It helps when stalking prey." The dimple deepened. "I don't mind you talking, but sometimes you forget to breathe, and I'd rather you didn't pass out right now."

"I didn't used to babble," she whispered. When would her brain return to normal?

"Never," Lucinda said, stomping bright red boots toward

the door as Vinnie followed with her gaze. "I give up. You're on your own." Lucinda wisped out of sight.

Raze tightened his hold. "What are you looking at?"

Vinnie turned back from the door. "A hallucination."

His frown flattened out and curved into a grin. "Oh." He caressed the nape of her neck. "Is he better looking than me?"

"Nobody is better looking than you." A blush warmed her cheekbones. "I mean—"

"Let's leave it at that. Who are you seeing? And talking to?"

"My stepmother, Lucinda." Vinnie sighed. "Before she died, we got along okay but weren't really close. Now she won't leave me alone."

Raze leaned in and rubbed his chin on top of her head. "Maybe your brain is trying to tell you something."

Yeah. To run like hell from the deadly soldier. "Perhaps, or maybe I'm just crazy. The drugs could've easily damaged my brain, which could lead to all sorts of disorders, including schizophrenia." As he rubbed her head, she relaxed into his hard chest. "I guess it could take a while for the drugs to completely leave my system."

"Let's go with the positive thought." Raze levered back and then swooped in, kissing her.

Tingles exploded down her body, and she kissed him back. Her body flushed, and her mind spun. Finally, he set her gently on the bed and stood. "I need to go figure some things out. What's your plan today?"

Pleasure tickled through her. They were sharing their days. Like a couple. "I'm starting work today as a counselor." In fact, she needed to get a move on.

He nodded and then paled.

She stood and inched toward him.

He swayed. "Shit."

She jumped out of bed and slid a shoulder beneath his arm. Yep. Scorpius sucked. "Not so tough now, are you?"

"No." He shut his eyes.

She helped him back to the bed. "You did just come out of the most dangerous infection to ever plague humans." How weak was he? God. Had she just totally taken advantage of an invalid? He sure hadn't felt ill when he'd been hammering inside her.

He lay down and took several deep breaths. "I'm fine. Just not quite at full strength."

Then they had to have sex when he was at 100 percent, because Raze at half strength had been freaking amazing. She shook her head to get rid of the thoughts and leaned over to feel his forehead. Perfectly cool. "You probably just need some soup. If I remember right—to be honest, I don't remember everything—it took about a week for me to get my strength back after Scorpius. Maybe it was two weeks. I'm not—"

"Vinnie."

She pressed her lips together. "Sorry," she mumbled.

"Don't be sorry." He pressed the palm of his hand against his forehead. "Fuck. When does the headache go away?"

She tugged the loose blanket up and over his chest. "Not sure. It's different for everyone, and most survivors get migraines once in a while." She'd wanted to cut her head off during the last one. "They're not that bad. You'll be fine."

"I'd kill for an aspirin."

This was the first time Raze had allowed her to see any vulnerability in him. Her heart warmed, and she moved closer to him. The fever had shaken him, but soon he'd have all his defenses shored up again. "What's your real name?"

"Raze." His hand dropped to the covers.

She'd help him whether he liked it or not, but she needed something. A small token to show that she mattered. That she was special to him. How pitiful was that? "Come on. Won't you tell me?"

His lips twitched. "On the lives of my ancestors, my name really is Raze. My dad's name was Ryan."

"Um, okay."

My mom had three great-uncles who helped to raise her way back when. Albert, Zeke, and Elton."

Humor bubbled up through Vinnie. "Raze. She combined their first names to create yours."

"Yes. In the military it turned out I was pretty good with a blade, so some rumor got started that Raze was a nickname for Razor, which it wasn't."

She smiled. "I won't tell anybody, I promise."

"I know." With that small movement toward trust, Raze Shadow dropped into sleep.

She smoothed his hair back, and once his breathing deepened, she leaned over to place a small kiss on his forehead. God, he was beautiful. Making sure to be gentle, she traced the strong contours of his face. Native American markers shaped him; she'd have to ask him where he got the blue eyes.

Her body felt both satiated and a little sore. She grinned and hustled to get dressed in jeans and a light sweater, yanking her hair into a ponytail. After brushing her teeth, she gave one last, rather longing look at the sleeping warrior. Could he be hers? She wasn't sure. Whatever secrets he held seemed to torture him.

She slipped out of the apartment and hurried down the hallway and stairs. The soup kitchen was nearly empty, while the smell of cooked cheese filled the room. Waving at a couple of men wiping card tables, picnic tables, and scrap tables, she headed into the infirmary. "Tace?"

Tace poked his head out of a back room, his hair ruffled. Was his hair getting darker? "You ready to get to work?"

"Yes." She walked past the former reception area, past

the two examination rooms, and beyond Lynne's lab to an office near the back door. Desk, shabby love seat, ragged rug over concrete, and an executive leather chair. She ran her hand over the buttery softness. "Nice."

"We stole it from a former attorney's office on the west side." Tace looked around. "Will this do?"

"Yes."

"Good." He handed over a scratched clipboard holding lined school paper. "Here's the list and order for today. I gave you an hour for lunch, and you end when you end. Some folks signed themselves up, and Jax ordered his top lieutenants to seek spots. I put us in."

She read the list. "Jax believes in psychotherapy?"

"I think he believes folks need help, and you're the best we've got. Plus, I'm sure he wants you to alert him with problems." The Texan sauntered in and dropped into a chair. "Sami is late, so why don't you do me first?"

Vinnie faltered and then followed him, sitting in the leather. It cupped her butt. "How are you feeling?"

He grinned, all charm. "I'm different since the infection, and I don't really care about being different. I like how much faster my brain works, and I have quicker reflexes. In fact, I can see what has to be done without emotion."

"So you think more than feel now, and you used to do the opposite." Vinnie crossed her legs. "Does that worry you?"

"No." His handsome face set into puzzled lines. "I'm not concerned. The reason I don't want to be a Ripper is because then I'd have to kill or be killed, and that seems unnecessary, you know? Also, I have OCD now. It's a pain in the ass."

She reached for a pad of paper on the small table and started to scribble notes. "Do you have any urges or craving to harm people?"

"Nope. Not at all." He sat back and extended his long legs. "Any urges I have are of the sexual nature."

She paused and took a moment to clear her throat. "How so?"

His expression didn't falter. "I always liked women and sex, so it's not that different. Let's just say my tastes have turned a little darker."

"Sadistic?" Vinnie didn't like labeling anything, but Tace obviously wanted clear conclusions, and she needed answers.

He grimaced but didn't blush. "I don't know. One of the women I've been seeing likes it rough, and I've enjoyed her, where before I would've stayed clear."

Vinnie nodded. "So long as it's consensual, why not explore? Do you want her to, ah, get rough with you?"

His blue eyes twinkled. "No. I like dishing it out, and she enjoys getting her ass paddled, but there's no emotion involved. Just sex."

"She's all right with that?" Vinnie asked.

Tace nodded. "Her rules, really. Said she's not interested in emotion or entanglements because survival is all that matters."

"Do you mind giving me her name?" Vinnie asked. She'd like to check on the woman to make sure Tace was giving the full truth.

"Julie Bernete. She's one of the inner territory doctors," Tace said smoothly. "Feel free to talk to her. I waive any confidentiality or stuff like that."

"All right. How is this different from before Scorpius?" Vinnie leaned back to appear relaxed and promote trust.

Tace's hands hung loosely between his knees. "Well, before, I'd wine and dine. Buy flowers, say ma'am a lot, and treat the woman like a princess. I mean, the end result was banging the headboard against the wall, but I never once went for the rougher stuff."

"Ever been in love?"

"Nope." Tace shrugged. "I wasn't opposed to love, but with the army and all, I kept relationships pretty simple."

"So you were satisfied with sweet and gentle?" she asked.

He grinned. "I'm not saying I didn't go for it, just that I didn't smack anybody's ass with a belt."

"Now that you are?" she asked, trying to sound professional and not gossipy. This was just fascinating.

He lost the smile. "To be honest, I'm not sure. There's something powerful and right about having a woman under me, bound, and helpless." He winced. "Not unwilling though, if that makes sense. If she's not into it, then I'm not interested in the slightest. God, I'm kinky now."

Vinnie bit back a smile. "For the time being, why not explore the kink? You have a willing partner, and this might just be a phase, Tace."

"If it isn't?" he asked, his eyes darkening even more.

She shrugged. "Then it isn't. You're not doing anything wrong so long as everything is consensual between you and your partner—and that's the key. Communication is paramount when you're exploring this way."

He nodded. "All right."

"Also, how about you keep a diary? I've found that exploring thoughts and feelings in a safe journal can help make sense of the world around us, especially with Scorpius changing everything." She kept her voice gentle.

"I'll think about it." Tace frowned.

A ruckus sounded from outside.

"Tace?" a female voice called.

Tace stood. "In here."

Boots clomped and Sami came into view.

"You're late," Tace said mildly, moving toward her.

She stepped aside. "Bite me."

He paused as he reached her and leaned in, all charm leaving his face. "Okay."

She shoved his chest, and he took a step back. "Knock it off."

He glanced at Vinnie. "The little soldier here has secrets, and it's time she told the truth."

Sami rolled her eyes. "Tace, I've been kicking your ass in training for months now. Do you want another beating?"

Vinnie bit back a smile.

He turned back to Sami, towering over the petite brunette. "One of these days, you're not going to win our little matches. The doc and I just figured out I like to spank women, so you might want to watch yourself." He pivoted and disappeared from sight.

Sami blushed a hard red and stalked inside. "Did he just threaten me?"

"Yes." Vinnie frowned toward the door. The medic had just shown more emotion, real emotion, in those thirty seconds than she'd seen from him yet. "But he likes his sexual encounters to be consensual, so I believe he was just messing with you." Which was interesting, now wasn't it?

Sami perched at the edge of the love seat. "Listen, Doc, it's great you're here and all, but I don't want to chat. I'm one of Jax's top lieutenants, I'm highly trained in karate and street fighting, and I used to be an LAPD rookie. That's all you need to know."

Vinnie sat back. The fact that Jax Mercury, supreme Alpha male, had trusted female lieutenants spoke even more for his character than the fact that he'd created Vanguard as a haven. "I'm not going to make you talk to me if you don't want to do so."

Sami smiled, making her look about eighteen. "Good." She stood and walked right out the door.

"Well," Lucinda huffed from behind the desk, "you're not very good at this shrink stuff."

Vinnie sighed. "I don't know. Most shrinks are nuts, you know? That's how they help people."

Lucinda cackled a laugh. "Well, then, you should be much better than you are. You're crazier than a loon."

Vinnie caught herself glaring at what would appear to be the wall to anybody watching. She *was* crazy.

A knock sounded, and a pale brunette edged into the entryway. "Dr. Wellington? My name is April, and I'm your next patient."

Vinnie forced a smile. "Come on in, and let's get to know each other." She'd try to help these Vanguard members while she had enough sanity to do so.

"That won't be long," Lucinda muttered. "You're falling off the deep end big-time, sister."

Chapter Sixteen

―――◦◦◉◦◦―――

Genius and insanity feed off each other . . .
and only one can truly survive.
—Dr. Vinnie Wellington, *Sociopaths*

Instead of dancing easily on the mat, Raze's feet dragged on the worn material, even as he threw punch after punch at the bag hanging from three heavy, rusted chains. He grunted with the effort, and his eyesight hazed more than once.

What in the hell had he been thinking the previous night? He'd slept with Vinnie. The sound of her sighing his name would remain with him the rest of his life. How could he put her in danger with Grey? What kind of a bastard would that make him? The very idea of hurting her made him hit the bag harder, even though his strength had already ebbed.

"I'm no doctor, but you're gonna pass out if you don't slow down," Jax drawled from the doorway of the basement training area.

Raze hit the bag again, following up with a fierce kick that nearly took him to his knees. Covering his pain, he turned to face Jax. "Want to go a round?"

Full of arrogance and amusement, a smile curved Jax's hard mouth.

Raze rolled his shoulders. "Is that a no?"

"If I wanted you dead, Shadow, I would've just shot you the other day after the Ripper bit you. Instead, I saved your life." The Vanguard leader sauntered into the room.

Warning ticked along Raze's scalp, followed by a healthy dose of shame. "Thanks for saving my life."

"You're welcome. Don't make me regret it." Jax glanced around. "When did you guys put up the punching bags?"

"Last week." They'd found the bags at an old gym near Malibu, of all places. "We were looking for medical supplies at the gyms and we found these as well as the free weights." Raze pointed to a set against the far wall.

The mats had been spread end to end before he'd joined Vanguard, and he'd never questioned where they'd come from. The room was big enough to have a weight section, a punching section, and a place for grappling. "What was this place before you created your headquarters?"

"Storage. The windows are too high and too small to provide egress, so the room wasn't compliant with occupancy laws, probably." Jax leaned against the wall and crossed his arms. "Good job during the attack from Twenty."

"Ah, thanks." The image of the dead kid flashed across Raze's mind. His chest ached.

"Sorry about the kid. That sucks." Jax studied him.

"Yeah, it totally sucks." Raze rubbed the back of his neck. "When does the Scorpius headache go away?"

"Not sure it ever completely does," Jax said.

Great. That's what everyone kept saying. "Why did you save me?" Raze asked. The Vanguard leader just could've left his ass for the Rippers to finish off.

Jax lifted a shoulder. "I like you, and you're a damn good soldier. Plus, my new Vanguard shrink-slash-profiler cares about you, and I didn't want to piss her off quite yet."

He liked that Jax was beginning to need Vinnie—the woman wanted to be needed. "You don't trust me."

"Of course not, but if you hadn't been here yesterday,

more people would be dead from the Twenty attack. More of my people," Jax said.

Raze nodded.

"Why won't you tell me why you're really here?" Jax asked.

"I'm here because there's nowhere else to go." That was kind of the truth.

Jax sighed. "I know the look of a guy on a mission, and I know the look of a guy clawing with bloody fingers at the end of his rope. Whatever is driving you, I can help."

God, everything in him wanted to trust Jax, but how could he gamble with his sister's life? The next time Raze met with Ash, he'd get more information, and then maybe he could go to the Vanguard soldiers with a solid plan. "I don't need help."

"Maybe not, but you wouldn't be keeping secrets unless there was a good reason to do so, and the only reason you won't level with me is because whatever you're planning will piss me off." Jax shook his head. "Which means that one of us is likely to end up dead, and I won't desert Lynne that way."

"Where does that leave us?" Raze asked evenly.

Jax's eyes darkened. "You have until tomorrow to give me the truth, or you're out of Vanguard. Take today and really look around at the people here. See if you can leave them. And then use the night, another one with Dr. Wellington, to see if you can forget her. If so, get the hell out."

Sami jogged into the room. "You guys fighting?"

Raze forced a smile for the petite soldier. Sami wore dark pants with an olive shirt, and she'd tamed her thick brown hair into two braids. "How old are you?" he blurted out.

She rolled her eyes. "Twenty-five, but I'm out of makeup. Regardless of age, I could kick your ass, Shadow."

Actually, she might have a chance at the moment. His knees wobbled, and invisible hammers pounded away inside his skull. "When I'm at full speed, we'll have to test that theory."

"If you stay," Tace Justice said, loping into the room, his tennis shoes leaving indentations in the mats.

Sami snorted. "Nice shoes."

Tace glanced down at the pristine white shoes. "A scouting party hit the edge of Bel Air last week. I like these. What's wrong with them?"

"You look like you're about to hit brunch at the country club." Jax snorted.

Sami laughed and even Tace grinned.

The moment slammed Raze in the solar plexus. The sense of camaraderie washed over him. The world sucked, and more enemies than they could count waited outside the Vanguard fence. But inside, they had this. They had one another. He opened his mouth, and a picture of Maureen learning to ride a bike popped into his head.

His mouth shut. He had to save his sister.

"Ah, where were you yesterday during the Twenty attack?" Raze focused on Jax. "I saw you come back in after I'd regained consciousness, but I didn't get the chance to talk to you."

Jax's upper lip curled. "There was a skirmish inner territory between the good Reverend Lighton and my soldiers."

Raze breathed out. "Seriously?"

Sami frowned. "Jax ordered them to take down a fence, which they have not done."

"I didn't think they would," Jax muttered. "Just needed time to do some digging to figure out a plan."

Sami nodded. "Reverend Lighton isn't even clergy. He was a contraceptive salesman from Portland before Scorpius attacked the world."

"He has found his calling," Jax drawled.

Raze pressed a hand against his left temple. "What's the deal?"

Sami rocked back on her heels. "I've been investigating

since yesterday. Turns out the reverend, as he's insisting on being called these days, has been issuing sermons the last months in private, and only to people he's now calling the Pure."

"The Pure?" Tace asked.

"Folks who haven't been infected by Scorpius," Jax said.

Sami gave a mock shudder. "That's creepy."

"Yes." Jax nodded. "I need somebody to go undercover to a sermon or two, but we're all survivors of Scorpius and won't be included. Are any of you close to an uninfected person?"

Raze shrugged. "Most of us don't know who has been infected and who hasn't."

Jax grimaced. "We could have mandatory testing, but I'm not ready to go there yet. It seems too draconian."

"What about April Snyder?" Tace asked. "She hasn't had the illness."

Jax stared at the far wall. "How is she doing?" The woman had lost her only daughter just a couple of weeks before, and she'd nearly taken her own life afterward.

"As well as can be expected," Sami said. "April helps with the kids and is now working on schedules for scouts as well as the soldiers. She's tough."

Raze breathed out. "That is tough. I see her with Lena a lot."

Tace nodded. "Lena has attached herself to April, and it has been good for her." He reached in a pocket and drew out a rock shaped a little like a heart. "The girl gave me this earlier. Any ideas?"

"So long as it ain't blue, I don't care," Jax said.

Raze grinned. Lena often gave Jax blue rocks shaped like hearts, or rocks with blue hearts painted on them, or drawings of blue hearts. Definitely related to Lynne Harmony. The odd thing was that Lena had started giving the little talismans to Jax long before Lynne had walked into his life.

Sami touched an earring in her left lobe. "Lena gave me this yesterday."

"What is it?" Jax asked.

"Just a pretty orange stone," Sami said.

Raze squinted. "That's a topaz. The birthstone of Scorpios."

Sami blinked. "How do you know that?"

"My sister was into astrology," Raze said. "She'd do my chart every year, whether I liked it or not." God, he missed her. He had to get her back. "Is your birthday in late October or early November?"

"No," Sami said. "I'm sure she just saw the pretty stone and gave it to me. You guys have to stop reading things into her gifts."

"I'm a Scorpio," Tace said dryly.

"Whatever." Sami focused back on Jax, her face flushing a pretty pink. "What's our plan with the Pure morons?"

"Dunno." Jax stretched his shoulders and winced. "They want to take over the three apartment buildings on the south side of Vanguard, they want soldiers, and they want autonomy."

Raze lifted an eyebrow. "Autonomy so long as we provide food, medical supplies, and protection?"

Jax grimaced. "That seems to be the request."

"If we refuse?" Tace asked.

"I think they're going to leave," Jax said.

"So let them leave." Raze shook out his left arm, trying to banish the weak tingles still attacking him. "If they want to create their own society, then they can."

"We've managed a head count, and twenty of the uninfected are children," Jax murmured. "Mostly orphans."

That changed things. "Tell anyone over the age of eighteen they can go, but the kids stay here. Or the kids without parents stay here," Raze said. A fight was coming about that—he could feel it. He needed to get his strength back and soon.

Sami nodded. "How many adults, and do you have a list?"

"No list yet, but I'm guessing about eighty adults," Jax said. "If I refuse to let them take the kids, there is going to be trouble."

Tace breathed out. "If they stay, and if we provide shelter, what do they offer? How many of the eighty are providing any sort of service to Vanguard?"

"I don't know. I guess we'll have to sit down at the negotiation table with the reverend," Jax muttered. "I don't like kids being used as bartering items, and I really don't like being held hostage by a prick seeking safety with my guns. But the kids matter, and we need to make sure everyone in his little flock is there willingly."

"Wyatt would've known," Sami said, her chest heaving as she spoke about a soldier they'd lost in battle recently.

"I know. Nobody has his connections throughout Vanguard," Jax said wearily. "I think Dr. Wellington is our best chance for creating a good community and keeping everyone in the loop."

"Then stop calling her Dr. Wellington," Raze said softly.

"Excuse me?" Jax asked, the muscles flexing in his crossed arms.

Why the hell was he getting involved? Raze shook his head. "She's fragile right now, and your using her title keeps her at a distance, when all she wants is to belong. You call your other lieutenants by their first names or nicknames. If you want a title for her, call her Doc."

"You sure have her figured out," Jax drawled.

"She's not exactly a closed book," Raze said. Why was he trying to smooth the path for Vinnie when he planned to kidnap her in two nights? Though if his plan succeeded, he'd have her right back in Vanguard within hours. "You have to make her feel at home before she can make others feel the same way."

"Good point," Jax said.

"She sure made you feel at home last night," Tace murmured. His face turned red. "Shit. Sorry. Sometimes my mouth is faster than my brain."

Raze stiffened. "Were we loud?"

Sami snorted. "Oh baby, oh baby, oh baby."

"I did not say that," Raze snapped.

"You groaned it." Jax chuckled.

Raze's neck heated and the fire spread to his face. "You guys are all assholes." Hopefully they wouldn't mess with Vinnie.

"I have more condoms in the infirmary," Tace said, then lost his grin. "Although there's bad news on the reproduction front. Two of our scouting teams branched out last night to refugee camps, and in both, several women had recently miscarried."

Raze stilled. "Women who'd become pregnant after surviving Scorpius?"

"Three after, one before, and no live births," Tace confirmed.

"Shit." Jax scrubbed a hand down his face. "If this is true, then I do see the reverend's need to separate his group from survivors. The uninfected might be humanity's only chance to continue."

"Everyone is gonna catch Scorpius at some point, so our better bet is to find a way to promote successful pregnancies," Tace said. "The bacteria lives both in survivors and on surfaces, so someday there won't be an uninfected person still alive."

Jax nodded. "That's what Lynne believes, too. She also thinks we'll find answers at the Bunker, if that place really exists."

"I found more references to it in the research materials

from the dental lab," Tace said. "Lynne and I are halfway through those documents."

Sami nudged Tace with her hip. "I have training with new scouts in a little while, so if you wanna train and get your ass kicked again, we have to get started." She pulled her arm across her chest in a classic stretch.

"Has Lynne trained lately?" Jax asked.

"I'm not a tattletale, Mercury," Sami countered, loosening her other arm.

"That's a no," Jax said. "I want you to train Lynne and Vinnie every day until they can take care of themselves. The president is hunting them both, and at some point, we're going to meet up with him again. You're on hand-to-hand, and Raze is on weapons. Get them up to speed."

"Roger that," Sami said. "But you both need to speak with your women about it, because neither one of them wants to train. They're both too involved in their jobs."

"They'll train," Jax said grimly.

Raze nodded. "President Atherton is crazy but very, very smart. If he wants them—and we know he does—they need to learn to fight dirty."

Like he did.

Chapter Seventeen

━━━━◅◆▻━━━━

*Controlling the behavior of others is a simple task,
controlling their thoughts is an impossible one.*

—Dr. Vinnie Wellington, *Perceptions*

Tace Justice followed Sami down the stairs to the main
gym, trying not to notice how tight her ass looked in the
yoga pants. They'd been training together for months, and
lately something felt different.

Hell. *He* was different.

The second she reached the mat, she turned and swept
his legs out from under him. He smacked the mats and
rolled. Damn it.

She bounced back, her hair flying, her smile wide. "When
are you going to be prepared?"

Tace circled her, looking for an opening. She'd been
kicking his butt for eons, and he'd had enough. It was time
to teach the little karate expert a lesson, but he wasn't quite
as fast as he wanted to be. Not yet. "You're asking for it."
He dodged in with a right cross.

She slid back easily and kicked up, nailing him under
the chin.

His head jerked back, and stars exploded behind his eyes.
"Damn it, Sami," he growled.

She chuckled.

He shook his head, trying to get his bearings. She moved, and he saw what she planned before she did it. As she struck with a straight on punch, he caught her fist in his hand. The sound of flesh on flesh echoed throughout the room.

Her pretty brown eyes widened, and she jerked free. A stream of irritated Spanish flowed from her full mouth.

He tried not to smile.

"You're getting faster," she murmured, dancing on the mats.

Faster, smarter, and stronger. "Hmmm," he agreed, focusing on her feet. All of a sudden, he could read her body language better.

"What do you think of Raze?" she asked, using a roundhouse kick to nail his ribs.

Pain exploded across Tace's torso. He hadn't seen that one coming, now had he? "He's fine." Truthfully, Tace didn't give a shit right now.

"I like him, but he has secrets."

Heat filled Tace's esophagus. "You like him?" Why would that bother Tace?

Sami rolled her eyes. "Not like him, like him. He's good in a fight, and he's helpful. Not sure about the secrets, though."

"Look who's talking." Tace swept with his left leg and caught her ankle.

She went down, rolled, and kicked up to his knee.

It buckled, and he went down, landing hard.

She jumped and perched on his chest, pressing both knees into his shoulders. "Pinned."

Damn it. One of these days, he was going to teach her a lesson. Apparently this wasn't the day. "If you need help training Lynne or Vinnie later, let me know." Tace gave Sami the victory and tapped the mat.

She grinned and rolled off him. "I could use the help, to

be honest. Neither one of them has a clue how to fight, and the president is definitely coming for them." She held a hand out to help him up.

Tace accepted the hand. This time. "I want a rematch tomorrow," he murmured.

She shrugged and headed for the doorway, her hips swaying. "Your funeral."

Maybe. Maybe not.

President Bret Atherton finished his tenth set of push-ups, moving with perfect precision and control. He'd always kept in shape, but since healing from the Scorpius bacterium, he'd become stronger and faster.

As had his enemies.

"Sir?" Vice President Lake strode into the makeshift gym, his jeans perfectly pressed. "I debriefed our scouts and have much to report."

Why in the world did the man spend time pressing pants? When Bret had ordered his men to reactivate the steam generators used by the mansion owners before commercial power became available, he was more concerned with light and protection than fashion. He gracefully rose and wiped his face with a towel, his gaze going to stunning Lake Tahoe outside. "You were right about this place."

"Yes, sir."

The lake in May sparkled with a chill, and that was fine with Bret. The world had gone cold.

He turned and shucked his sweats and shirt for faded jeans and a black button-down shirt. While he sometimes still wore suits for occasions, he liked to be comfortable, so jeans were his go-to. After this meeting he'd take a long, hot shower. His enemies didn't have heated showers, now did they?

Bret moved out of the gym, through a gathering room,

and into what now served as a conference room. During the mansion's heyday, the long, paneled space had been a dining room for the rich. The family who'd owned the mansion had eventually sold it to the California Park service, and then it had become a place for weddings, gatherings, and tourists.

With acreage, the lake, and many outbuildings, the mansion was the perfect place for his western headquarters. Plus, it was close to Vanguard territory, the Mercenaries, Twenty, two large farms, and the spot where he suspected the Bunker to be.

He had to find that place.

An aide—a pretty one with very long legs—handed him a ledger with perfect neat rows. "Sir." She turned on a heel and clip-clopped in the opposite direction.

He continued past the conference room to his office, which had served as the first owner's study. Dark paneling covered the walls and ceilings in intricate designs, while two full walls of windows opened to incredible views of the lake and surrounding trees. He sat in an antique leather chair and set his papers on the mahogany desk.

Lake sat across from him.

"How many scouts have returned?" Bret asked.

"Seven so far, sir." Lake rested his wrists on the wooden arms of his guest chair, his posture loose, his feet flat on the floor.

Bret lifted an eyebrow. "From that position, how quickly can you be up and on the attack?"

"Seconds," Lake said without a pause. "I won't let anybody get to you. Ever."

Not for the first time, Bret wondered if he could take Lake in a fight now that Scorpius had granted him new strength and speed. "Please report."

Lake's eyes darkened as if he followed Bret's thoughts. "The first scout reported back from Twenty. They launched a retaliatory attack on the Vanguard headquarters, much as we suggested, but the attackers failed to return with intel."

Irritation clawed up Bret's esophagus. "We have no new intel?"

"No, sir."

Damn it. "How am I going to get Lynne and Vivienne back without proper intel regarding Vanguard?" Those Twenty gang members were morons.

Frown lines marred Lake's too-smooth face. "I understand you've always wanted Dr. Harmony back for personal reasons, but I thought you'd planned to kill Dr. Wellington anyway."

Bret pressed his lips together. "Lynne is mine, and I need her expertise once we find the Bunker." The woman had to pay for defying him first, though. "Dr. Wellington is psychic and much smarter than I gave her credit for. I believe she can help me to find the Bunker." Plus, he had promised he'd kill her, and he always kept his promises. He'd held her captive for weeks, and she hadn't come close to breaking. He had to admire that in a woman.

Lake nodded. "There's more. I had a scout reach out to a survivor camp outside of Vegas, and Jax Mercury is circulating drawings of his brother, who's missing."

Bret paused. "Did you obtain a picture?"

"Yes."

"Excellent. Have all of our resources looking for the man, too. We want to find him before Mercury does. Wouldn't that be an excellent bargaining chip."

Lake smiled. "Of course. Also, we had two scouts keeping close track of the Mercenaries, and I'm having them draw out their territory along the coastline. The Mercs have taken over the pier, several nurseries, and an agricultural research center at UC Santa Barbara."

Bret leaned forward. "They have food."

"Not only do they have food, but they have the means to grow more. The greenhouses in that region are phenomenal." Lake eyed the snow still frosting part of the grounds outside. "Two other scouts found farms, and we'll discuss them later, but you requested concrete news on the Mercs."

"Yes. Vanguard is the enemy of the United States, and I need to know if the Mercs will join with us, or if they must be destroyed as well." Bret flexed his left hand. He'd practiced boxing with Lake the night before, and bruises had formed.

"The Mercs are strong, and the compound is regulated with military precision. Our scouts captured one of the soldiers and, after some persuading, he talked. Apparently the Mercs have a mole in the Vanguard territory."

Bret sat up. "Excuse me?"

"Yes." Lake almost smiled. "Greyson Storm, the leader of the Mercs, has acquired the sister of a Vanguard elite soldier. Raze Shadow is his name."

"Shadow." Bret rubbed his chin. "He's a soldier with Vanguard?"

Lake shook his head. "Shadow is posing as a Vanguard soldier, and he's supposed to trade Dr. Wellington for his sister sometime later this week."

"Where's the sister being held?" Bret asked.

"Unknown at this point."

"Plans?" Bret asked.

Lake cleared his throat. "I've sent a force of six men to Mercenary territory to discover the location of the woman. If there's an easy grab, I told them to take her and come here."

"She'll probably help our men. She's got to be in hell with the Mercs, no question." Bret flipped the page of his notebook. "Continue your report."

* * *

Maureen Shadow peered out at the moonlight glimmering on the too-calm Pacific ocean. Sure, waves rolled in, but after the continuous rain of the last month, the peacefulness seemed like a warning. Like a prelude to an explosion.

She sat on her bed in what was once a luxurious villa that probably had rented for twenty thousand dollars a week. Soothing beach colors decorated her plush room, from the expensive duvet cover to the landscapes covering the walls. Her sliding glass door was open, leading out to the spacious deck and down to the beach. The scents of salt and sand blew inside. A palmlike fan took up most of the ceiling, silent and unused.

She was using candles to light the room, although there were generators in case of emergency. Wasn't the entire world one big emergency zone now?

Not too long ago, she would've been taking in a movie with a bunch of friends at such a time. Her friends were dead, and movies were gone. She rubbed her chest above her heart. Losing so many good people had hurt, and the pain had yet to go away. Maybe it never would.

A sharp rap on her door jerked her out of her head. "You still up?" a male voice called.

She eyed the door. Perhaps if she pretended to be asleep, he would leave her the hell alone. She just couldn't get a take on him, and that meant he was beyond her experience. A bad guy or an evil one.

"I know you're up. Open the door, or I will." Greyson Storm didn't bluff, and it wouldn't take much for his size fourteen boot to kick open the door.

"It's unlocked," she snapped, her entire body going into overdrive. The knife she'd stolen from a soldier the day before lay heavy against her thigh. She'd have to strike fast and go for a vulnerable soft spot when she finally decided to use it. But she had yet to see either a vulnerable or a soft area to Greyson. No way would she win a fight with him, so she should probably get rid of the Mercenary leader and find somebody else to fight. A guard to the north. Her captors wouldn't expect her to run to the north.

The door opened. "The cooks said you missed dinner earlier." He stepped inside, the master of the castle, tall and broad. Dangerous.

She met his gaze, rethinking her plan. If she could incapacitate him, just for a couple of hours, she could possibly get free. Should she jump up and stab him? Or wait until he got closer? She'd never stabbed anybody before. Starting with the most dangerous man she'd ever met didn't seem like a great idea, but she was rapidly running out of options. "What?" she asked when he continued to look at her.

"I asked if you'd eaten dinner," he said.

"No. I'm not hungry."

His eyes, an odd combination of gray and green, focused on her. "Are you ill?"

"No."

His chin lifted. Once again, he hadn't bothered to shave, and dark whiskers shadowed his chin. On Greyson, the look was edgy and masculine. "We're not going through this again, are we?"

She rolled her eyes. Since her captivity, she'd tried everything from escaping to refusing to eat, and he'd thwarted her at every turn. "I'm just not hungry, Grey. Stop being a dick."

One dark eyebrow rose. "Name-calling is a new one for you."

So was attempted murder. Or rather *murder*, if she succeeded. "You are a dick, and I'm sick of playing nice."

He smiled, then, a flash of white against his bronze face. Shockingly handsome in an I'm-about-to-kill-you way, the smile lent a certain charm to the sense of danger surrounding him. "This has been you playing nice? You knocked two of my guys out yesterday."

"They should've been concentrating on guarding the perimeter," she said primly. "They're both fine, I'm sure."

"Yeah, but they want your blood. Bad." Amusement competed with the warning in his eyes.

They probably did want to retaliate. She tilted her head to the side and studied him. "Then I suggest you control your men. I doubt my brother will make that trade you want so badly if I'm damaged." She hoped. There weren't any other women in the Mercenary camp, and she'd caught more than one of the men staring at her tits. Only Greyson's firm leash on his men had kept her safe, and she knew it.

"Oh, Raze will take you damaged, and don't you forget it," Greyson said silkily, his broad form filling the entire doorway.

She forced a smile. "I think you're full of shit." Her second curse word in an hour. It was a new record for her.

He stepped into the room, bringing the scent of ocean and man. "You're pushing tonight, pretty girl."

She stood and stepped his way, lifting her chin. For two weeks, she'd been held captive, and not once had he lifted a hand to her. In fact, he made sure she had privacy and food. Yet something about him inspired caution—even fear. In a world full of predators, Greyson Storm stood out as something dangerous.

She drew in air. "Do you think I don't hear what goes on? What you did with those three teenage refugees yesterday who wanted asylum?" Three girls, all around fourteen years old and prepared to do whatever they had to do for food and shelter. "I heard every word." She'd been sick about it ever since and needed to understand what had happened to those girls.

He breathed out, his nostrils flaring. "You don't know what you're talking about. It's a dangerous world, and they're lucky to have survived this long."

Oh, she was finished being frightened by him. She moved

toward him, the knife in her hand hidden by her thigh. "Where are the girls?" she hissed.

Greyson's face went blank.

She shivered but held her ground.

"Like I said, you don't know anything." He towered over her by at least a foot, his body harder than rock. A vein lined the hard cords of his neck. "I suggest you worry about yourself."

She'd never been able to do that, and she needed him pissed so he'd go and leave her alone. Then she'd put her plan into motion and attack another guard. She wouldn't win against him. "I know you're a monster, Grey. How much of one?" When he'd kidnapped her, he'd done so easily and without causing a bruise. Would he have allowed those young girls to be harmed? It was unthinkable, but she didn't know him. Not at all.

He leaned down until his nose almost touched hers. "Your only concern is yourself. For the rest of it, mind your own damn business."

"I very well might kill you." If she moved an inch, his mouth would be on hers. She immediately shook the thought away. "Because there is no way my brother will bring Vinnie Wellington here to you. He wouldn't sacrifice an innocent woman. Not even to save me."

His gaze bored into hers. "I disagree. I barely knew your brother in the military, but his loyalty was well understood. I bet he'd do anything for his baby sister."

"Why do you want this woman so badly?" Maureen asked for the umpteenth time.

"None of your business."

Was this a lover's spat? The idea kicked Maureen in the stomach, and she had no clue why. "If you lost your girlfriend, that's your own damn problem. Leave me and my family out of it."

His gaze dropped to her mouth. "I've never met the woman, so there's no need to sound jealous, pet."

Fire rushed through her, sparking temper. "Screw you, Greyson."

"It occurs to me," he said thoughtfully, "that you're picking a fight right now. You did the same thing yesterday, I stormed off, and then you attacked two of the guards. What are you planning right now?"

She stepped back and out of his atmosphere. Her lungs seized. "Nothing."

"Then I suggest you make a move with that knife in your hand. Let's see where we end up, shall we?" On the last, he lunged.

Chapter Eighteen

Without the shadow, we can't find the light.
—Dr. Franklin X. Harmony, *Philosophies*

Vinnie tossed in the bed, her mind spinning, her body aching. The first resulted from a full day of being bombarded by other people's feelings, and the second from the energetic tussle of the night before. Raze Shadow knew how to play a woman's body like he'd invented the entire concept of orgasms.

Moonlight streamed in through the broken blinds, and a slight breeze wafted as well. The rainy season had ended, and soon heat would pound them. For now, the weather refreshed instead of punished. That would change.

Heavy boot steps sounded outside the apartment, and she stilled.

The door opened, and Raze slipped inside. His face remained in shadow, but she knew his form and how he moved. Graceful and quiet, like a jungle cat, and yet with a weariness he failed to hide.

He set two guns and three knives quietly on the counter.

She watched him silently, allowing her breath to even out, as if she slept. The atmosphere changed with him inside, becoming heavy and electric. He overwhelmed the apartment, projecting his mood.

Yet she couldn't quite read him.

He yanked his shirt off, revealing hard, smooth muscle. The moonlight captured the ripped ridges and play of strength as he moved, his hands going to his belt as he kicked off his boots.

Her lungs heated, and she had to subdue her breath to keep it even.

His jeans hit the floor, and he stood, clad only in black boxers.

Her mouth watered.

Not seeming to notice her watchfulness, he opened a cupboard and reached high for a bottle of some type of whiskey. A tumbler followed. He poured a generous glass and took both to the sofa, dropping something she couldn't see on the table. Sitting, he tossed back the entire glass and then poured a second.

His bare feet settled on the table, and he crossed his ankles, lounging with a soft sigh.

The muted light played across his strong profile, leaving the other half of him in darkness, which he seemed to prefer. Just who was this man? She'd known him a little over a week, and she'd touched that stunning body. But who was he, really? Did he even know? What tortured him so?

He looked her way, sipping his whiskey.

She didn't move.

He took another drink and set his head back on the sofa, closing his eyes. "You know, I'm not one of those guys," he murmured.

She blinked. How did he know she was awake? "What guys?"

"The ones who'll warn you off for your own good. Who'll take the blue balls over hurting you."

She bit back a juvenile snort. Blue balls? "You're not going to protect me from myself?"

"Hell no. You're smart, you're strong, and you're a survivor. You can live with whatever decision you make." He took another healthy drink of whiskey.

"I get the feeling you're trying to convince yourself of those facts more than reassure me," she whispered.

He sighed. "My job is to protect you from any external threat. You have to protect yourself internally."

"Somehow I don't think you're talking about contraception," she drawled.

"No."

She might be a little nutty right now, and her instincts might be fried, but even she knew when a guy warned a girl that he'd break her heart, he'd definitely break her heart. "Maybe I'm not as fond of you as you think."

His feet hit the floor, and he sat up, his eyes opening. "I'm getting fuckin' tired of the subtext here. It's like living in *Jane Eyre*."

"I would've gone with *Pride and Prejudice*," she said.

He ground his palm against his left eye. "Stop being clever."

"I think it's a natural state."

He swore beneath his breath.

Fine. "What do you want from me, Raze? Absolution? Guarantees? Forgiveness?"

He dropped his hand and studied her. "I want to put my face between your legs again and make you scream my name. Twice."

Heat flushed through her so quickly, she gasped. "That certainly lacked subtext."

"I want to pound into you so hard we both forget about the world."

She gulped.

"I want you turned around, beneath me, knees spread

wide, face in the pillow, my hands at your hips, my dick so far inside you I'll never be free, while I smack your ass until you come."

More words like that, and she wouldn't need his help reaching an orgasm. She pressed her thighs together. Why did such obvious danger draw her so? Even before the illness and the drugs, she would've been intrigued by Raze Shadow. But this need? This overwhelming, painful, frightening need for him? That was from already having had a taste.

One taste and one night . . . and she craved to have him again.

Was it the same for him? Was that why he was drinking so late and warning her off? Did he know they'd combust? While he'd claimed he'd never warn her off, he was trying to do just that with his crass words. Too bad he'd aroused her to the point she could barely move without moaning.

"What are you so afraid of?" she murmured.

He barked out a laugh and stood, deliberately setting the glass near the bottle. "We don't have enough time to go through that list. Make a decision now."

She could play coy and pretend she didn't understand his meaning. There was a freedom in having already slept with him; the uncertainty of whether or not he wanted her was gone. The energy pouring off him should give her pause. Instead, it intrigued her. *He* intrigued her. "I have received your warning. Now come to bed. We'll deal with the world tomorrow."

He didn't twitch, but a tension swelled from him to choke the room. He seemed to vibrate. Several seconds ticked by, and he reached for something on the table.

Ah. Condoms. What she'd been unable to see. He'd tossed condoms on the table. "You sure?" he asked.

"Yes. Make me say your name," she said.

He reached the bed in long strides. "Scream my name,"

he whispered, lifting the covers and jerking her to her knees with one hand around her arm. "I said *scream*."

Chilly air assailed her a second before his mouth descended and captured hers. It wasn't a kiss. Not from the first touch could it be considered a kiss.

His lips were hard, his tongue demanding, his hold unrelenting. He tasted of whiskey and determined male, which should've sent warning bells blaring through her. Instead, the harder he pushed, the more he took, the hotter the stirring desire attacked her. Instead of the slow burn of the night before, fire bombarded her from within, sparking each nerve and shutting down her mind.

For the moment, she wasn't a doctor or a lost soul or a crazy woman. She was all female being consumed by a primal male too far gone to stop.

That thought, that reality, forced her beyond desire to desperate need.

He ripped her shirt in two and dragged it off her without releasing her lips. Her breath caught, and he still didn't grant her a reprieve, his tongue sweeping inside her mouth in a blatant claim. His palm flattened between her shoulder blades, pressing her bare flesh into his, holding her exactly where he wanted her.

Her nipples hardened against his chest, and she moaned into his mouth.

Even then, he didn't halt the determined assault on her lips. She kissed him back, trying to keep up, finally just accepting what he was giving. So much and so hard. Her body shook with need, and she burrowed closer into his warmth, into his fierce strength. A thumb at her jaw forced her mouth wider, and he took more, his taste burned forever on her tongue.

Every instinct inside her wanted to struggle against his dominance, if for no other reason than to push him farther. She curled her nails into his torso and tried to pull away.

He growled a warning that vibrated through her mouth and down her entire body, zinging erotic points on the way. The hand on her back moved up, and he threaded his fingers through her hair, jerking her head down, forcing her to arch her back. He followed her, his mouth still working hers, bending over her.

His knee landed on the bed and slid up, pressing between her bent legs. Minishocks licked through her abdomen.

She gasped into his mouth, helpless in his hold. He pressed harder, and her thighs naturally widened. He controlled her easily, his hand at her nape, his knee between her legs, bending her back. Her hand dropped from his chest to the bed, behind her butt, where she tried to find some sort of balance.

"Raze." She spoke into his mouth.

He paused, his lips still over hers, his eyes right above hers. Awareness slowly cleared the lust from the blue.

Relief flowed through her.

The awareness turned to focus and then determination.

Her relief blew to bits. She blinked, and adrenaline, the fight-or-flight kind, spread through her to compete with desire. She couldn't handle him in this state, and she knew it.

He lifted just enough to leave a millimeter between their mouths. "Too late, baby."

She did a full-body shiver.

His lips tipped, his gaze knowing. Keeping her in the tenuous position, he slid his hand down her flanks, over her abdomen, and inside her panties.

Pleasure clawed through her.

He slid one finger inside her very wet folds. "Well, then." Removing his hand, he tugged her back up on her knees. "Take 'em off, Vinnie."

She pushed off the mattress and regained her balance while on her knees. "No," she whispered, tilting her head to the side, keeping him squarely in her sights.

His chin lifted.

She smiled, meeting his gaze directly.

Slowly, his eyes darkening, he shook his head. "Don't do this. Take them off."

Her nostrils flared. She was so far out of her head, she'd never make her way back. If the badass wanted her panties, he could take them. "Do it yourself."

She never saw him move. One second, she was facing him so bravely. The next, the entire room tilted, and she swung around, landing on her hands and knees, her panties ripped off. A hard, very hard, smack echoed from his hand on her ass.

She cried out, half laughing, and tingles spread through her extremities. "Raze—"

The crinkle of a condom wrapper stopped her entire world. "Don't. Move," he ordered.

Her arms trembled from her wrists to her shoulders. He was behind her, and she couldn't see anything but the dingy wall on the other side of the bed. Firm hands grabbed her hips.

She sucked in air.

He slid inside her, inch by inch, taking his time but not slowing down. Her body flexed around him, taking him in, pleasure with a hint of pain.

Finally, he pushed all the way inside, his groin flush against her ass. "Are you all right?" he whispered, his voice low and hoarse.

She closed her eyes as sensation after sensation bombarded her. Even overcome, even in this state, he paused to check on her. He would never convince her he wasn't one of the good guys. "I'm fine," she croaked.

"Good." He manacled her nape and pushed. "Down."

She tossed her head, sending her hair flying, but he didn't relent. Finally, she lowered her cheek to the pillow. He released her neck and ran his palm down her back, delivering a stinging slap to her butt.

A surprised laugh escaped her.

He chuckled. "Only you would laugh."

Was it just her, or was that fondness in his gravelly voice? She clenched her sex around his dick.

He audibly sucked in air. "You wanna play, Doc?"

She craned her neck, cheek still on the pillow, and looked over her shoulder. "You up to it?" she asked.

His lids half-lowered, but those incredible blue eyes still glowed. His bronze face settled as if sculpted into harsh lines, while his full mouth quirked. His nostrils flared like any predator's on a hunt. "Let's find out."

He brought both of his knees onto the bed and then shoved her forward with his hips before reaching around her thighs and spreading her knees farther apart. Her weight fell fully on her arms and face, and she tried to shove back.

One hard hand planted in the middle of her shoulder blades.

She. Couldn't. Move.

Her thighs quivered, and more wetness spilled from her. The ache between her legs spiraled out, making her entire lower body clench in the need of a release. "Raze."

"Say please," he murmured.

She stilled.

"Now."

She had to bite her lip to keep from begging. Tremors swept through her. "No."

Smack.

This one centered right in the middle of her butt and spread warmth. She arched as much as she could and cried out. "Please." The word came unbidden and from way beyond the moment.

He gripped her hips again and slid out, only to power right back in. God. It was too much. The man, unleashed, was way too much. His tempo and power increased, and she closed her eyes just to feel, her face burrowing into the pillow. Hard and fast, he hammered inside her, bombarding her with a pleasure too sharp to be real.

Coils unfolded inside her, throwing sparks.

She held her breath.

The world detonated, flashing streaks behind her eyes. White-hot pleasure rode waves through her entire body, exploding out from deep inside, where his cock suddenly held still and jerked hard. The orgasm took her over, and a loud wail echoed through the apartment.

Finally, what seemed like a long time later, her body relaxed into mush.

He kissed her left shoulder and then withdrew. As his body left hers, she murmured a protest. Then her eyelids flashed open. "Did I just scream your name?" God. How loud had she been?

He returned from probably taking care of the condom and lay down, tugging her into his side. She reached down and pulled up the covers. "Um, did I yell?" she asked.

"Yes. It kind of sounded like my name," he rumbled, placing an absent kiss on her forehead. "Go to sleep, baby."

Nobody in her entire life had called her *baby*. It took a guy like him, one dangerous and deadly, to even think of trying it. As she struggled to think of a proper retort, her eyelids shut, and her breathing smoothed out. "Raze," she murmured, crashing right into sleep.

Chapter Nineteen

*Our deepest desires are often ones
we'd never admit aloud.*

—Dr. Vinnie Wellington, *Perceptions*

Raze watched the ceiling and held Vinnie as she slept, his
mind troubled and his chest aching. God, she was something. Sweet and wild and brilliant . . . and fragile. So
fuckin' fragile, he had no right touching her. The woman
wouldn't survive in the Mercenary camp, so he had to find
another way to save Maureen.

God. Maureen. What was happening to her right now?
Raze had been assured no harm would come to her if he followed the plan, and he had to believe that fact, or he'd go
crazy. Thus far, he'd played along, so Greyson had no reason
to harm Moe.

Thunder rolled outside, and lightning zagged. Here Raze
had thought the rainy season had ended. Well, one more
night of collecting water was just another blessing.

He gingerly moved Vinnie off his arm and slid from the
bed. She rolled over, still out cold. He swallowed and quickly
dressed, arming himself with the two guns, three knives,
and pack concealing a water-ski rope he'd hidden in a lower
cupboard. He turned to take one last look at her. That light

hair splayed over the pillow, while her skin glowed with a translucent tint. She barely made a bump under the covers. He couldn't watch her and mentally prepare himself for what he had to do, so he exited the apartment and jogged down the hallway to the old vestibule.

Jax Mercury stepped through the mess hall doorway, his hair ruffled, his eyes weary. "You on patrol?"

"Yes. Couldn't sleep, so I thought I'd scout." Raze zipped up his leather jacket.

"Take a partner," Jax ordered, moving past him and heading up the steps. "Remember what it feels like to work with people instead of alone. You're still out of here tomorrow if you don't come clean about everything."

"Of course," Raze said, waiting until the Vanguard leader had disappeared from sight. Hunching his shoulders, he shoved out into the drizzle and walked across puddles to the fence. A quick whistle from him—the correct one—and the gate opened. He nodded to the darkness and strode beyond the downed vehicles and tires to the scraggly weeds.

A brick apartment building stood silent and dark across the road. They had to figure out how to take it down. Rippers could easily be hiding inside, and a clear view for Vanguard would provide much more security.

They. If he stayed, he wouldn't be considered part of Vanguard.

Unless . . .

He kept to the shadows and soon left Vanguard territory. Abandoned shops and little stores lined his way, all with broken windows or busted doors. A noise near a former jewelry store caught his attention, and he paused, facing the door.

A fully grown male lion padded outside, its eyes glowing golden in the night.

Holy fuck. He'd heard Marvin roar late at night, but he'd never caught a glimpse of the massive beast. It was much larger than he would've thought. Had Vanguard continued leaving him meat at night? God, Raze hoped so.

Marvin stared at him for a moment and then flicked his tail, turning toward Vanguard.

Raze let out his breath. He gave a shudder, then turned and hustled in the opposite direction from the lion. Within thirty minutes, he reached Luke's Bar.

Ash was inside, sitting on the bar, waiting. "About fucking time. You're late."

Raze's boots crunched shattered glass, irritation heating his breath. "Where's Grey?"

"Busy. He couldn't make it." Ash blew a bubble with grape-scented gum. "I was hoping you'd bring the bitch."

Muscles tightened down Raze's back at the language. "I'm here for the fuckin' plan." He looked around and tried to listen for other breaths. "Who am I supposed to coordinate with?"

"Me." Ash grinned and revealed yellowed teeth.

Raze rolled his eyes. "You're a lackey, Ash. Who am I working with here?" He had to make sure Ash was alone.

Ash shoved himself off the bar, his boots scattering dirt as he landed. "You're working with me, dumbass. It's just me. Stop wasting time. Grey gets antsy if I'm late, and when he's pissed, it's bad." Ash gave a mock shudder. "I can't imagine what he's doing to your sister right now while you're dicking around with me."

Raze moved in, fast as a whip, and grabbed Ash by the neck. Rage tried to take hold, but he shoved it down, going cold. "Do you know what I did in the military?" he asked, shoving the asshole back and leaning into his face.

Ash clawed Raze's scarred arm, his eyes bugging out. "No."

"Anything I needed to do." Raze increased the pressure on Ash's windpipe and drew out a knife. "Now you and I are gonna have a little talk, and if you need persuading, I can torture you for at least three days before you'll die. It's a honed skill."

Ash paled, and his nails dug in hard. "You can't hurt me. You touch me, and Grey will kill your sister. With pain. He likes to hurt women."

Raze kept cold and shut out all of Ash's words. The bastard's pulse beat rapidly, and his breath panted out of his skinny chest. "I'll carve you like a turkey. Where's my sister?"

"I don't know," Ash croaked, his breath scented with grape.

"Then it's gonna be a long night for you." Raze lifted the idiot by the neck and slammed him down on what was left of the bar. Then he turned and threw Ash into the jukebox. The greaseball hit, and glass shattered.

Ash groaned and thrashed on the ground.

Raze jumped for him, lifted him, and deftly used the water-ski rope to shackle Ash to the jukebox.

Ash struggled, kicking out, his arms useless.

Raze casually punched him in the jaw.

Ash's head jerked back and forth, his blood-shot eyes widening. "What the fuck do you think you're doing?" he spat, blood dribbling from his mouth.

Raze shrugged out of his leather jacket and rolled up his sleeves. He swallowed twice and settled into the calmness required for the job. Taking his time, he leaned down and withdrew a glinting double-edged knife from his boot.

Ash's eyes bugged out, and he struggled against the restraints. "Wait a minute. Just wait a minute here."

Raze kept all expression off his face and ignored the nausea suddenly swirling in his belly. "You know, this kind of thing comes right back." He shrugged. "I figured I'd have to work up to cutting you, but I'm already in the zone." He stepped in and sliced Ash's shirt from hem to neck without touching skin. The dirty material fell to the sides.

Ash coughed, and his eyes filled with tears. "If I don't make it back to Merc territory on time, Grey will kill your sister. And he'll enjoy it."

Raze nodded thoughtfully, his gaze on Ash's neck. "I considered that, but it's a risk I'll have to take. He's gonna wonder if a Ripper or two got to you. My guess is that he'll wait until the rendezvous night, and if I don't show, then he'll take action with my sister."

Ash gulped in air. "So you're going to kill me no matter what."

Raze lifted his gaze to meet Ash's directly. Too many people had died in the world. "No. I absolutely don't want to kill you. Tell me what I want to know—all of it—and I'll let you go."

Ash shook his head and snot bubbled out of his nose. "That's a lie. You won't let me tell Grey about this."

Raze chuckled. "Oh, if you tell him, you're dead. If he discovers how easy it is to subdue you and get answers, he'll know what a liability you are. He'll cut off your head and feed it to the dogs as an example to his men." Probably. Truth be told, Raze didn't know shit about Greyson Storm.

Ash's chest heaved as he tried to control his breathing.

Raze cocked his head to the side and ran his blade down the side of Ash's neck. The idiot flinched and nearly got cut. The fear of torture, of pain, was often worse than the actual thing. "You could always switch loyalties," Raze murmured. "Work with me on getting my sister back, and I'll find you a place in Vanguard."

Ash snorted. "Jax Mercury is going to rip your heart from your chest when he finds out you've been working with the Mercs. You can't help me with Vanguard."

So Ash wasn't a complete moron. Good to know. "Jax has more of a capacity for forgiveness than you know, and he'd understand my trying to save my sister." Not a chance in hell. The second Jax found out, Vanguard became Raze's enemy. So far, Vanguard's enemies all had met with terrible, if well deserved, deaths. "If you don't want to work with me, you're still gonna tell me everything I need to know." Raze allowed the tip of the blade to puncture Ash's neck.

Ash stiffened and tried uselessly to pull away from the knife. A dot of blood rolled down his jugular. "I'm just doing my job."

"So am I," Raze countered. "My sister is mine to protect, and you're keeping her from me. Let's start easy. You came with a message, so why don't you give me that?"

Ash struggled uselessly against the bindings, his greasy hair scattering the tempered red and yellow glass from the jukebox. "I was supposed to give you the location for the exchange of Dr. Wellington and your sister."

"Where and when?" Raze snarled.

Ash blinked rapidly. "The location of the trade is halfway between here and Merc territory in Thousand Oaks."

Made sense. It got Raze far enough from Vanguard to be vulnerable but didn't let him see anything in Merc territory. "Where?"

"The Civic Arts Plaza."

Also a good plan—plenty of hiding and sniper positions for Greyson to use. If he used them. What little Raze had learned about the Merc leader showed the guy was a wild card full of surprises. "What's his plan for coverage there?"

Ash violently shook his head. "I don't know. Really. I'm not privy to his plans."

Raze wouldn't let this moron know his plans, either. "Not sure I believe you." He pressed the blade in.

Ash sucked in air and tried to draw back. "Honest. I'd tell you. Grey doesn't tell me shit."

Oh, Ash was definitely expendable. Raze nodded. His primary objective was to meet with Greyson at the rendezvous point and save Maureen. If that didn't work, he needed to know more about headquarters. "Okay. Say I believe you. Where is my sister being held in Merc territory?"

Ash sniffed loudly. "I don't know much. She's kept in the main headquarters with Grey."

Raze growled. "Where's the main headquarters?"

"Come on, man. I can't tell you. I'd be a dead man," Ash pleaded.

Raze sighed and drew a long line from Ash's neck to his belly, making a very shallow cut—more like a scratch.

Ash screamed.

Raze slapped a hand over the man's mouth and leaned in. "One more sound, and I'll find something in this rat's nest to gag you with. It won't be pretty."

Ash gurgled and then subsided.

Raze removed his hand. "We've already established you don't have to tell Grey shit when you get back, and I've promised I won't kill you if you give me the information I want. If you don't, you're gonna feel pain you can't even imagine, and by the time you die, you'll thank me for it."

Fear rolled off the Mercenary scout. Ash shook his head. "This isn't fair."

Raze barked out a laugh. "Fair is dead. Work with me. I won't hurt you."

Ash's body went limp. "Fine."

God, that was easy. "Tell me about Maureen."

"The main headquarters is the Pacific Beach Club on Goleta Beach." Ash snorted snot up his nose again.

Raze narrowed his gaze. "They can see attackers from each direction down the beach, and I'm assuming mansions are behind and to the sides? More good vantage points."

"Yeah. The pier is down the way, so there's fresh fish to eat. There are tons of nurseries and greenhouses from UC Santa Barbara, too." Once Ash gave his cooperation, he did it completely, now didn't he?

"Where Maureen can continue her work and grow food

for him?" Raze drawled. Hell. That was a fucking brilliant location for a camp.

"Yeah."

Raze leaned back. "How many men does Grey have?"

Ash relaxed and kept his gaze on the knife at Raze's side. "About a hundred, I think. All trained, all dangerous. Only a few women, and they're all attached."

"Attached or sex slaves?" Raze asked, bile rising in his throat.

Ash shrugged. "Never paid attention. But they're not passed around, if that's what you're asking."

"Is Maureen?" Raze asked evenly, his chest heating.

"Not that I know of." Panic filled Ash's eyes as Raze straightened. "Honest. She's in the beach mansion with Grey and a few other top soldiers, and the rest of us rarely see her. I've only seen her once, and that was last week."

Raze lifted an eyebrow.

Ash scrambled. "She looked fine. Pretty girl with dark hair and even bluer eyes than yours. Looked like the girl next door." His gaze darted around the dismal bar. "She was reading some papers and muttering about crop growth. Seemed more distracted than scared of anything."

Perhaps Greyson wanted her for her knowledge and ability to cross-pollinate edible plants. Raze breathed out, his vision clearing. Moe had to be all right. "Good. You're doing a good job, Ash. Now we're going to go over Merc territory, and you're going to tell me everything."

Ash nodded.

A ruckus sounded from outside.

Raze turned just as two men rushed inside, both wearing torn boxer shorts, both foaming at the mouth. Blood covered their bodies, and dried fur and blood matted their lips. Their eyes were crazed. Rippers.

Ash screamed.

Shit. The first Ripper rammed into Raze. He ducked and brought up his blade, piercing the Ripper's neck and wrenching his knife to the side. The guy spit out blood, gurgled, and fell to the ground.

Raze turned, but the other Ripper had already bitten through Ash's neck and was chomping on muscle and cartilage. Ash sagged in death, his eyes wide and filled with shocked horror. The Ripper pivoted, chewing. Raze drew a gun and shot the guy three times in the chest. He fell with a soft sigh.

Damn it. "Sorry, Ash," Raze murmured, looking at the dead Merc scout. "I really would've let you go." He said a quick prayer for the fallen and turned to jog out the door. Dawn would soon arrive, and he didn't have time to properly bury anybody. If the Mercs sent somebody after Ash, they'd find the Rippers and assume Raze had already left. Hopefully.

Now that he knew the location of the exchange point as well as where Maureen was being held in Merc territory, things had changed. Finally, he had intel. He had about forty hours to figure out how to set a trap for Greyson in Thousand Oaks and get Maureen to safety without putting Vinnie in danger. God help them all.

Chapter Twenty

We study sociopaths to better understand ourselves.

— Dr. Vinnie Wellington, *Sociopaths*

Vinnie stepped into her office while sipping a cup of way-too-strong coffee. Raze had been gone when she'd awoken, but he was probably out on patrol. The morning felt odd without him in it. She was getting too attached way too quickly. Time to regroup.

"Girlfriend? You need to get yourself a gag," Lynne Harmony murmured from her perch on the love seat.

Vinnie faltered and then continued in to flop into her leather chair. "I screamed his name. He said I was going to scream his name, and I actually did it." She shook her head, and prickly heat climbed into her face. "I have never, in my entire life, screamed during sex. I mean, not even once."

Lynne chuckled and pushed her long hair away from her classic face. "You're not the first, and I doubt you'll be the last woman who gets embarrassed around here. The walls are thin, and a few of us are forming couples, so it's going to happen."

"Forming couples?" Vinnie looked at the rather famous scientist over her cheap coffee mug. "That's what we're calling it?"

Lynne smiled, her green eyes sparkling. "Sounds better than hooking up with wild, dangerous, deadly men in this postapocalyptic hell we're all living in."

Vinnie chuckled and leaned forward. "Do you think that's it? I mean, that everything is amplified so much more because of the world ending? I mean, we could die any minute. So sex, feelings, anger . . . it's all just bigger and more overwhelming than before?"

Lynne nodded. "I do think that. In my mind, when I'm rational, I do believe that's a factor. But when I'm with Jax, when we're together and he's all, well, Jax . . . then I'm not sure. Maybe it's the men we're with now, you know? Even before Scorpius, Jax was intense, and I'm thinking Raze was as well. Perhaps it's the men and not the apocalypse."

"That should be a bumper sticker." Vinnie snorted. "I mean, if we still all drove cars every day."

"T-shirts. We could make T-shirts." Lynne reached for a steaming mug decorated with a picture of Einstein. "Extreme situations lead to extreme emotions," she murmured thoughtfully.

"Plus, there's safety being tied to a warrior during war, you know?"

The scientist had obviously given the matter some thought. "Biological imperative," Vinnie agreed, studying the woman. "Do you think you'd feel the same about Jax if the world hadn't ended?"

Lynne took a deep sip, and color slid into her cheeks. "I actually do. He's smart, strong, and honorable. I would've loved him even if our biggest struggle was how to balance the checkbook every month." She leaned back and kicked her jean-clad legs out to cross her tennis shoes at the ankles. "Yet there's something about this world now where we see more clearly who somebody really is."

Vinnie lifted an eyebrow. "Meaning?"

Lynne shrugged. "When things are at their worse, true character is revealed. Jax is a survivor and so is Raze. But they go beyond making sure they survive to actually saving and shielding other people. Character."

"The apocalypse has revealed heroes," Vinnie said softly. She'd been in bed with a hero just hours before. A real one.

"Exactly," Lynne answered.

A timid knock sounded, and little Lena slid inside. Vinnie had seen the young girl around the mess hall but had kept her distance, waiting for the child to want to approach her. She sat up and smiled at the petite girl. "Hi, Lena. I've been hoping to meet you. Would you like to sit with us?"

Onyx eyes widened, and the girl shook her blond head. She wore a pretty pink blouse beneath a denim jumper. Reaching in a pocket, she drew out a piece of glass to hand to Lynne.

"Thank you," Lynne said, taking it. She smiled. "It's a broken microscope slide. You know I work with microscopes."

The girl nodded and reached into another pocket.

Vinnie's breath heated. What would her gift be? She'd heard so many stories about Lena's odd gifts and how they related to personal characteristics of the receiver that the little girl shouldn't know about. Hopefully Vinnie's gift wouldn't be a broken watch, showing her time was up. Lena handed over a tiny green soldier that had been nearly rent in two. "Ah, thank you." What the hell?

Lena hummed.

Images slammed into Vinnie's brain. A little girl alone in a big house with a shaggy dog. She went with the thought. "Did you have a dog, sweetheart? One with brown eyes and lots and lots of hair?"

Lena's eyes widened. She smiled and nodded before turning and scampering from the room.

"How did you know that?" Lynne asked.

Vinnie cleared her throat. Was she psychic? Could she read thought patterns all of a sudden? The possibility seemed to exist, but she wasn't ready to share that fact. "Just a guess. Wanted to get to know her."

Lynne sat back. "Uh-huh. I'll let you off with that lame explanation for the time being. Unlike some folks here, I don't think Lena has any extrasensory abilities. I just think she listens to everything. I'm a scientist, so she gave me this. You're obviously with Raze, so she gave you a soldier." Lynne swallowed, her gaze not leaving the figurine.

"Right." Vinnie cleared her throat and set the soldier down. "My question is: Did she find it like this, or did she cut the soldier nearly in two?" There was no doubt something was tearing Raze apart, pulling him in different directions.

"I'm sure she found it." Lynne took a deep swallow of her drink, her eyes not quite meeting Vinnie's.

Vinnie crossed her legs. "All right. Down to business. Let's talk."

"No." Lynne shook her head. "I mean, I want to talk, but not as patient and shrink. I need a friend, and we have a lot in common, so I just want to girl talk."

Warmth spread through Vinnie's torso. What a kind offer. She so missed the friends she'd had before Scorpius took them all away. "I'd like a friend. Okay. That works for me."

"Good. I'm totally frustrated I haven't been able to find a way to allow folks to permanently create vitamin B in their bodies, and I'm pissed off I don't have a lab to work in. I need a functioning lab." Lynne gritted her teeth.

Apparently they were talking about business and not boys anyway. "What about the Bunker? It exists, right?" Vinnie asked.

"I think so. We just have to find it." Lynne's face flushed with color. "And Jax is driving me crazy with his bossiness. 'Sleep, Lynne. Eat, Lynne. Fuck me, Lynne.'" She grinned. "Maybe the last one is usually my idea."

Vinnie chuckled and settled in for girl talk.

"And the other thing: Jax told Raze he has to leave by tonight if he doesn't level with everyone about what's going on with him. Why he's here, and where that letter is he talked about when he thought he might die." Lynne sobered. "I figured you should know about the ultimatum."

Raze had to leave? Vinnie shook her head. There had to be some way to help him. Why wouldn't he just level with everybody? The idea of him leaving made her chest feel hollow.

"Blue?" a male and very impatient voice echoed through the infirmary.

Lynne sighed. "What?" she hollered.

Jax Mercury appeared in the doorway wearing combat gear and a pissed off expression. "I said to meet me for breakfast."

"I don't work for you," Lynne said mildly.

Vinnie leaned back in her chair. Her new friend sure liked to mess with fire.

"Fair enough." Jax took two steps inside, ducked, and hauled Lynne over one broad shoulder. She landed with a muffled *oomph*. Jax turned. "See you later, Doc." The two disappeared, with Lynne yelling in Latin.

Ah, Latin. A truly lost language. Vinnie rubbed her chin. Raze had to leave? Why the hell didn't he just tell the truth? She kicked back in her chair and mulled it over. Wait a minute. Where would Raze hide a letter? If she were Raze . . . she knew. Oh, she could guess exactly where he had hidden it. She jumped up and set her coffee down, heading for the back door.

A spring breeze wandered over her as she shoved outside. The rain had ebbed, leaving the cracked concrete wet but drying quickly. She hustled down the rutted road, passing people on their way to different work locations, until she reached her former apartment building. The wet weeds dampened her jeans as she walked around the building to the back courtyard, easily opening her sliding glass door.

The smell of mildew and dust assailed her.

She had to pause before stepping inside. Goodness. She hadn't had a nightmare since she'd started sleeping with Raze Shadow. How could she have forgotten the nightmares already? This place had been full of them.

Steeling her shoulders, she crossed inside, and her knees wobbled. Damn it. She needed to grow a pair. Sucking in musty air, she searched the sofa, the former bathroom, the bed, and finally reached the kitchen. She opened the stove, and there it was. A folded piece of paper. Raze must've left it there when he'd helped her to move.

Her hand shook as she drew it out. One word, drawn in pencil, was on the outside. *Jax*

Her stomach lurched, but she took the letter. The walls closed in on her, and she all but tripped trying to get outside. Leaning against the crumbling brick, she straightened the precise folds to read.

Jax,

   If you're reading this, I'm gone. I've taken Dr. Wellington to the Mercs, but I swear to God, I'll bring her back. The leader of the Mercenaries has my sister and is insisting on a trade. I don't think he wants to harm Vinnie, and I vow I'll bring her back.

   If you're reading this because I'm dead, remember I helped you once, and go get my sister. Her name is Maureen Shadow, and she's an innocent.

                    Fight on,
                    Raze

Well. A hollow pain slammed into her chest. Vinnie hunched over, as if she'd been punched in the solar plexus.

Then she carefully refolded the paper. The man had nice penmanship, if nothing else. A sister. Yeah, that explained it. His motivation. The question was what she'd do with the information. Her heart hurt a little, but not nearly as much as it should. Her instincts told her Raze had been fighting himself the entire time, and no way would he have really kidnapped her.

Of course, she'd been wrong before.

He had invited her outside of Vanguard territory just a few nights ago. Had he planned to turn her over at that time? What about now? She certainly hadn't slept with him to gain safety, but could he leave her with the Mercs now that they'd become close? Maybe not close, but closer? Lovers?

"You are such a moron," Lucinda said, bouncing from around the corner and settling in a bunch of waist-high weeds. "I told you he was bad news."

Vinnie sighed. "Why do you only show up when I'm thinking about being with Raze? I mean, what's up with that?"

Lucinda tossed sprinkles through the air. "I'm your hallucination, doll. If you're seeing me when you're around Raze, then that should tell you something."

"It tells me that I'm crazy and the drugs ruined my brain," Vinnie answered, feeling about a thousand years old. "I can't imagine he'd really try to kidnap me and then give me to the Mercs. How could he do that?"

"His sister?" Lucinda ran her thin hands over her white hair, and blue streaks emerged throughout the long strands. "I'm just taking a stab in the dark here, considering that's what his note says. Maybe he's in love with the Merc leader? No, that can't be it. Perhaps he wants to stick it to Jax? Nope. Probably not that, either. I guess I'd go with the sister as an explanation."

"Only I would have a smart-ass bitch for a hallucination," Vinnie snapped, leaning her head back.

"Again, I come from your imagination. So you're really the smart-ass bitch."

"You are," Vinnie countered and then groaned. She was actually having a spat with a hallucination. "What the heck am I going to do now?" She was hurt enough that she wanted to confront Raze right now—after kicking him in the balls.

"I like the kick-in-the-balls idea, but he's bigger and stronger than you," Lucinda sang in a high octave.

Vinnie blanched. "So?"

"So? Make sure he can't knock you out or cart your ass out the front door en route to Mercenary land." Lucinda poofed out of sight.

"I should at least get the last word with my own hallucination," Vinnie muttered. She pushed away from the building, stopping cold at the sight of a line of men at the edge of the weeds. "Excuse me?"

Reverend Lighton stood in the middle of the group, all dressed in nice pants with button-down shirts. "Hello, Doctor Wellington."

Vinnie discreetly tucked the letter in her back pocket, her instincts humming. "Can I help you with something?"

"You're trespassing," said Lighton, not unkindly.

She nodded, her heart thrumming into a quicker beat. All lined up, the men looked like a threat, despite the nice clothing. "I wanted to make sure I didn't leave anything behind when I moved out of this apartment."

"I understand. You've been infected by the plague, right?" He continued speaking as if they were attending a nice tea together.

"Yes." Would they turn against her?

The men next to him settled their stances.

Vinnie fought the urge to take a step back. If they did

something bizarre and attacked her, she could get back inside and lock the door. Of course, they could always break the glass. "Why do you ask?" she murmured.

"Just making sure. We're having to separate into two groups to protect the Pure, as I'm sure you understand." His eyes took on an odd glow. Or maybe it was just a trick of the light.

Vinnie shook her head, her profiling skills kicking in. "I don't understand. We need to work together to survive this. At some point, we'll need to move north to more fertile land, and a better climate." While the summer was great in LA, there were drought years more often than not, and they needed water to live. Professional curiosity reared up in her. "Do you think you're chosen, Reverend?"

He lifted his chin. "It's not a matter of opinion. Anybody spared by the bacteria is chosen, and I've been anointed as the leader of the Pure. Survival is all that matters."

In her time as an FBI agent, she'd studied cults and their leaders. This guy was almost textbook, and there would be no reasoning with him since she was not one of the Pure. "We all want to survive." She had to find common ground with him to start a real dialogue.

He nodded. "Yes, but only the Pure will survive. You know that survivors can't procreate, right? In less than a century, the last Scorpius victim will pass on, and the Pure will inherit the earth."

Not the meek, huh? Vinnie eyed the men on either side of him. "Your flock?"

He chuckled, the sound filled with charm. "My friends. My family, in fact. I'm not starting a cult."

Oh, this was definitely a cult. "Why aren't you flanked by women?" she asked. "You don't have female soldiers?"

One of the guys rolled his eyes.

The Reverend smiled. "No. Women know their place in the Pure."

Vinnie lifted her head, and a chill swept down her back. "What exactly does that mean?"

"You don't need to worry about it," the reverend said. "Now it's time for you to return to Vanguard territory and leave the Pure. Even though we haven't fenced all of it yet, these blocks of Vanguard are now ours."

Lynne Harmony sauntered around the building, tripping on a weed and then righting herself. "I don't believe that's been decided, Reverend."

The men fanned out, their expressions immediately darkening.

Vinnie instinctively moved toward her new friend. "I thought you were eating breakfast."

"Something came up for Jax, and I saw you sneak out the back door." Lynne inched her way forward, and soon the women stood shoulder to shoulder, facing the rapidly angering group. "Looks like you found a little excitement."

"Yes," Vinnie said, her breath quickening. "Don't suppose you're armed?" she whispered.

Lynne nodded.

Good. That was good.

"Of course, I'm a complete klutz," Lynne whispered. "But I have a knife in my boot."

The reverend studied them. "Ladies? It's time for you to go home."

"Doctors." Lynne pressed her hands on her hips. "We're both doctors, buddy. Unlike you with your new title, we actually earned ours."

Vinnie elbowed her. "Let's not antagonize the narcissist," she hissed.

Lynne lifted her head. "I'd like to understand more about your women and how they know their place. What's going on there, gentlemen?"

"The Pure is not your concern." The reverend motioned

for his boys to part. "Go back now, please, and do not return to our territory."

Lynne opened her mouth, no doubt to argue, but Vinnie grabbed her arm and tugged her to the road. "Let's regroup when we're not facing down five twitchy men." She didn't allow Lynne to halt and kept on walking down the road, finally releasing a sigh of relief when the men didn't follow them.

"For a petite little thing, you sure have a good grip," Lynne murmured, tugging her arm free. "How crazy is that guy?"

"As a cult leader, I'd say he's motivated, ordained, and buck-assed nuts," Vinnie said.

Lynne chortled. "Is that your professional opinion?"

Vinnie nodded. "Close enough."

Lynne slipped an arm through Vinnie's. "I saw you reading a letter. It had to be the mysterious one from Raze. What did it say?"

Vinnie pressed her lips together, wanting to confide in her friend but needing to give Raze options. "I'd prefer to discuss it with Raze first, if you don't mind." Then maybe she could talk Raze into going to Jax.

Lynne sighed. "Fine, but I can only give you the day. At that point, I have to tell Mercury. My loyalty is to him."

Vinnie nodded. "Agreed. For now, we have a meeting to get to, and we'd better report on the Pure. I'm worried about the women and kids, and maybe some of the other men. That guy has an agenda that might include taking out Scorpius survivors. He's looney."

Lynne barked out a laugh. "Is a shrink supposed to use that term?"

Vinnie shrugged. "Only when it fits. And in this situation, believe me, it fits."

Chapter Twenty-One

***

Every girl wants a hero at her side.

—Dr. Vinnie Wellington, *Perceptions*

Raze kicked back in the chair in the Vanguard meeting room as the rest of the group filed in. Somebody had brought in an executive conference table with inlaid oak paneling that morning. The thing probably weighed a ton and looked as out of place in the dismal room as a tuxedo or ball gown would have.

Vinnie sat across from him, next to Lynne, not meeting his eyes. Had he been too rough with her the previous night? He tried to get her attention, but she focused steadfastly on Jax, who stood near the head of the table.

Sami sat at the foot, and Tace loped inside to pull out the chair next to Raze. "Where'd we get the fancy table?" Tace murmured, shoving the last bite of what looked like a Pop-Tart into his mouth.

Lynne stood and crossed to a rickety card table holding coffee. "Jax told a scouting group to get more tables for the mess hall, as well as for the dining room inner territory, and they got their wires crossed." She poured a glass and absently stirred in what looked like brown sugar.

Jax sighed. "I meant picnic tables or even kitchen tables."

He frowned at the decadent monstrosity. "This is big enough to fit us all, though."

Raze pushed away from the table and crossed to drop into Lynne's vacated seat next to Vinnie. She stiffened and still didn't look at him.

Lynne smirked and kept stirring as she walked around the table to claim his former seat.

"Reports," Jax said, remaining on his feet. "Tace."

Tace leaned forward. "Five new cases of Scorpius inner territory hospital. Two died yesterday, three still hanging on. Vitamin B stock is holding steady. We have four hundred and twenty people who need monthly injections, and at that rate, we have enough B to last one more month."

"That's good," Jax said.

"Not really." Tace shook his head. "When new folks get the fever, or when people show up fighting the fever, which keeps happening, we have to give them at least five doses during the dangerous phase. At this rate, going on statistics, we're out of B in three weeks."

Raze slid his boot beneath Vinnie's chair to touch her foot, and she kicked it away. He bit back a grin.

"Blue?" Jax asked.

Lynne sipped her coffee. "Tace and I are about three-fourths through the newest research, and it's confirming two things. First, with the right concoction of the mutated squid that turned my heart blue, combined with several substances, we can make an inoculation of sorts so we won't need injections any longer. With the right lab, which I do not have."

"And second?" Jax asked, rubbing the back of his neck.

"I think the Bunker does exist. There are too many references to it in the lab documents, and there are shipping manifests where important samples came from a place just called 'TB.' It's out there, and it probably has not only a working lab but samples of the mutated squid." Lynne tapped her fingers on the table. "Our prime mission has to be finding the Bunker. Period."

Raze tugged on Vinnie's hair, and she jerked her head free. His eyebrows lifted of their own accord.

Jax nodded. "Noted. Sami?"

The pretty brunette twirled a knife in her nimble hands. "We just finished training a new group of scouts. They're all older than sixteen, but man, some of them are young. New missions will focus on food, weapons, and medicine. Like usual. The self-defense training is going well, but the Pure group has backed out of all involvement."

"Raze?" Jax asked.

Raze breathed out. "Ripper attack last night, as I already told you. These were rough and tumble—crazy with the drive to kill. I'm concerned there are more organized Ripper groups out there being led by smart, logical, calculating sociopaths, and they're going to hit us from a surprise direction."

"I agree," Jax said. "Right now, the president is the Ripper I'm most concerned with, but we need to keep our ears to the ground for other threats."

"What about sending out scouts to encampments?" Raze asked. "When I was traveling west, I stopped often to get news. You'd be surprised at how many nomads out there are going from camp to camp, trading wares."

"Come up with a strategic proposal, and we'll work on it," Jax said. "Any news on the Mercs?"

"No," Raze said, nudging Vinnie's chair with his knee.

She kept her back to him and her face to Jax.

Jax eyed the two. "Vinnie? News?"

She jerked. "Um, I've been meeting with people and trying to help. No threats to report." She cleared her throat. "Except Lynne and I had a run-in with Reverend Lighton as well as a few of his men. And I emphasize the word *men* for a reason."

Raze grabbed Vinnie's chair and spun it in his direction. "You did what?"

Jax's gaze slashed to Lynne. "What?"

Lynne cleared her throat. "Vinnie and I decided to take a walk because it stopped raining, and we ended up in what's now considered Pure territory. The reverend nicely told us to leave."

Raze's body clenched, and he rolled Vinnie's chair flush against his. "Did he threaten you?"

Vinnie shook her head, tried to turn her chair around, and gave up with a muffled curse. "Not really. I mean, he said not to come back, but it wasn't exactly a threat."

"It was a threat," Lynne countered. "He tried to intimidate us with talk of purity and survival, and he had four other guys with him. Only guys. He said Pure women know their place."

"That'd be convenient," Raze snapped.

Both Lynne and Vinnie turned harsh glares on him.

He ignored Lynne and met Vinnie's gaze evenly.

Vinnie lowered her chin in pure defiance. "We need to get inside that group to see what's going on. If there are women or kids being abused in this new world order of his, we need to stop it."

Jax cleared his throat.

Raze reluctantly allowed Vinnie to turn her chair. Oh, they were nowhere finished with this discussion.

"I created Vanguard to be a safe place for its citizens," Jax said. "There should never be a threat inner territory, and you should all be able to freely move around. This is a problem."

"What do you want to do about it?" Sami asked. "I think we should kick the reverend and his flock out."

"Not with women and kids, if they want to stay," Jax said. He drew out a chair and sat. "Suggestions?"

Vinnie leaned forward. "We need to meet with the

members of the Pure individually to see what they want to do. Make sure nobody is being coerced."

Jax nodded. "I agree. We still don't have any idea who's involved and what kind of weaponry they've accumulated. I know what's missing from the storage units, but these folks might have been scouting and hiding weapons for months."

Tace nodded. "I have no clue who has been infected and who hasn't, so I don't know who's in the flock. Many of his so-called order could be our soldiers. They're armed, and they know how to fight," Tace said.

"So even if I decided to kick them out, we don't know how spread out they are or who the members are. Damn it." Jax slammed his fist on the table. "It's bad enough what's left of the government is going to launch an attack on us, not to mention Twenty and other rogue gangs and the fuckin' Mercs up north, but now I have organized resistance *inside* Vanguard?"

"We need a mole," Raze said.

Jax clasped his hands on the table. "All right. We move forward on both fronts. Who's close to April Snyder?"

Vinnie nodded. "I'm not close to her, but she was one of the people who came in yesterday."

"Did she mention Pure?" Jax asked.

"No. She talked about loss and pain." Like most people. "She seemed so alone, I don't think she's part of any group."

Jax wiped bruises on his knuckles. "Okay. Tace? Set up a meeting with the good reverend here at headquarters to happen tomorrow after we have more information. He comes to us. Raze? Please find April Snyder and send her in right now. We'll meet with her to see if she's up to work-ing with us. Doc Vinnie? I'd like you to stay here and profile her while we chat. That's different from meeting with her as a shrink, right?"

"Definitely," Vinnie murmured. She straightened in her chair.

Raze could almost see the wheels in her head turning as she realized that Vanguard needed her. She'd finally found a calling in this new world. Her small smile lifted his heart and warmed him throughout.

"What about me?" Lynne asked, dropping her plastic cup in the garbage.

"Keep researching. I don't want you near the reverend with that blue heart. Not right now anyway. We might put you two together later and let the doc watch and profile." Jax kicked back. "Raze? I believe we have a meeting around suppertime?"

Raze pushed away from the table. The meeting where he was supposed to confess all to Jax. "Yep. See you then." He had to figure out a way to put Jax off for the night, so he could go find Maureen and bring her home. For now, Raze had another woman to deal with. He pulled out her chair. "Vinnie? We need to talk."

"I need her here," Jax said levelly. "As soon as we're finished with April Snyder, you two can chat."

Vinnie turned then and looked at Raze for the first time that afternoon. To call her gaze chilly would be a gross understatement. "You can count on it."

Raze paused. Why did that sound like a threat?

The room temporarily cleared, leaving only Vinnie and Jax. "Thank you," she said as he slid a full cup of coffee between her hands. A battery-operated warmer had kept the coffee warm all afternoon. "Can we afford the battery usage?"

"Byron says we can," Jax said, blowing on his cup and retaking his seat. "Have you met him? Brilliant seventeen-year-old nerd who's going to be a father. Hopefully. He can create batteries out of nothing, but he can't remember to sheath his dick. Knocked up a sixteen-year-old girl."

Vinnie nodded. "I've seen them around. Cute kids. Besides, since when do teenagers remember condoms? Really."

"Good point." Jax straightened as April Snyder walked into the room. "Hi."

April hovered near the doorway, a pretty woman with sad blue eyes and classic features. She appeared to be in her early thirties. "You wanted to speak with me?"

"Yes." Jax's voice gentled. "Would you come in and sit down?"

April sat down and crossed her arms in a clearly defensive posture.

"It's okay," Vinnie murmured, keeping her voice soothing. "Jax just has a couple of questions and a job for you to do, but only if you're interested. He needs some help."

April's arms uncrossed, and she leaned forward just a little. "Oh. I'm glad to help."

Jax glanced from Vinnie to April, his gaze thoughtful. "Are you familiar with Reverend Lighton and his, ah, group?"

April straightened, and a tinge of pink colored her high cheekbones. "Um, well, I know who they are."

Jax's gaze narrowed. "Have they approached you?"

Vinnie leaned back to draw his attention. He needed to be gentle with April.

April swallowed. "Yes, the group has approached me."

"When and how?" Jax asked.

April glanced at Vinnie.

"It's okay, April. You haven't done anything wrong." Vinnie reached out and patted April's arm.

April's head snapped up. "About three weeks ago, before my daughter passed, a woman named Violet struck up a conversation with me about Scorpius. She hadn't been infected, and neither had I, and we talked about how likely it would be for us to catch the bacteria."

"Go on," Jax said quietly.

"Well, that was about it. Just a conversation, you know?" April drummed her trimmed fingernails on the table. "Then a few days after my daughter's funeral, the reverend approached me and offered to pray with me for her soul."

"Was he alone?" Vinnie asked, distaste for the man filling her mouth. How dare he prey on a grieving mother?

April nodded. "Yes. He was very comforting, and praying for my baby did make me feel a little bit better. Not really, but I felt like I was at least doing something, you know?"

A muscle ticked in Jax's jaw.

Vinnie gave a minuscule nod. Taking advantage of the woman's grief had been a rotten and manipulative thing to do. Unless maybe the reverend really had been trying to ease April's pain. Who knew? "So he was of help to you?"

April frowned. "I thought so."

"But?" Jax prompted, anger etching into the hard planes of his face.

"I'm not sure," April said slowly. "At first, we prayed for Haylee. Then his prayers turned to those people who haven't been infected by Scorpius and a plea to keep them, ah, pure. It was a little odd."

"He made you uncomfortable?" Jax asked.

April lifted a shoulder. "I'm not sure. Just breathing hurts some days, you know?"

Vinnie studied her. Clear eyes, sad but smart. Good posture, steely spine. But she'd been through so much; asking her to do more might break her. Or it might help her to survive.

Jax leaned forward. "Has the reverend invited you to any of his sermons?"

"No, but Violet has mentioned their support group. She

says the reverend preaches to them, and it gives her hope. Anything that gives hope these days has to have value." April faced Jax bravely. "Why, Jax?"

"I need somebody to infiltrate the sermons and see what the hell is going on," Jax said.

"Why?" April breathed.

Vinnie tried to measure the woman's strength. The last thing she wanted to do was cause more pain for April. "We're not sure all of the reverend's members are there willingly. We don't even know who the members are, and we're concerned."

April frowned. "Why can't you go to a sermon?"

"Only folks who haven't been infected with Scorpius are invited," Vinnie said.

April bit her lip. "Oh. What information exactly do you need?"

"How many kids are involved, and are the members, or whatever we're calling them, there willingly? Finally, I need a list of names. Who exactly am I dealing with here?" Jax muttered.

Vinnie leaned forward. "This is optional. If you're not up to the task, then there's no obligation for you to attend. You've been through a lot, more than I can even imagine, and you certainly don't have to put your neck out there right now. The job you're doing with the organizational schedules is more helpful than you know."

April rubbed her chin. "Do you really think the church is hurting people?"

Jax flattened one hand on the table. "My fear is that people are being coerced into joining, especially women and kids. I have to know they're safe and free. My plan is to send in someone to observe and then also to meet with the leaders and any members I can find."

April's blue eyes hardened. "You think the reverend is forming some sort of cult that harms women and kids?"

"We have no clue what he's doing." Jax studied her. "He wants to be separate from Vanguard, and if we let him go, I have to make sure everyone who goes with him wants to do so."

April swallowed. "I'll do it."

"Wait a minute," Vinnie said. "Really think about it."

"Why? If people are in danger, and all I have to do is attend a sermon or two, why the heck shouldn't I?" April's chin lifted. "It's too late to save my child, but there are other kids out there who might need help. So I'll help."

Admiration welled through Vinnie. "Fair enough."

Jax kicked back. "All right, April. If you do this, it's your Op. What's your plan?"

"Um." April blinked several times, thoughts scattering across her face. "I'm supposed to help with the second dinner shift tonight inner territory, and I think Violet is on the schedule, too. I'll bring up the topic of God and church with her and see where it goes."

Jax frowned. "Violet is still working with Vanguard?"

"Yeah, but now that I think of it, she spends time finding out who's been infected and who hasn't." April shoved tendrils of hair from her face. "Do you think she's recruiting for their group?"

"That's exactly what I think," Jax said. "Are you sure you're up to this?"

April pushed back from the table. "I don't have anything to lose, Jax." With a sad smile aimed at Vinnie, she turned and strode gracefully from the room.

Jax sighed. "Fuck."

Vinnie lifted an eyebrow. "She's strong."

Jax shook his head. "Nobody is that strong. We may be making a colossal mistake sending her into that group. What if the sermon makes sense to her?"

"Then we'll help her at that point." Vinnie pressed her thumb into her aching temple. "How long has the good reverend been putting his little group together?"

"Three months tops. Does that matter?"

Vinnie rested her chin on her hand. "Yeah. Three months is more than long enough to create a cult atmosphere, especially when hell has descended all around us. Who would know more about him and his group?"

"Wyatt." Jax sighed. "Unfortunately, he's dead."

Vinnie had arrived at Vanguard after Wyatt had already passed. "Is there anybody Wyatt spoke with or worked with much? Somebody has to know more about the reverend."

"I don't think anybody does and that's my concern. The guy has built a following by staying under the radar, which makes me wonder about his agenda." Jax grimaced and reached behind himself to draw a Glock out of his waistband. He placed the deadly gun on the table with a thunk.

Vinnie eyed the weapon. "What's our best-case scenario?"

"We don't have one," Jax said wearily.

Interesting. Vinnie relaxed back in her chair, her gaze on the Vanguard leader. His face was rugged, his body hard, and his right arm scarred. Slashes, white and rough, cut down from his upper arm and over his hand. "What happened?" she asked.

He looked down at the old scars. "Punched through glass and burning metal, trying to save a buddy when a land mine took out our vehicle."

"Did you save him?"

"No." Jax's honey-brown eyes turned darker. "He's one of many I failed to save."

If that didn't speak volumes about Jax Mercury's internal struggle, nothing would. "Is that why you created Vanguard?" In a world where the strong overcame the weak, and too many people were forced into victimhood, creating a safe haven took unbelievable conviction.

"No." Jax pushed back from the table. "I created Vanguard because it needed to be created." He turned and strode for the doorway. "Please keep an eye on April. She trusts you."

Vinnie stared at the empty doorway. Great job, there. One personal question, and she'd made the Vanguard leader all but run away. Had she owed him a report on Raze's letter? Probably. But Lynne had given her the day to speak to Raze, and she was going to take it.

What she was going to say, she had no clue. Her heart hurt, and her temples ached with unacknowledged anger. It burned inside her, getting hotter and hotter. She'd never been known for her temper.

Until now.

Before the world had disintegrated, she would've dropped Raze Shadow like an old pair of shoes. But now, well, she still trusted him. She believed he wouldn't really have betrayed her. Was she nuts? Or was this love?

Or had the world changed so much that his actions weren't a true betrayal?

Jax poked his head back in. "I have to go talk to Lynne right now, but we can touch base later about April and the plan. For now, I'm not sure if Raze has talked to you about my ultimatum, but I meant it. He's out if he doesn't come clean about his motivations and priorities. I suggest you talk to him as soon as he gets back from his scouting."

Her smile even felt angry. "I fully plan on it."

Chapter Twenty-Two

One doesn't need a coffer of advanced degrees
to understand why opposites attract.

—Dr. Franklin X. Harmony, *Philosophies*

Lynne Harmony awoke with a start and turned over on the sofa, sending papers scattering and finding Jax staring at her. He stood above her, a dangerous man in combat gear, focused solely on her. "What?" she mumbled.

"While I'm glad you're taking a nap, you were crying out. Is everything all right?"

She'd had a raging headache and had decided to work in their apartment for a while. When had she fallen asleep. "Of course. I'm fine. I have bad dreams sometimes. You know that." She tried to keep his gaze, but it cost her.

His pupils narrowed. "What aren't you telling me?"

She might have been avoiding him by working in the apartment. Sometimes she forgot how smart he was and how well he already knew her. "I don't know what you're talking about."

He didn't speak. Those bourbon colored eyes narrowed, and the muscles in his chest flexed.

How could a look be so intimidating? For goodness' sake. Her gaze shifted and landed on her father's journal, near the counter. Her father had been a brilliant scientist, and he'd often recorded his thoughts. She hadn't read it for a while. "Maybe I'll read a bit."

Jax bent and lifted her, striding toward the bed to pin her beneath him on the mattress. "Blue? In this new, postapocalyptic world, the rules have changed. You get that, right?"

Tingles rushed through her. His hard body bracketed her in warmth, and her breath caught. "Yes." Her gaze dropped to his lips.

"You're lying to me, and I don't like it." He settled between her legs, pressing just enough to catch her interest.

Her body pulsed. "I'm not lying." She just wasn't giving him the entire truth. Oh, she'd tell him about the letter she'd seen Vinnie grab, but not until Vinnie had a chance to speak with Raze. Lynne didn't know what was going on, but the couple deserved a small window of time to do the right thing, and she wanted her new friendship with Vinnie to last. Jax would kick their door down to get the letter. "Don't accuse me of being untruthful."

He grasped her arms and lifted them above her head, flattening them under his.

She couldn't move.

Her body trembled, and her nipples peaked.

"Tell me all of it." His order came with warmth and warning.

"No." She widened her legs and rubbed against him. Sparks rolled through her, caressing each nerve.

His head tilted just enough to be threatening. "Last time you defied me, you got spanked with a belt."

She lifted an eyebrow. "I've learned to fight since then."

"No, you haven't," he whispered, brushing his mouth across hers. "What are you hiding?"

"I'll tell you later tonight." She nipped his bottom lip. "Give me a few hours. You have to trust me, Mercury."

He breathed out and studied her. "I do trust you. More than anybody else in life."

She smiled. "Then believe me."

"All right." He leaned down and kissed her, going deep.

The sense of coming home careened through her, along with liquid desire. When he lifted his head, she waited until he focused on her gaze. "I love you, Jax. Everything you are and have done and will be."

He closed his eyes and dropped his head to her neck to place a kiss at her jugular. "You're my heart, Blue."

"Good. You have got to stop threatening me with the belt." She wrapped her fingers through his, even though she couldn't move her hands off the bed.

He levered himself back. "You're right, and I won't do it again. Though if I remember right, you do like being tied with it."

Well, now, that had been an adventure. She forced a frown. "Hmmm. I don't recall that."

His lip quirked. "Maybe I'll have to remind you."

God, she hoped he would. At the very least, she'd bought Vinnie a few hours to talk some sense into Raze Shadow. After dinner, Lynne would have to level with Jax about the letter. For now, she was going to enjoy her late afternoon. While she'd never solve the puzzle of how she'd found love in such dire circumstances, she'd learned to accept the good in her new life.

Whether he liked it or not, whether he understood it or not, Jax was good.

After a cold dinner of canned ravioli, Vinnie went up to the apartment and straightened the place. The area smelled like Raze, all male with the hint of forest. He was supposed to return by suppertime, but sometimes the scouting trips took a while. Finally, she lay down on the big bed, just for a moment, and closed her eyes.

She drifted along until fine whiskey heated through her veins. Her body hummed, and her mouth tingled. She opened her eyes, caught a flash of blue, and then gasped as Raze's mouth enveloped hers.

Passion uncoiled inside her, taking over, making her pulse. She struggled to focus, but his tongue swept inside her mouth, and then all she could do was enjoy the moment. He kissed her deep, taking his time, propelling her into desire.

Something, a thought, tickled in the back of her brain, but sleep turned to need so quickly, she banished doubt.

His nimble fingers unbuttoned her shirt right before he swept off her pants.

She moved against his bare skin and hard erection. Her body ached, more than ready for him. Her heart thumped, and emotion filled her heart with Raze Shadow.

Almost frantic, she explored him. All hard ridges, smooth muscle, and raw strength. He rolled her over, and she had one second to appreciate the fact that he wore a condom before he shoved hard inside her.

She arched and sighed, accepting him, finally feeling appeased. Then he started to move. Her need shot right back up, sharper than before. "Raze," she murmured, sliding her hands through his thick hair.

He pounded inside her, no preliminaries, giving as much as he took. His blue eyes tracked her, focused and glittering.

The orgasm attacked her from nowhere, flaring the room white-hot and forcing her eyelids closed. She gripped him hard, holding tight. With a final shove, his body jerked inside hers.

What the heck? A smile tickled her mouth. They came down at the same time, both panting.

He leaned back, still inside her. "Did you have a nice nap?" he asked, his voice gravelly.

She laughed. A full-on, relaxed, satisfied laugh. "Waking up was better."

"Good." He smoothed the hair back from her face, his large hand gentle.

Reality crept back in. She breathed out and sobered. "Um."

"Um what, sweetheart?" he whispered, dropping a kiss on her nose.

Sweetheart. She liked that. A lot. "I found your letter, and I know about your sister."

The energy in the room changed faster than a lightning strike.

Raze pulled out of her so quickly, Vinnie's eyelids slid open. He rolled off the bed and stalked into the bathroom, no doubt disposing of the condom. Too bad the bathroom wasn't functional.

Seconds later, he returned, seemingly unconcerned by his nudity.

His face had lost the slumbering pleasure she'd glimpsed on it moments ago, leaving hard and pissed in its place.

"Ah, shoot." She tugged the sheet up and then sat, covering her still-humming body. A chill shook her. "I didn't mean to blurt that out."

"Where's the letter?" he asked evenly, his eyes glowing with a light she couldn't quite read.

She pointed to her jeans. "Back pocket."

He grasped her jeans and tore out the letter. "You read this."

"Yep. It's very sweet."

"Sweet?" His face darkened even further. "What the fuck, Vinnie? Seriously. What the fuck?"

Man, he could go from satiated to furious very quickly.

That was quite a temper. "What?" She pulled her knees up and wrapped her arms around them.

"Are you crazy?"

"Maybe." But she'd gone into this one with her eyes wide open.

He dug a fist into his eye. "You slept with me. Why the fuck did you sleep with me? Did you think sex would keep me from turning you over to Grey?"

Hurt ticked in her chest. "You're the one who woke me up with the kissy face."

He glowered. "Are you trying to manipulate me?"

"Of course not. Geez, Raze. If I wanted safety, I would've gone to Jax with the letter immediately. Sleeping with you doesn't guarantee my safety."

Oops. She would've thought it was impossible, but his fury darkened even more. "It doesn't?" He sounded like he'd bitten, chewed, and swallowed shards of glass. In fact, he sounded like the glass was still in his throat. "Really."

She swallowed. "Um, listen. I—"

"Stop talking. For the love of God, stop talking before I beat you." His hand shook as he reached for his jeans.

She snorted.

He stilled.

She smashed her lips together, but a small laugh escaped. Then another. Then she started laughing so hard, tears filled her eyes.

He watched her, his expression an intriguing mix of rage and incredulousness.

Finally, she hiccupped twice. "Sorry about that." She cleared her throat. "There's no way you'd beat me." The man had apparently forgotten she was a profiler. Perhaps the most experienced one still living.

He cocked his head to the side in a curiously dangerous move. "Maybe you didn't profile me as well as you thought."

Well, he did have the hint of a wild card to him. "You're angry because I know your real agenda?"

"Damn it. I'm pissed as hell."

"Why?" It wasn't like she'd snooped through his stuff. She'd gone back to her former apartment.

He gripped her arms and lifted her onto her knees. "You found a letter saying I planned to turn you over to the Mercs." At her nod, he hissed in his breath. "Instead of running to Jax and telling all, you come up here and take a nap? Then you let me roll you over and fuck you senseless?" His voice rose on the last.

Temper roared through her. She shoved him, and he released her arms. "Listen, jackwad." Her voice shook. "I found the letter and came up here to discuss it with you. I don't need Jax to tell me what to do. Finally, this most recent fuck wasn't good enough to make me remotely senseless."

His head jerked back. "Excuse me?"

If danger had a tone, he'd just used it. She deliberately lifted one shoulder. "Eh. You've done better." What the holy hell was she doing, poking the beast? She couldn't help it. He was just so damn arrogant and scary. "I'm a very good profiler, and while I know you're a big bad with a history, I don't think you'd kidnap me and turn me over to the Mercs."

He glowered. "Oh. Don't you?"

She wavered and then straightened her spine, even though she was naked and on her knees. "No. Besides, Lynne knows about the letter, too. My guess is that you have about thirty minutes to find Jax and confess all, or she'll do it for you."

Raze's eyes glittered. "At least that's somewhat of a backup plan."

She shook her head. "Wait a minute. You're angry I didn't turn you in?"

"Yes," he exploded. "My God! The world is a dangerous place, and there's a chance I'm not gonna be here tomorrow to cover your ass. So you need to cover your ass and protect yourself, no matter what."

She chuckled.

His face flushed a deep red. On most guys, it would look like a heart attack was imminent. Not Raze. Not even close. His fury was darker, dangerous. Raw and primal in a way that had her quickly biting her lip. No laughing. No more laughing.

She breathed out. "You're mad because I didn't turn you in, and I need to do things like turn you in because you may not be here to protect me tomorrow."

"Exactly."

She just gaped. The man had gone and totally lost his mind. "Are you listening to yourself?" she whispered.

He headed for the couch to yank up faded jeans. He turned while drawing down a black Metallica T-shirt. "Stay here."

She scrambled out of bed and hurriedly dressed. "I'm coming with you."

He stepped toward her, and she hastily retreated, falling on the bed to sit.

"Stay. Here."

"N-no." Her stupid voice quivered, but she stood again. "There's less of a chance that Jax will shoot you in the head if I'm standing next to you."

Raze's head tilted just enough to be threatening. Incredibly thoughtful, deliberately threatening. "Not gonna say it again."

That probably didn't mean he was going to agree with her if she argued. "We need to come up with a plan," she croaked.

"I have a plan, finally. My last meeting with the Mercs gave me the location of the next meet. Tonight I'll go get

Maureen, and I'll bring her back here." He turned on his heel.

Vinnie rushed after him and smashed right into his back when he stopped moving.

He pivoted and lifted her by the arms.

"Eek." Shock stilled her for precious moments as he walked backward, grabbing a belt from a pile of discarded clothing on the way. She struggled then, panic consuming her.

He set her down on her ass beneath the window, not hard but definitely not gentle. Quick, smooth movements had him easily tying her to the rickety, useless old radiator. He sat back on his haunches, surveying his handiwork.

"You goddamstupidmotherfucker," she spat.

He stilled. His lips tipped almost in a smile.

She kicked out and nailed him in the thigh.

He stopped smiling. "Man, you're a handful." Leaning in, he fisted her hair and held her face right beneath him. His heated breath brushed her lips, and his fiery gaze warmed her entire body. "If I make it back, you and I are gonna have a little chat. You might want to reflect on the fact that I've tamed wilder animals than you." He pressed a hard kiss on her lips, turned, and strode out the door before she could say a word.

Fury burned through her like a flash fire. She pulled against the restraint, but it held fast. Oh, she was going to kill him.

Chapter Twenty-Three

*Behavior is the most important aspect
in studying the true nature of man.*

—Dr. Vinnie Wellington, *Sociopaths*

Raze found Jax pounding on a punching bag in the basement. His movements were fluid and fast . . . and his strikes were aimed to kill instead of subdue. "Jax."

Jax stopped and turned, sweat rolling down his face. "Where's Vinnie?"

"Tied up." Raze hadn't regained his full strength after having the fever, and he knew it. But he was fast, and his training for the military matched Jax's. If they fought to the death, it'd be close. Hell, they might both die. "I told her I wanted to speak with you alone. Where's Lynne?"

"Sleeping. She's working too hard." Jax rolled his neck. He'd left his hands and knuckles bare for his boxing session, and they were already turning purple.

"You're one tough bastard," Raze murmured.

Jax lifted an eyebrow. "What's it going to be? You telling me all, trying to kill me, or leaving?"

"Are those my only three options?" Raze drawled, his body settling.

"Yes."

Raze leaned against the doorframe. "How about option four?"

"Go on."

"I leave tonight, do the mission I'd intended, and then return tomorrow?" Raze lifted his chin. "Then we go on, and I serve Vanguard and its people." It shocked him how much he wanted to do just that. Wanted to belong and find a place in this new world for himself.

Jax shook out his scarred right arm. "I want to read the letter. Lynne said Vinnie found it."

Raze nodded and reached into his back pocket to draw it out. He handed it to Jax.

Jax slowly unfolded the worn paper and read, his expression revealing nothing. Finally, he refolded the note and handed it back to Raze.

"Well?" Raze asked, shoving it in his front pocket.

Jax struck with a right cross, followed up by a left to the gut.

Pain exploded in Raze's face and torso. He bent over and grunted, instinctively lifting with an uppercut that jerked Jax's head back with an audible snap.

Jax kicked Raze's knee in a sweep, ducking as Raze aimed a punch for his temple.

Raze roared as agony split his knee and jumped Jax in a tackle, tumbling them both to the mat. They rolled, both punching, both trying to find leverage with their feet.

The fight lasted nearly thirty minutes. Neither tried for a kill shot, but pain remained on the table, and both men were more than willing to cause it.

At some point, Tace and Sami entered the room. Tace blocked the door, his gaze intent, watching them. Sami slid to the floor, her legs extended, and munched on what smelled like popcorn. A few times Raze could see her wince, but she didn't make a move to stop the fight.

Raze leaped backward to his feet, his vision fading, his muscles protesting. Jax jumped up and rushed him.

At that point, Tace stepped between the two men. "Enough."

"Get the fuck out of the way," Jax snapped, punching around Tace to hit Raze in his aching jaw.

"Yeah." Raze pivoted and bent his leg, kicking around Tace.

"Stop it right this second!" Lynne Harmony yelled from the doorway. She ran inside and wedged herself between Tace and Jax.

Raze stilled. He couldn't hurt the little scientist. Small hands grabbed his shirt and yanked him back. He turned and looked down at Vinnie. "How the hell did you get free?"

The promise to kill him all but glowed in her eyes. "Lynne dropped by to see how our talk went."

"I need to get a lock for the damn door." Raze wiped sweat and blood off his chin. Now that he'd stopped moving, his entire body throbbed in agony. There wasn't a square inch of him that wasn't bruised or battered. "How about the scientists get the hell out of here, and we finish our talk, Jax?"

"Damn good idea." Jax walked right into Lynne, forcing her to back toward the doorway.

She planted both hands on his chest, seeming not to care about the blood and sweat. "I am not leaving."

Vinnie nodded vigorously. "You tell him, sister."

Jax looked over his shoulder at the profiler. "I'm glad you two have bonded. Now go mind your own damn business."

Lynne poked him in the chest. "You *are* my business."

Vinnie cleared her throat but didn't move an inch. "This entire situation is my business, considering the Mercenaries are willing to kidnap women and blackmail soldiers in order to get me. The question is, why do they want me?"

Raze paused. He'd spent more than one sleepless night trying to figure that out. "You were with the president for weeks. Maybe the Mercs think you have information."

"What info—" Tace asked, turning around. "The Bunker. Everyone is looking for the Bunker, and it's not unthinkable to believe the president knows where it is. He did travel from DC to Nevada. Maybe visiting LA was just a pit stop to acquire Lynne, and then he planned to move to his prime objective. Perhaps he's heading to the Bunker."

Raze's shoulders settled. His lower back hammered with pain. "Are we done fighting?" He looked over Vinnie's head.

Jax glanced over his shoulder. "I could go a few more rounds."

"Me too," Raze drawled.

Sami shoved off the mat. "Enough testosterone. You both have big dicks—let's stop comparing them."

"They both *are* big dicks," Tace said.

Sami grinned. "Yeah. That."

Raze looked down at Vinnie. "I told you to stay in the apartment."

Pain rippled up his shin. He blinked and looked down. She'd kicked him. His mouth dropped open.

She put both hands on her hips.

"Vinnie," he murmured.

Pain. Sharp and right in the same spot. She'd kicked him *again*. He moved into her, his hands wrapping around her elbows and lifting.

"Wait a minute." Jax sighed. He shook out his hand, and blood sprayed. "Everyone needs to cool off before we deal with the personal shit. Put the shrink down, Shadow."

Raze's shoulders tightened, and he met the Vanguard leader's gaze evenly, keeping his hands where he damn well wanted them. "I'll deal with my woman as I see fit, Mercury."

"*Your* woman? I don't think so." Vinnie's gasp should've warned him, but he was too busy playing chicken with Jax. She moved, just enough to jerk her knee up, and his balls exploded. He dropped her and bent over, gasping for air and trying not to puke. Bile rose in his throat, and his intestines spasmed right up through his gut.

Fury swept through him so quickly he forgot, very briefly, about the pain.

Vinnie sprang into action, turning and running full bore for the stairs.

He moved to follow her, and Jax stopped him with one hand planted on his chest.

"She kneed me in the nuts," Raze growled, his voice a little wheezy.

Jax snorted. "I saw. The doc has a mean streak." He glanced at Lynne. "Go make sure she's okay, and meet us in the conference room with the ridiculous table in fifteen minutes."

Lynne's brow furrowed, and she looked from Jax to Raze and then back again. "I can't let you guys kill each other."

Raze's body pulsated with the need to go after Vinnie and let the beast living deep down inside him loose. The rational part of him, the civilized man he'd tried to become, whispered to calm down before he found her. Fuck reason. He shoved against Jax.

Jax returned the shove, and Raze braced his back. "We're going to shower, and then we're going to have a calm meeting about how to deal with the Mercs," Jax said through gritted teeth.

Raze shifted his shoulders, fully intending to punch the Vanguard leader in the head again.

Tace clapped both hands, edges in, on Raze's biceps.

Pain ricocheted deep. "No more fighting. I'm fresh, and neither one of you wants to take me on," the medic murmured. "Shower time, and let's figure out the Mercs."

"I don't need your help with the Mercs," Raze snapped.

"Too fuckin' bad." Jax nodded to Lynne, and she turned to go after Vinnie. "We need to come up with a plan, just in case you survive the next couple of hours."

Raze stiffened. "You're going to take a shot at killing me?"

"Oh, hell no," the Vanguard leader said almost cheerfully through a busted lip. "I bet fifty to one odds the good doc rips off your dick and beats you to death with it. Anybody want to bet?"

Both Sami and Tace shook their heads.

Raze bit back a sharp retort and moved with the group toward the stairs. The overwhelming sense of camaraderie settled around him again. These soldiers and this time . . . they were his. Oh, he and Vinnie were going to have one hell of a discussion that night. It was time the good doc met the real him.

She'd kicked him. *Three* times. Never in her life, not once, had Vinnie Wellington resorted to violence. When she'd seen the look of retribution in Raze's eyes, she'd finally found caution and had run for her life. The problem was, she had nowhere to go.

Footsteps tapped behind her, and she stopped, whirling around.

Lynne grinned. "Oh, you're so gonna pay for that one."

"I know," Vinnie whispered.

Lynne shrugged. "He deserved it, and man, was it funny."

"He's going to kill me," Vinnie said, her hands shaking.

"Nah. He might make you pay, but he'll let you live." Lynne slid her arm through Vinnie's and tugged her around the landing to the next flight of stairs. "The guys are showering off the blood and sweat, and then we're meeting in the conference room to discuss the Mercs. You don't have to be there, but considering you're the prize . . ."

"I definitely need to be there." Vinnie's head swam.

Lynne tripped, and Vinnie helped her to remain upright. "Sorry. I'm a little clumsy," Lynne said as they reached the second level.

"I hadn't noticed," Vinnie lied, her legs moving of their own accord.

"That's kind of you." Lynne shoved open her door and pulled Vinnie inside. Her apartment had the same configuration as Raze's place, but touches of whimsy and decoration warmed the area. Lynne opened a cupboard and pulled out a bottle of silver tequila.

Vinnie shook her head. "I don't think—"

"Girl? You just kicked one of the most highly trained soldiers in the current world right in the nards." Lynne grabbed two shot glasses and poured. "One shot will give you courage for the meeting we're about to have." She handed over a glass.

Vinnie eyed the clear liquid. What the hell. She tipped it back, and the alcohol burned down her throat. She coughed. "That is not the good stuff."

Lynne took her shot. "Not even close," she agreed, her eyes watering. "Whoa. Man. That stuff might destroy our livers, but at least then you won't have to face Raze."

Warmth spread throughout Vinnie's belly. She wanted another shot, but it had been so long since she'd had alcohol, she didn't reach for the bottle. "I'm not afraid of Raze."

Lynne wheezed twice. "Really?"

"Sure. Why would I be? He's been mostly kind to me during my time here." Sure, that was before she'd kicked his balls. Hmm.

Lynne shook her head. "Um, yeah, but he's been secretly

planning to kidnap you and turn you over to the enemy. The kindness and the charm? I'm thinking initially it was used to disarm you and gain your trust, and then he felt guilty."

Vinnie cleared her throat. Her tongue felt like she'd swallowed boiling mints. "So?"

"So? He's no longer trying to gain your trust, and now that he's come clean, he's not feeling guilty." Lynne shook her head. "I know you. Hell, I kind of am you."

The room swayed just a little. "Huh?"

Lynne sighed. "You're with him, right?"

"Well, kind of. I mean, we have had sex, but we're on equal footing." She was educated and trained, damn it.

Lynne snorted and then quickly covered her nose. "Oh man. Then he belted you to a radiator so you'd stay where he put you."

Vinnie opened her mouth and then closed it again. Good point. "That doesn't mean anything. He was ticked, and he needed to face Jax without interference." Man, that sounded lame.

A knowingness lightened Lynne's eyes. "The old world and the old rules are gone. I mean, if guys like ours even followed those rules in the first place, which I kind of doubt."

Vinnie pressed both hands to her hips. "You're okay with being tied to radiators? I mean, the famous Dr. Harmony, educated and brilliant, is just fine and dandy with dating a Neanderthal?" She shook her head. "I don't believe it. Not for a second do I believe you're all right with being man-handled."

Lynne breathed out. "Of course not. Well, unless there's something kinky involved."

"It's odd, though. I mean, they're over-the-top bossy when it comes to safety. We should be burning our bras and shooting these guys." Vinnie worked through the issue in her mind. "Yet they have no trouble working side by side with female soldiers."

Lynne nodded. "I've analyzed that as well. When there's time for thought and debate, fairness and reason win out. But in crisis situations, their atavistic sides trump everything else."

"So the more backward they act, the more they care?" Vinnie grinned.

Lynne snorted. "As wrong as that sounds . . . yeah. In a crisis situation, anyway." She waved the issue away. "Society will rebuild, and we'll be stronger than before."

"Good." At least they were on the same page.

"But right now, we're in limbo, and I'm just saying that kicking a guy like Raze in the nuts, in front of his friends, might be an unwise move with repercussions." Lynne reached for a leather-bound journal on the counter.

"He won't hurt me," Vinnie said. "I won't let him."

Lynne smacked her arm, her hand glancing off. "Good on you, sister. That's the spirit."

Vinnie faltered. "What would Jax do?"

Lynne sniffed. "We'd talk it out like rational adults, but we've made a commitment to each other." Her eyes didn't quite meet Vinnie's. "Though he has a long way to go with the whole sharing of feelings and not being a throwback."

Vinnie chuckled. "I do hope we don't have to go through the entire suffrage movement postapocalyptic."

"Ha! Well, considering three out of Jax's five elite lieutenants are women, you, me, and Sami, I'd say we're going to be fine."

Vinnie straightened. "I'm not one of Jax's lieutenants yet."

"Sure you are, or you wouldn't be invited to the big meetings." Lynne smiled.

Vinnie grinned, and warmth bloomed in her chest. "I'm a lieutenant." She *belonged*. "You're right. Those big bad men do treat women as equals. Well, ones they don't date."

Lynne shuddered. "As opposed to the creepy way the Pure seems to be treating women."

"That's true." Vinnie tapped her lip. "Very true."

Lynne handed over the journal. "This was my father's journal, and he has some terrific insights into science, love, and the combination of the two. Why don't you read it for some fun and relaxation?"

Vinnie felt the worn leather. Her friend had just entrusted her with a prized possession, and surprising tears pricked the back of her eyes. "Thank you. I'll take good care of it before bringing it back."

"I know." Lynne tossed an arm over Vinnie's shoulders, wobbling slightly. "Let's go meet our men."

Chapter Twenty-Four

———◆◆◆———

The camaraderie found amongst soldiers
gives strength to get the job done.

  —Dr. Vinnie Wellington, *Perceptions*

Raze cut Tace a killing look across the conference table. "I do not need ice for my balls. Stop offering."

Tace grinned and drew out a chair to sit. "Just tryin' to help, pard."

Sometime in the very near future, that Texan accent was going to get the medic punched in the face.

Jax waited patiently at the head of the table, taking turns between glaring at the empty doorway and glowering at Raze. Bruises mottled the left side of his face, while his right side sported a darkening black eye. A small cut near his chin had stopped bleeding but still looked red and painful.

Raze grinned and then winced when his busted lip protested.

Vinnie and Lynne stumbled through the doorway.

Raze leaned back. Vinnie's hair cascaded wildly over her shoulders, and a very pretty pink blush colored her classic features. Her blue eyes were watery and a little unfocused.

He stood and grasped her arm, leading her to sit next to

him before she could take a seat across the table. To his surprise, she followed easily and sat, both hands holding a leather bound journal.

The smell of tequila wafted up.

Jax yanked out the chair to his right. "Lynne?"

She inched across the room and dropped into the seat, turning a brilliant smile on the Vanguard leader.

Raze turned Vinnie's chair so she had to face him. "Have you been drinking?"

She shook her head and hiccupped. Damn, she was adorable. Sexy and adorable.

Sami snorted from the end of the table, where she had her boots firmly planted as she kicked back in the executive chair. "It's not nice to drink alone."

"Just one shot," Lynne slurred, her eyes nevertheless alert. "It has been so long, I guess it really affected us."

"We'll talk about it later." Jax shook his head. "Raze? Tell us everything you know about the Mercs."

Raze left his hand on Vinnie's chair, wanting to explore this new aspect of her later—now was the time to work. He needed to trust Jax and his guys with the Mercs. So he took a deep breath and related everything Ash had told him, as well as what he'd picked up on his own through the last few months. "I don't think the Mercs want to harm Vinnie, but I don't trust their long-term plans after they get the information they want from her."

"There's only one way to find out," Vinnie mumbled.

Raze shook his head. "No. Now that I finally know where the exchange is supposed to take place, I'm going in to get Maureen, and you're staying here. It's too risky to turn you over. It's not going to happen."

Her eyes widened. "You've agreed already. It's the only way to find your sister."

"No," Raze said.

Jax nodded. "Agreed. You, Sami, and I will go in fast and

stealthy." He stood and walked over to where a bunch of pictures showed the Civic Center.

Raze eyed the pictures. "What I wouldn't give for an air attack."

"Amen to that," Jax said absently.

Vinnie slapped her hands on the table. "I should go to the rendezvous point, and we should negotiate from there." She turned her gaze on Raze. "Greyson Storm wants information from me, and I'm happy to tell him what I know, which isn't much. I can convince him of that, he'll turn over your sister, and then we can all live safely behind Vanguard walls."

Raze barked out a laugh, with Jax not far behind with his own chortle.

Vinnie's lips turned down, and her chin jutted out. "What is so funny?"

Lynne elbowed Jax in the gut, and he stopped laughing, cutting her a warning look. Then he focused back on Vinnie. "Doc? Greyson Storm ain't letting you go if he gets his hands on you. Like it or not, you're a valuable commodity with your knowledge of sociopaths and the president."

Vinnie sat back, her frown deepening.

"In addition, I'm thinking Shadow here has figured out the same thing about his sister. Does she have value to Greyson?" Jax drawled.

Irritation clawed through Raze. "Yes."

"Why?" Sami asked from behind her boots.

Raze sighed. "Maureen is one of the top agriculture and food growth specialists in the world. She was working at the university on a research grant to grow food for undeveloped countries."

"Food. Well. That's not very important," Jax said, a snap in his voice.

Raze couldn't blame him for the anger. "I know. She's valuable as more than a bargaining chip. Even if we pretend to trade Vinnie, no way will Greyson let Maureen go. It'd be like you letting Harmony go."

Lynne lifted an eyebrow. "That's because he adores me."

Raze shook his head. "Adoration or not, there's no way the Vanguard leader lets Blue Heart leave, even if she wanted to go."

Lynne glowered. "That's not true." She twisted to face Jax. "Right?"

He met her gaze. "We'll discuss it later."

Her head lifted, and awareness dawned. "You bet your ass we will."

Jax gave Raze a killing look. "What do you know about Greyson Storm?"

"He's ex-military sniper. I knew of him, and he knew of me, but that's about it. I believe he was one of the best," Raze said.

"How did he get your sister?" Lynne asked, scooting her chair away from Jax's.

"She stayed at the University to continue her work, knowing the country would need viable new food sources. Greyson captured her there, I believe." Raze forced fear out of his gut. His sister was fine. She had to be.

Jax yanked Lynne's chair back in place. "He took your sister, knowing of your ability to hunt and track anybody. He figured you'd be able to get your hands on Vinnie."

Raze leaned back and fingered the pounding bruise on his forearm. "That and the fact that I worked with the FBI right when Scorpius started making serial killers. I was reassigned, and I took care of some of the worst." He didn't need to go into details. If there was somebody to hunt, he was the guy, and the government had known it. "There's a good chance Greyson believes Vinnie and I crossed paths."

"But we hadn't," Vinnie said.

"That you knew of," Raze drawled. "I took point in

Charleston when you were trying to capture the Ripper who'd killed all of those roller hockey players."

Her mouth dropped open. "We didn't catch him. He ended up dead."

"Yeah," Raze said softly.

She leaned back, her eyes widening as she must've realized he'd taken the shot. "Did you see me?"

"Yes. Part of my orders were to ensure your safety. Then I got called to work with the Brigade in Colorado, and I left. Next thing I heard, about two months later, was that the president had you and Greyson wanted you." At that point, his entire focus had changed.

Jax leaned forward. "Wait a minute. Are you AWOL?"

Raze shrugged. "Hell if I know. The government has broken down. The Brigade is still alive and kicking, but I was just on co-assignment with them." The Brigade had been created as a first line of defense against Scorpius; now they'd branched out to protect key infrastructure. Who knew if they still existed or even answered to the president. "The military is fractured, and the president's elite force, which answers directly to him, is small and primarily comprised of former Secret Service agents."

Jax nodded.

"Besides," Raze murmured, "if I'm AWOL, you and Tace probably are as well."

Vinnie leaned forward. "The best plan is for me to head to the rendezvous point, meet Greyson, talk to him, and then go from there. Maybe he doesn't have to turn over your sister. Perhaps she wants to stay with the Mercs and continue her work in their territory. The key is to make sure she's willing and that nobody has hurt her."

Raze breathed out. "It's too risky."

"We could cover her," Sami said. "If there's a way to reach an agreement with the Mercs, some sort of postapocalyptic treaty, shouldn't we try? I know it's risky, but the payoff could be huge for us."

Lynne nodded. "Especially if they have food resources. That's huge right now."

"Who knows what type of fuel and even medicinal provisions they've picked up from the university," Tace said. He sat back. "I hate the thought of bending to blackmail, but if there's a chance for cooperation, having the Mercs as an ally when Twenty and the president's elite force attack would be a definite plus."

Raze shook his head. "Absolutely not. I was wrong to even consider a trade in the first place."

"Not your decision," Vinnie countered. "It's mine." She looked toward Jax. "Plus, how do you know the Mercs are bad? I mean, the president has put out misinformation before. Perhaps he's spreading rumors not only about the Mercs but about Vanguard."

Jax studied her thoughtfully. "Keeping us from becoming allies would certainly fit his agenda."

Vinnie nodded. "My job was to profile the most dangerous sociopaths in our world, and I was good at it. I found them, and I captured them, and then I studied them. Meeting with Greyson Storm doesn't scare me."

Raze pulled her chair back. "You're not in a fully protected prison facing a shackled convict, damn it. Greyson is dangerous."

"I know," Vinnie said, reaching out to pat his hand. "This isn't just about helping you or getting your sister back, although that's a good goal. This is bigger. Aligning with the Mercs gives us strength, and if they do have food and medicine . . ."

Damn it. He should've just gone himself the night before.

Jax studied everyone. "All right. We need two plans. The first, a plan for meeting Greyson on his terms in Thousand Oaks. If that goes bad, we need a secondary backup plan for taking his headquarters."

Sami eyed the map. "The doc has a good point about rumors. The Mercs have a terrible reputation, but do we know any details? They're known to hunt and kill and fiercely protect their territory, but we're known for the same things."

Raze fought the urge to tie Vinnie to the radiator again. This was his fault. If anything happened to her, he'd live with the pain forever. He shook his head. "That's the fucking problem. We don't truly know a damn thing about them."

"We're about to find out," Jax said. "We'll meet and strategize after lunch. Everyone be back in an hour."

Raze sure as hell didn't like how the meeting had gone, but he was taking the reprieve to have a little chat with Vinnie, whether she liked it or not. To avoid an argument in front of everybody, he smoothly stood and lifted her, tossing her easily over his shoulder.

She yelped.

He didn't have a claim on her, not one strong enough to prevent her from going on a mission. But there was no doubt in his mind that a claim would be forthcoming, and it was time they set some ground rules.

She stilled for the briefest of shocked seconds and then punched him square in the kidneys.

His responsive smack on her tight ass echoed through the entire first floor.

She struggled like a crazy woman as he made his way out of the offices and upstairs to their apartment, where he swung her over and tossed her stubborn butt on the bed.

The woman bounced twice. "You are a damn Neanderthal who needs to enter this century," she yelled, flipping the leather-bound book onto the bed next to her.

He crossed his arms and gave her his most intimidating look.

She glared right back.

"I don't have a right to forbid you to go on this mission."

If he could figure out a way to go on his own before Jax's plan came to fruition, he'd do it.

"Damn straight," Vinnie spat, shoving to her feet.

Hot blades pierced inside his chest. "I'm asking you not to go," he bellowed, his ears ringing with temper.

Her chin lowered, and raw fury darkened her stunning eyes. "Too fucking bad." Her voice lowered to pure challenge.

"Oh, baby." He had no idea where they stood, but she was about to find herself buck-assed naked with him sprawled over her. He didn't have the right. He needed to earn the right. Even though he wanted to quash her stubbornness, he wanted her with him more. On his side and having his back. Obeying him out of loyalty alone. "This is a dangerous world, and I call the shots with missions."

She lifted an eyebrow. "We're not a couple, Shadow."

His last name. She always used his last name when she was trying to distance herself from him. "I think we are." He didn't understand it, and they'd happened way too quickly, but they were together. Period.

"You wanted to sacrifice me," she said, hurt glimmering with the anger in her eyes.

"Until I fucking met you," he ground out. Not for a second would he have been able to turn her over to Grey, and she damn well knew it. "Now I'm willing to take a risk with my own sister's life just to keep you safe. That has to count for something."

Vinnie paused. "That counts for a lot. But it doesn't give you license to make my decisions."

"What does?" he asked softly.

She blinked several times. "Nothing does." Slowly, she lifted a shoulder. "It's not who I am."

He rubbed his battered chin. "When it comes to military missions, when it comes to safety, there has to be a chain of command." If he was crazy enough to allow her on the mission, then she couldn't question him if he gave an order. "You understand that, right?"

She swallowed. "I think so."

That meant no. "Submitting to me doesn't make you weak," he whispered. "It shows strength."

Her chin jerked up. "I'm not submissive."

Ah. There it was. The crux of the issue. He could handle this. "Okay. New terminology. If we're on a mission, or if we're in danger, you're the dominant one if you do as I say."

She chortled. "That makes no sense."

"Neither does courting danger just to spite me or show me your independence," he said evenly. He knew, with every fiber of his being, that threatening her to gain compliance would backfire. Yet truth was truth. "You can push me all you want, you can even get away once with kicking me in the balls. But, baby, you go on a mission and ignore my directives, and I ain't going to go easy."

She shook her head. "I have a brain, Raze."

"Yes, I know. An impressive brain." There had to be a way to get into her head and make her see reason. The mere idea of anything harming her made him want to punch through the nearest wall. "How many close-combat situations have you experienced?"

"None." Her mouth tightened.

"Right. So logically, it makes sense to listen to those with experience."

She huffed out a breath. "We're not talking about me being an idiot on a mission. We're talking about you being bossy, overprotective, and overbearing just because we've slept together. You're the one whose focus is fractured, not me."

Damn if she hadn't just nailed him with the truth. He nodded, falling into acceptance. "Right. You're right."

Triumph lit her eyes.

"So here it is. If you do one thing—and I mean one little titch of a thing—to put yourself in danger on this mission, or if you disobey one order of mine, I swear to fucking God I'll make sure my focus is never fractioned again." He let the truth flow.

She frowned. "Meaning what?"

He finally let her see the guy he rarely allowed himself to be. "I'll tie you to that bed, I'll shackle you to that radiator, I'll beat your ass until you can't walk . . . in order to keep you safe and keep you here."

She drew back. "You're a chauvinistic asshole."

He shrugged, his focus finally narrowing and settling. "So be it. I'm Raze. Nice to meet you."

Chapter Twenty-Five

The brain is the most powerful
of all weapons . . . except a sledgehammer.

—Dr. Franklin X. Harmony, *Philosophies*

Vinnie stretched her toes in her borrowed tennis shoes as she jogged down the stairs to the gym. After spending two more hours in the conference room, she knew the plan backward and forward.

Now, under Jax's orders, she was being trained by Raze in some very quick self-defense moves. "I think this is a waste of time," she muttered again, stomping in front of him and down the rough steps.

"That's unfortunate," he said, his breath brushing the back of her hair.

Yeah, it definitely was. Allowing Raze to put his hands on her would end up with her breathless, turned on, and probably pissed off. Not a comfortable way to be.

She squished across the old mats and then turned around, shaking out her arms. "I don't see why Sami couldn't train me just as well."

"She could have," Raze said, shutting the door. "I told her I wanted to train you."

"Oh." Vinnie took a couple of steps in retreat. "I know you don't want me to go and meet with the Mercs."

"Yep."

"So why are you training me?" She tried to keep the hurt out of her chest.

He stalked closer, all intent and all male. "Because I care about you, and the idea of you being harmed makes me want to blow up the entire Mercenary organization just to ensure your safety."

The words hit her dead center. She held out a hand. "Please don't be sweet. I can't take sweet."

His lips tipped. "I know you have to be focused and slightly pissed, or you're going to get scared. But you do not get to be pissed at me. We have to work together."

"You want to shackle me to a radiator again. *Oh, baby.* I am pissed at you." And slightly, very slightly intrigued. She'd never admit that, no matter what.

He nodded. "I get that, but you need to get a few things, too. You're going to have to accept the mission and the parameters, and you need to be focused and not angry. Especially at me."

She could be angry at whomever she wished, but that wasn't how to get into his head. "All right, that's good. Since we're finally being real and talking, I think we should talk about us."

His left eyebrow lifted, and with his face bruised, he looked like a pirate about to plunder. "All right."

Oh, it was time for her to gain the upper hand. With a guy like him, there was a surefire way to get him to back the hell off. "I like you, and you're a strong partner to have."

He straightened, moving his torso back and away from her. "Huh?"

She nodded vigorously, even feeling mean. "Yep. I want the whole enchilada. You know. Hearth and home—and I think you're a good bet."

He may have paled a little bit.

"Because we're building civilization as well, I want to get married before we continue any sexual encounters. Any chance you could find a ring on a scouting mission?" She put a hopeful expression on.

He studied her, and the moments ticked by. "Sure."

It took every ounce of control she had to stay still. "Su-sure?"

"Yeah." He moved in, his hands cupping her face. "You're right. We do have to worry about civilization, and here in Vanguard, we're safe. We'll get married right away."

Holy shit. She opened her mouth to argue.

His descended, and he kissed her deep. Electricity zinged through her torso, bounced around, and landed in her girly parts. When she'd forgotten how to think, he lifted his head. "During the ceremony, you're gonna vow to obey, baby." Amusement glittered in his eyes.

Warmth exploded in her chest. "Oh, you—you—" She kicked him in the shin.

The pop to her ass shocked her.

He grinned. "Nice try, and I guess it's time you learned I retaliate . . . considering we're getting married and all."

Maybe faking him out hadn't been such a great idea. "I will never marry you," she hissed, her face heating.

"Too late." He released her. "You proposed, and I said yes." He turned, his gaze thoughtful. "In fact, we could actually use our marriage to meet with the good reverend, couldn't we? Get in with him by talking about a wedding."

She breathed out, her nostrils flaring. In panic? Could nostrils flare in panic? "Wait a minute. I was just messing with you."

"I know." He rolled his shoulders back. "But I like the idea of you being my obedient little wife."

"Knock it off," she ordered through gritted teeth.

He studied her head to toe. "Yep. Just perfect."

She looked for something to throw, but the free weights seemed kind of heavy.

"I'm not kidding about meeting with the reverend," Raze said.

She shook her head. "It's too soon. With April joining his church, and Jax offering to sit down and talk, our hitting up the reverend would be too much. Besides, neither of us is Pure."

Raze frowned, thoughts scattering across his sculpted face. "You're right." He shrugged. "I guess we'll just have to ask Jax to marry us. I'll write the vows, and you find a nice dress."

She fought the urge to tackle him, mostly because she'd lose the fight. "Stop teasing me."

He shook his head. "Sorry, baby. You proposed, I said yes, and now we have a binding contract. You will be mine."

Enough of this silliness. Maybe if she ignored him, he'd stop it. She'd tried to mess with his head, and it had totally backfired on her. For now, she needed to learn a couple of defense moves in case things went south on her first and probably only mission.

She looked around and shuddered. "Is this where the bodies are buried?" Her voice echoed off the dirty walls.

"We burn the bodies, remember?" He winced.

She nodded. "Not funny, considering it's probably true." She glanced at the bright blue gym mats covering the floor. "Those are actually nice."

"From the school on Chalice Street. Jax said they raided it right off." Raze rolled his neck. "You should've already been down here training. From the second you arrived in Vanguard, you should've been training."

She huffed out a breath. "My work is more important."

"If we're attacked and you die without fighting back, then you can't work."

She sighed. "You really don't like me right now."

He paused. "I'm doing this because I like you. By failing to prepare, you're preparing to fail."

Temper rippled through her. "You're quoting Benjamin Franklin? Really?"

He grinned. "I've been hanging out with Jax too much."

The Vanguard leader loved his quotations, now didn't he? "Fair enough."

"Attack me."

"Oh, I'd love to," she said grimly. "Anything goes?"

"Yep, but keep in mind, I'm fighting, too. You nail my boys, *again*, and you're not going to like the results."

She stepped onto the mat and turned around to face him. "I'll take my chances."

He gestured in a come-and-get-it motion. "Let's go."

She frowned and carefully settled her stance, one foot slightly behind the other. Then she shook out her shoulders. Finally, her hands rose and fisted.

"What the hell are you doing?" he asked.

"Getting ready."

He shook his head, irritation wrinkling his nose. "I said to attack me. You don't pause and get ready. You fucking attack."

"Fine." She rolled her eyes. Taking several moments to think, she finally launched herself at him, head down, trying for a tackle.

He caught her easily, lifting her up, shaking his head. "No. Definitely no." Setting her down, he took two steps back. "Okay. I want you to attack when I give the order, but this time move instantly. There isn't time to stop and think and plan. You have to fight."

She frowned and blew hair out of her eyes. "I'm a psychologist."

"Not today." He gave her a second to get her balance. "Attack."

She threw herself at him, turning, her shoulder colliding

with his chest. He grabbed her biceps, lifted her, and then put her down flat on the mat, sprawling over her. Her legs kicked ineffectually, and her hands slapped the mat. Her thighs widened to allow him more room, and heat slid through her entire body. As she struggled, her breasts rubbed against his chest, providing a breath-stealing friction. Finally, she stilled. If she moved one more inch, she'd combust. "How was that?"

He laughed. A true, genuine, honest, and deep laugh. "Really, really bad."

She gaped. His laugh, the full one, was sexy as hell. Masculine.

He sobered, but the smile remained. "You kinda suck."

She blew out air. "That's what I was trying to tell you. My time is better spent digging into people's minds. It's too late to train in self-defense."

He lost the smile. "What a rational, scientific, reasonable approach to survival."

She gave him a look. "I do not appreciate the sarcasm."

He pressed into the vee of her legs. "You need to know how to get free and run if anybody grabs you in Thousand Oaks."

Her eyes wanted to roll back in her head from pure pleasure. "Somehow I don't think they'll jump on me like this."

"True."

"I'll be fine." She'd take a gun and a couple of knives. "One night of training isn't going to do me any good."

"You're wrong, and while I don't agree with your going on this mission, I'm going to make sure you're prepared. By the end of the night, you'll know how to break several holds and cause major damage to an attacker. You have no choice." He nipped her bottom lip.

The bite held pain and warning. She blinked. "Raze?"

"I like you. I like being right here," he said quietly, his

gaze intense. "Remember that during the next several hours."

What did that mean? "Um—"

He rolled them both and stood, easily planting her on her feet. "If somebody grabs you, it's going to be like this." Twirling her around, he slid an arm beneath hers and grabbed her neck, yanking her back into his hard chest. "Get free."

She took a breath and kicked back. His weight shifted, he lifted, and started moving her toward the door.

Panicking, she struggled against him, her shoulders feeling like they were bouncing off a boulder. She kicked and shook, slapping back, not slowing his stride at all.

He paused at the doorway, set her down, and smacked her sharply on the ass.

Pain rippled through her lower back, and she turned, her hand going to her smarting butt. "What the hell?"

He cocked a head to the side, no give on his hard face. "Every time you let me get you to the doorway, you're feeling my palm."

Her mouth gaped open. "You have got to be kidding me."

"Nope. You need motivation, and I'm happy to provide that." He looked down several inches at her. "If you can get through the doorway by yourself at any point, then we're finished training."

Oh, she was feeling more than a little motivation. Was there any way she could actually knock him out? She eyed the closed door. "Open the door, then."

He reached behind his hip and opened the door about six inches. "Get back across the room."

Yeah, she was so going to make him pay. Turning on a tennis shoe, she moved back to the middle of the mat and settled her knees.

He moved for her, straight on, not even trying to hide his attack.

She kicked out. He grabbed her arms and flipped her over his shoulder. The breath whooshed out of her lungs. Three long strides and they reached the doorway. This smack made her groan out loud and rushed her temper hard and fast to the surface. He put her down and she punched out.

His hand enclosed her fist with a loud smack. "Middle of the mat. Now."

Jerking free, she stomped back to the middle.

He crossed his arms. "Are you ready to learn a couple of moves now?"

She glared at him. "Fine. But don't be surprised when I knock you on your ass."

"Looking forward to it." His chin lowered, and he moved toward her again.

Chapter Twenty-Six

*A sociopath's behavior is often in
opposition to his true thoughts.*

—Dr. Vinnie Wellington, *Sociopaths*

Morning light shone through windows set in the far wall
of the conference room. It was really a war room. Interesting. Maybe Jax called it the conference room just to keep
everyone calm. Raze kicked back in his chair and kept his
face blank.

"That's good. Look scary and thoughtful," Jax said, not
looking up from a stack of papers set on the opulent table.

Raze rolled his eyes.

"I saw that." Jax shook his head.

Raze drummed his fingers on the table. He and Jax sat
on one side, waiting for the good reverend to show up.
Everyone else had somehow gotten out of this stupid duty.
"We have more important things to deal with today."

"Not really." Jax set down a piece of paper and looked
up. "We're not supposed to meet Greyson Storm until midnight, so we might as well get some work finished today.
How was training last night?"

Shitty, and it had left him with a hard-on that had tortured
him all night. After Vinnie had finally gotten past him, he'd

sent her to bed, and he'd spent most of the night scouting Vanguard territory for threats. "The training went fine," Raze said. "Vinnie can break a few holds and run if necessary, and today Tace is teaching her how to shoot to kill." If Raze had been forced to spend one more minute smelling her sweet scent of calla lilies, he would've finished the training session with her naked. "I still think it's a mistake to take her."

"She wants to go, and I think she has a point. If she tells Greyson what he wants to know, then there's no reason for him to continue hunting her. Also, if the meeting somehow does lead to an alliance, we'll have the edge against the president and his forces." Jax cut an irritated look at the empty doorway. "Bastard is late."

The burn scars on Raze's arm ached like a storm was coming. "If Maureen is of value to Grey—and I think she is—then he's not going to willingly trade her."

"Agreed." Jax kept his gaze on the door. "Our goal is to get your sister, protect Vinnie, and figure out Grey. If we have to kill him to meet our first two goals, then so be it. But again, if there's a chance we can form an alliance with the Mercs, we'd be crazy not to at least try to work things out."

Vinnie crossed into the room wearing a pretty yellow skirt with a silky blouse.

Raze straightened, his body thrumming to life. "What are you doing here?"

She ignored him and moved to the end of the table.

"Jax?" Raze rumbled.

"Leave your personal shit at the door. She's a profiler, and we need her," Jax said.

Vinnie sat and hissed out a breath.

Jax turned her way. "You okay?"

"Fine," she said through gritted teeth. "Just a little tender from training last night."

Jax nodded. "It'll get better. Those are unused muscles, and the more you train, the tougher you'll get. The key is to take those sore muscles and use them again."

Raze pressed his lips together to keep from smiling. It wasn't her muscles that were smarting.

Vinnie shot him a death glare.

Reverend Lighton strode inside, all purpose. His hair was slicked back, and he'd donned a pair of designer glasses. The guy probably had perfect eyesight. "Thank you for meeting with me." He didn't offer to shake hands.

"Take a seat," Jax said, pointing to a chair on the opposite side of the table.

Lighton pulled out a chair with his gloved hands. Nice, leather gloves.

Jax blinked almost in slow motion. "Afraid of germs, are we?"

Lighton nodded. "I'm sorry, but yes. Scorpius lives not only in humans but on surfaces just like any bacteria, right?"

"Right." A muscle ticked in Jax's jaw.

So the guy had kept gloves off last time in order to draw them in. Hadn't worked, now had it?

Lighton grimaced toward Raze. "I heard you had been infected, and I offer my condolences. You would've made a good member of my congregation."

"I'm still kicking," Raze said, throwing threat into his voice.

Lighton turned toward Vinnie. "Dr. Wellington. I've never asked, but I've assumed. You're a carrier of Scorpius, correct?"

"Enough. What do you want, Lighton?" Jax asked.

Raze nodded. Leaving off the guy's new title would put him on the defensive, and they needed him off-center a little bit.

Lighton's lip twisted. "The Pure would like an autonomous area in the southeast corner of Vanguard territory. In addition to the three blocks of apartments, we'd like to claim the other two blocks, extending our territory to the far corner."

"You want to expand the fence?" Raze muttered.

"Yes. Complete autonomy. Our soldiers would continue to patrol with yours, of course." Lighton kept his gloved hands in his lap.

Vinnie leaned forward, her gaze thoughtful. "Would your soldiers also patrol your proposed borders?"

"Of course," Lighton said.

"What if somebody trespassed?" Vinnie asked.

The reverend smiled, revealing smooth, white teeth. Very white. "We'll figure out those kinds of details at a later date. Right now, we're discussing autonomy."

Jax crossed his arms. "As I understand it, you're asking me to share my resources, including protection, with a group of folks who want to close themselves off from the rest of us. Who want our food, our medicine, our guns . . . for what? What exactly are you giving back here, buddy?"

The reverend nodded in what seemed like understanding. Intelligence and determination glowed in his eyes. "That's a fair question. Like I said, our soldiers still work with you, and our scouts still go on missions."

"Not enough," Jax drawled.

The reverend breathed out slowly. "Listen, I know it doesn't seem fair, but what about the bigger picture? Don't you understand the responsibility we have to humanity as a whole? We might differ on the reason God wiped the earth clean, but we have to agree that preserving human life is paramount." Lighton's voice deepened.

The guy showed a charisma that probably motivated his little flock from the pulpit.

"What do you mean?" Jax asked.

"Babies," Lighton said. "God has made it clear that Scorpius results in death, either now or in a few decades.

Infected women can't carry babies to term. Only the pure, only the uninfected, shall be here in a hundred years."

Vinnie paled but didn't speak.

Raze had a very clear image of himself reaching across the table and choking Lighton out with one hand. He smiled.

Lighton leaned back in his chair, his eyes widening.

Jax shook his head. "That's a rumor, and it's too early to know if it's true. I'm sure there are plenty of pregnant Scorpius survivors out there."

"They won't make it to term," Lighton said, his conciliatory tone at odds with the triumphant gleam in his eye. "You know it as well as I do."

"Is that why you've become a reverend?" Vinnie asked.

"God called me," Lighton said simply. "I have a duty to my people."

Vinnie smiled. "It must be nice to have a calling in this world."

He nodded. "It is. With a calling comes great responsibility."

"About that." Jax cocked his head to the side. "What are the rules of the Pure? I mean, all churches, all organizations, have structure, right?"

Lighton focused solely on Jax, his face losing its charm. "I'm afraid that's private, Master Sergeant Mercury."

Interesting that Lighton had used Jax's military designation. Raze glanced at Vinnie to catch her reaction, but her expression remained calm and vaguely interested. She probably made a hell of a shrink.

Jax lost his patience. "Listen, Lighton. Every single person in this territory is a member of Vanguard, and I rule this territory, all of it."

So much for negotiating. Raze went on alert.

Lighton shook his head. "Not anymore."

Jax lifted an eyebrow—slow and sure. "Meaning?"

"Meaning, if you don't agree to our terms, we're leaving."

Lighton held up a hand to halt Jax's response. "I mean no disrespect, but I have to protect the uninfected."

Jax nodded. "I'm fine with you leaving with your group."

Vinnie leaned forward to speak and then stopped at whatever she saw on Jax's face.

"However, I want to speak with each and every member of your organization before they walk through the fence. Without you present." Jax crossed his arms. "If I get even a hint that you're forcing people to belong to your church and leave the safety of Vanguard, you end up three feet under. Make that six."

Death threats? Raze made sure his gaze conveyed support for the Vanguard leader, keeping it focused on Lighton, who'd flushed an interesting shade of red.

Jax shoved his chair back from the table. "Get me a complete list of your members and who's planning to leave Vanguard with you. Vinnie will schedule exit interviews."

Raze stood, showing muscle and agreement.

Lighton pushed back from the table, and Vinnie held up a hand. "Do you mind remaining and speaking with me, Reverend? Perhaps I can ease the way here. I have a few questions." Her voice remained low and soothing.

Jax turned to Raze.

Raze didn't like it. Not one bit. But Vinnie could probably get Lighton off the defensive and gain some information. He nodded. "I'll be right outside." The last was said for the reverend's benefit.

Jax led the way out the door and shut it. After moving across the outer room, he leaned against the wall. "Well? What do you think?"

"I'm not a shrink, but if I were, I'd call that guy a narcissistic asshole," Raze said.

Jax nodded, eyeing the closed door. "The question remains whether he's dangerous or not." He paced toward a weapons locker and then back. "He seems to believe his nonsense, which might make him unstable."

"Has April Snyder infiltrated the group yet?" Raze asked.

"Tomorrow." Jax ran a hand through his hair. "She worked with Violet last night in the mess hall and told her how lost she is, how lonely, which is probably the fuckin' truth."

"Yeah. Violet bit?"

"Violet invited April to a meeting tomorrow morning. Our spy is on the way in."

Raze shook his head. "Our newest spy is a young, grieving widow, and our biggest benefit in the next mission is a slightly crazy shrink who's willing to sacrifice herself for the greater good. Your soldiers, the top three, are Tace, who's going dark, Sami, who's hiding more secrets than I was, and me, a guy you don't trust."

Jax nodded. "Yeah. I get it. I'm fucked."

Vinnie glanced toward the coffeepot in the corner. "Would you like some coffee, Reverend?"

Lighton smiled and smoothed down his black pants. "No, thank you."

She'd known he'd avoid the germs, but the polite language provided clues. "Do you mind telling me about your congregation?"

He eyed her, once more in control now that the Vanguard soldiers had left. "We're just a group who believes there's a reason we were spared the Scorpius infection. God has a plan for us."

"That must be nice." She clasped her hands together on the smooth wood.

"It is, but it's also frightening," Lighton said. He leaned forward, and this close, freckles showed on his smooth skin. "We've been given the tools to survive, but it's up to us to use them, you know? It's up to me to lead and keep my people safe."

"Why you?" Vinnie asked, settling right back into profiling as if she'd returned home. Her focus sharpened, and her shoulders finally relaxed.

He tugged on his leather gloves, straightening the fingers. "I don't know. One day, I just knew I had to do something. That night I dreamed God talked to me." He laughed, the sound deep and self-effacing. "You're a shrink, so you have to believe that's crazy. But what if?"

She lowered her chin, as if contemplating his claims.

"Do you believe in God? Many scientists don't," he said.

"I do believe," she murmured. "I don't see how anybody can look at either the human body or the cosmos and believe for a second that it all happened by chance."

He nodded. "Exactly. If there's a God, then why wouldn't he talk to some people? Some special people?"

"You're special?" she asked.

He grinned again. "Well, God talked to me, so I'm thinking that yes, I am."

Man, he could be charming. She smiled back, encouraging him. "The foundation of your church is your mission to protect the uninfected so humanity can continue?" she asked.

"Yes."

"What if there's an uninfected person who doesn't want to join your church?" Vinnie asked.

"Then they don't join," he said simply. "I'm not forcing men to do anything."

Intriguing phrasing. "What about women?"

He stiffened. "Women either, but I think they need to be protected more than ever these days. Too many have been victimized as the strong have overcome the weak."

How paternalistic. "Even here inside Vanguard? You think women need to be protected here?" she asked.

He clucked his tongue. "Asks the woman who has a guard dog waiting right outside to make sure she's safe."

Her breath heated. "I work for Vanguard at headquarters. That comes with protection regardless of sex." Although, that wasn't why Raze waited outside.

Lighton lifted his chin, and his upper lip curled. "Do you think you could leave? If we asked you to accompany the Pure, do you honestly believe Mercury would let you, the president's profiler, leave Vanguard?"

She blinked. "I'm free to leave." The words rang hollow.

"No. You're not, and you know it." Lighton pushed back from the table and stood. "You're every bit as much of a prisoner here as is Lynne Harmony, whether either one of you likes it or not."

"That's not true." Vinnie stood, her breath catching.

Lighton sneered. "You're telling me that Blue Heart is free to up and go? That Mercury will open the fence for her? You're delusional. While I believe the survivors of Scorpius are ultimately doomed, many people out there think she has a possible cure for the disease in her blue blood. Or at least she has the knowledge to create permanent B for survivors . . . if she finds a lab."

"We're rebuilding civilization slowly," Vinnie countered. "We believe in the freedom of the individual to make his or her own choices. Are you, or are you not, forcing women to belong to the Pure?"

"I am not."

She couldn't tell if he was lying. "Is God?"

He scowled. "Don't be ridiculous."

She shook her head. "It's too dangerous outside these fences for you and your people. There has to be a way for you to work with Jax."

"I thought so, too, but now I realize we need to make a pilgrimage outside this place." His eyes glowed a dark blue.

She frowned. "Where? Where will you go?"

He smiled then, his charm back in place. "Oh, we're going to the Bunker. It's out there, and it's waiting for the Pure."

She gaped. "You know where the Bunker is?"

"No, but you do, right?" He smiled. "The president had to have told you during your time with him."

Where the hell had this guy gotten all his information? While rumors about the Bunker had been spread far and wide, not many people knew that the president had kidnapped Vinnie. She shook her head. "If the Bunker exists, I have no idea where it might be."

"That's unfortunate." Lighton turned on faded brown loafers for the door. "I guess God will have to show us the way, then."

Chapter Twenty-Seven

―――•◉•―――

A true hero would never consider himself as such.

—Dr. Vinnie Wellington, *Perceptions*

It was a mistake to take three vehicles. Too much gas, too much noise. Raze kept his temper at a slow simmer as he drove the battered truck with Vinnie sitting across the seat. Jax followed on a dirt bike, while Tace and Sami brought up the rear in another truck.

The plan was to hide all three within running distance just in case the Mercs took out one or two of the machines.

A warm breeze, even at the midnight hour, promised the warmth of the oncoming summer. The moon shone bright and strong over the deserted land, its glow illuminating rusting car carcasses lining each side of the once busy 101.

"Is the good reverend crazy?" Raze asked, twisting the wheel to avoid a downed ice cream truck.

"Define crazy," Vinnie said, planting her tennis shoes on the dash. "He's determined, and he's focused. I haven't met with him enough to really diagnose him, but if I had, I think I'd discover that he suffers from either narcissistic personality disorder or borderline personality disorder. Or something else. Who knows?"

"So he's nuts."

"Not really." She wrapped her arms around her legs and rested her chin between her knees.

"Lean back, sweetheart." He winced. Calling her an endearment would backfire.

"Kiss my ass," she muttered, not moving.

He nodded. Yep. Backfire. "We're on a mission, Vinnie. Put your legs down and your back to the seat just in case we hit something." All he needed was for her to get hurt while outside the Vanguard walls. "Obey me, or I'm taking you back." Which was what he wanted to do anyway.

She gave a long-suffering sigh and dropped her feet to the floor. "You are so bossy. I bet you have a disorder or two."

"Of that, I have no doubt." He kept an eye on Jax in his side mirror. The Vanguard leader rode a bike like he'd been born on one. "Do you think Lighton is dangerous?"

"Yes. If his beliefs are threatened, or if the Pure don't follow his lead, I think he might resort to violence." She wiped her hands on her jeans. "I wish we could provide April Snyder with some sort of backup while she's attending church services."

"Me too." Raze drove around what looked like a satellite dish in the middle of the interstate. "I don't know who we can trust."

"That's because you're a hidden-agenda kind of guy," she muttered.

"No, I'm not."

"Right."

He glanced her way. "I lied to protect my sister. When I got to know Jax and you, I changed my plans."

"Whatever. If I wanted to leave Vanguard, could I? Would Mercury let me go?" she asked.

A hollow emptiness ached in Raze's chest. "You have your freedom, I'm sure. While Jax definitely needs you to do your job, and while he thinks you might be able to unlock the secret of the Bunker, I don't think he'd force you to stay."

She breathed out. "All right."

"Are you thinking of leaving?" If so, he'd really pegged her wrong.

"No."

"Good."

She turned, her knee bending on the bench seat, her gaze sharp on his. "Would you try to stop me?"

He liked that. That she used the word *try*. There was a right answer. He knew there was a right answer, but he'd just said he was finished keeping secrets. "Yes."

"Damn it, Raze. You're no better than the Reverend Lighton." She wrinkled her nose.

"I never said I was better than him," Raze said. He kept his hold firm on the steering wheel but still looked her way. "Listen. I don't know what's going on between us, and I don't know what'll happen next, but what's happened already happened, and that means something."

A cute frown drew down her brows. "You mean sex?"

"It was more than sex, and you know it."

Even in the meager light, he could see pink flood her face. "I did not sleep with you to get something more, you idiot."

"I know." The woman couldn't be any less manipulative. Period. "Yet it did create something, whether you like it or not." They hadn't made promises or a commitment, but he'd been inside her, and she'd cried out his name. To him, that meant he protected her, which he couldn't do without Vanguard. And considering his initial plan had been to turn her over to the Mercs, he owed her. "Could we fight about this later? We're almost at Thousand Oaks."

She huffed back in her seat. "I could leave if I wanted to."

He sighed. "Fine." Then he'd have to follow her all over hell and back just to make sure she stayed safe. If their training session the previous night had taught him anything, it was that she was a creature of thought and not action. Though he liked that about her, it would get her killed on the outside. "You're a free, independent woman."

She snorted. "You're an ass."

The woman was into name-calling all of a sudden. "Speaking of which, how is yours?" he drawled.

She sucked in air.

He tried not to grin. His training methods had proved effective finally, but she had to be sore. He tried really hard to feel bad about that. "You're right, by the way. I am an ass."

"Acknowledging that fact gets you no points. Changing that fact might."

He breathed out. "Thanks, but I'm good." If smacking her butt a few times kept her thinking and moving when danger eventually came, he could live with being an ass.

Her mumbled retort included a creative litany of more names.

He pulled into an alley about six blocks from the meeting point at the Thousand Oaks Civic Center and cut the engine. "Just a quick double-check. You have your gun and knives?"

"Yes." Her voice trembled just a little.

"If you pull your gun . . ."

"I shoot. Pull and shoot." She wiped her hands again. "I know what to do."

He nodded. "If there's shooting, you run. I'll get Maureen and follow you back here. No matter what, you protect yourself." He'd cover her back. "Let's go."

She nodded and jumped from the truck. He waited for her to reach him and then started at a brisk pace, keeping her in the shadows and slightly behind him.

Jax, Tace, and Sami would approach from different directions.

They passed an unmoving pool full of stagnant water. The fountains were silent now, but at one time, the area had been spectacular.

He made sure they stayed away from the steps and motioned for Vinnie to crouch near a column. He turned to look for sniper positions. Finding a couple, he reached out and moved her closer to the building, where the shadows covered her position. Hopefully Tace had found a good spot without running into a Merc.

While Raze didn't think Greyson's plan was to shoot Vinnie, he wasn't taking that chance.

His heart thumped hard, and his blood roared through his veins. Adrenaline swamped his system. Damn it. The smell of calla lilies was sending him into overdrive. Focus. He had to focus.

Several deep breaths later, and he went cold. Good. He kept an eye on Vinnie. She tugged down the bulletproof vest and did some sort of weird shimmy inside it, no doubt trying to get comfortable.

A form stepped away from a nearby column. "Shadow."

"Greyson." Raze went on full alert. He'd only seen the guy once across a small camp, but he recognized him. Dark hair, light eyes, rugged features. Hopefully Raze's team was in place. How many men had Grey brought? "Where's my sister?"

"Contained nearby," Greyson said, most of his body still in the dark.

Raze strained his ears but couldn't hear any signs of life. "If she's dead—"

"She's not." Grey stepped into the moonlight. He stood well over six feet and was muscled tight. The energy rolling from him was coiled and smooth.

Raze moved toward him, noting they stood eye-to-eye. "We didn't know each other in the service."

"Just by reputation, although I did see you once in the desert across a camp." Grey appeared relaxed and on alert at the same time. "I have snipers in three positions and men surrounding us."

"As do I," Raze said smoothly.

Grey glanced around the nearby rooftops. "Maybe, maybe not. Did you kill Ash?"

"No," Raze said truthfully. "Rippers got him. Saw the body."

"Figures." Grey paused, his voice dark and gravelly. "I want the woman."

Raze leaned in. "Why? Why do you want Dr. Wellington so badly that you'd kidnap a fellow soldier's sister?"

"Your sister was in the right place at the right time, and her insight into food production has been invaluable. I'll be sad to let her go." A gun tucked into Greyson's hip glinted in the night. "As for the doctor, that's my business."

"I think it's my business." Vinnie stepped out from behind the column, her gun pointed at Greyson's neck. Not his chest, not his head, but his neck, just like she'd been taught. "I'm Dr. Wellington. What the fuck do you want from me?"

Vinnie kept her aim steady, even though her knees wobbled. Maybe the f word had been too much. Yeah, it probably had, but perhaps she'd sounded tough? Not classy, but tough. She'd always—

Man. Now her thoughts rambled like her mouth. She had to concentrate, damn it.

Greyson Storm was very tall and looked like a soldier with flak boots, black jacket, and worn jeans. He held himself much the same as Raze did—graceful and watchful. Even now, with the moon shining down, she couldn't place his expression. "Doctor."

She nodded. "What can I do for you?"

"Come with me." He held out a large hand. "The second we reach my truck, I'll let Maureen Shadow go." His voice remained steady, as did his gaze. This guy was a trained liar, but she was the best of the best. His eyes ticked a little, and his chin was down slightly.

She shook her head. "He's lying," she whispered to Raze.

Raze instantly drew his gun. "Get behind me."

She inched closer to him but remained in the open with her gun trained on Greyson. "Where's Maureen?" she whispered, her heart aching in her chest.

Greyson dropped his hand. "She's close by, but I won't free her until you come with me."

"She's not here, or if she is, he doesn't intend to turn her over." Vinnie set her stance and tried to keep from freaking out any more than she already was. "Why do you want me so badly?"

Greyson studied her for the briefest of moments. "Zach Barter."

Vinnie's head jerked. The crazy Ripper who'd purposely infected Lynne Harmony with the Scorpius bacteria cure? "Excuse me?"

"You chased him, right?" Greyson asked.

Raze didn't look her way and kept his gun trained on the threat. "Not another word."

Just a few more. "I did chase him," Vinnie said slowly. In fact, Barter had been one of her first Ripper cases when she'd still worked for the FBI. A former scientist, Barter was brilliant and crazy. He'd worked with the initial CDC team when the outbreak had first occurred, had gotten infected, and then had gone crazy. His boldest move was to try to kill Lynne Harmony, but he'd turned her heart blue instead. "Why are you asking about Zach Barter?"

"I just want to know where he is. Tell me where he is, and I give you Maureen." Greyson's body didn't tense in the slightest, despite the guns pointed at him. "Now."

She swallowed. "We're at a standstill. I do know where Barter is right at this moment. Well, where he was a week ago, anyway." Her voice hitched a little, and she hoped he thought it was from fear and not because she was bluffing. At the moment, she had no idea where Barter was or if he even still lived. She edged closer to Raze just in case one of them needed to fire.

"Tell me where he is, and we're done," Greyson said, tension swelling from him.

"No," Vinnie said softly. "However, we'd like to negotiate an alliance with you."

"Yeah?" Interest glimmered in the Merc leader's eyes.

"Yes. What do you say?" she asked.

"Tell me where Barter is, and we'll negotiate," Greyson said.

She shook her head. "I don't know."

Greyson lifted his left hand. Men came from every direction, at least ten of them, all with guns.

The ground exploded all around them, dirt popping up. The men surrounding them scattered like rats, jumping out of the way. Raze leaped sideways, catching Vinnie in a tackle and slamming her to the ground. She fell hard, the wind swooshing from her lungs.

"Up." Raze grabbed her vest and yanked her up and in front of him, shoving her into a run. Bullets pinged all around them. "I think it's Tace, but I'm not sure he's the only one firing."

"Raze!" a female voice yelled.

Raze paused and half-turned. "Moe?" he yelled.

A red truck careened by with a woman in the passenger seat struggling furiously against some man. The truck continued on, flipping around the corner.

Jax came running from the left, shooting at the fleeing Mercs.

Bullets continued to ping the earth.

A motorcycle roared to life, and Greyson rode out from

behind part of the building, following the truck. His soldiers ran, and three more vehicles started up.

"Fuck." Raze turned just as a beat-up pickup careened around the corner and screeched to a halt with Sami driving. "Get in," she yelled.

Raze pushed Vinnie toward Jax. "Get her to safety." He turned and leaped into the truck.

"Hell no." Vinnie shoved Jax in the stomach and turned to follow Raze into the cab. She flew over his lap and landed next to Sami. "Go, go, go." Raze yanked the door closed.

Sami punched the gas, and the truck leaped forward, following the motorcycle. "Did Tace manage to hit anybody from the sniper's position?"

Raze shook his head. "I don't think so, but he did save our asses. Faster, Sami. We're losing them."

Vinnie coughed. God, they had to hurry. Up ahead, she could barely see the taillights of the motorcycle. The truck was already out of sight.

Sami slammed her foot down on the accelerator.

Vinnie scrambled to keep her seat. "Was that Moe? Really?"

"Yeah." Raze's jaw clenched hard enough it had to hurt. "She was so fucking close. We have to get her." Panic edged his strong voice.

Vinnie nodded, her fingers digging into the worn cloth of the seat. "She's alive. We'll get her."

The motorcycles turned around a sharp corner. Sami had to slow down and then punch it.

Greyson Storm stood in the center of the street, legs wide, gun pointed at them.

"Shit," Sami said, jerking the wheel.

Gunfire plowed into their front tire, and the truck swerved wildly. Vinnie screamed, her hands going to the dash. The truck smashed against a solid brick building. Metal crunched, and glass blew in every direction.

Pain exploded through her body. Her head jerked back, and she fell sideways into Raze. Without missing a beat, he kicked open the door, already firing toward the street.

Her head rang, and her body ached. She struggled to shove her way out of the vehicle. Her feet hit the ground, and then she kept on going down. The last sound she heard before darkness claimed her was Raze yelling her name.

Chapter Twenty-Eight

*It's a fallacy to believe that man is at his
most dangerous when he has nothing to lose . . .
the most ferocious of predators emerges
when a man has everything to lose.*

—Dr. Franklin X. Harmony, *Philosophies*

His sister was gone. Raze looked wildly around and saw
Vinnie on the ground next to the demolished truck, her light
hair splayed out. He bit back a bellow and rushed to lift her
off the ground. "Sami?" he asked.

The soldier shoved herself off the cracked sidewalk and
rubbed dirt from her pants. "I'm all right. Banged up, but
okay." She looked around and wiped blood off her cheek.
"This area isn't safe, and the truck is toast. How bad is
the doc?"

Raze held the small blonde. Vinnie was breathing evenly,
and her color was still good. "She's out but she's breathing.
Let's get back to the Civic Center." The sooner they returned
to Jax and Tace, and sooner Raze could go after his sister.
He leaned down and nuzzled Vinnie's neck. "Baby?
Wake up."

She didn't move.

Panic heated his chest, and he took several deep breaths.

"Let's get her to Tace." Maybe the medic would know how to reawaken her.

"Follow me," Sami said, loping into a jog.

Raze followed, holding Vinnie against his chest, trying to put one foot in front of the other with some semblance of control. His hip ached, and his head pounded from the crash. "Vinnie, wake up," he whispered.

She didn't obey.

Hadn't they had a nice talk about her obeying him? From now on, she was to fucking stay in Vanguard territory, away from threats. Greyson could've killed them by shooting the tires. Oh, the Merc leader was going to die and painfully.

Vinnie groaned.

Raze stopped and dropped to his knees, holding her as Sami stopped a few yards ahead. "Vinnie? Open your eyes, sweetheart."

Her dark eyelashes twitched, and her eyes opened, filling with tears. "Raze," she whispered.

He pulled her into his chest, and some of the rock caught in his chest eased. "You okay?"

"No," she sniffed, putting one hand to her temple. "My head hurts." She blinked several times and looked around. "Did we get Maureen?"

"No." Raze stood back up, the blood roaring through his veins. "We will, though." He moved back into a fast walk and followed Sami through back alleys and deserted streets, keeping his ears focused for any threat. After about a mile, Vinnie struggled in his arms. "I think I can walk," she said.

He looked down and studied her. Good color, clear eyes. If she walked, then his hands would be free for defense. "Okay." He set her on her feet and waited until she'd gained her balance. "You good?"

"Yes." She turned toward Sami. "Let's go."

It took several hours, but they finally reached the Civic

Center, where Jax and Tace were impatiently searching the area.

"About fucking time," Jax muttered, glancing up at the rapidly lightening sky.

Raze nodded.

"Keep to back roads and away from streets," Jax ordered. "Too many gang members cover this area still."

They all piled into the truck while Jax jumped back on his bike.

Raze sat with Vinnie on his lap. "How's your head?" he asked.

"Fine," Vinnie said, rubbing her temples. "I'm so sorry we didn't get Maureen."

Tace jerked the wheel to the right to avoid a dead dog, and Raze tightened his hold on Vinnie. "We will." At that point, Greyson Storm was gonna die.

They made it to Vanguard around noon. After making sure Vinnie was all right, Raze talked her into sleeping for the rest of the day. Sami also headed to bed to recuperate.

While Raze wanted to rest, his mind was too alert, so he spent the entire remainder of the day planning an attack on Merc territory. They'd go in the next night, when everyone had recovered, and there would be no mercy.

Night had fallen, and he still didn't want to go to sleep. Every time he tried to shut his eyes, he saw his sister's desperate face. So he once again scrutinized the satellite map taped to the whiteboard in the conference room. Approaching Greyson from the beach was a dangerous idea. Rooftops would be better, but with Grey's history as a sniper, he probably had all the vantage points covered.

"How's Vinnie?" Jax asked, crossing into the room with two glasses of what looked like whiskey. The Vanguard leader had been absent most of the day, dealing with different scavenger groups.

"Vinnie is better. Headache, but Tace doesn't think she has a concussion." Raze scrubbed his whiskered chin. At some point, he was going to have to shave. "She's still sleeping and should be all right tomorrow."

Jax studied him. "It's almost ten at night. Have you eaten today?"

"Not hungry."

"Fine." Jax slid a glass across the table. "Nourishment."

Raze grasped the glass and downed the alcohol. It splashed into his empty stomach and burned. "Thanks."

"You okay, Shadow?"

"Yes." He partially turned to face the Vanguard leader head-on. A slow burn was building inside him, and at some point, he was going to detonate. For now, he had himself under control, and he could plan. If he just kept his emotions tamped down, he could do this. "I may try to hit Greyson from the rooftops."

Jax studied the picture. "Where'd we get satellite pics?"

"Byron found them in the loot from the inner city library." The same stack of materials in which Raze had discovered the books written by Vinnie.

"Ah." Jax stepped up to the image. "You could go rooftop after rooftop, but here you're going to have to descend and then climb this fence." He pointed out the area. "It's the only way to reach the beach house, if that's where he's really keeping your sister."

"Yeah."

Jax shook his head. "I'm really sorry we didn't get her, man."

"I will," Raze said, his jaw hurting from clenching it so hard.

"It's a *we* situation. Let's come up with an assault plan, and we'll go in tomorrow night." Jax drank down his whiskey in one smooth swallow. "I think a force of three: you, me, and Sami. I'd like to keep Tace here if possible, but I'm sure he'll want to go."

"A combat medic's needed more here," Raze said. "Medical personnel—the ones trained with blood and guts—are few and far between. You're right to try to protect him."

"He doesn't like it."

"He likes shooting, hunting, and hard-core hand-to-hand," Raze drawled. "Scorpius changed him, I'm sure."

Jax nodded. "How about you? How are you feeling?"

"Fine, Mom."

"Seriously."

Raze settled his chest and took inventory. "I'm about at three-quarters strength, and my head aches constantly. My temper is right on the surface, but that could be stress about Maureen. I get tired easily—too easily—but my reflexes seem sharper."

"Yep. Scorpius. You'll be at full strength and not need nearly as much rest as you used to . . . in about a couple of weeks." Jax tapped a finger on the map. "I sent scouts out the minute we returned today to report back about Mercenary territory. In case a big move is made."

"I saw them go," Raze said. "I appreciate it."

Jax shrugged. "If we're going in, I'd like to at least have an idea of the lay of the land."

"You don't have to go. This is my fight." Raze stared back at the map.

"You're Vanguard. That makes it my fight."

Emotions roared to the surface, and Raze breathed out evenly. "Vanguard it is, then," he said, feeling the words deeper than the moment. He wanted to belong, and he wanted to trust again. Hell. He needed to be part of something bigger than himself in this new and dangerous world. *Better* than himself. He glanced at the Vanguard tattoo winding over Jax's shoulders. "I'd like to get tagged before we go."

Jax stilled and was silent for a moment. "You mean it?"

Raze faced him fully, studying the lines. Vanguard was spelled out in gang-like font in the middle of a shield which was bisected by a sword. The handle of the sword, he noticed, was actually a scorpion. "I mean it. Full Vanguard tattoo."

Jax's chin lifted. "Brothers, then. Good." He smiled. "Let's go find Tace. He's an artist, but I have to warn you, these days he doesn't mind inflicting a little pain."

Raze grimaced. "Great." At least physical pain would distract him from the torturous images flowing through his brain. Would Greyson take last night's failure out on Maureen? The Mercenary leader had threatened to kill her if Raze failed to cooperate.

Was his little sister still breathing?

Vinnie poked her head in. Bruises mottled her forehead, and a scrape lined her fragile jaw. "I just wanted to pop in and see how everyone is doing." She spoke to Jax but kept her gaze on Raze, searching his face, no doubt for a hint that he was about to explode.

Jax nodded.

Raze crossed his arms. "I thought you were sleeping."

"I was, and then I decided I should get to work." Her blue eyes held steely determination. "I'll be in my office if either of you need me." Just as she left, a ruckus sounded, and three scouts jogged into the room.

"Byron?" Jax asked a young kid with fogging glasses.

Byron frowned and shook out his wet hair. "We scouted Merc territory." He faltered, his gaze going to Raze.

"And?" Raze said, his chest becoming too tight for his skin.

Byron looked at Jax.

"Byron. What did you find?" Raze snapped.

The kid paled. "We took to the alleys for better angles, and Jon went in from the beach. Behind the big house, where we think headquarters is, they were, um, burying somebody. In a makeshift cemetery."

There was a roaring in Raze's ears. The kid's mouth kept moving, but he couldn't hear the words.

Jax grabbed his arm. "We shot at soldiers last night, and it's a dangerous world. We don't know it was her."

"We need to go. Now." Raze moved for the door.

Jax yanked him back. "It's too late tonight, and you know it. It'd be morning by the time we got there."

Raze fought him, and Jax shoved him against a wall. "Listen to me, Shadow. I know what I'm doing. We'll prepare and go in first thing tomorrow night . . . under darkness."

Raze blinked and stopped fighting. "Maureen," he whispered.

"She's okay," Jax said, releasing him. "Greyson has nothing to gain by killing her and everything to win by keeping her alive. It wasn't her."

The man was correct. It'd be suicide to try and take Greyson's headquarters during daylight. Raze nodded numbly. He had to get out of there. Air. He needed air, damn it. "I'll be back. Need to check the fence. We'll work on a plan tomorrow morning and infiltrate Merc territory tomorrow night." She had to be okay. He couldn't have failed her. God, what if Moe was dead?

It was his fault.

He jerked free from Jax and all but ran out the door and into the rain.

Vinnie hustled through Vanguard headquarters after Lynne had given her the bad news about the scouting party. The burial couldn't have been for Maureen. It just couldn't have been. Vinnie clomped through the rain to the outside fence and slipped through an opening.

"Go back inside," Jax said suddenly from her left.

She yelped and jumped, catching her shoe on a rock as she came down.

He sighed and grasped her elbow until she steadied her stance. "Like I said, get out of this crazy weather. Leave Shadow alone for the night."

"I can't," she faltered, unable to lie in the face of Jax's hard gaze. "Which way did he go?"

Jax studied her, rain sliding down the sharp contours of his face. The rain had slicked back his dark hair, giving him a predatory look that showed his rough upbringing. "I tracked him to the cemetery, and then he went to the abandoned apartment building across the way."

Vinnie wiped rain from her eyes. "You were covering his back."

Jax lifted a shoulder. "If I were covering yours, I'd force you back inside. Raze needs some alone time to deal with demons and plan for tomorrow night."

"I don't need your help." She gentled her statement with a smile. "Thank you anyway."

Jax shook his head. "You're not mine to stop, but I wish you'd listen."

"Give me a break," she muttered.

He lifted a shoulder. "You don't know guys like Raze, but I guess it's time you did. I've given you my best advice. The area is secure, and you'll safe from Twenty or anybody else. Well, except for Raze and maybe that lion. But this is a mistake."

She lifted her head. "It's my mistake to make." He was wrong. He didn't know Raze like she did. Even so, anxiety fluttered awake inside her abdomen. "Thanks, Jax."

He handed over a flashlight. "Try not to fall into a hole."

Without another word, he turned on his combat boot and strolled back inside.

Vinnie sniffed and pushed sopping-wet hair from her forehead. Keeping the flashlight beam low on the ground, she moved carefully, acutely aware of each hole and shattered rock as she slid out of the main gate, which was slightly open but well-guarded. The guards didn't stop her.

She tripped and regained her balance. All she needed right now was to break an ankle. The rain assaulted her, and a chilled wind dug past her wet shirt to bite her skin. Yet she forged on, making it through the two lines of downed cars, giving a nod to each guard she passed. Nobody tried to stop her until she reached the far end of the biggest Mack truck.

"This is a mistake," Sami said, gun down, her head protected by a ball cap. "Trust me, girlfriend. Go wait in your nice, warm bedroom for your man to get his shit together. You can't save him."

Vinnie paused. "None of us can save one another. I know that. But I can help him."

Sami snorted. "You don't believe that."

"I do." Vinnie patted Sami's arm. "Thanks, though." She pointed her flashlight back to the ground and ran across what probably was once a busy street in a downtrodden area. Her shoes squished in mud as she hurried by a burned-out truck. Should she go through the front door or the side fire escape? Probably the fire escape. Water splashed up her legs as she rushed toward the rear of the building and ran full force into Raze Shadow. She bounced off his hard chest, and only his hands on her arms kept her from falling on her butt.

"What the fuck are you doing here?" His hands tightened until pain rippled through her forearms. He glanced over her shoulder. "Has there been a breach?"

"No." She gulped down air and shook rain from her hair. "I was looking for you."

He stilled. His head lowered. His gaze glittered through the rain. "I scouted for a few miles, just walking, and now I'm here trying to figure out how to take down this place without any explosives."

She swallowed. "You could burn it."

"I don't think the brick would burn." He studied her. "You left the safety of the compound by yourself in this weather?"

"Um, yeah." Her knees quivered. "I was looking for you."

He pivoted and lifted her up against the worn brick building, not very gently. "You were looking for me." He leaned in, heat from his body giving warning instead of warmth. "Are you fucking kidding me?"

"Nope." She went for flip because he was scaring the ever-living shit out of her. Enough violence pulsated in his rigid muscles to make the air around them resonate with a tension rivaling the storm.

Rain poured from the roof, landing next to them. "Why?" he asked.

She shrugged, acutely aware of being a foot off the ground. Rough brick scratched her back, and rain smattered her head, but the only thing that mattered was Raze. "I thought you might need me."

He straightened. His eyebrows drew down, and he blinked. "What am I going to do with you?"

She settled against the building and gripped his hips with her knees. Shrugging slightly from his hold, she pressed a hand over his heart. "Being so close to your sister and then losing her had to be terrifying. There aren't any words to take the pain away." Hell, she knew how bad life could cut. "You have to believe we'll get her back." Before meeting him, she wouldn't have used those words.

He studied her, a series of emotions finally crossing his face. Fury, pain, confusion. So many emotions and so quickly. His chin lowered. "Vinnie." Then his lips were on hers. Not gentle and definitely not sweet. He kissed her so hard her head hit the wall, and still he pressed. She opened her mouth in defense, and he went deeper with a low groan.

Rawness pulsed from him, digging through her, setting her on fire. Her mind reeled, and her body ruled. She shoved her hands beneath his shirt, caressing up, filling her palms with male and man. So much desperate strength.

His tongue took hers, claiming her mouth in a way that even felt primitive. She gyrated against him, the ache between her legs demanding relief. Nobody had ever treated her with such roughness and desperation. As if he was claiming her on every level and giving himself back in ways he'd never be able to say.

Only Raze Shadow could make her feel like this.

He slapped a hand to the brick by her head, his mouth continuing the assault; his free hand yanked down her wet shirt to palm her breast. Demanding and warm, he squeezed and then moved to her other breast. Electricity, sparking and alive, zipped down to burn her clit. Too much. Way too much.

His teeth sank into her bottom lip. Excitement flared her nerves to the point of pain.

She gyrated against him, her nails cutting into his chest. "Raze, please."

Through the scent of rain, he smelled wild and free. Totally male. He lifted her higher, and his mouth took her breast, sucking hard. Alive and rough, his tongue flicked her nipple before moving to the other one. "So fucking pretty," he murmured against her. "Hold on."

Desire quivered her into a mass of need. Her feet hit the wet pavement, and he yanked her jeans down her legs. She scratched down his ripped abs and frantically released his belt, shoving down. He helped, kicking his pants to the side.

Both hands grabbed her ass, she left the ground again, and he thrust himself inside her. Pain edged with carnal pleasure rippled inside her, and her internal walls gripped him tight in a hold that went beyond her mere body.

She threw back her head, taking even more of him. All of him.

"Look at me." The fingers at her ass squeezed, and one brushed her anus.

She stiffened, trying to focus, and opened her eyes. Everything in her stilled, quieted, as if waiting. He watched her, his eyes glittering with a light deeper than hunger.

Balls-deep inside her, holding her against the wall, he took her mouth in a brutal kiss so deep a miniorgasm rocked through her core. His grip tightened, and he released her bruised mouth, his lips remaining a second away. "You came out here, Vinnie."

She blinked, her breasts aching. "I know," she breathed.

"Your choice, but there's no going back." His nose was so close it nearly touched hers, and everything—man, everything—glowed in his eyes. "Understand?"

She did. On some level she couldn't quantify, couldn't explain, she knew exactly what he was claiming. "I understand," she whispered.

Satisfaction and determination were stamped hard on his deadly face. "Good. Every inch of you is mine. Get me?"

It was a declaration she should fight. Reason with. But her body rioted, craving for him consuming all thought, and she tightened her sex around him. "Yes."

His lids dropped to half-mast, giving him a dangerous look that only increased her hunger. One hand spread out over her ass, and the other slid up to clamp on the nape of her neck. He tilted her, just enough, and started to power into her.

Energy rushed into her, rolling through her, crashing an orgasm into her from nowhere. She cried out, digging her hands into his shoulders to keep from flying away. He wrapped over her even more, keeping her from hitting the building, somehow holding her weight exactly where he wanted her. So damn strong. He hammered into her, his lips on her neck, his body enfolding her.

Faster and harder, he battered her clit, each impact flicking a sensation of energy through her that stole her breath. Holding her in place, he hit a spot inside her that arched her entire body. Lava sparked through her, and she exploded. White flashed behind her eyes, and her body gyrated with the crashing waves. She gripped him tight, rippling along his length. Finally, wrung out to the point of going limp, she relaxed into his hold.

He stilled, pushed home hard, and came with her name on his lips.

Chapter Twenty-Nine

God, this world needs heroes.

—Dr. Vinnie Wellington, *Perceptions*

The morning light cascaded through the windows as Raze paced the conference room like a caged animal. He needed to go, and now, but that would be a colossal mistake. In a world filled with Rippers, displaced gang members, and wild animals . . . darkness was his only ally. The sun had only been up for a couple of hours, but if he looked at the map of Santa Barbara for one more minute, he was going to start yelling his head off.

His night of wild sex with Vinnie had taken the edge off physically, but now his chest ached. What the hell was he going to do with her? She'd burrowed so far inside him, he didn't feel whole unless she was next to him. For hours after they'd returned to the apartment, he'd listened to her sleep.

Leaving her had pissed him right off, even though he'd headed straight to work. Now he could barely concentrate. So he pivoted on one boot and headed through the building to the infirmary.

Tace looked up from the receptionist counter. Lines of

fatigue cut into the sides of his mouth, and red colored the whites of his eyes. "Do you have an appointment, sir?"

Raze snorted. "You look like shit."

"Can't sleep." Tace pushed back from the desk. "Since Scorpius, I can't sleep. Lynne thinks it has something to do with the lack of vitamin B during the initial infection."

Raze winced. "Don't people need sleep to keep sane?"

"Yep. Maybe that's part of the insanity issue, you know? Lack of sleep." Tace stood and turned back toward the examination rooms. "Jax said you wanna get tagged."

Raze faltered. "Um, yeah, but I'd rather you had some rest first."

Tace chuckled. "Don't be a pussy. I've drawn the Vanguard tat on at least two dozen bodies and won't screw up your pretty skin."

Raze's steps slowed, but he continued on. In case he didn't make it back from the Merc attack, he wanted to belong. A little ink in his skin didn't change much, but at least he'd be part of Vanguard for a few hours. It had been so long since he'd belonged anywhere. "All right." He entered the room and sat on a torn examination table that had lost most of its padding. "Just don't screw it up."

Tace opened a worn cardboard box and drew out ink and needles. "We actually raided a top-of-the-line shop a few blocks over, so no worries. The Vanguard tat will look good. Where do you want it?"

"Left bicep." Raze yanked off his shirt.

"I could do a sleeve on your right forearm to cover the burn scars," Tace said casually, wiping off Raze's arm with a cloth that almost appeared clean. "What's the story there?"

Raze glanced down. "Barn fire. I was twelve and Moe was eight. She was playing inside, and I went in after her. A burning rafter fell, broke my arm, and burned me to shit." Maureen had been nearly inconsolable, and had spent the entire time he'd been in a cast bringing him presents and haranguing their mother to make more cookies.

"You grew up on a farm?" Tace asked.

"Yeah. Wyoming." Raze held still as Tace went to work on his other arm.

Jax loped into the room and flipped a chair around to straddle it. "Gettin' the tat, huh?"

Heat threatened to climb into Raze's face. "Yeah. I said I was going to. It's definite."

Jax studied him, gaze intent. "Good."

Tace kept working. "We'll get your sister back. She's okay, and we'll get her. Family."

Raze nodded, his chest heating. Family. With every stitch of ink, Vanguard was becoming family as well. "You'll like Maureen. She's smart and fearless." From day one, when he'd looked at the tiny pink bundle, he'd vowed to protect her. "She has to be safe."

"She will be, brother." Jax said the words, his dark eyes nearly glowing.

Brother. Yeah. Raze leaned back and let Tace work away.

Nearly three hours later, he'd been tagged. He glanced at the intricate and strong lines. "That's that, then." It meant more than he could say that Jax and Tace had stayed with him the entire time. Sami had poked her head in, nodded approval, and returned to scouting duty.

He had a home.

Shrugging his shirt on, he finally relaxed into the new reality. "I should get to work."

April Snyder suddenly hovered at the doorway. "Jax? Do you have a minute?"

"Yeah." Jax pushed off the chair and turned it. "Have a seat. Let's hear it." He waited until April sat before bellowing, "Vinnie? Get down here."

Vinnie strode inside wearing a pretty pink blouse and dark jeans. "For goodness' sake. Stop yelling."

"Sorry." The Vanguard leader strode toward the far side of the room to lean against the wall. "April? How was church?"

The petite brunette scrunched up her face. "Different. I mean, the sermon was strong, and the reverend very charismatic. But the message was one of survival at all costs."

Raze tried not to focus on Vinnie as she stood in the doorway, her attention on April. In the light of day, she was even sexier than the night before. Just the thought of him taking her against that brick wall hardened his groin. Things had changed.

Jax mulled over the situation. "Did he threaten violence?"

April shook her head. "No, but he did stress sacrifice. Of what kind, I don't know."

"What else?" Tace asked, standing and stretching his back.

"There's a hierarchy," April said. "The reverend is at the top, and he has four bishops who flank him—two on each side. Men only." She leaned forward on the rickety chair. "There's a study session for the men scheduled after church, and there are also women's studies, but those are led by one of the bishops."

"That's odd," Vinnie murmured. "Even the women's studies aren't led by women. Very odd."

April nodded. "I thought so, too. You have to be a full member of the church to be invited to the studies as well as to other meetings I couldn't quite get a handle on."

"How do you become a full member of the church?" Vinnie asked, thoughts flitting across her face.

"I don't know." April flattened graceful hands on her jeans. "I went into the situation acting unsure if I wanted to be there, so I thought if I tried to become a full member all of a sudden, they'd be suspicious."

"Good call," Raze said, smiling.

She didn't smile back. "Thanks."

Had he ever seen the woman smile? Doubtful. Her eyes were so sad, his own chest hurt. "What happens next?" Raze asked.

She licked her lips. "Reverend Lighton asked if I'd like to meet with him tomorrow morning for coffee just to chat. I figure that's the next step to joining the congregation."

"How many people heard the sermon?" Vinnie asked.

April shook her head. "I don't know. It took place in what used to be a common room in the middle apartment complex, and there were three sections, all separated by heavy curtains. I was in a small section for guests, and Violet sat with me. There were only eight of us there."

"I don't like the secrecy of that," Jax muttered, a frown deepening between his eyes. "I need you to talk to Violet some more. They're recruiting you, so wait until she approaches you, and then ask questions. She'll expect you to be curious, so that's okay. But don't seek her out. Let her find you."

"Okay." April drew something out of her pocket.

"What's that?" Vinnie asked, craning her head.

"A silver cross." April opened her hand to show a small cross. "Lena gave it to me this morning before church."

Vinnie smiled. "That was nice of her."

April stared down at the jewelry. "Sure, but I didn't tell Lena I was going to church. She had no clue."

A chill scattered down Raze's back.

Nobody spoke.

Maureen Shadow missed her knife. He'd confiscated the blade from her during their last altercation. So close. So damn close. The look on her brother's face when he'd heard her voice would haunt her until the day she died. She should've killed Grey Storm the first chance she'd gotten.

As if she could.

She breathed out, her chest shuddering. How the hell could she get free? Moving to the open door of her room, she could see patrols already combing the beach. If she ran, they'd spot her within seconds.

Huffing out a breath, she sat on her bed in the Mercenary mansion, the outside French doors wide open, the ocean rolling in to the sand as if the world was all right again.

A knock on her door had her sitting bolt upright and stiffening her entire body. "Go fuck yourself," she snapped.

Greyson Storm walked inside wearing faded jeans and a white tank top that did nothing but enhance the powerful muscles down his arms and chest. "That's quite a mouth you've got on you." His eyes sizzled a pissed-off combination of gray and green that sent a clear warning. "I've sent a scout to meet with your brother again."

She crossed her arms. "You're such a dick."

He crossed his arms. "I liked your silent treatment better."

"Too bad." She glared at him. "Where are those girls from the other day? Do you enslave kids here?" The few soldiers she'd seen had all been men. What happened to the women? What would happen to her now?

"I don't enslave anybody, and those girls are none of your business." He leaned back against the door. "The scout is going to set up another exchange for Dr. Wellington, and this time, either it goes smoothly, or I plug your brother in the head with a nine mil. I like the smaller caliber. They bounce around a little."

Her chin lowered. "I hope I'll be the one carrying the bullet that gets you."

"I doubt it." He shrugged. "If you are, best of luck to you. Much better trained forces than you have tried."

She shook her head. "I won't cooperate with you."

"I'm not giving you a choice." He leaned against the

doorjamb. "We're scheduling another meet tomorrow night, and this is the last chance. If it goes south, I'm killing your brother and making sure you never step outside Merc territory again."

She couldn't read him well enough to know if he was bluffing or dead serious. "You told your scout you'd kill me."

"I lied. You're much too valuable to kill; we need food resources. However, I certainly don't have to take the good care of you that I have." He gestured around the comfortable room. "Believe me, there are far worse places I could put you."

She stood and faced him. "If you harm my brother, I will never help you grow food."

He jerked his head to the side in an oddly dangerous move. "You'd be surprised how easily I could make you want to please me."

The words and cadence carried a vaguely sexual tone. Stockholm Syndrome. Yeah, that was it. She was actually starting to think she knew this bastard. "You've misread me," she said smoothly. "Right now you hold the cards, I get that. But at some point, when you least suspect it, I'll hold your life in my hands."

His chin lowered, and interest flared in his eyes. "Do tell."

"And I'll let you drop right through," she said.

He smiled then, a flash of amusement across his hard face. "Listen and listen good. We get to the meet, you behave and help get the doctor in the truck, and then you live a life of luxury here working on food."

"You never intended to turn me over," she murmured.

"No. Like I said, you're too valuable." He turned to go.

She coughed. "My brother will never let that happen. He'll die before he lets you take either Dr. Wellington or me."

Greyson looked over his shoulder, his jaw set. "I know."

He shut the door without another word, and his heavy boot steps echoed down the tile outside.

Vinnie eyed Raze's new Vanguard tattoo with interest. While the skin was raised and red, the outline of the Vanguard symbol stood in proud relief. Maybe she'd get one, too. Perhaps on her lower back, right above her butt?

The outside door clanged. "Mercury? We have a visitor," a male voice called out.

Jax frowned and headed out the door, followed by the rest of them.

They reached the entrance to the soup kitchen, the big one that looked out on what used to be a parking area. Two Vanguard soldiers flanked a tall black man dressed in bloody jeans and a ripped T-shirt.

"Who the hell are you?" Jax asked.

"Damon Winter," the guy answered, his voice beyond deep. He appeared to be in his early thirties with angled features and a scar across his neck.

Jax moved closer, motioning April back. "What's with the blood?"

Winter looked down at his jeans. "Ran into some trouble on the way here. Pack of Rippers." He frowned, his dark eyes shadowed. "When did the crazy ones, the wild ones, start running in packs?"

Jax shook his head. "I'm about to shoot you so you don't have to ponder philosophy."

Winter nodded. "Fair enough. Greyson Storm sent me with a message. The meet is back on, at Merc territory this time. We figure you know where it is by now. If not, I'll draw you a map."

"Is my sister alive?" Raze asked, his voice vibrating.

Winter frowned. "Yeah, of course."

"Who was buried earlier today?" Jax asked.

Winter blanched. "A couple of soldiers. Not Maureen. So listen, come to headquarters with the doc. If you don't show with the doctor . . ."

"What?" Raze asked softly, stepping around Jax and heading toward the messenger. "What happens then?"

Winter smiled with smooth white teeth, flashing a dimple in his left cheek. "You must be Shadow. I've met your sister, and she has the same eyes." He held up a hand when Raze pivoted to punch. "Literally. I've met her. As in 'hi, how are you, I'm Damon.' She's fine, man. Not a bruise on her."

Raze paused. "You could be lying."

Winter sighed. "Yeah, I could, but I'm not. Grey has no desire to hurt her, but he'll do what he has to do, so cooperating with him is your best bet." He glanced around, and his gaze landed on Vinnie and April. "One of you the doc?"

Raze shook his head. "The doc didn't make it last night."

Winter rubbed the back of his neck. "Man, I hope that isn't true. You need the doc, or Grey has no reason to keep your sister alive. I'm supposed to tell you that Greyson has to get a visual on the doc, or he's ending your sister. You show up without the doctor, and it's a done deal. Greyson doesn't mess around, guys."

"I'm the doctor." Vinnie stepped forward, her voice sure and strong.

Raze cut her a hard look.

She ignored him. "Why does Greyson want the location for Zach Barter so badly?"

Winter grimaced. "The guy isn't much for sharing, you know? I can give you my word that Greyson just wants to talk to you—that's all he wants. But he'll do anything to find Zach Barter. Who is the guy, anyway?"

Nobody answered him.

Jax nodded to the soldiers. "Take our new friend here downstairs."

"To the gym?" Vinnie asked, moving forward.

Raze stopped her with a hand on her arm. "The gym is a nice place to talk." Beyond the gym were a few old storage rooms that were used for different purposes. One even had a drain in the floor.

Winter stiffened and then eyed Vinnie. "There's no need for torture, guys. I came with an offer for a second chance, and I've told you everything I know."

"We'll see." Jax jerked his head, and the two soldiers grabbed Winter's arms.

"Wait." Vinnie tried to move forward again, but Raze pulled her to his side. "Don't hurt him. That's not who we are."

The soldiers turned and propelled Winter through the mess hall and to the stairs leading to the basement. To the guy's credit, he didn't fight them.

Vinnie turned toward Raze, her mouth opened to argue, just as gunfire pattered from inner territory.

Chapter Thirty

We all have a hero and a villain in us . . .
it's up to us who wins the battle.

—Dr. Vinnie Wellington, *Perceptions*

Vinnie turned and ran for the back door, dodging around tables, yards behind Jax, Raze, and Tace. All three of them somehow managed to pull guns from somewhere on their bodies without a pause in their strides. The door had already closed when she and April reached it.

They ran out onto what had been an alley, quickly turning left to follow the racing men. Soldiers on patrol emerged from around buildings and street corners as they all ran toward the gunfire and the Pure apartment buildings. The fence remained in place.

A row of former crack houses shared the road with the new Pure territory, and the group took cover to the side of the nearest one.

"Status?" Jax asked the Vanguard soldiers.

The first guy was bleeding from a shoulder wound, but it didn't seem to be holding him back any. "We called for Lighton to get out here and explain why the fence was still up, and instead, somebody started shooting."

"What kinds of weapons do they have?" Jax snapped.

"Dunno," Tace said, crouching against the peeling paint. "And we don't know who the members are, so we have no clue how many soldiers they have."

"Even one would've given them access to the armory," Jax muttered. "A couple of them, and they could've taken anything they wanted. We've just started keeping track of weapons, and our system sucks."

Tace nodded. "Yeah, but we have the good stuff locked down. So they probably have guns but no explosives or grenades."

"We have grenades?" Vinnie asked.

Raze nudged her farther back, along with April. "Yes, but not many."

Jax cleared his throat. "Lighton? Get the fuck out here."

"Maybe I should negotiate," Vinnie said, ignoring Raze and moving up toward Jax. "I've had negotiator training. I mean, I wasn't an expert, and I've never negotiated during a standoff, but I did take a class, and I have worked with sociopaths. In fact—"

"Okay." Jax brought her to his side, keeping her protected between him and the house. "You'll probably do a better job than me, considering I want to cut off his balls and make him eat them."

"I won't start with that." She cleared her throat. "Reverend Lighton? It's Dr. Wellington. We need to talk." Her voice easily carried across the street to the rambling apartment building. She tried to move out and be seen, but Jax blocked her way with his body.

"Stay covered, Doc." His gun remained pointed at the silent building.

Raze crept up on his other side, crouched low, his gun also out and aimed.

"Reverend?" Vinnie called again.

A cracked window on the bottom floor slowly slid up. "Dr. Wellington? Please step forward so I can see you."

Jax grabbed her arm when she tried. "Sorry, Lighton. The doctor is staying out of the line of fire. She can hear you just fine while being covered from your bullets."

"My bullets?" Lighton yelled. "I didn't shoot first. Your guys did."

Jax glanced at the soldiers, who quickly shook their heads. "Not true. However, what now?"

Vinnie elbowed him, and he snapped his mouth shut. "Reverend? Is anybody hurt in there?" Her first step needed to be finding any injured. Hopefully no kids had been hurt.

"Would you care? You only want to help Scorpius survivors," Lighton called.

She tried to inch forward just a little, and Raze stepped forward, his head shaking.

Fine. She'd just raise her voice. "Not true. I'm a doctor, a medical professional, and I want to help anybody who needs it. Is there anybody in your apartment building who needs medical assistance?" she called out, the hair on her neck rising.

"No." Heavy curtains covered Lighton's placement. "We just want to be left alone."

What was he, Greta Garbo? Vinnie kept her voice pleasant. "That's certainly your right, within reason, but you have to understand we have concerns. How do we know you don't have prisoners in there?"

Jax nodded.

"Everyone here wants to be here," Lighton called out.

"I'm not taking your word for that," Jax yelled. "I want a list of your people, and I want to speak with each and every one of them. Then we'll figure out if you can remain within my territory or not."

Vinnie fought the urge to punch Jax in the jaw. He wasn't helping in the slightest. "Zip your lip," she whispered.

He frowned at her.

"Reverend? We have concerns. How many citizens do you have in there?" she called.

"About seventy," he answered. "All here willingly."

Vinnie leaned closer to Jax and Raze. "You have records of everyone living in Vanguard?"

Jax nodded. "Yes. We instituted a record-keeping program right off the bat, and Sami has been in charge of take-ins since. We don't know who's been infected and who hasn't, but we know who lives in Vanguard territory."

Vinnie breathed out. "This is actually good. While we're in this standoff, do a Vanguard-wide roll call to see who's outside the fences. Then we'll know for sure who's inside, even if he's not telling the full truth. He just did us a huge favor."

"Unless not all of his members are in there." Jax turned to Tace and April. "You two find Sami and get her master list. Have her organize everyone into groups to go building by building and check people off. Don't forget the soldiers outside. There are seven square miles to check, as well as several of the vantage points outside the fence, and I think our numbers are more than five hundred. The sooner the better on this, folks." Tace and April both nodded and inched to the rear of the house before running back to headquarters.

"Now we have to think of a way to keep him talking and not doing anything crazy," Vinnie whispered. "If he's challenged, and if he's losing ground, I don't know how stable he really is. Or rather, how unstable."

"Do you think he'll order a mass suicide or something?" Jax asked, his face darkening.

Vinnie shook her head. "I don't think so, because his focus is on continuing the human race with uninfected survivors. He doesn't have illusions of a god calling him home. He wants to be king right here on earth. To do that, he needs subjects."

"Good." Jax's shoulders relaxed. "Is he smart?"

"Yes." Vinnie pushed dandelion fuzz out of her hair. The sun shone down, and sweat dotted her forehead. "I think he's very smart and charming. Charismatic."

"A smart guy would've left several of his followers in key positions outside of the fence," Jax said.

Vinnie nodded. "If this is planned, then yes, you're right. But there's a chance the shooting wasn't planned."

"Why would he lie about who shot first?" Jax asked.

It was all about perception and power. "To save face with his people. He needs them to be scared, so they follow him for safety. If you did start shooting, unprovoked, into homes where children live, then you're scary. He's their savior, and you're their threat." She needed to play into that dynamic. "Reverend? Your followers are frightened, and I'm sure you want them to feel safe."

"They feel safe behind our new walls," Lighton returned. "So long as they're away from the bacteria and the carriers, they have a chance to live a long and healthy life."

"I can't fucking believe this," Jax hissed quietly. "I have an armed camp inside Vanguard. With guns pointed out, and kids somewhere inside. How the hell did this happen?"

Vinnie swallowed. "These are scary times, and the reverend hit upon that. He's not wrong in that the uninfected are probably better off away from us. Most of them, if infected, will die. The survivors will either go insane or possibly be unable to have kids. Wouldn't you want to find a safe haven away from Scorpius if you had a chance?"

Jax frowned. "This isn't the way to do it."

"I know." She rubbed her chin. "What *is* the way to do it? I doubt most of them are soldiers, so on their own, they wouldn't be safe. We have the best chance of finding the Bunker, with Lynne's brain and research, so leaving us would be a bad idea."

"Shooting at us is a worse idea," Raze muttered.

Vinnie nodded. "Reverend? Is there a way we could reach an agreement here that everyone can live with? I understand your need to keep the uninfected away from germs, but you must understand Jax's need to make sure everyone inside is there willingly."

Silence reigned for several moments.

"All right. If you want proof, I'll send you proof," the reverend called.

The front door opened, and seven women filed out. Four were noticeably pregnant. They all had long hair and wore full skirts beneath heavy sweaters.

Jax breathed out next to her. "Shit."

Two of the women, the ones most obviously pregnant, walked up to the fence.

"I'm here of my own volition," the first one said, while the second one nodded vigorously. The remaining women stood behind them, not speaking, no expression on their faces.

Jax half-turned toward her. "I could not be more creeped out right now," he whispered.

She swallowed, and her stomach hurt. "We'd like to interview each member of your group individually. If you haven't coerced anybody, that should be all right with you, Reverend," she called out.

A whistle echoed from inside the building.

En masse, the women all turned and marched back inside without a backward glance.

"Did they just react to a whistle?" Jax snapped.

Vinnie stared at the empty front lawn of the apartment building, just beyond the fence. She had no words. "I wonder if seven has significance in his new religion." There were seven women. That probably meant something, but only the reverend could explain what.

The reverend reached out to close his window.

"Wait a minute, please," Vinnie called. "We need more than that, and you know it, Reverend. While I understand your concern regarding germs and contamination, there has to be something we can work out. There has to be somebody you trust enough to come inside and speak with your people."

"There isn't," he answered.

She stepped into the sun. Raze and Jax both tensed, crowding in. "We have to work together. You have no access to food or medicine or even weapons if you lock yourselves behind that fence. Let's negotiate. Please?" Pandering to his obvious ego was working better than any of Jax's threats, but she'd managed to get a threat or two in there. It was true. How did the reverend hope to survive by locking them all out?

Silence came from the secured area for several moments. Finally, the curtains parted again. "I'll agree to discuss the issue, but we're going to want concessions on your part as well."

Raze lifted an eyebrow, and Vinnie shook her head. She had no clue where the reverend was going. "What kind of concessions?"

"You'll see when we talk. For your liaison, we demand April Snyder, because she hasn't been infected," Lighton yelled.

Jax shook his head. "I don't think she's up to that."

"How about if I accompany April?" Vinnie called.

Raze stepped even closer to her, and the heat of his body rivaled the sun now beating down. "Absolutely not."

"You don't have a vote," Vinnie said beneath her breath.

"Oh baby. You gave me more than a vote last night, and don't think for a second you didn't," he returned.

Jax looked from one to the other. "Give me a break, you two. I have a possible hostage situation going on right now."

"Would you let Lynne go in there?" Raze shot back.

"Hell no." Jax turned his focus back to the reverend.

The curtains parted. "I'm sorry, Dr. Wellington, but you're a carrier. As much as I wish you weren't, you're a danger to my people. You may not accompany Ms. Snyder," Lighton yelled.

"Good answer," Raze muttered.

Vinnie tried to take a deep breath. Standing between Raze and Jax was like being bracketed by raging wolves barely leashed. The tension pouring from the men on either side of her sped up her heart and stole her breath. If anybody could avoid a disaster, it was her, but she needed to control the Vanguard men as much as the reverend. "Everyone just calm down. If there are hostages in there, then we need to pacify the reverend and not instigate a bigger problem."

Jax's lips flattened out. "Shadow? I'm going to need an infiltration plan that somehow takes into account the safety of children and civilians."

Raze nodded. "A sniper shot for Lighton would work, but we don't know what would happen then. What if there's a number two just waiting to take control? At least we know the name of this guy."

"Copy that." Jax wiped sweat off his forehead.

Vinnie shook her head. "Guys, we can't go in, and we can't wait them out and starve them. There are kids in there."

"With the right team, we could go in." Raze craned his neck. "But there are three buildings, so we'd need quite a force to do it. And what if some of our soldiers actually belong to the reverend?"

Vinnie took a steadying breath. "Reverend? We really want to work with you. You have no choice but to work with us, so let's figure it out. Remember, you're inside Vanguard territory."

Lighton's chuckle wafted through the stagnant day. "You think you hold all the cards."

"No, sir." Hell, not even close. There were kids and civilians in there. "We don't."

"You're right about that," Lighton said.

She closed her eyes. "I know you must have food, medicine, and weapons." He had this planned, so he would've at least obtained enough provisions to hold them for a while. "Which is good. We don't want any of your people going hungry or getting sick."

"That's not all I have," Lighton said, his voice rising just enough to give Vinnie pause.

She listened for more, but nothing came. "All right. What else do you have?"

"Well, I have all the vitamin B in our possession. We cleared out the three medical arenas earlier today."

"Fuck," Jax muttered. "Shots aren't due for a few more days. We wouldn't have even looked." He stared down at the ground, thoughts flying across his tough face. "We'll have to go in and get those. The uninfected don't even need the B. What if he just goes ahead and pours it all out?"

The hair on the back of Vinnie's neck rose. "That's not all he has. There's something in his voice . . . it's bad. I feel like it's bad. I don't know what, but that's not all." She let her voice rise. "That's quite a bold move, Reverend."

"Somewhat," he returned.

She went with her gut. "What else do you have to bargain with?" He had more than the B. She could tell.

"Well, I guess the best chip I'm holding would be Dr. Lynne Harmony. I can't believe you haven't missed her yet."

Jax flew into motion, Raze intercepted him, and both men crashed into the side of the house. Vinnie backed away as Jax fought furiously and Raze contained him.

"Stop it." Raze shook the Vanguard leader. "That's what he wants. Don't give him what he wants." Raze leaned in. "We'll get her out. Have soldiers cover the entire territory, and I'll come up with a plan. Trust me. I'm Vanguard now."

Chapter Thirty-One

*A brother made in battle is
as strong as one made in blood.*

—Dr. Franklin X. Harmony, *Philosophies*

Raze immediately took control of the situation, motioning to the soldiers. "Get backup and cover every exit. Vinnie, you keep talking. See if you can get a visual on Lynne."

Vinnie nodded.

Raze yanked Jax away from the house and got in his face. "We have to make sure she's there, and then we need a plan. We'll get her. I promise."

Jax nodded, his eyes beyond wild.

Raze motioned for a soldier to hustle over. "Keep the doctor covered, and don't let her make a move toward the house." The soldier nodded, and Raze eyed Vinnie. "Find out what Lighton wants, but stay in the shadows where he can't shoot at you. We'll be back."

Jax paused. "You're right. Let's make sure she's not in her lab." He sprang into a run.

Raze tore after Jax as he ran through Vanguard territory toward the soldier infirmary. They cleared the back door together and reached Lynne's lab. Papers were scattered haphazardly, as if she'd spent a late night reading through reports.

Jax stopped cold and shot a hand through his hair. "She's not here."

"No." There had been no reason for Lighton to lie.

"How?" Jax strode out of the room, fury coming off him like steam. "How did they get her from this room and across six blocks without anybody knowing?"

"A hidden gun to her rib cage, and she would've looked like she was out for a stroll." Raze followed him through the mess hall and toward the stairs, meeting Sami on the way in from patrolling.

She took one look at Jax's face. "What's happened?"

"Lighton took Lynne and has barricaded himself in the back corner apartments," Raze said tersely.

Sami's mouth gaped open. "We goin' in?"

Jax nodded. "Yeah. We're goin' in." He hesitated at the stairs. "Shadow?"

Raze paused, his mind reeling. He needed to leave within ten minutes to make the meeting with Greyson on time. Fear for both Maureen and Lynne nearly tore him in two.

God. What should he do? *Think, damn it.*

He settled into the moment, his mind calculating scenarios. The tattoo ached on his arm. *Vanguard.* "Let's send Grey's man back to him with a new plan. We meet tomorrow night. That gives us the next few hours to create mission parameters to reclaim Lynne without harming anybody."

"You sure?" Jax asked, his gaze remaining on the stairs.

Raze's Vanguard tattoo pounded on his arm, reminding him of his allegiance. He could negotiate more time for Maureen, but Lynne was in immediate danger. This had to work out. "I'm sure. Grey wants to negotiate, so he'll give us a night without doing anything drastic. Especially if we explain to Winter what's going on."

"Without explaining," Jax muttered.

Sami wiped a smudge off her chin. "Who's Winter?"

"Down here." Jax jogged down the stairs and filled her in on the way as Raze took up the rear.

Two guys stood guard outside a room on the far side of the gym. Jax shoved inside.

Winter was shackled to a folding chair, his hands behind his back. He slouched in the chair, his legs extended on the worn concrete. His ankles had been duct taped.

Raze sighed. "Duct tape?"

Jax shrugged.

Winter lifted an eyebrow. "You two appear a little . . . stressed."

Sami edged inside. "He's seriously good-looking—like a combination of Shamar Moore and Duane Johnson."

Winter grinned. "That's mighty kind of you."

Raze cocked his head to the side. "Who the hell are you?" Most guys would at least be sweating a bit, considering only one bare light bulb hung from the ceiling and showed dots of blood on the concrete walls.

"Damon Winter," Winter said. "I already told you my name."

One of the guards flipped a badge on a lanyard toward Jax, who caught it. He glanced down. "LAPD."

"Yep. Well, I used to be," Winter said.

Raze eyed Sami. The soldier had gone pale. "Aren't you LAPD, too?" he asked.

She nodded. "I was."

Winter frowned and studied her. "I don't recognize you."

"Did you know every LAPD officer?" she asked.

"Of course not," Winter said.

Raze frowned, his instincts humming. "We're letting you go."

Winter lifted one dark eyebrow. "Why?"

"There's an internal issue going on, and we can't meet Greyson tonight," Jax said. "Go back to your territory, and tell him we'll be there tomorrow night with Dr. Wellington. If he tries to double-cross us, or if he harms Maureen Shadow in any way, I'll blow up his entire world."

Raze drew a knife from his boot and bent to slice through the duct tape. He circled the chair and unlocked the cuffs. "I'll take it out on you," he whispered into Winter's ear.

Winter looked over his shoulder, his gaze relaxed. "Nobody wants to hurt your sister, man."

"That had better be true," Raze said. He hefted Winter from the chair. "Let's get you an escort at least through Vanguard territory." They all hustled up the stairs, and Raze handed the ex-cop off to a couple of soldiers.

Winter looked over his shoulder. "Don't make a move without the doctor, Shadow. Greyson demanded to see her, and the man doesn't bluff."

Raze didn't answer and turned to follow Jax into the conference room to a wall map of the Vanguard territory. "Sami? It's odd you didn't know each other," Jax said.

"Maybe he wasn't really LAPD," the woman said easily.

"His badge and the ID with his badge showed his picture." Jax scrutinized the map. "We'll discuss it more later. For now, we need a plan. Raze?"

Raze shook his head. "There are three buildings with multiple floors containing kids and civilians. We don't know where anybody is except for Lighton." Raze moved closer to the map. "I could take him out, but we don't know what happens next."

Sami nodded. "They might panic and hurt Lynne, or they might just panic and let her go."

Raze shook his head. "Right now, negotiation is still the best tactic. We don't know the layout or what kind of forces they have inside. Hell, we don't know anything, and it's not like we have the resources to find out."

Jax nodded. "We'll keep negotiating for now, but I need a rescue plan just in case."

Raze headed over to the weapons lockers. "We have flash grenades, tear gas, and tactical gear. If we go in, we need to hit all three buildings simultaneously."

Jax crossed his arms. "Who do we have? I mean, who's trained well enough to engage in this type of mission?"

Raze shook his head. "You, me, Sami, Tace, and about five others, I think. Byron is smart enough to catch on quickly, but ten soldiers is still a small force to take three buildings."

"What if we just took the front building?" Sami asked. "If Lighton is there, don't you think Lynne is there somewhere?"

"Probably. Let's ask Vinnie to profile him." Raze reached for a combat vest and quickly shoved grenades and extra clips in the pockets. He grabbed a piece of paper and made notes. "Jax and I will return and back up Vinnie. Sami, here's a list of who you need to gather to go in. Make sure Byron is with either Jax or me."

Jax pointed to the map. "We'll need to cut through the Vanguard perimeter fence out of sight of the buildings. Any thoughts?"

Raze nodded. He'd patrolled the fence more than any other soldier. "Yep. I know right where to breach." He forced thoughts of Winter, Greyson, and Maureen out of his mind.

One crisis at a time.

Vinnie kept her shoulder against the rough wood of the crumbling house while Jax's soldier covered her. "Reverend? I'd like proof of life for Dr. Harmony, please." If nothing else, Vinnie needed a location for the scientist. She wouldn't be able to keep Jax from going in for long, so the more intel she gleaned, the better.

"Vinnie?" Lynne called out from the open window. "I'm fine. Just having a nice chat with the reverend."

"Good." Vinnie breathed out. Thank God Lynne was all right. "So what's the deal, Reverend? What do you want?"

"I knew you'd be the sensible one," Lighton called. "My needs are very simple. We'll turn over Dr. Harmony and all of the supply of vitamin B in exchange for the contents of warehouses three and four."

"I'm unfamiliar with those warehouses," Vinnie called. She hadn't belonged to Vanguard long enough to know all the details. "What's in them?"

"Food and medical supplies," Lighton yelled. "Enough to last my people a year. During that time, we'll work within Vanguard, but we want autonomy, much like the Native American reservations used to have within the United States."

Vinnie blinked. "You're taking a huge risk trying to negotiate by taking hostages."

Lighton coughed. "Jax Mercury is a criminal, and he understands loss. This is the only way I could've gotten his attention."

Vinnie shook her head, out of sight. Lighton had created one hell of an enemy with this stunt, but first things first. "If I speak with Jax about the warehouses, will you let Lynne go?"

"Not until the provisions are inside Pure territory," Lighton yelled.

Raze and Jax suddenly came up on her side. She explained Lighton's demands to them.

Jax eyed the still curtains. "Depleting those warehouses will put the remaining Vanguard citizens in danger. We need those medical supplies and food." He craned his neck, his gaze narrowing. "Did you see Lynne?"

"No, but I heard her. She sounded all right," Vinnie said.

"Do you think he'll hurt her?" Jax asked.

Vinnie ran through what she knew of Lighton. "I think he's off-center, and this is scarier than he thought. While I don't believe he'll purposely harm her, he's on edge and may make a mistake."

"She could get caught in the crossfire if we go in," Jax said.

Raze scrubbed his face. "If we infiltrate through that isolated point to the east, I can go through the window, but I'll have to take down Lighton to do it."

A muscle ticked in Jax's jaw. "Give me your whole plan."

Raze nodded. "Vinnie keeps Lighton talking while we go around back. Ten of us infiltrate the fence. We send four to the front and back of the southern buildings just to cover the exits. You lead a team of five in through the rear entrance of the main apartment building, while I take out Lighton in the window."

Vinnie's heart rose in her throat. "Lighton is armed."

"Yeah." Raze kept his gaze on Jax. "It's risky. We can continue to negotiate, or you can hand over the provisions. Even if we hand them over, we can probably get them back once Lynne is free."

"If he sets her free," Vinnie said, her mind spinning. "She's infected, I know, but she's valuable with her medical experience and her blue heart."

"You don't think he'll let her go?" Jax asked.

Vinnie looked toward the quiet brick building. "Not unless he has to. This entire situation was planned out too well to have just happened. He's narcissistic, and he thinks he's much smarter than the rest of us. I just can't say how far he'll go."

Jax grimaced. "That's what I figured. Okay."

The group of eight jogged up from the rear of the house. Jax motioned to Raze. "Everyone behind the house for orders. Vinnie? Please keep Lighton talking as much as you can, and get a visual on Lynne if possible." He turned toward the soldiers.

Raze bent down and swept his mouth across hers. "This will be okay."

Tears pricked her eyes. What if she was wrong about Lighton? What if he wanted to kill Lynne? What if infiltrating the building got Raze or Jax or one of the other soldiers shot? "This is so up in the air," she whispered.

He kissed her harder. "It'll be okay. Settle yourself, and just talk to him. You can do it." Raze waited for her shaky nod before he turned and strode out of sight around the decrepit house.

"Reverend? I really would like to see for myself that Lynne is unharmed." Vinnie calmed her voice.

"You're welcome to scale the fence," Lighton yelled back.

"I can't talk Mercury into giving you all of his medical supplies without being able to prove that Lynne's okay." Vinnie stepped into the sunshine. "Just one glimpse."

"Sorry, but she's busy," Lighton said.

"Where is she?" Vinnie asked.

Lighton didn't answer.

Vinnie let a couple of minutes tick by. "Reverend? Do you have any other hostages?"

"Where's Jax Mercury?" Lighton called out. "It's time I started negotiating with him."

Vinnie squinted but couldn't see inside the room. "He went to check the warehouses you were interested in." That might sound like the truth. "He was concerned about the medical provisions and wanted to see what he could spare without putting the rest of us in danger."

"You have five minutes to find Jax Mercury, or I'm

going to start cutting off Blue Heart's fingers one by one and throwing them into the street."

So much for the question of whether or not he was dangerous.

Raze appeared to the left of the apartment building, on the other side of the chain-link fence. Vinnie kept her gaze straightforward on the open window. "Jax will be here in a minute," she called.

"Good," Lighton responded.

Raze crept up the side and toward the reverend's open window, staying low. He paused at the corner.

Vinnie stepped full into the sunlight. "Reverend? I know you don't want to hurt anybody. Please work with me."

The curtains didn't move.

Frustration clawed up her throat. "Besides medicine, I know where the antibacterial supplies are locked down. If you let me see Lynne, I'll add those to your pot," she said.

The curtains shifted, and Lighton came into view.

She nodded.

At her nod, Raze moved. In less than two seconds, all hell broke loose.

Chapter Thirty-Two

*In our field, we're not supposed to use
the word "crazy." Yet sometimes, the term just fits.*

—Dr. Vinnie Wellington, *Sociopaths*

Raze rolled and came up firing, hitting Reverend Lighton dead center. Lighton's eyes widened, and he fell back, blood bursting from his chest.

Without missing a beat, Raze leaped through the window face-first, slammed into a wooden floor, rolled and jumped up, gun sweeping. Nobody else was in the empty room.

Gunfire pinged from outside the room, and a woman screamed, high and loud.

Lighton stared up at the ceiling, his eyes open in death.

Raze didn't need to check for a pulse. He inched the door open, his gun ready, his body on full alert.

Another scream echoed from down the hallway.

He edged outside, trying to see through the smoke. Had Jax thrown a flash grenade? "Mercury!" he bellowed. Where the hell was everybody?

"Jax?" a female voice yelled from the next door.

Raze kicked it open and swept inside, going low.

Lynne Harmony sat bound to a chair, a pink scarf around

her hands and rope around her torso. Her green eyes glowed dark in her pale face.

Raze hustled toward her and cut the bindings. "You okay?"

She stood. "I'm fine. This building is mostly empty. The civilians are in the two other apartment buildings."

"Weapons?" Raze asked, drawing her toward the door.

"Lighton has some, and he has two soldiers also armed." Lynne stumbled, and Raze reached back to steady her. "Thanks."

Raze nudged the door open to see Mercury stomping down the hallway, his gun on a tall blond guy with a goatee. "Lynne's here. She's safe."

Jax shoved the blond man toward Raze, who pivoted and put the guy into the wall, face-first. The guy struggled, but Raze planted the barrel of his gun at the base of his neck, and he stopped moving. Smart.

Jax kept going right into Lynne and enfolded her. "You okay?" he whispered.

Her arms wrapped around his waist. "I'm fine." She peered around him toward Raze. "That's Joe Bentley. He tried to talk Lighton into letting me go."

Raze decreased the pressure of his barrel into Bentley's neck. "He wasn't successful."

Lynne stepped away from Jax. "No, but he tried. From the little I saw, he has a good grasp on the people here." She looked around, her gaze wide. "Where's Lighton? He'll come out shooting."

"He's not coming," Raze said, whipping Bentley around. "Talk."

Bentley's glasses wobbled on his thin nose. "The reverend lost it. All of a sudden, he told everyone to get to the residences. I saw Dr. Harmony, and then I saw the gun at her ribs, so I got everyone out of here." He swallowed, and his Adam's apple bobbed.

Lynne nodded vigorously. "That's true."

"Then I came back and tried to talk Lighton into letting her go and dropping the weapons." Bentley shoved his glasses into place. "I was heading out back to try to find Mercury when everything seemed to explode."

Raze stepped back and let Bentley go. "I guess you live."

Bentley's blue eyes widened. "Um, thanks."

Jax's soldiers all came into sight. He cleared his throat. "Bentley? I want a list of every member of your congregation. Tace? Get a crew and take down the fence around this place."

Bentley held up a hand. "Wait a minute. I don't agree with Lighton's methods, but we do want to remain separate for our own safety. We have pregnant women who will lose their babies if they're infected."

Jax breathed out. He studied Bentley. "It looks like you're the new leader of Pure, and I'm fine with that, but no fence. It comes down."

Bentley opened his mouth to argue, and Raze stepped in again. Bentley's lips closed.

Jax tugged Lynne to his side. "We can discuss the situation, and I won't force your people in proximity with survivors, but there's a lot of work to do before we're all on the same page. Talk to your people, and make sure they understand that they'll each be interviewed, alone, within the next week. After that, we'll figure things out."

Bentley nodded.

"For now, bring that fence down," Jax ordered.

Tace turned and motioned for a couple of the soldiers to follow him.

Jax pulled Lynne toward the hallway. "Let's get out of here and come up with a plan to deal with these people. Tomorrow night, after we get your sister back, Raze."

Raze breathed in, for the first time in way too long, not feeling alone. "I like having the extra night to plan."

Jax grimaced as they walked into the bright sun. "I agree, but I wouldn't have minded a few hours with Damon Winter to get some information about Merc territory. As it is, we're going in blind."

Raze looked around at the smoky hallway. "Not our first time."

Jax shook his head. "Good point." He strode across the weeds and dropped a kiss on Lynne's head.

Tace was already using wire cutters to destroy the fence, and they slid through.

Vinnie ran up and flew into Raze's chest. He wrapped his arms around her, breathing in the scent of calla lilies. "I'm okay," he murmured, rubbing his chin on top of her head. "So is Lynne. Almost everyone is okay."

Jax paused. "Tace? Set troops on the fence. We need somebody to . . ."

Tace looked up, his pupils narrowing. "Ah. Yeah, okay. I'll take care of Lighton." He tossed the cutters to one of the soldiers and turned to head back inside.

Raze paused. "I'll help." Considering he'd shot Lighton, he should help to clean up the mess.

Tace waved over his shoulder. "I don't need help. Go figure out a plan for us tomorrow night. I want in, and nobody is going to keep me out this time, medic or not." He kept talking as he entered the building, and his voice faded slowly.

"He's talking to himself," Jax said slowly, his brow furrowing.

"Most of us do," Vinnie said, her gaze somber. "I'm sorry, Raze."

He blinked. "Huh?"

"Sorry you had to . . ."

Ah. He pulled her into his side. "It's my job, sweetheart. I'm sorry we had to get you involved." The pretty shrink shouldn't have to occupy sociopaths and stand in danger while he did his job. They'd have to work on that later. For now, he wanted her away from the area.

Jax must've been of like mind, because he was all but dragging Lynne through the empty streets, past the showers, and into the main headquarters building. "How many people did you see there?" he asked, dropping into a chair in the mess hall.

She shrugged and sat. "Not many. The main apartment building is serving as a kind of corporate headquarters for the Pure. Or at least, it was."

Vinnie trooped along at Raze's side, her pallor still a little alarming.

"Bentley seems like a nice guy," Jax said. "You're sure he tried to convince Lighton to let you go?"

Lynne nodded. "Yeah. He was mostly worried about the Pure."

Vinnie pressed a hand to her stomach. "I wouldn't mind interviewing him later this week. Just to get a feeling for him."

"You got it, Doc," Jax said. "For now, we should all eat. Then we'll come up with a plan to infiltrate Mercenary territory." He stepped in front of Raze and grabbed him for a hard hug. "I owe you."

Raze smacked his back and moved away. "It's all good."

Jax shook his head, his dark eyes swirling with emotion. "No. You put off your mission for Lynne, and then you went through a window. My loyalty is yours."

Raze nodded, his chest filling. That meant something. "Ditto."

Jax settled. "Winter said that the doc has to come, and it's your call if she does or not."

Raze lost his appetite. The plan he'd come up with before Winter had shown had included Vinnie staying nice and safe in Vanguard territory. The woman wasn't bait, damn it. He'd die for either his sister or for Vinnie, and this mission would put both of their lives on the line.

There had to be another way.

"President Atherton?" Lake's voice carried through the mansion with more excitement than Bret had ever heard from him.

"Just a second." Bret rolled off the blonde and ignored her murmur of protest. The secretary had long legs and nice tits, and she didn't talk too much. He gave her a smile as he stood next to the bed. "I have work, but we can continue this later."

She stretched in the large bed and nodded, covering a yawn with her hand.

"So get back to work," he said, pulling on his jeans and shirt.

Her glare was kind of pretty as she huffed from the bed.

If the woman thought fucking him would get her anything other than a couple of orgasms, she'd sorely misread him. In fact, she was just a temporary indulgence and apparently didn't know it. Maybe he should find his fun elsewhere.

There was a time he couldn't get it up without thinking of Lynne Harmony. Thank God that time was over.

Finished dressing, he forgot all about the blonde in bed and exited the bedroom, startled at finding Lake right outside. "You okay?"

Lake nodded his buzz-cut head. "Yes. We intercepted a Mercenary scout earlier this morning, and it looks like there's going to be a meeting between the Mercs and Vanguard later tonight."

Bret finished tucking in his shirt. "Sound like a setup?"

"No, sir." Lake's startling blue eyes darkened. "It took three hours of persuasion to get the scout to say a word. This is real, and it's happening."

Bret nodded. "That is excellent. What is the meeting?"

"The scout seemed to believe that there was going to be an exchange of Vivienne Wellington for Raze Shadow's sister." Lake kept at perfect attention, even in the hallway.

"What do you think?"

"Don't know." Lake frowned. "But I know how badly you want Vivienne Wellington back, so we should create a plan."

Bret's entire body hardened at the thought of having the profiler in shackles again. This time, oh this time, he'd use her. In every way possible. He smiled. "Fate is finally smiling on us again." He turned and loped down the hallway. "I've never created a torture room before." There was a shed on the other side of the property that had held rather interesting tools.

He rubbed his hands together. "Can't wait to see you, Doctor Wellington."

Vinnie finished rubbing lotion into her arms and nearly groaned at the decadence. A scouting party had found a whole box of lotion and toiletries on that morning's mission, and one of the women had tossed Vinnie a tube after dinner.

The sense of belonging felt even better than the lotion.

The door opened, and Raze walked in. He'd stopped even pretending he was going to bunk with Tace and had even started mixing his clothes up with hers. Though he'd acted fine with his decision to kill Reverend Lighton, shadows darkened his eyes, and a vein bulged in his neck.

He felt the pain of causing death, even if he wouldn't admit it.

She smiled and pushed off the sofa.

He lifted his head and sniffed the air. "What is that?"

She smiled and held out the tube. "Lotion. Real lotion. Can you believe it?"

He lifted an eyebrow. "No?"

She shook her head. "It's a miracle. The world right now smells like roses."

"I prefer calla lilies," he said, dropping his bulletproof vest on the chair.

"Um, okay." She fought the urge to go to him, although the need to soothe him dug deep and took hold. They hadn't had the talk. The other night had been intense—incredibly so—and something had shifted inside her for him. For them. But she didn't know how he felt, and considering he was worried to death about his sister, now didn't seem to be the time to talk about it.

"What in the world is going through your head?" he rumbled, setting his guns and knives on top of the fridge.

She swallowed. "Nothing. Just thinking about the mission." Yeah, she was a total chicken.

"I still think you should stay here," he said, turning around, sans any weapons. Well, any metal weapons. The guy was a weapon himself, now wasn't he? He sure moved like one.

She shook her head. "My staying here would just exacerbate the problem. Only I can convince Greyson Storm that I have no clue where Zach Barter is, you know? The president didn't even know. Once Greyson has the truth, once he sees it in my eyes, he'll let your sister go."

"Maybe."

"And if he doesn't, then we'll go with plan B. My presence is necessary to lull him into our trap." She sounded like a Bond villain, for goodness' sake. "I know we're going on instinct here, but I think he'll work with us. He'd make an excellent ally against the president."

Raze nodded. "What else were you thinking about?"

She blinked. "Huh?"

"You have the worst poker face I've ever seen," he murmured, tension rolling off him.

"God, he's a hottie." Lucinda popped out of the fridge.

Vinnie gasped and took a step back. She quickly recovered and smoothed down her jeans.

Raze frowned. "What the hell?"

"Although I don't like his potty mouth," Lucinda muttered, waving a sparkling wand around. "Look. I'm the good witch."

Vinnie pressed her lips together. Her chest started to ache. It had been a couple of days since Lucinda had appeared, and she'd let herself believe she'd healed. That the damage to her brain had somehow gotten better. "Nothing. Just jumpy, I guess."

Raze looked toward the fridge. "You seeing people again?"

Vinnie's shoulders hunched. "Yes."

He looked back toward her. "That's okay. At least you know it's a hallucination, right?"

She nodded.

"Well, then, you know the difference between reality and fantasy," he said, kicking off his boots.

"For now." At some point, what if she lost that distinction? Hell. What if she wasn't even talking to Raze right now? He could be downstairs with Jax, still coming up with a plan, and she might be—

"Vinnie." He studied her. "Get out of your head, baby. You're gonna be okay. I promise."

"I may be psychic. With all the brain tweaks, I may actually be able to read the thoughts or emotions of other people." She had to share that fact with somebody.

His eyebrows went up. "Interesting. We'll have to explore that later."

His acceptance of her oddities warmed her throughout. "Where are we?" she blurted out.

He straightened. "You, ah, don't know where we are? In Vanguard territory?"

Heat flushed up her neck and into her face, making her cheeks burn. "Of course I know where we are. What I meant to ask, even though it's really bad timing, is where are we? It's odd, and I know we have to save your sister, but last night, something changed for me, and I was wondering if it changed for you. Not a huge change, but more like a shift. You know, the—"

"Vinnie." He stepped into her and cupped her cheeks. "My entire life shifted the second I carried you out of that storage room in Las Vegas last week."

Well. now. If that wasn't the sweetest statement ever. "For the better?"

He chuckled. "Yeah. For the better." He leaned down and caught her mouth, his lips gentle and firm. The kiss went from slow burn to flash fire, and he wrapped an arm around her waist, pulling her into the long contours of his hard body.

She closed her eyes and allowed herself just to feel. A few moments of forgetting reality wouldn't hurt anything.

The kiss went on, and he smoothly removed her shirt.

Her eyelids flew open, and she glanced toward the kitchen. Lucinda had taken off. Good.

Vinnie stepped in and grabbed the hem of his shirt, struggling to get it over his head. He ducked to help her out.

The next day would bring fear and possibly pain, but tonight, they had this. They had each other, and she was going to show him what that meant. Words rambled together for her, but when he touched her, she settled. The entire world calmed and once again made sense.

She leaned in and kissed his strong torso. His heart beat steadily beneath her mouth, and she stretched up on her toes to kiss the strong column of his neck. "I'm so glad you found me."

He tangled his hand in her hair and drew her head back.

Those glorious eyes had turned the color of a magical moonlight, deep and blue. "Me too."

Neither one of them pretended they were talking about Las Vegas.

He bent and lifted her, carrying her easily toward the bed. Her pants hit the floor, and soon his joined them. He sprawled out on top of her, warming her from head to toe.

Her breath caught at the look in his eyes.

Strong and absolute . . . and for her. That look was for her and her only. "Raze," she murmured, running her fingers through his hair.

He nodded. "Yeah." Then he leaned down and kissed her again, so much emotion in the taste, tears sprang to her eyes.

Somehow he rolled on a condom, and then he was pushing inside her, filling her almost too full. He took his time, staking more than his claim, each inch a testament to a hopeful tomorrow.

Finally, he paused, his body fully embedded in hers.

He smoothed the hair away from her face and placed gentle kisses on her nose, her chin, and her mouth. "You have to stay safe tomorrow. I need you."

The words, such simple words from such a strong man, wrapped around her heart and warmed her forever. She opened her mouth to reply, and his descended, cutting off her breath and then her thoughts.

As he kissed her, as he held her, he began to thrust, taking her high and hot. Her thighs trembled, and she clasped her ankles at the small of his back.

He pounded harder, his kiss never losing strength, his body protecting hers.

Energy flushed through her, winding out, and her body arched in an orgasm so strong, she forgot how to breathe. She was just coming down when he ground against her, his body shuddering.

Tears slid down her cheeks.

He kissed them away, a brutal man showing such incredible gentleness.

Her heart burst, way too full.

Tomorrow, they'd go on a mission against an unknown enemy. What if she was wrong, and Greyson was more dangerous than she'd thought? Doubts about her sanity and ability to think clearly assailed her.

This might be their last night together.

Raze ditched the condom and rolled her over, spooning his big body around her. Warmth and security wafted around, providing shelter in a world gone dark and lonely. "It's not too late to back out," he murmured sleepily at her ear.

She blinked, staring at the far wall, her body thrumming in contentment while her mind rolled with reality. For the first time since Scorpius had blanketed the world, she had found her place in it. With a soldier, a complex fighter, a man she'd need a lifetime to truly know.

He was giving her a chance to protect herself and wait at home for him. But his best chance for survival was to work with her.

She shook her head, her hair winding across his arm. "No. It's much too late to back out."

Once again, neither one of them pretended she was talking about anything other than the two of them. They were bound together, no matter what, and the thought kept her awake for a very long time.

She couldn't lose him just as she'd finally found him.

Chapter Thirty-Three

Trust is the ultimate leap of faith.

—Dr. Vinnie Wellington, *Perceptions*

"This is an interesting development," Vinnie murmured, her gaze on three well-worn dune buggies.

Raze nodded, his lips tipping with humorless determination. "Yeah. Greyson is expecting us to approach through the university streets, and these will take him somewhat by surprise."

Vinnie pointed to the big missile things mounted on top of each buggy. "If not, those will."

"Bazookas." Now Raze did smile, but it was more chilling than reassuring.

"Ah." The sun was slowly going down over the Pacific. After a day of going over the plan and of training with weapons, they'd finally set out, driving through crumbling neighborhoods to the south of Merc territory. The beach stretched on in each direction, white, sandy, and empty. "Where'd we get the dune buggies?"

"We've had scouts looking for some since we first discovered the location of the Mercenary camp," Jax said, jogging up beside them. "Each one is supposed to have helmets, which will protect not only your head but your eyes from the sand. Can't provide any protection from bullets except for the vests you're already wearing."

The heaviness of the vests was a constant reminder of the danger they courted.

Raze frowned. "You don't have to come with us."

She rolled her eyes. "I'm a trained FBI profiler with some negotiation experience. For Pete's sake. We have *bazookas*." Apparently there was a reason the Vanguard leader kept his warehouses locked and guarded. Who knew what else Jax had hidden away?

Raze jerked his head at Jax. "Let's just keep in mind that we don't want to blow up my sister."

Jax nodded. "Copy that."

"They'll have the beach secured," Raze said.

"Not as well as the streets," Jax said. "Teams of two. You and Vinnie, Tace and Sami, Me and Byron. If this goes south, that's all the casualties we can afford."

Byron swallowed and looked younger than his seventeen years. He jerked a fluorescent helmet over his head.

Vinnie tried to give him an encouraging smile, but her lips trembled. Perhaps bringing a teenager had been a bad idea, but Jax seemed to be grooming the kid for a top position in Vanguard.

Stay safe, she mouthed.

Byron nodded, his brown eyes serious. "The lights are amped. I hate to waste them, but we'll need to make a statement without using the weaponry. If they shoot at the lights, we have a decision to make."

"Nobody returns fire unless I order it," Jax said tersely.

"They won't be expecting us from the beach," Raze said. "Surprise is our best option. We'll have to put the guards down."

Jax nodded. "Affirmative. Let's try to keep them alive because we hope to negotiate."

"I'll do my best." Raze reached past the bars for a helmet

to toss to Vinnie. "Put it on." She gave him a look but tucked it over her head. It smelled like salt and sea, which wasn't so bad. She took Raze's hand and stepped into the buggy, allowing him to secure all the buckles across her chest.

"They'll see us coming," Jax said, squinting down the beach.

"Hopefully they won't shoot." Raze slid inside the buggy. "Let's get this over with."

Jax nodded and ran for the other vehicle.

Vinnie glanced at Raze. "Helmet?" Her voice came out tinny in the helmet.

He shook his head and slid protective glasses over his eyes, his gun already in one hand. "Hold on." He turned the engine over, and the three vehicles drew closer together and began spinning down the beach.

If they hadn't been heading for a showdown to meet a kidnapper, it might've been fun. The buggy bounced over dunes, throwing sand. Vinnie clutched the padded bars, her stomach spinning. Each dip and fall jarred her entire body, and soon her lower back began to ache.

After about thirty minutes of riding, Jax gave some weird hand signal. Byron gripped the bars next to him, his face looking pale through the helmet's visor.

Vinnie tapped Raze's arm and tried to focus on his face.

"Merc territory," he yelled.

Her heart just dropped. The sun had disappeared, and only a thin strip of pink remained across the still-light blue sky. Dusk was already falling and soon would take over the heavens.

A man ran out from behind a rock wall, and Jax turned his buggy, heading right for the guy. The vehicle hit the man, throwing him up and over the roll bar. Raze swung around and was flying out of his seat before his buggy completely stopped. The forced stop threw Vinnie against her restraints, and she cried out, her chest blooming in pain.

Raze reached the guy and punched him in the face three times. The guy slumped to the beach, out cold.

Vinnie gaped and drew off her helmet.

Blood had sprayed across Raze's shirt, and a couple of drops marred his chin. His eyes went beyond cold to merciless. He didn't speak as he jumped back inside the buggy and turned it around, heading north again.

Vinnie held tight to her helmet, her pulse ticking so fast her veins ached. She blinked against flying sand but couldn't make herself put the helmet back on.

They encountered three more soldiers, and the element of surprise and a quick attack took care of each of them. One did get off a shot, but it ricocheted harmlessly against a fender. They left the downed guards on the beach, figuring at some point they'd wake up and walk it off.

Finally, Raze tensed next to her and tossed his eyeglasses to the sand. "Remember the plan?" he yelled.

She dropped her helmet to the ground. Both hands went to the restraints, and she paused, waiting for the signal.

Jax drove up on the left, and Tace on the right. Almost in slow motion, as if they'd choreographed it, all three vehicles turned and came to a complete stop, facing a sprawling brown beach bungalow.

Vinnie ripped open her seat belt and jumped out of the buggy, running to the rear to duck down out of sight. She took her gun from where it had been strapped to her leg, disengaged the safety, and drew several deep breaths. She edged to the side and craned her neck to see what was happening.

Lights set atop the roll bars flipped on and flooded the beach house, illuminating a fire pit surrounded by empty chairs.

Then they waited. And waited.

Raze, Jax, and Tace stood to the side of their vehicles,

guns out, near the loaded bazookas. Sami and Byron covered the rear, just like Vinnie.

Finally, Greyson Storm stepped out from the building, his hand wrapped around the bicep of a petite woman. Even from a distance, her blue eyes were recognizable as similar to Raze's. "This is a nice surprise," the man said, his voice easily carrying over the sand and surf. "Are those bazookas?"

"Yes," Raze snapped back. "Moe? You okay?"

Guns suddenly emerged from every window, from the rooftop, and from around the house. At least two dozen barrels all pointed at Raze.

"I'm fine, Raze." Moe held perfectly still, no doubt wanting to keep things from escalating. "Dune buggies, huh?"

"Let my sister go, Grey." Raze settled his stance, and sand sprayed.

"Where's the doctor?" Greyson asked.

Vinnie faltered and then stepped forward. "I'm right here. Let Maureen go, and I'm happy to speak with you as long as you like."

Raze stiffened even further. "Get back down."

"No. This is what I do." She moved up next to him. "You don't want to hurt anybody, do you, Greyson?"

The massive man cocked his head to the side. "I wouldn't mind hurting the asshats who have bazookas pointed at my home, Dr. Wellington. However, I have no desire to harm either you or Maureen Shadow, if that's what you're asking."

Well, it was sort of what she'd been asking. She stepped up to Raze's side. "How about we meet in the middle? You and Maureen meet with Raze and me? We can have a nice chat with all these guns trained on us."

"And bazookas," Greyson said wryly.

"Yes," Vinnie said.

Greyson apparently gave the idea some consideration.

"No guns. Drop yours, Shadow." As they watched, Greyson removed a gun from his waistband and set it on a table.

Vinnie nodded at Raze. "That's a good sign," she whispered.

Raze cut her a look but took his guns out to place them on the buggy seat. "Not giving up my knives," he muttered under his breath.

Vinnie set her gun on the seat and then slipped her hand through Raze's arm. "Let's go." She sank into the soft sand, trying to maneuver Raze toward the middle of the beach.

He smoothly set her partially behind him and led the way. "If anybody shoots, you duck and cover," he ordered.

"Okay," she whispered.

Greyson and Maureen moved off the porch and onto the sand, Greyson keeping his hand around Moe's arm. The couples walked toward each other like some weird beach-bum square dance.

Finally, they met in the middle. Vinnie nodded to Moe. "Hi."

Raze reached out and tugged his sister's hair, his gaze intense and more than a little pissed. "You okay, wild one?"

She nodded. "I am. Nobody hurt me, Raze."

"It's so nice to see you two together. I mean, Raze is all man, but I can see him in your face. Or your face in his. I mean, you're very feminine, but it's cool too—" Vinnie blurted out. She slapped her hand over her mouth. Now wasn't the time to start talking endlessly.

Maureen's eyes widened. "Let's relax. We're all on the same side. Well, kind of."

Raze kept his gaze on Greyson. The two men stood about the same height, both wearing threatening expressions.

Greyson lowered his chin. "Dr. Wellington? Where is Zach Barter?"

Vinnie shook her head. "Why do you think I know?"

"My intel reports he's at the Bunker, and you know where that is." Greyson took a small step toward her, and Raze growled.

Growled? Vinnie frowned at him. "Knock it off. I said we'd talk as long as he needs. Listen, Greyson." She put on her most serene expression while her twitching legs longed to run away from all the guns. "I don't know where the Bunker is."

"You chased the initial Scorpius sociopaths, right?" Greyson asked.

"Yes." Vinnie tried to listen for the soldiers behind her. They seemed to be holding tight. Good.

"You caught some," Greyson said.

She nodded.

"They were sent to the Bunker," he added.

She shook her head. "No. They were sent to jails to await trial. Nobody had heard of the Bunker at that point. At least none of my contacts in the FBI ever mentioned the Bunker to me."

Greyson sighed. "Then you spent a few weeks with President Atherton in Vegas, right?"

"Yeah, but he wanted information about the Bunker, too. He thought I was psychic and could tell him. I'm not and I didn't." She lifted her hands. "I'm really sorry, but I don't have the information you want."

Maureen snorted. "You kidnapped me for nothing. Serves you right."

Greyson studied Vinnie, not saying a word. She let him. After a while, he sighed. "You really don't know."

"No, but I'm hoping we'll find out soon," she said. "We're looking for it, same as you. I know we can work together here and form some sort of alliance."

Greyson leveled a look at Raze. "I'll consider an alliance,

but right now we seem to have a problem. Your doctor doesn't do me much good, and your sister does. She stays."

Raze stiffened. "Not a chance in hell."

There was a moment of tense silence. Without warning, the Mercenary beach headquarters exploded out in a massive fireball, throwing debris and bodies across the sand.

Chapter Thirty-Four

*I think anybody willing to put their thoughts
to paper is a little bit nutty.*

—Dr. Vinnie Wellington, *Perceptions*

Raze reacted instantly, going for both Vinnie and Maureen.
Greyson beat him to Maureen, tackling her to the ground
and covering her with his body. Raze flattened himself over
Vinnie as several more explosions rocked the beach.

Gunfire echoed from every direction. Fuck.

Greyson rolled and all but tossed Maureen, still on
her hands and knees, at Raze. "Cover her," the Merc leader
bellowed, turning and running full bore for the burning
house. A man careened outside, his body on fire, his
screams shrill. Greyson lunged at him and took him down,
patting out the flames with his hands.

Raze grabbed Moe by the scruff of her neck while half-
lifting Vinnie and shoved them both against the dune buggy.
He turned to see Jax exchanging fire with several men
coming out of the water.

What the holy hell? Raze squinted. Boats. Rubber boats.

The night seemed to slow, and he focused. Threats in
front and behind him. To the sides, he wasn't sure. There

were Mercs out there, as well as this new attacker, and none of them were on his side. Only one thing to do. He lifted Vinnie into the dune buggy and then did the same with Moe, handing her his gun. "Vinnie, drive south to where we left the trucks. Moe, fire at anybody who moves, and keep firing."

Both women opened their mouths to argue, and he held up a hand. "We're trained for this and you're not. If you're here, I'm not concentrating. Go. Now."

Vinnie gave him one last look and pressed her foot on the pedal. The vehicle whizzed around, and she punched it.

Two men in black gave chase along the beach, and one started firing toward the women.

Raze shot him between the eyes and then took the other guy out with a neck shot. Jax slammed his back against Raze's. "What the hell?"

"New player." Raze eyed Sami and Tace as they ducked behind a dune buggy and fired at any advancing soldiers. Byron lay on the ground. "Byron's down." He jumped into spraying bullets and grabbed the kid, dragging him between the two remaining buggies. Jax covered him, spraying fire.

Sami took a hit to the shoulder and fell back with a sharp cry. Tace pivoted and took the shooter out before dropping. "Sami." He yanked off his belt and tied it around her upper arm. "Hold still."

Tears streaked down her dirty face, but she shoved him away and turned, her gun out.

Three more explosions blew nearby houses to the heavens.

"Cover," Raze yelled at Jax as he ran his hands over Byron's body. Blood marred the kid's temple, and Raze turned his head to the side. "Looks like a graze." But to the temple? Might be bad. He stood and immediately fired toward the water. His gaze ran the beach, and in the far distance, he caught sight of the dune buggy ripping wildly along. A rubber boat, its motor revving, followed on the water.

"Hurry up," he muttered, his gaze on the two women.

The buggy jumped over a dune and slid sideways. Vinnie corrected quickly, getting back on track.

The driver of the boat floored it, passing the buggy and moving quickly south on the water.

No, no, no. Raze partially stood.

The boat turned, cutting through the water and up the sand. Three men jumped out as if they'd practiced the maneuver a hundred times, running for the buggy, firing.

Vinnie jerked the wheel, and the vehicle flipped in the sand, going end over end.

Raze's gut dropped. Had they had time to put on the belts? No bodies went flying, but he couldn't see.

The men from the boat grabbed both women, carrying them into the boat.

Panic ripped down his throat. He jumped across the buggy and started running full bore, yelling at the top of his lungs.

A bullet whizzed by his head, but he didn't slow down. He had to get to Vinnie and Moe before that boat took off. Pain exploded in his upper arm, but he didn't stop.

More bullets.

A hard body tackled him to the sand, and he came up swinging.

"Get down!" Greyson yelled, tackling him again. He lifted his head and started firing toward the water.

Raze shoved him off and rolled over, firing from behind a slight mound of sand. He took two guys down. The roar of the boat motor echoed over the water, and the guys in black drove out and away.

He watched them, his chest imploding. The other two boats turned back to sea.

Bodies littered the beach. Some attackers in black, and some of the Mercs. Raze turned his head to the side.

Greyson Storm watched the retreating boats, fury darkening his face, promise lowering his chin. "We'll get them back. I swear to God, we'll get Moe and the doctor back."

"I should kill you right now." Raze turned and pressed his gun to Greyson's temple.

Grey turned, his gaze determined. "Kill me after we get them back. I have resources you need."

Fire crackled in the background, burning down Merc territory. Jax stomped over, blood flowing down his left arm. "You okay?"

"No." Raze rolled and stood, as did Greyson. "Who the hell was that?" Had they just wanted women, or had they targeted those two? Or one of those two? "How are we even going to know where to look?" His gut hurt so bad he wanted to puke.

Jax's jaw clenched. "I recognized one of the guys. Vice President Lake."

"What?" Greyson snapped.

Raze drew in air. "The president has them."

Vinnie tried unsuccessfully to free her wrists from the ropes while Maureen did the same, sitting across the truck bed from her. After the quick boat ride, they'd been locked in the back of a small moving truck. "Are you all right?" Vinnie asked, her entire body aching.

"Yeah. I hit my shoulder when we rolled, but I think it's just bruised." Moe kicked her legs out and eyed the door. "I bet the lock is good."

"I'm sure it's solid." Vinnie coughed. "Did you hear what they said?"

"That they're taking us to the president?" Moe nodded. "That's bad, right? I've heard rumors, but you never know what's true anymore."

"It's true." Vinnie swallowed down bile. "Atherton is crazy with a sociopathic mean streak."

Moe tapped her head against the wall. "Wonderful. Just great." Tears filled her eyes. "Right now, Vanguard and the Mercenaries are trying to kill each other and probably don't even know we're gone."

"Maybe they'll work together," Vinnie said softly. "I saw Greyson Storm tackle you and protect you from the explosion."

"I'm an asset to him," Moe said dully. "You have no idea how they treat women there."

Vinnie sucked in air. "Oh God, I'm so sorry. I didn't know. Are you okay? We—"

Maureen held up a hand. "Geez. I'm fine. Nobody hurt me."

Vinnie frowned. "Um, okay."

"A few days ago, there were three teenage girls, and they were scared and wanted shelter. I heard a couple of the guys making jokes about what to do with them, and then they just disappeared. I don't know what happened to them." Pain etched into Moe's face.

Vinnie gave up on the rope. "Three girls? Two blonds and a redhead?"

Moe jerked her head. "I just saw them for a minute, but yeah, that sounds right. How did you know?"

The truck bounced, and Vinnie scrambled to keep her balance. "They showed up outside of the Vanguard fence a few days ago, looking for help. Some guy in a truck dropped them off and left. We took them in, and they hadn't been harmed."

Maureen's mouth dropped open and then shut. Her gaze turned thoughtful. "Interesting."

Vinnie leaned forward. "The Mercs have a bad reputation, but have you seen anything bad happen? Really?"

"No." Maureen twisted her wrists, but the ropes appeared secure. "Doesn't mean something bad hasn't happened, though."

"True. Although, I can see Greyson being pretty pissed his headquarters got blown up and wanting revenge. Maybe he'll work with Raze and Vanguard for that reason alone." Vinnie scrambled up on her knees and tried to bounce to the back door. Pain rippled up her legs. "Though we have to find a way out of here first." She didn't want to scare Maureen, but President Atherton liked to inflict pain.

Moe nodded and pushed herself backward with her legs until her shoulders hit the door. She struggled to stand.

Vinnie did the same and tried to turn the knob with her bound hands. Nothing.

The truck hit another bump, and they both went flying. Vinnie landed on her side, and pain ripped through her ribs. Maureen sprawled next to her, swearing up a storm. They both shoved themselves to seated positions again.

"We have to get free," Vinnie whispered.

"We will." Maureen nodded. "You really don't know where the Bunker is?"

"No. No clue." Vinnie scratched her chin on her shoulder. "Did anything, um, ah, happen between you and Greyson?"

Moe's eyes widened. "God no. He kidnapped me."

"Yeah. That's true." Vinnie cleared her throat. "It's just, when the world blew up, his first reaction was to cover you."

Pink tinged Moe's face. "My brother covered you."

"He aimed for both of us," Vinnie returned.

Maureen studied her. "Is there something going on between you and my brother?"

What an odd time to have this conversation. "Yes."

"Wow."

Vinnie half-shrugged and then winced when her shoulder pulled.

The truck took a series of turns.

Vinnie's breath caught.

"We'll stop for the night to avoid Rippers," Maureen whispered. "They probably have a secured location."

Vinnie nodded.

"Don't worry. The president won't be there. I'm sure he's wherever their main headquarters is," Moe said.

Vinnie shook her head. "No. He wouldn't have fought on the beach, but he'd definitely want to be at the next location. It's who he is." God, she couldn't face him again. Her time with Atherton was still a drugged blur, and she couldn't bear to repeat it. She'd been tied and shackled like an animal. She swallowed.

"It's okay," Maureen whispered. "I promise. I'm here for you."

The truck stopped, something creaked, the vehicle moved again, and then the engine was cut.

Vinnie fought the urge to crab walk to the far wall and scramble away from the door. Instead, she forced herself to stand.

The door opened, and Vice President Lake stood in muted lantern light. He'd kept his blond hair buzz-cut short, and his blue eyes were the coldest things she'd ever seen. "Dr. Wellington. How nice to have you with us again."

Fear careened through her entire body. "I could've gone forever without seeing you again," she snapped, her chin up.

He smiled. "Get out of the truck."

She moved toward him, her skin crawling when he lifted her down to a cement floor. A garage door slowly closed next to them. Lake reached for Moe and set her next to Vinnie. "Let's go inside, shall we?" He gestured the way, as if inviting them to tea.

Vinnie's knees shook, but she strode ahead and entered a kitchen decorated with tons of birdhouses.

President Bret Atherton leaned against a cheery blue counter, using a knife to cut into an apple. His thick hair had grown to his collar, and he filled out his button-down shirt with streamlined strength. His hard-cut jaw ticked, and he smiled. "Ah, Dr. Wellington. I have more drugs for you."

Chapter Thirty-Five

━━━◉◎◉━━━

Evil can exist on its own without
any medical diagnosis. I know it's true.

—Dr. Vinnie Wellington, *Sociopaths*

Vinnie couldn't breathe. She locked her legs to keep from falling. Bret Atherton was in front of her.

Maureen stepped forward to partially block her. "So you're the president."

Bret nodded and looked Maureen up and down. "You're pretty, but I don't need pretty right now." He looked beyond her to Lake. "Take her out front and shoot her in the head. Dump her body close to the beach. That should keep anybody following us very busy."

Lake grabbed Moe's arm.

She jerked away.

"Wait," Vinnie said, panic clawing down her throat. "This is Maureen Shadow, one of the foremost agricultural experts in the world. She has food sources and knows how to splice genes to make more. She's famous, Bret."

The president's gaze narrowed on Moe. "We do need food."

Vinnie nodded. Should she say that Maureen was sister to one of the top Vanguard lieutenants and would make a good bargaining chip? Would that keep Maureen alive? Or would Bret kill her to distract the Vanguard gang? It was too much of a risk to say anything else, especially because he seemed to be considering Moe's skills. "We definitely will need food to survive," she said.

"Is that all true?" Bret asked.

Maureen shrugged. "Simplistically put, yes. I study crops, soil, and how to increase yields. And yes, I can splice and dice and create supercrops if needed."

Bret cut into his apple.

Vinnie flinched.

He smiled. "I didn't get the chance to know you last time like I want to this time." He leaned in. "I was enamored of another woman and couldn't take the time to appreciate Vivienne here." He frowned. "How is my ex?"

Vinnie swallowed.

Bret twirled the knife around. "Start talking, or I stab your friend."

"Lynne is fine but would be better with a working lab." Vinnie tried to focus on the sociopath. "Do you have a working lab? I mean, have you found the Bunker?"

His nostrils flared, and a dark gleam filled his eyes. "Not yet. But this time you're going to tap into your psychic abilities, and we're going to find it together." He flashed sharp teeth. "I can motivate you better than last time, I think. You seem to like the farmer next to you. I'll cut pieces off her until you find the Bunker for me." He ate a piece of apple off the knife and chewed, his gaze turning thoughtful. "That's what was wrong last time. No motivation."

Lake shoved Vinnie between the shoulder blades, and she stumbled forward. "Where do you want them?" Lake asked.

Bret frowned. "Let's go into the living room and chat."

Vinnie looked around what had been a high-end suburban home. "Where are we?"

"Safe house for the night," Bret answered, leading the way into an enormous great room with vaulted ceilings and expensive leather furniture. "We'll head out at first light for my west coast headquarters. You'll like it there. Maybe." He sat and smoothed down his dark jeans.

Vinnie sat next to Moe on a matching sofa. "Have you been able to reorganize the military yet?" she asked, trying to keep off the topic of torturing Maureen.

Bret's lips flattened. "Slow to get back on track, but we're getting closer. My elite force now heads up the four branches of the military, which all answer to me. I've had a little trouble locating the Brigade, but I'll find them soon." His gaze moved around.

Moe rubbed her bound hands on her jeans. "Wasn't the Brigade the first line of defense against Scorpius? Didn't they head out to vulnerable spots like nuclear plants to try to get things under control?"

"Yes." Bret sniffed. "We lost touch, and I think they might've gone rogue. Or been eaten by Rippers." The last possibility seemed to cheer him. "There's also a chance they found the Bunker."

Moe tugged on her restraints again. "How is it possible you don't know the location of the Bunker, if it really exists? You're the president."

He sighed. "Yes, I know. But my swearing-in ceremony wasn't the norm. The president and VP died, and I was next in line as speaker of the house. Let's just say there wasn't time to transfer the launch codes or important information." He cut off another piece of the apple.

The fresh apple.

Vinnie studied the food.

He smiled. "Nursery close by headquarters. Has apple trees."

Maureen nodded. "We have some in green houses outside of campus."

Bret pursed his lips and looked her over again. "I know the Bunker exists because I've found enough references to it in communications and budget bills. It's on the west coast, and I'm sure we'll find it soon." He kicked back as if relaxing after a hard day's work. "We need the resources in the Bunker to protect the country. At some point, I'm expecting an attack from overseas. It's possible one of our enemies wasn't hit by Scorpius as hard as we were. They may be regrouping now and could strike any minute."

There was enough truth in the statement that Vinnie's mind reeled. The guy might be a sociopath, but that didn't make him wrong. One thing at a time, though. "Do we even have a working government?"

"Just the elite force, led by me, and the military." Bret picked lint off his jeans. "At some point, we'll institute another Congress, but right now it's more of a military operation. Survival, if you will."

Two men patrolled outside the window, and Vinnie caught a flash of purple. "Is the Twenty gang still working for you?"

"We're using what's left of them as foot soldiers," Bret said. "We allow them to keep their colors on, and they do as we say. They're expendable, as I'm sure you've noticed."

A chill whispered through her. "You sent those Twenty kids the other day to attack Vanguard."

"Yep. I take it the kids didn't make it?" Bret asked.

"No," Vinnie whispered.

He shrugged. "It was worth a shot. I'm sorry to hear that Jax Mercury is still walking among the living. Is Lynne still enamored of him?"

Vinnie didn't twitch.

"She always was a tramp." Bret set the apple down and peered at both women. "I need to lead by example as we rebuild our society, and to do so, I require a first lady."

Vinnie shoved back in the sofa. "Lynne is never coming back to you."

He shook his head. "Blue Heart can't be my first lady. I understand that now." He leaned forward, his forehead smoothing out. "Don't get me wrong. Someday I'm going to catch up with her, and I'll rip that blue heart right out of her body. But I can't be seen with her."

Vinnie glanced at Moe. "Um."

He nodded, as if reaching a decision. "I can only have one. We'll take the night and figure out which one of you will be the more valuable to me and the country as a whole. It's the country that matters, and we must make sacrifices. One of you will become my first lady, and the other will be shot in the head and left for Vanguard to find." He smiled up at Lake.

Lake stood at attention near the doorway, effectively blocking any exit. "That's a fine idea, sir."

Vinnie swallowed and could feel Moe tremble next to her. Was it possible to find a way out of this?

Bret glanced at a shiny wristwatch. "The clock is ticking." He looked up and smiled. "Who wants to live?"

The air chilled several degrees, and Vinnie eyed the knife still in Bret's hand. If she could get to it, she'd still have to deal with Lake, who stood watch over the entire room. Her knees tensed, and she mentally ran through a plan.

The windows burst in, and glass sprayed. "Down," she yelled, using her shoulder to knock Maureen to the carpet. Something flashed, and her head jerked back as she lost her hearing.

Smoke filled the room, and darkness swam toward her.

Raze leaped through the window, his boots crunching glass. The flash grenade had thrown up smoke, but it quickly dissipated.

Vice President Lake stood near the sofa, a knife to Vinnie's neck. He held her up by her hair, even as she swayed in place, her eyelids obviously struggling to remain open.

Maureen lay on the ground, not moving.

Men poured in, guns out, already firing. Raze plugged two between the eyes and hit another center mass. Three more ran in from the doorway, and Greyson shot two from the window before jumping inside.

Outside the sound of a firefight ripped through the quiet subdivision as Jax, Tace, Sami, and Damon Winter tried to keep the president's soldiers occupied.

The president was nowhere to be seen. The bastard must've made a run for it when the explosion occurred.

Lake backed against a wall, keeping his knife steady on Vinnie's neck.

Her eyes focused on Raze.

"Where's the president?" Raze asked.

Lake smiled. "He was escorted to safety at the first sign of threat. He's the president of the United States, asshole."

In other words, the coward ran out the back door. Raze centered and focused, trying not to look at his sister prone on the floor.

Greyson kept his gun on Lake and crept forward, crouching to feel her neck. "Steady pulse. She's unconscious." He stood and aimed his gun.

Raze nodded and angled to the other side so they could flank Lake. Greyson remained next to Moe.

Lake shook his head. "You might get off the shot, but I'll shove this knife in so quickly it won't matter."

Smoke and fiery debris wafted through the air.

"Let her go, and we won't kill you," Raze said.

President Atherton appeared in the doorway. "The house is secure, but there's a fight outside." He pointed a gun at Raze, moving to the side to keep Grey in his sights.

"Sir? I've got this. Please return to the guards," Lake said, moving so Vinnie's head covered his neck and part of his face.

Atherton's chin lowered. "They breached my head-quarters, which is treason."

Lake nodded. "Yes, but tonight might not be the time to take them in. We're not at the main headquarters."

Bret sighed. "All right. Let's give them something to deal with." He turned his aim toward Maureen and fired.

"No!" Greyson flattened himself over Maureen, his body shuddering with the impact. Blood sprayed up in a grace-ful arc.

Raze fired at the president, who threw himself back into the hallway.

Lake jerked Vinnie up on her toes and backed to the doorway. She struggled and kicked. "Sorry about this," he said. He sliced the knife across her neck and shoved her toward Raze, turning and running.

"Vinnie!" Raze bellowed, leaping for her.

Blood flowed from her neck. Her eyes widened, and her hand covered the wound.

"Let me see." Panic engulfed him, and his vision hazed. He moved her hands and gently wiped. "God. Oh, God." The knife had cut into her lower neck and slashed across her vest. When she'd struggled, she'd probably saved her own life. "It's bad but it isn't going to kill you." He breathed out, and his hands shook. "We'll need to close it." The jugular hadn't been impacted. Thank God.

She nodded.

"Tace?" Raze yelled.

The screech of tires ripped through the streets outside. More gunfire. Seconds later, maybe longer, silence reigned.

Raze called for Tace again.

The medic popped up at the window, blood on his face. "What?"

"We need a doctor." Raze angled to the side to check on Greyson.

The Merc leader slowly stood and helped a wavering Maureen to the sofa. Blood flowed from his left arm.

Raze frowned. "Did you get shot twice in the same arm?"

Greyson dropped next to Maureen. "Yes. Being allies with you so far has sucked." He rested his head back and closed his eyes.

"We are not allies, asshole." Raze would deal with the Merc leader once he had Vinnie and Maureen safe.

Maureen rubbed the purple bruise already forming on her forehead. "Raze."

He nodded and all but lifted Vinnie toward a chair, keeping pressure on her wound. "I missed you too, Moe."

Tace jumped into the room just as Jax came through the door where Lake and the president had disappeared. "The house is secured," Jax said. "They shot out our tires, and the president got away. Bastard."

Tace nodded. "I'll find a sewing kit, or maybe even a first-aid kit. Everyone hold tight."

The feeling of Vinnie's warm blood on Raze's hand made him want to kill somebody. "Hold on, sweetheart. You'll be okay."

"I know," she croaked. "Thank you for rescuing us."

Tears filled his eyes, and he gave a chuckle. "Anytime. I love you, you know."

Her body jerked. "Yeah, I know. I love you, too."

Greyson partially turned to Maureen. "Your brother is a total sap."

Maureen's smile was a bit shaky. "He gets passive aggressive sometimes, too. She doesn't know what she's getting into."

Tace returned with an impressive-looking first-aid kit and started sewing everybody up.

Vinnie held tight to Raze's hand, and every time she winced, he felt the pain in his own neck. He tried to distract her. "Greyson? What's up with you, the Bunker, and Zach Barter?"

Grey sighed. "Listen. I'm fine with creating an alliance between our people, but that doesn't make us confidants."

"So much for trust," Raze muttered. "I'm still shooting you later."

"You can try." Greyson nodded. "Trust has to be earned. This is a start."

Tace stepped back and studied Vinnie's stitches. "Damn good job, if I say so myself." He turned. "Do I save Greyson or let him bleed out?"

Jax covered the window. "Save his ass. He has information we might need. Raze can kill him later if he chooses."

Raze eyed his sister, so pale on the sofa.

Vinnie glanced up and then gave him a nudge. "Go."

He moved and gently lifted Moe, tucking her into him for a hug. "I've been looking so hard for you."

She leaned back, tears in her eyes. "I knew you'd find me."

Finally. His sister was safe.

Chapter Thirty-Six

I like you just the way you are—crazy or not.

—Raze Shadow

Vinnie limped across the small apartment, her entire body aching, her heart full. Home. They'd made it back home to Vanguard territory, and she hoped to never leave again. Of course, that wasn't possible.

Raze followed her and shut the door. "How's the neck?"

"Hurts." She turned and smiled. Then she sobered. Ah, hell.

"So you went and got yourself stabbed?" Lucinda bounced next to Raze, wearing an eighties aerobics outfit, complete with bright purple leg warmers and a matching headband. "I told you he'd be dangerous."

Vinnie rolled her eyes. "Go away, Lucinda. I'm tired."

"Well." Lucinda puffed out of sight.

Raze lifted an eyebrow.

Vinnie shrugged. Keeping secrets seemed like a waste of time. "She's gone now."

Raze eyed the area next to him before heading for Vinnie and backing her toward the bed. "Good. There are things I want to do to you, soft and gentle ones because you're injured, that I'd rather she didn't see."

Vinnie smiled and let him set her down on the firm mattress. "You don't mind that I'm nuts?"

"I adore you the way you are, crazy or not." He grinned. "Definitely crazy, though."

She chuckled and rolled right into his strong body, careful to avoid the bandage on his bicep from the bullet wound. "We found Maureen."

"Yeah." Raze ran a hand down Vinnie's hair. "Sorry about the whole plan to kidnap you."

She licked along his neck. "You're forgiven." Especially because he hadn't done it. "You didn't have to be so bossy with your sister earlier." The man had all but forced Maureen to accompany them to Vanguard territory.

Raze sighed. "I just got her back here."

"Yeah, but those nurseries are her babies, and we all need food. Her work is in Merc territory." Vinnie kept the rest of her thoughts to herself. She'd seen the way Maureen had looked at Greyson when she'd discovered the guy had jumped in front of a bullet for her. "We're allies now, right?"

"Hell, no. I'm glad Grey and Damon went to inspect the damage to their territory and assess casualties. It's gonna be a bad day for them." Raze kissed the top of Vinnie's head. "Maureen is staying here for the time being. We'll figure out a safe way for her to continue her work. Oh, and I'm still killing Greyson the second he's no longer useful."

Vinnie wondered what Maureen would have to say about that. Vinnie sighed and let her body relax. "I can't believe you guys caught up to us so quickly."

"We used the dune buggies and followed the boats. When I saw them load you guys into a truck, it was all I could do not to stop it. But Jax was right. Hot-wiring a truck and taking the president by surprise was a better move." Raze sighed. "I wish I could've ended that bastard, though. He's safe at his new headquarters, wherever that is."

"Oh, we'll get him." Vinnie tried to sound positive. If the

military actually answered to Bret, then it was a long shot. But that was a concern for another day. "I heard that Sami and Byron are both recuperating."

"Yeah. That kid was great in the fight, and so was Sami. I owe them," Raze said.

"We both do." She needed to tell him everything she was feeling. "You keep saving me, Raze." The man was a hero, and more importantly, he was her hero.

"Of course. I love you."

Those words. How those words filled her. Life was dangerous and full of uncertainties, but for now, Vinnie was safe and with the man she loved. "I love you too, you know."

He leaned back, his blue eyes sizzling. "You had better. Um, remember when you were trying to mess with my head and said we should get married?"

Her silly heart fluttered. "Sure."

"I meant it. When I said yes, I meant it." He brushed a kiss across her nose. "I want you, all of you, as completely as I can get you. That means marriage and same name. Mine."

Her chest swelled with what had to be happiness. "You sound a mite possessive, Shadow," she murmured, running her hands through his thick hair.

"Just a mite?" He grinned. "I want full on, totally possessive. What do you say?"

Somehow, in this time and this place, it was the most romantic proposal she could even imagine. "I say yes."

He leaned down and kissed her, going deep, so much love in the movement that tears filled her eyes. "Don't forget you promised to obey," he murmured against her mouth.

She grinned and nipped his bottom lip. "I most certainly did not."

"Hmm." His incredible blue eyes darkened. "We'll have to work on that, then."

He could tease all he wanted. Somehow, in the darkness the world had become, fate had given her this man. This wounded, brave, dangerous and honorable man. "I love you, Raze Shadow."

His gaze showed her everything she'd ever wanted to see. "I love you, too. Whatever happens, Vinnie. It's you and me. Forever."

Read on for a taste of Rebecca Zanetti's
next Realm Enforcers novel,

WICKED KISS,

coming in digital and POD formats
from Lyrical Press this July!

So far, the magical world of Ireland pretty much sucked eggs. Her dreams of rolling hills, rugged men, and wild adventures had given away to facts that tilted her universe, spun it around, and spiked it headfirst into the ground.

The world held too many secrets.

Tori Monzelle leaned her shoulders against the cold metal wall of the van and tried to blink through the blindfold turning the interior dark. Nothing. The carpet in the rear of the van smelled fresh and new, but she sat on the floor, her knees drawn up and her hands tied behind her back.

The sounds of drizzling rain and honking horns filtered inside, while two men breathed from the front seats. She hadn't recognized either one of them when they'd arrived at the penthouse just an hour before. For an entire week she'd been held hostage in various luxurious locales after having been kidnapped from Seattle.

Had it only been a week since she'd learned the world wasn't as she'd thought?

Witches, vampires, and demons existed. As in *really existed.*

They were just different species from humans, apparently. So far she'd seen witches create fireballs and throw them, and she'd met a demon who'd shown her his fangs. She had to go on faith that vampires really existed, but at this point, why not believe?

She cleared her throat. "Listen, jackasses. I'm about done with this entire kidnapping scenario." It had to be the oddest kidnapping of all time, with her being flown across the globe and then put up in zillion-dollar penthouses for a week. "I promise not to tell anybody that supernatural beings exist. Just let me go."

A snort came from the front seat. "Supernatural," one of the men muttered.

Her chest heated. "All right, so you think you're natural. Then how about I refrain from announcing that your species even exists?"

Another snort.

What a dick. Fine. "Are you witches, demons, or vampires?" If she had to guess, they were witches.

No answer.

The van swerved and she knocked her head against the side. "Damn it." It was time to get free. "Let me go, you morons. This is international kidnapping." Did witches care about international laws? Her shoulders shook and a welcome anger soared through her.

The van jerked.

"What the hell?" one of the guys snapped.

They tilted.

Something sputtered. The engine?

An explosion rocked the day and the van spun. Her temple smacked the metal, and she rolled to the other side across the carpet. Breath swooshed from her lungs. Pain pounded in her head, and she blinked behind the blindfold.

The van stopped cold, and she rolled toward the front, her legs scrambling. Her forehead brushed the carpet and she shook her head, dislodging the blindfold.

Doors opened and grunts sounded. Men fighting. Punches being thrown.

The back doors opened and light flooded inside.

She turned just as hands manacled her ankles and dragged

her toward the street. Kicking out, she struggled furiously, her eyes adjusting and focusing on this new threat. A ski mask completely covered the guy's head, leaving only his eyes and mouth revealed. With the light behind him, she couldn't even make out the color of his irises.

His strong grip didn't relent and he easily pulled her toward the edge, dropping her legs toward the ground.

She threw a shoulder into his rock-hard abs and stood. He was at least a foot taller than she and definitely cut hard.

Everything in her screamed to get the hell out of the area and make a run for it. She was smart, she was tough, and she could handle the situation. No time to think. Tori leaped up and shot a quick kick to his face. While he was tall and fit, he probably wasn't expecting a fight.

He snagged her ankle an inch from his jaw, thus preventing the impact. Using her momentum to pull her forward, he manacled his other hand behind her thigh and lifted, tossing her over his shoulder in one incredibly smooth motion.

Her rib cage slammed into solid muscle, knocking the wind from her lungs.

One firm hand clamped across her thighs and he turned, moving into a jog. The sound of men fighting behind them had her lifting her head to see more men in ski masks battling the two guys from the van.

Then her captor turned a corner and ran through an alley, easily holding her in place.

"Let me go," she gasped, pulling on the restraints holding her hands. Cobbled stones flew by below, while cool air brushed across her skin. Rain continued to patter down, matting her hair to her face.

He didn't answer and took two more turns, finally ending up in yet another alley next to a shiny black motorcycle. Her hair swooshed as he ducked his shoulder and planted her on her feet. Firm hands flipped her around, and something sliced through her bindings.

Blood rushed into her hands and she winced, pivoting back around. "Who are you?" She slid one foot slightly back in an attack position.

He reached out and tugged the blindfold completely off her head before ripping off his ski mask.

Adam Dunne stood before her, legs braced, no expression on his hard face. Rain dripped from his thick black hair and irritation glittered in his spectacular green eyes. That expression seemed to live on him. He was some sort of brilliant scientist, definitely a brainiac, and he always appeared annoyed.

She blinked twice. "Adam?"

He crossed his arms. "It has been nearly impossible to find you."

His deep voice shot right through her to land in very private places. Then the angry tone caught her. She slammed her hands against her hips. "And that's my fault? Your stupid people, the fucking witches, *kidnapped* me."

Witches. Holy crap. Adam Dunne was a witch. Sure, she'd figured that out a week ago, but with him standing right in front of her, she had to face reality.

The man looked like a badass vigilante and not some brilliant otherworldly being. For the rescue he'd worn a black T-shirt, ripped jeans, and motorcycle boots. Definitely not his usual pressed slacks and button-down silk shirt.

His sizzling green eyes darkened. "I have about an hour to get you to a plane and out of this country, so you'll be quiet, *for once*, and you'll follow orders."

She pressed her lips together. No matter how badly she wanted to punch him in the face, she wanted to get out of the country even more. "Fine."

He lifted an eyebrow. "We're getting on the bike, heading to the airport, and then you're flying to Seattle. You don't know who rescued you and you haven't seen me in weeks."

She swallowed. "How much trouble are you in if we get caught?"

He turned and grabbed a helmet off the bike. "Treason and death sentence."

Everything in her softened. He'd risked his life for her. Sure, his brother was dating her sister, but even so. "Thank you."

He turned and shoved the helmet at her. "Don't thank me. Just do what I tell you."

Man, what a jerk. Nearly biting through her tongue to keep from lashing out, she shoved the helmet on her head.

He did the same and swung a leg over the bike, holding out a hand to help her.

She ignored him and levered herself over the bike and into place, anger flowing through her. Why did he have to be such a dick? She'd wanted to thank him, that's all.

He ignited the engine. It sputtered. He stiffened and tried again.

Hell. She closed her eyes and tried to calm her temper. They had to get out of there. *Work, bike. Damn it, work.* The more she tried to concentrate, the more irritated she became.

He twisted the throttle again, and this time nothing happened.

Damn it. Why the hell did this always happen to her? What was wrong with her? "It won't work. If it's broken, it won't work." She tugged off the helmet and slid off the bike.

He turned toward her. "The bike ran just fine an hour ago."

She shrugged, her face heating. No way was she telling him about her oddity. "I know the sound of an engine that's not coming back to life and so do you."

He frowned and tried the bike again. Nothing. "All right." He swung his leg over and stood, reaching for a buzzing cell phone and pushing a button. "I have a problem," he said.

"The woman has been tagged," came an urgent male voice. "There's a tracker and you have about five minutes until the Guard gets there." Keys clacking echoed across the line. "Get rid of the tag and find safety. I'll be in touch with new coordinates as soon as I can." The line went dead.

Adam surveyed her from head to toe, reaching for her shirt.

She slapped at his hands. "What are you doing?"

He sighed. "You've been tagged and I don't know where. Strip, baby."

Baby? Did he just call her baby? Wait a minute. "Strip?"

"Now." A muscle ticked in his powerful jaw. "Our tags are minute and could be anywhere on you." He dug both hands through her hair, tugging just enough to flood her with unwelcome tingles. "Not in your hair."

"I am not stripping," she said through clenched teeth, her body doing a full tremble.

He lowered his head until his nose almost touched hers. "Take everything off or I'll do it for you."

She blinked.

He gave a barely perceptible eye roll and turned around, pulling off his T-shirt. "Drop the clothes and put this on. It'll cover you for the time being."

Muscles rippled in his back.

Her mouth went dry.

"Now, Victoria. We have to hurry."

The urgency in his voice got through to her. She shucked her clothes, kicking off her socks and shoes, shivering in the light rain. The second her jeans hit the ground, she reached for his shirt and tugged it over her head. The soft material fell below her thighs and surrounded her with the scent of male.

He turned around, and yep. His bare chest was even more spectacular than his back. "Everything off? Bra and panties?"

Did Adam Dunne just use the word *panties*? A slightly hysterical giggle bubbled up from her abdomen and she shoved it ruthlessly down. "Yes."

"Good." He took her hand. "Sorry about the bare feet, but we'll get you replacement clothes soon. For now, we have to run."

A car screeched to a stop outside the alley.

"Bullocks. They're here," he muttered, launching into a run down the alley. "Hurry, and don't look back."

Panic seized her and she held firm to his hand, her bare feet slapping hard cobblestones.

A fireball careened past her, smashing into the brick building above her and raining down debris. She screamed.

Adam stopped and shoved her behind him, dark blue plasma forming down his arms as he pivoted to fight.

She gulped in air and peered around him as three men, each forming a different color plasma ball, all stalked toward them from the street.

"Run, Victoria," Adam ordered.

**Don't miss the next book in the
Scorpius Syndrome series,**

Justice Ascending,

coming next February!

Before surviving the Scorpius bacterium, Tace Justice was a good ol' Texas cowboy who served his country and loved his mama. After Scorpius, the world became dark, dangerous, and deadly—and so did he. The Vanguard medic is stronger, faster, and smarter than before, but he's lost the line between right and wrong. His passion is absolute, and when he focuses it on one woman, there's no turning back for either of them. . . .

Sami Steel has been fighting to survive right alongside Tace, convincing the Vanguard soldiers she's one of them. In truth, Sami is a former hacker turned government agent who worked at the Bunker, where scientists stored both contaminants and cures. Only she knows the location, and she's not telling. Yet when sexual fire explodes between her and Tace, she'll face even that hell again to save him.

**"Thrilling post-apocalyptic romance
at its dark, sizzling best!"
—Lara Adrian**